THE BEGINNING PLACE . . .

A path of sorts seemed to lead Nimbulan to a doorway in the center of the south wall of the building. His next step sent him flying backward into a bed of thistles. His staff lay ten feet in front of him. What kind of force was strong enough to separate him from his staff?

"Nimbulan!" Quinnault helped him up. He brushed some of the excess mud from Nimbulan's already filthy clothes. "What happened?"

"I don't . . . don't know." Nimbulan clutched his temple to keep the world from spinning away from him. "One minute I was on solid ground, the next I was flying through the air."

(You trespassed where your kind are not welcome.) A shadowy mist rose up between the two men and the monastery.

"Who are you?" Quinnault addressed the air. "I am Lord of this island. This is my land, and I may walk where I will! Show yourself to your rightful lord."

(I recognize no lord. I am the guardian of the beginning place.) The mist, crowded with gray and purple shadows, shaped itself into the vague outline of a man, twice the height of a normal man. *(I guard these hallowed grounds against all who would misuse the power that begins and ends here. The Stargods gifted this power to the people of Kardia Hodos for the good of all. I guard against misuse—intentional or accidental. Be gone!)*

Be sure to read these magnificent
DAW Fantasy Novels by
IRENE RADFORD

The Dragon Nimbus:
THE GLASS DRAGON (Book 1)
THE PERFECT PRINCESS (Book 2)
THE LONELIEST MAGICIAN (Book 3)

The Dragon Nimbus History:
THE DRAGON'S TOUCHSTONE (Book 1)

The Dragon Nimbus History

IRENE RADFORD

DAW BOOKS, INC.
DONALD A. WOLLHEIM, FOUNDER
375 Hudson Street, New York, NY 10014
ELIZABETH R. WOLLHEIM
SHEILA E. GILBERT
PUBLISHERS

Cover art by John Howe.
Interior map by Michael Gilbert.
DAW Book Collectors No. 1059.

First Printing, June 1997

1 2 3 4 5 6 7 8 9

DAW TRADEMARK REGISTERED
U.S. PAT. OFF. AND FOREIGN COUNTRIES
—MARCA REGISTRADA
HECHO EN U.S.A.

PRINTED IN THE U.S.A.

For Benjamin Colin
my little baby boy
who knew all about flywackets
before I did.

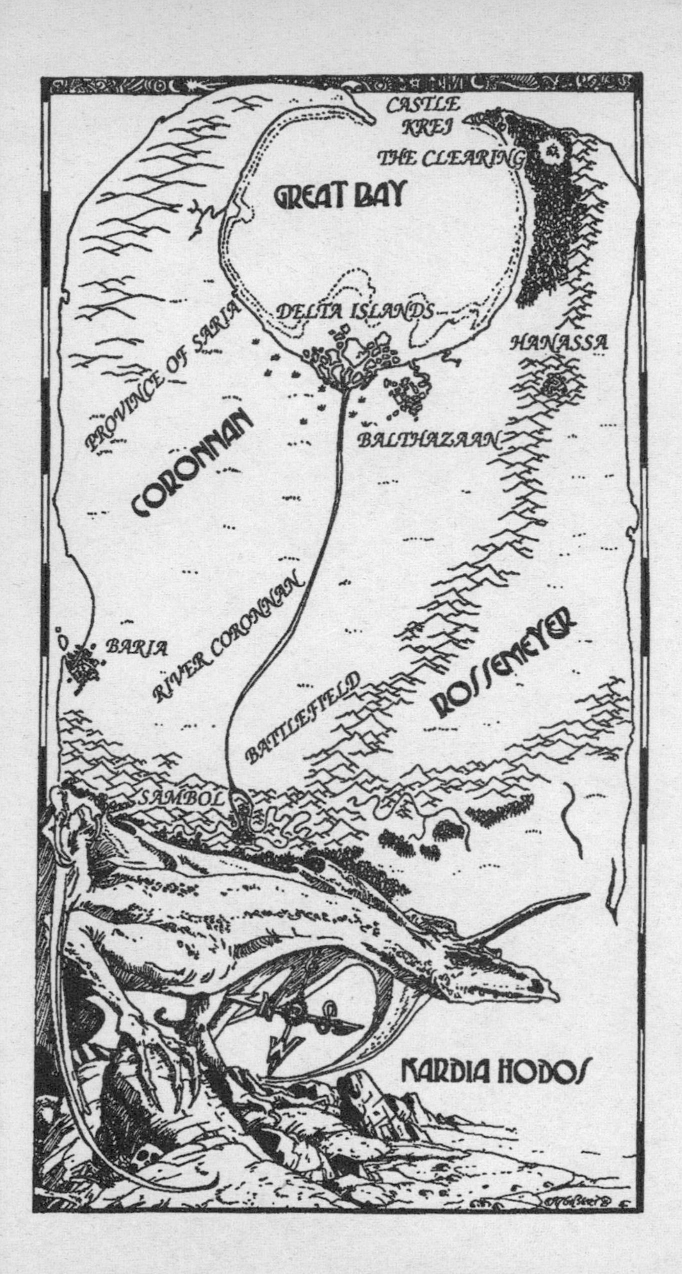
CASTLE KREI
THE CLEARING
GREAT BAY
DELTA ISLANDS
PROVINCE OF SARIA
HANASSA
CORONNAN
BALTHAZAAN
BARIA
RIVER CORONNAN
ROSSEMEYER
BATTLEFIELD
SAMBOL
KARDIA HODOS

PROLOGUE

A lovely rising thermal current caught Shayla's wing as she glided one last time from the mountains to the Great Bay. A hundred dragon lengths below her, white-caps danced on the gentle spring breeze. Sunlight sparkled on the water, reflecting rainbows from her nearly transparent wing.

Mandelphs darted in and out of the water in a game of "catch me if you can." One youngster leaped through a rainbow, laughing.

Join us, crystal-furred dragon. Play with us, the intelligent water-dwellers chirped. *Dragons cast interesting shadows and offer new hurdles to leap over and dive under. More interesting since you are nearly invisible.*

(Thank you, friends. Not today,) Shayla declined. Her lair was a long way away and the twenty babies growing inside her had become too large for her to be confident of her mobility. Tonight she would feast on a fat cow and build her nest. For the next few moons her five mates would feed and pamper her while she could not fly. At any other time, except during mating, she wouldn't tolerate the presence of her consorts within her hunting territory. The male dragons wouldn't tolerate each other except during the cooperative effort to support their gravid mate.

Five fathers for her first litter of twenty dragonets. Pride swelled through her. The more fathers, the larger and stronger the litter.

She widened her circle of flight inland, enjoying the changing air temperatures against her wings. The Great Bay dissolved into a chain of islands then merged into a solid landmass split by a mighty river.

Curiosity sharpened her FarSight to spy on the humans who inhabited this land. A bustle of activity in a wide-open space below drew her attention. She dropped lower to spy on the strangely intelligent, yet sadly immature race who had invaded this planet several millennia ago.

One of the humans below threw a ball of bright magic across a field. The ball arced upward and burst into thousands of glittering shards.

Sharp burning pain snaked from the tip of Shayla's tail, up to her haunches, numbing her muscles as it progressed. Without the maneuvering balance of her tail, she fell into a downward spin. Startled, she didn't immediately compensate with stretched wings and extended limbs.

Too late! Another pain spiraled around her left rear leg. Muscles jerked out of control. She lost another dozen dragon lengths in altitude.

Too low. Dangerously low. The humans came into sharper view without the aid of FarSight. A cloud of magic residue hung above them. As this fact registered in her mind, more magic flashed across the field, adding to the residue. She barely escaped a responding flash that hurled upward from the edge of the meadow before it fell toward the opposite side of the open space.

A magic duel! How dare these puny humans battle with forces they couldn't control!

Flame burst from her mouth with a roar of rage. She refocused her FarSight, seeking a victim to atone for this outrage against her body and the forces of nature.

Spells of varying complexity and strength continued blasting back and forth between the men. None looked up to see the source of her flame. They ignored her fair warning.

She dropped heavily through the air as a new pain reminded her sharply of the weight within her womb. No! Her babies weren't ready. No nest awaited them in her distant lair.

A new spell lanced upward. She veered sharply right, barely avoiding it. Fire burst forth as she bellowed her outrage. She folded her wings and plunged into a dive.

Her wing membranes snapped open at the last minute as she shifted and fought to regain height. Her flames drenched the field, turning the entire army, stubble, and nearby trees to ash. No sense of triumph followed the obliteration of the threat. The pain in her womb enveloped all thought.

Shayla swung upward, slow and unwieldy with the extra weight in her womb. Greedy flames from the burning battlefield singed her belly. The babies twisted and fought for exit.

Not yet. Not until she found safe haven.

Where? Oh, where could she go? If she accessed the void long enough to find her lair, the babies would never survive the birthing. The void between the planes of existence would choke crucial air, light, and warmth from both her and her babies.

Who could shelter her? None of the males. Their lairs were small caves, barely large enough to secrete a single dragon; all of them too far away.

(I come,) an ancient dragon voice hailed her.

Iianthe. The oldest dragon of all and the only purple-tip known to have ever existed.

Shayla stretched her wings a little under the guidance of the telepathic voice, and she gained a little more control. But she kept dropping. She had make headway. East. Where the mountains met the sea. Iianthe's lair, huge, designed to house many litters of baby dragons.

Barely skimming the tops of the trees, Shayla forced her wings to keep going. Her belly cramped in time with her downstrokes.

Iianthe appeared beneath her. His right wing supported the dragging leg that threatened her balance and her altitude. With the injured limb tucked back where it belonged, they gained elevation.

Everblue treetops receded from view. One dragon length, then two and three. They caught an updraft and glided East to safety.

The plateau in front of Iianthe's lair appeared before her, almost level with her sagging legs.

A heavy, awkward landing sent her nose into the spring beside the cave opening. Exhausted, she lay there, wishing she could cry as humans did.

Iianthe landed beside her, almost as tired as she. Near the end of his span, he'd lived longer than any living dragon could remember. Without moving, he crooned a *Song* of healing that only she could hear.

She could walk, a little, far enough to get inside the cave where a nest of leaves and soft sheep's wool awaited. Had Iianthe known she would need the nest?

No matter. She collapsed upon the bed as the first baby dragon squeezed from the protection of her womb into the waiting nest—an undersized mass of wiggling limbs the color of dark pewter. The tiniest hint of red touched its wingtips and the nubs of horns. A male. Alive and squalling for food already.

Shayla licked the last of the afterbirth from her son's fur. She paused a moment while she panted in rhythm with her labor. The miracle of new life filled her with awe. She stared at the tiny form in wonder.

Two more mewling dragonets made an abrupt entrance. Twin purple-tips. Purples! Rarest of all dragon colors, assigned only to personalities of great power or wisdom. What strange portent did their birth signify?

The cramping pains did not abate.

(My replacement is born. I must die now. There can only be one purple-tip alive at any given time,) Iianthe said from the cave entrance.

Shayla waited through the birth of two more dragonets before answering the hovering dragon.

(Do not fly into the void just yet, wise one. We need your advice. The humans must be punished!)

(Your mates must not interfere. 'Tis not their destiny. This is a matter to be settled between your babies and the human magicians.) Iianthe heaved a weary sigh. *(My next existence awaits, I must guard the beginning place of magic. The humans will find it within a century. Only those worthy of the power must find it.)*

(The intruders have grown too strong, without the maturity of the centuries to guide them. They weave magic they cannot control,) Shayla reminded him. *(The beginning place needs a powerful guardian until humans can use the magic properly.)*

('Twas foretold long ago by Purple Dragons wiser than I that your children must teach the humans what they need to know.) Iianthe's voice faded as he backed out of the lair entrance.

(But they are twins. Which one takes your place and which must be destroyed?) Shayla panicked. Her babies

were too small, not ready to grasp their destiny. Who would take on the task of dropping the extra purple-tip baby from the void into the Great Bay—to live or die as fate decided.

(Seek answers in the void. Until you know the destinies of both purple-tips, do nothing to either. Perhaps they have been chosen by the fates to solve the problem with the humans.) Iianthe gathered his wings for one last burst of energy and disappeared into the void. *(I can die now, Shayla. The lair is yours.)* Iianthe's voice faded.

Shayla caught a glimpse of winking amethyst crystal in the distant blackness that opened before her but did not touch her.

Shayla's wing folded protectively over all six pewter-colored dragonets that lived. Four males and the asexual twin purple-tips. No females. She pushed aside fourteen dead babies. No more infants awaited birth. A new kind of pain swelled within her. She lifted her muzzle in a mournful wail that pierced the silence and echoed through the mountains of Kardia Hodos. The sound lingered and replayed itself as sorrow overtook all of the dragons. The future seemed bleak indeed.

Too many dragons fell victim to the wild and aggressive humans who hated and feared all they did not understand.

Shayla nuzzled each of her babies, willing them all to live and grow. She had time to make a decision about the redundant purple-tip. Time to find a way to save both. Time to plot and persuade before dragonkind took drastic action.

CHAPTER 1

Eighteen Years Later

"Don't do it, Keegan. Don't try that spell, boy!" Nimbulan yelled across the din of the battle. He projected his words with magic above the noise of death and destruction.

Keegan, Nimbulan's former apprentice, ignored the command, if he heard it at all. On a slight mound, opposite the raging battle from Nimbulan, the young man wove his hands in a stylized, intricate pattern.

"That spell draws its symmetry from stars that disappear at midnight! Dawn is but a few heartbeats away." Nimbulan tried once more to warn his opponent. He climbed onto the stump of a tree that had been blasted by magic gone awry during a battle on this same field nearly twenty years before. No one had survived the fires then. Neither would they survive Keegan's spell.

False dawn shimmered on the horizon, barely discernible beyond the witchlight that illumined the two armies battling between the mages. If Keegan continued to weave his magic one heartbeat past sunrise, the spell would go rogue with disastrous results.

Keegan's chant became a steady, rhythmic incantation. It slid under and around the noise of seasoned troops slashing and hacking at each other. Nimbulan watched as Lord Hanic's men wielded their weapons in time with the words of the spell chanted by Keegan. The front line of Lord Kammeryl's troops sagged and gave ground in the same rhythm. Nimbulan thought furiously about how to protect Kammeryl's men. He had to stop Keegan's spell before it drew too much power from the sun, rather than a balance of moon and stars.

All day and most of the night the battle had raged. Keegan's spell was a desperate attempt to tip the balance.

Nimbulan ran the words of the spell past his memory. Keegan had said them correctly. The spell would begin as planned. Keegan sought to encase Nimbulan and his army in a stasis field, unable to move or protect themselves. Lord Hanic's smaller army could then slaughter Lord Kammeryl's troops at leisure. If the spell worked.

But the light of the sun was so much stronger than the stars. Keegan's magic would distort and destroy all of them. "No, Keegan. No," Nimbulan moaned.

Perverted by the fading moon and stars, the stasis field would freeze all life within ten leagues, including the grass, air, and river. Nimbulan's belly chilled at a vision of winds from all of Kardia Hodos rushing to fill the vacuum created by the spell. Tornadoes, dry hurricanes, all manner of catastrophic storms would wreak havoc across half the planet.

Keegan was too young and too arrogant about his talent to realize the dangers of his actions. He wanted only to win this battle.

"I can't let you do it, Keegan," Nimbulan mumbled as he rammed his staff into the Kardia to steady his own spell. He raised his left hand, palm outward, fingers slightly curved to weave the energy of the Kardia. Trickles of magic power meandered up the twisted grain of wood into his palm. Not enough. The ley lines that fed his magic were empty. He needed fuel for his inborn magic talent.

Nimbulan snapped his fingers impatiently. A fat green leaf with pink veins appeared in his hands. A leaf of the Tambootie, the tree of magic. He licked the essential oils from the veins and spine as his mind formed words and images of a great wall surrounding Keegan.

Fire burst upon Nimbulan's tongue. He chewed the leaf eagerly. Colors sang through his blood and into his eyes. Ugly sounds of battle faded, and the Tambootie took hold of his talent. His raised palm tingled, ready to weave his magic into a protective spell.

Keegan completed the last hand motions and singsong words. The chant lingered in the air just below hearing level.

Power began to vibrate within Nimbulan. Time slowed.

Keegan wound a spell into a tight wad and drew back

his arm to hurl his magic outward with all the might of his youthful body.

Nimbulan's invisible wall rose out of the depths of the Kardia.

Keegan's spell crashed into it. Power erupted. The shield buckled. Sparkling shadows flitted along the wall.

Thunder rolled. Lightning flashed. Sparks flew in all directions. A crack spiderwebbed around the wall of magic from the point of impact with Keegan's spell. Natural green fire, unholy red, magical blue, and blinding yellow followed the crack lines and sprayed backward into Keegan's eyes. A momentary outline of a winged form spewing fire appeared on the damaged shield, then vanished, taking the fire with it.

"A dragon! We've been cursed by a dragon!" men from both armies cried at the fleeting shadow as they threw down their arms and fled.

"Yieee!" Keegan screamed. His own spell backlashed and knocked him flat, drenching him with magic gone awry.

The battle stopped. Both armies froze in awe and fear.

Nimbulan covered his ears. His apprentice's screams reverberated deep in his skull.

* * *

The screams echoed a distant time when he'd heard another apprentice scream in pain and desperation.

He'd been thirteen at the time, a new journeyman. Most boys didn't pass Druulin's arduous magical tasks to become journeymen until they were much older and better trained. Ackerly, his best friend and fellow apprentice, had recently failed Druulin's tests for the third time.

And been beaten for it.

Druulin's rages and beatings formed an expected part of the boy's life. The hot-tempered and often irrational Master Magician claimed he taught his apprentices defensive mechanisms by flailing them with various magic tortures.

The day Ackerly failed his journeyman tests for the final time, Druulin took a mundane whip to the boy's back.

Seven apprentices and journeymen stared in horror at the viciousness of Druulin's attack. Only Nimbulan found the courage to wrap Ackerly in defensive armor with one spell and freeze Druulin's right hand mid-stroke with another.

"A few days in the dungeon without food or light will cure you both of insolence!" Druulin said between gritted teeth. His eyes narrowed in speculation, noting the precise moment Nimbulan began to tire. He broke the spell and quickly cast another to compel both Nimbulan and Ackerly into obedience.

He prodded the boys with the whip handle until they marched down the spiraling stairs. Down they marched, from Druulin's private study and bedchamber on the top floor, past the common workroom and dormitory, down another flight to the ground floor past the kitchens with the enticing smell of supper cooking.

Nimbulan's mouth watered at the thought of fresh bread and meat. The two spells, thrown without preparation, had drained him. He needed food and rest to replenish his magic. His knees weakened as they marched down yet another flight of stairs into the storage cellars.

Druulin conjured a small ball of witchlight to keep himself from stumbling on the damp stone steps. The light didn't extend to help Nimbulan and Ackerly.

Nimbulan tried to step carefully and avoid slipping. A fall now could result in nasty broken bones at the bottom of the steep flight.

Ackerly wobbled and clung to the wall for support. His face was gray with pain and his back bled through his torn tunic. A night in the dirty dampness of the dungeons would probably infect the wounds.

Nimbulan ached for his friend. He didn't dare give in to the tears that clogged his throat and made his eyes burn.

At last, they staggered off the last step into total blackness—as black as the void except for Druulin's tiny wisp of witchlight. The old magician shoved the boys forward into a tiny room, then slammed a heavy door closed before releasing the compulsion spell. "Think about your crimes against me, you ambitious little upstarts. When you are hungry enough and sick enough to apologize, I'll think about letting you have some light and food."

The little glow of witchlight vanished. An ominous series of clicks signaled a locking spell on the door. Druulin's retreating footsteps faded quickly.

Ackerly collapsed upon a heap of rags in one corner, moaning and crying. Nimbulan felt his friend's forehead. No fever yet. "We've got to get out of here, Acker."

"Not yet. Not until Druulin settles down for the night with his liquor." Even in pain and defeat, Ackerly thought ahead better than Nimbulan.

"What then? I don't think I have enough strength left to break his locking spell." Nimbulan snapped his fingers and produced a little witchlight. He looked carefully at the lock but couldn't figure out the spell. Quickly he doused the light as his stomach turned over. He was so hungry he was queasy.

"Rest a little, Lan. Then you can open the door with magic, and we'll sneak out and steal some food. We'll come back and relock the door. Druulin will never know the difference." Ackerly shifted uncomfortably.

"We'll also steal some medicine. We can't let those wounds fester." Nimbulan wiped his running nose and eyes on his sleeve. The dungeon was colder and wetter than he remembered from the last time he'd been punished. He wished he knew some healing spells. Ackerly really needed help.

He'd never known Druulin to lose control of his temper so badly before.

"Maybe we could run away together when we get out?" Nimbulan asked. Hope of escape from Druulin's tyranny filled him with a quivering warmth.

"Where would we go? No other magician will take us on since our parents gave us to Druulin. Even masters of other trades won't take us on until Druulin releases us. And he won't let you go ever, Lan. You're too good a magician. He needs you to correct his mistakes," Ackerly replied between sobs.

"Then I'll have to take care of you. You could settle nearby—but not so close Druulin would find you," Nimbulan offered. The hope in his belly turned into a cold fearful lump. Neither of them would ever get away from Druulin. The old man intimidated all the mundanes for miles around. They'd betray Ackerly's presence.

"What will I do? Magic is the only thing I know and that not very well," Ackerly asked.

"You know lots more, Acker," Nimbulan soothed his

friend. "You think ahead and plan much better than any of us."

"But I can't do the great magic. That's what makes a Battlemage," Ackerly protested. "That's why Druulin got so mad when I failed the tests. He needs stronger apprentices to make up for his failings. He's getting too old to do it on his own."

"Apprentices and journeymen helping the Master Magician is what makes a Battlemage. Not one man alone," Nimbulan mused. "When I'm a full Battlemage, I'll make you my chief assistant, Acker. We'll be a team. Just like always. Remember the time Boojlin and Caasser ganged up on us and pelted us with rotten eggs all the way from the kitchen to the cellar? You were the one who thought up the idea of the bucket of water atop the door. When they opened the door, the bucket fell right on top of them. They both nearly drowned . . ." The two boys smothered their giggles at the memory of the two older bullies spluttering and choking as repeated cascades of ice cold water caught them unawares.

Druulin had discovered the mess and made all four of them clean it up, and do without breakfast the next morning for wasting supplies and magic.

"We'd never have escaped Boojlin and Caasser if you hadn't thought of the water bucket," Nimbulan whispered through his giggles.

"But you were the one who had the magic to hold the water up there without a bucket, and keep it coming," Ackerly reminded him.

"See, that's what I mean. We're a team. We'll always be a team. Now help me figure out this locking spell."

Thirty-six years later, Ackerly was still Nimbulan's chief assistant, and they never beat their apprentices or made them go hungry. So why had Keegan run away? Why had the boy felt he had to prove himself a better Battlemage than Nimbulan before he was fully trained?

Guilt piled on top of Nimbulan's grief.

* * *

"Why, boy? Why'd you have to push me to kill you?" Nimbulan shuddered in the cold mist that drifted over the now silent battlefield. The first rays of dawn almost pierced the gloom of fading witchlight. Clumps of sparkling moisture shimmered and wavered in the golden light, like the ghosts of the dead men who littered this unlucky wheat field. Would the victims of this battle haunt the site for generations to come?

Nearly twenty years ago, two other armies had fought on this same field. Indiscriminate and uncontrolled magic had killed them all. Troops, lords, magicians, and camp followers, all reduced to ashes in a moment of screaming agony. The stump he stood upon now, an ancient elm tree so large three men holding hands couldn't span its girth, had been toppled and blasted to ash by that same magic. A stroke of luck had sent Nimbulan and Ackerly elsewhere that same day. But not today.

Druulin, Boojlin, and Caasser had been among the thousands who had died that day, eighteen years ago.

Today Nimbulan had been forced to murder his most promising apprentice with magic in order to save the few men who still lived at the end of this most recent battle.

Thousands more dead would haunt this field now.

Nothing stirred within Nimbulan's narrow field of vision. No one cried for help or solace. A peculiar mound of ashes on the rise opposite him silently taunted him with warped magic.

Ashes that had once been Keegan.

"I called you 'son.' " His words dissipated with the mist as a chill wind blew up from the river, half a league away.

The only response was a twisting groan of eternal pain that lay trapped in the ashes.

"I'll never have a son of my body. You could have filled that aching hole in my life, Keegan."

He'd have to liberate the ghost. A father's duty. No one else was left. Trapped, unable to pass on to the void between the planes of existence, the boy's spirit begged him for release.

Nimbulan leaned heavily upon his staff, feeling twice his forty-nine years, as exhaustion drowned him.

Many men had died on both sides of the fray. Many more suffered wounds so severe they shouldn't live. For the first time in almost three decades as a Battlemage,

Nimbulan wondered if the victory won by Warlord Kammeryl d'Astrismos was worth the cost.

Keegan was dead. "You should have been my successor, boy. Not my enemy. What lured you to hire on as a Battlemage before your training was complete?"

Placing one foot wearily in front of the other, Nimbulan trudged across the field toward the opposite rise. He had to avert his eyes from the carnage around him. Recognition of a corpse or wounded friend might deter him from his mission. Many of the soldiers had died an honorable death at the hands of an enemy. Many more had died from the volleys of magic lobbed back and forth across the battlefield by the magicians. *He* was as guilty as Keegan for their deaths. The lords may have called the men to battle, but the magicians working behind them determined who won and who lost; who lived and who died.

Nimbulan stumbled and nearly fell over a dead man. Blood and mud obscured a uniform or identifying crest.

"Keegan and I did this to you." He shifted the outflung arms of the corpse into a more natural position. "Go in peace. Find your next existence and happiness," he murmured the death prayer, too numb to do more.

He supported Lord Kammeryl d'Astrismos, the one lord who might unify Coronnan. Time and again the rival lords proved that peace could only be achieved at the tremendous cost of war. He tried wrapping a cloak of justification around his emotions and failed miserably.

He trudged up the hillock to where Keegan had stood. "The Stargods would never forgive me if I made you suffer the hell of your own spell backlashed against you, son," Nimbulan sighed as he planted his tall staff beside the mound of ashes. "I would never forgive myself."

Tongues of unholy red flame licked outward from the still smoldering ashes. Sparks tried to reignite a life from the residue. Each time the essence of Keegan found an anchor, his final spell doused it.

Echoes of torment lingered in the air.

Nimbulan stretched out his hand, palm toward the pile of ashes, fingers curved as if capturing the essence of Keegan as he tried escaping his unholy prison.

He had no strength to summon magic from the depths of Kardia Hodos to work this one last spell. Nimbulan's bond with the four elements, Kardia, Air, Fire, and Water which together with the cardinal directions formed the *gaia,* had shriveled with the death and destruction wrought this day and night.

The spirit in the ashes writhed again. An irritating burn crawled all over Nimbulan's sensitized nerves. He resisted the urge to douse them both with water.

" 'Twouldn't soothe either of us."

"Come, Lan, sup and rest before you discharge this final duty." A new voice intruded upon the magician's weary thoughts. "Perhaps if I grind a few Tambootie leaves into your meal, you will feel better."

"I've used enough of the weed today, Ackerly," Nimbulan replied to his assistant. "I need food and rest, not drugs. When this spell is finished, I'll be able to rest."

"At least wait a while before you weave this spell. The boy's spirit deserves to linger in torment for a time. Perhaps he will be less impatient for power in his next existence if he suffers in a hell of his own making."

" 'Tis a hell of my making! I'll not wish that fate on any man." *And I loved you, Keegan.*

"Had he waited 'til his powers were fully grown, you'd not have defeated him. We are both getting old," Ackerly grumbled. "Old and losing our stamina. That ungrateful youngster wouldn't have wasted his strength liberating your soul from a pile of ashes." Ackerly lifted his foot to scatter the residue with a kick.

"No!" Nimbulan pushed him aside to keep him from spreading Keegan's soul too thin to regather and liberate.

"I like to think my apprentice would do me this one last service. I tried to teach him respect for others and for the power we wield."

"He only wanted to learn the spells; not the *right* way to use them," Ackerly spat. "Go back to your pavilion, Nimbulan. Let me perform this chore. I may not be a great magician who can weave the Kardia into my spells, but I can send this ungrateful wretch where he belongs."

" 'Tis my responsibility. I caused his final spell to backlash." Nimbulan shored up his sagging willpower. Ackerly's manner suggested an animosity toward Keegan that would stand in the way of a proper weaving. Nimbulan could have plucked Ackerly's true intentions and the source of his grievance from his mind. He wouldn't.

"I'll speed the boy on his way to his next existence. Druulin wouldn't have bothered. You know as well as I that *I* must do this."

CHAPTER 2

Nimbulan rummaged in the pockets of his formal robes for a small wand of the Tambootie tree affixed with a perfect faceted crystal.

Sadly, he looked through the crystal into the pile of ashes and chanted.

"Walk with me, son of my learning,
Walk with me one final time.
Walk with me the paths of life,
Walk with me to the place of your yearning."

"Greedy wretch doesn't deserve this." Ackerly turned aside, grumbling under his breath.

Nimbulan ignored his companion as his mind sought a deeper contact with the essence of his apprentice. Bright green flames and burning pain flashed from the crystal into his weary eyes.

One deep breath, hold three counts, let go three counts. A second breath filled his lungs and released. On the third inhalation he found access to the void between the planes of existence. His spirit lifted free of his weary body and found solace in the black nothingness. A second soul stood beside him, dim and unformed.

Coils of pulsing colors that represented the lives of all the souls Nimbulan had encountered in the nearly fifty years of his current existence sprang into view. A silver umbilical, tinged with blue, symbolized his own life. It wound away from his sight into a tangle of life forces.

Seeing others represented in symbolic colors was easy. Only once had Nimbulan glimpsed the full texture of his own life and aura—during the day and the night of his rite of passage into adulthood. On the eve of his twelfth birthday, his tutors sent him to a windowless stone room, with only a Tambootie wood fire for heat and light. His trance, induced by the mind-altering smoke, had been deep and profound. After thirty-six years as a magician, he still didn't understand the reflections of reality that he had seen. But ever afterward, he knew the true colors of his life-pulse in the void. A rare achievement.

Now, during his saddest trip into the void, he saw life forces of clear crystal, reflecting all colors dancing around him. The crystal dominated the tangle of symbolic lives. He'd never seen them before—didn't know who they represented.

Beside him the dim essence of a fading soul drifted away. The red umbilical dulled toward gray.

Nimbulan had to weave Keegan's life force into the tangle of umbilicals soon, or he'd be lost forever, denied his next existence.

"Walk with me, son of my learning,
Eternal pain is not your due.
My silver path to you I lend,
Walk with me a path we are earning.

Walk with me, son of my learning,
Walk with me one final time.
Find with me the paths of life.
Walk with me till seasons cease turning."

A great shuddering possessed Nimbulan. The red chain beside him regained color and vibrancy. It coiled up through him, encasing Nimbulan's silvery-blue umbilical. All of their knowledge joined, their memories twined, and their secrets unfolded. They were one man, one life force, one mind.

The vast tangle of life forces shifted and collapsed into images of men, generations of men, marching in intricate patterns, sometimes peaceful, sometimes at odds with each other. Magicians ringed the intricate dance patterns, calling directions to the men. He became a part of the vision, manipulating the resisting lords. The patterns swirled into violence, became the battle he had just fought and dozens of other battles, each indistinguishable from the other. Battle after battle, he lobbed spells into the fray at random. Death and destruction sent waves of revulsion through him. And still he sent men to their deaths with his magic.

He watched men step away from the vision of battle, ready to retire and reform the balance of the dance patterns. Nimbulan wanted to join them, but he found himself pulling them back into the asymmetrical violence. . . .

Keegan's essence burst free of his mentor and sped outward into the knot of pulsing lives, leaving Nimbulan alone with access only to his own thoughts and memories. The vision faded. A sour taste lingered.

A vibrant red umbilical wrapped around Nimbulan, urging him to follow deeper into the void.

Symmetrical patterns. Balance. Harmony.

Keegan beckoned to him to walk beside him in intimate friendship, as father and son, till the seasons ceased their turning.

Nimbulan moved with the compelling vision, stretching to unite with other life-pulses as well.

Unity. Peace. If only . . .

An invisible barrier slammed down in front of him, blocking the enticing vision.

(Go back, human. 'Tis not your time!) Unknown voices resounded throughout the eternal blackness. (*Premature joining with the void is forbidden. Go back now, lest your immortal soul be torn from you and cast aside.*)

Nimbulan dropped back into his body with an ungraceful thump. The aches in his joints still hurt, but his soul felt lighter.

"I hope I never have to do that again, Ackerly. Something happened in the void—something important to all of us. But I couldn't quite grasp it. I almost followed Keegan into my next existence."

"Never think that, Master. What would Lord Kammeryl do without you?"

"He'd find another magician. Yes, yes, I know, suicide is forbidden, Ackerly." The Stargods had firmly reminded him of that. "But there is knowledge in the void. A vision slid around me, begging me to learn. I didn't have time to do more than glimpse the edges of the lesson."

"What? What did the Stargods show you?" Ackerly leaned forward eagerly.

"I'm not certain. I need time and solitude to meditate."

"Neither of which are you likely to have soon. Lord Kammeryl comes." Ackerly pointed to a broad man with the reddish lights of his Stargod ancestors in his hair. Their employer marched determinedly across the field toward them.

"Is that Quinnault de Tanos, the Peacemaker, behind him?" Hope brightened inside Nimbulan at sight of the tall figure gliding in the wake of Kammeryl d'Astrismos' powerful form. De Tanos' blond head shone in the dawn light like a golden aura of pure energy. The minor lord, who had studied for the priesthood until he assumed responsibility for his clan, was known for his wisdom and might help Nimbulan understand his vision in the void.

"Meddlesome priest. Why doesn't de Tanos stay in his monastery and count the stars?" Ackerly complained. "We don't need his version of peace to win this war."

"Priest no longer, but an anointed lord," Nimbulan replied.

"Lord of a miserable chain of islands in the river and a farm on the mainland—not even a proper fortress. He commands no armies and leads no men. No one respects his meddling in the name of peace." Ackerly spat on the ground beside his boot. "Compromise and treaties won't find us a new king. Only a warlord who can defeat all rivals will unite Coronnan under one crown."

"I used to believe that, too," Nimbulan whispered. He needed to think and think hard.

"Go back to your pavilion, Lan. Sup and rest while I divert Lord Kammeryl and the failed priest."

"Find Kammeryl a woman." Nimbulan suggested. Their employer's aura roiled like an unbalanced storm cloud—*like the patterns of men dancing in the void when they stepped out of the planned formation into violence. . . .* Splotches of black marred the layers of orange, green, and yellow energy surrounding d'Astrismos. 'Twas always thus before and after a battle. Only the camp followers soothed the violent outpouring energy of his mind and body.

"Make sure it's a willing woman and not a young girl under a compulsion," Nimbulan added.

"He prefers the girls. He'll linger longer with them. They cost less."

"A woman, Ackerly. Find him a camp follower who knows the payment, and the cost, beforehand."

Behind a delusion of thickening mist and smoke from the funeral pyres, Nimbulan withdrew.

"*Stargods,* help me interpret your vision correctly!"

* * *

A cold wet nose touched Myrilandel's cheek. She opened one heavy eye, shrugging her shoulders against the predawn chill. Her dream of flying high over the Great Bay vanished, leaving her curiously empty.

"Good morning, Mistress Badger," she responded to a second prodding from the animal's nose. "Thank you for the use of your burrow. I'll be on my way." She took one extra moment to rub sleep-sand from her eyes and dragged herself from the tight confines of the badger's home.

The joy of greeting a new morning filled the emptiness, and she forgot all but her excitement at facing a new day, a new adventure.

"Grrrr," Mistress Badger said, urging Myri to hurry. Dawn approached, and clearly the bristle-furred creature wanted to sleep.

"One more moment." Myri crouched in the den opening and reached back inside for her familiar and her pack before Mistress Badger could dash to her bed.

"Merawk?" Amaranth protested the abrupt move. The flywacket peered at Myri through the narrowed slits of his eyes and extended his claws for balance. A hint of heaving within his black fur released his feathered wings in automatic response to Myri's awkward grasp.

"You don't need to scratch, Amaranth!" Myri batted at the flywacket's offending claws. Half cat, half falcon, Amaranth usually exhibited the best qualities of both creatures. But for the first few moments after awakening, he was as cranky as Old Magretha, the witchwoman who had raised them both.

Myri dropped Amaranth beyond the badger's reach and stepped aside. He settled into a morning wash, pointedly ignoring her. The badger waddled into the narrow opening without a backward glance.

"Thanks again, Mistress Badger. 'Twas the snuggest nest I've had since I began this quest." Too long ago, with only her magic talent tugging her toward some distant place and anonymous voices in her head to guide her. *(East,)*, they said. *(You will find a safe home in the East.)*

She stood, brushing dirt and twigs from her leaf-green overgown. Her fingers provided the only comb for her silver-blonde hair. Out of long habit she braided the length of hair and coiled it beneath a kerchief. People accepted her more readily if they didn't notice her strange coloring right off.

A sense of wrongness buzzed like a bee around her head. She rotated her shoulders, hands held slightly away from her to catch the wind in her sleeves. The magic within her coiled, eager to spring forth in healing. Slowly she walked in a circle, waiting for her magic to point out the direction. North by East—not due East as the voices urged her. Stronger and more compelling than the voices. Something terrible awaited her. Close.

A chill breeze and her own uneasiness sent lumbird bumps up her spine. "My cloak!" Healing always left her weak and unbalanced. She didn't dare approach a spell without the means to warm herself later. She reached back into the den for the thick woolen garment. Her hand closed on the fabric just as Mistress Badger claimed it for her nest.

Myri tugged. The badger sank her claws into her prize. "I can't afford to let you keep it." She pulled harder. The sound of rending cloth sent her heart sinking. "I've no way to replace it, Mistress Badger. And I don't have your thick fur to keep me warm."

The fabric sprang free of the animal's grasp. Myri dragged it out into the glow of false dawn. She examined her peat-brown cloak with sensitive fingertips. Her fingernail caught on a small rip near the side seam. She found no other damage.

Eagerly she turned East to face the rising sun at its equinox. The sense of wrongness intensified, disrupting her joy at greeting the morning.

Just over the next hill, due North, lay a village. The

triple Pylon at the exact center of the community stood ready for fruit and flower decorations. All of Coronnan would celebrate the change of season today. Dancing. Feasting. Games. Especially dancing. Men and women weaving intricate patterns around the Equinox Pylon in ancient rituals that thanked the Stargods for the harvest and prayed for an easy Winter.

Myri and Amaranth had escaped Magretha's vigilant eye every Spring and Autumn for as long as she could remember to watch and participate in the dancing.

Did she need to heal someone in the village?"

(East. Go East. We will give you safety and rest. Do not turn aside.)

"I want to go to the village," Myri replied to the voices in her head. "They might need me." Why shouldn't she run away from her quest for just a few hours? She'd followed the compulsion to go East for over a moon now. Surely whatever called her could wait a little longer. As long as the first dance at least.

She doubted they'd allow her to dance in this village. The patterns required equal numbers of men and women to balance the forces of nature. Unlike the Spring Equinox Festival, partners of the harvest dance were usually determined long before the celebration date. But she wanted to watch, to tap her foot in rhythm with the music and sing along with the age-old tunes.

Myri ran up the hill to catch a first glimpse of people emerging from their homes as the sun crossed the horizon.

The wind joined her healing talent and circled around her in a fierce howl, pushing her back East by Southeast. Lumbird bumps marched up and down her arms. Wordless pleas carried by the moving air begged her to follow without delay.

Her talent threatened to drag her due North faster than she could run.

(Save your strength. Put aside your talent until you have more training. Go East. East and a little South, avoid the North.) The voices took on a pleading tone. *(Do not linger in this area. There is danger to you.)* The voices urged her to alter her route.

She sat down on the damp grass in protest. Her talent and the anonymous voices warred within her every time she encountered people who needed her healing. She was getting tired of the compulsion always choosing her path for her.

"I want to watch the dancing for a few moments."

The wind died. Her talent still reached out, sensing pain and suffering, but no longer dragging her in its wake. The voices silenced for a moment.

She straightened her skirts and draped her cloak over her shoulders, spreading her arms just a little so the cloak billowed behind her like a giant wing.

"Let's go Amaranth. Maybe we can share a cup of cider and a crust of new bread."

Her mouth watered. Dry journey rations and creek water didn't seem enough right now. Her stomach growled in agreement.

A distant drum sounded the rhythm of a pulse—softly at first, but gathering volume and tempo with each beat. Myri hurried over the crest of the hill. She didn't want to miss a moment of the first dance of thanksgiving. For four years now she'd participated in the dancing wherever she and Magretha made their home. This ritual offering of the first and best of the harvest, of all those dedicated to the Stargods, seemed the most important. Spring festivals, with all their emphasis on fertility, tended to be wild, drunken affairs. Autumn rituals brought people into harmony with the Stargods as they displayed their gratitude and reverence for the season's bounty.

She lifted her voice in a song that followed the same cadence as the drum.

The Kardia pulsed beneath her bare feet in unison with her song and the drum. Feminine voices from the village joined hers as people burst from the huts, wearing their brightest and newest clothing.

"Mew?" Amaranth asked in his cat voice. He wove a path of protection around and between her ankles. His sides heaved again and a wingtip protruded from the concealing folds of skin and fur. His preparation for flight revealed the depth of his agitation.

Myri came to an abrupt halt at the edge of the common.

"Yes, Amaranth. I know something is not right here." Myri bent to scratch his ears. His mild protective spell extended to her.

A circle of pounded dirt around the Equinox Pylon bespoke of many generations of ritual dances. Nine men, nine women, nine drummers, and nine children must circle the decorated three-times-three poles of the Pylon. Only healthy people filled with life and joy should participate in the dance. Nine, the sacred number of the Stargods. Always nines and always a balance of male and female.

But only one man joined the women, and he half crippled. Beardless boys, their faces set in dutiful concentration, filled the positions of the other men. A solitary ancient woman, well-past childbearing held a padded stick over the solitary drum. The young women in their prime seemed most out of place. None appeared pregnant from the Vernal Equinox fertility rituals.

None of them.

Because there were no men.

"Where did they all go? 'Tis not yet the season for them to go away hunting. Surely no plague would kill only men." Myri sought an explanation for the out-of-balance dancers.

The rhythm of the single drum faltered. Faces turned toward Myri and her black cat. Silence stretched across the bowl of the village until the hills themselves begged for the return of the drumbeat. Pain poured from the eyes of every dancer. They knew the unbalanced numbers. Then the old woman slammed her padded stick against the skin-covered hoop of the drum. She beat again and a third time. The rhythm returned. A flute joined in. Dancers moved in the ancient pattern.

Step, hop, clap, hop. Stamp three times in a circle. Step together, step, hop. Clap, clap, clap.

The voices joining the festival dance slowed to a dirge. Many of those in the circle of dancers wept openly. Still the dance continued. Step, hop, clap, hop.

"Where is the thanksgiving and the joy?" Myri asked the empty sky. "Where are the men?"

(The plague that took them is called war,) the voices said inside her head. *(Go now, quickly, before the plague catches you, too. You must delay no longer. Come East. We will protect you from war.)*

Myri whirled from the sad sight of the Equinox ritual,

choosing a direction at random. The rhythm of the drum continued to beat in her head. *No more men. No more men. No more men.* Up one hill, and another, and yet another, she ran, trying desperately to escape the horror of a village without men. Men to plow and plant, to hunt and sire new babies.

No more men. No more men.

The drum seemed to follow her, louder and louder. Her heart sped with the effort of her running. The drum increased its tempo to match.

(Turn away. turn to the East and South!) the voices pleaded. *(You are going the wrong way!)*

She held her hands over her ears. The throbbing sounds grew louder yet and so did the voices. The farther she ran, the closer she came to the source of the pulse. Amaranth flew circles over her head, mewling his concern for her.

As she crested the third hill, Amaranth dropped awkwardly to the ground, as stunned as she.

She stumbled across the body of a dead man. Blank eyes stared at her, his face twisted in pain. Blood covered his torso from a deep sword slash that split him nearly in two.

'Twasn't the drum that had followed her. She'd run away from a feeble attempt to celebrate life toward death and destruction.

"Pass in peace to your next existence." She closed his eyes with her left hand as she crossed herself with her right.

Below her, in a broad river meadow, lay thousands of men, dead and dying. Hideously wounded and needing her help.

Two generations of men, wasted.

The compulsion to heal pulled her feet toward the horrors.

(Turn away now, before you fall so deeply into a healing spell we can't pull you out. Save yourself. You need more training. More maturity and wisdom.)

"I can't run away from these men. They need me!"

Normally one healing spell dragged her spirit so low she needed a full day of rest and solitude to recover. Below her lay thousands of men needing her.

The drum continued to pound in her ears. *No more men. No more men.*

She had to save some of them. Some of them at least had to return to the villages.

No more men.

Healing drained the very life out of her, pouring it into her patients.

"I have to heal them. I have to try. What good am I if I don't give my talent to those who need me?"

(You will die.)

"Then I will die now rather than later. I have to do this."

CHAPTER 3

Myri pushed through the mist and the smoke hovering over the battlefield toward the core of pain that called to her. The intense suffering ahead made her talent reach out in healing comfort without conscious thought or preparation. She reeled the tendrils of power back within herself.

Screams pierced her heart. The stench of blood and fear embraced her and drew her deeper into the aura of pain and agony. And yet more pain and horror.

(Resist their call. Conserve your strength. Leave now before their pain swallows you whole. We will protect you, give you a home. You must come East now.)

"I can't leave them. They need me." She moved swiftly through the ranks of dead and dying. Her passing touch would only numb the injuries for a little, not truly cure. She would be drained before she reached those she could save.

Outside the hospital pavilion a young trooper stared at row after row of wounded men awaiting the attention of the healers. Myri grabbed his sleeve, yanking him away from the paralysis of bewilderment. His close-cropped hair that would fit neatly under a helmet identified him as a common soldier, not an officer or noble. He needed something to do.

"Hot water, lots of hot water. And bandages. Set your comrades to tearing up cloth—clean shirts and undergarments," she ordered him.

Desperate to relieve the pain all around her, Myri slapped the young man's face. "Do it. Now!" He shook himself free of whatever trance his mind had settled into.

"Yes, ma'am." His hand moved upward. Almost a salute, not quite a tug of his forelock. "Lots of hot water and bandages," he repeated.

"And get some of your friends to start washing these men. I can't heal them if I can't find their wounds beneath the mud and the blood." The patients would feel better for the attention until she had time to deal with them.

The young man dashed off.

"Younger than I am," Myri whispered. "But I can't call him a boy. Not after what he's lived through in this battle." She moved into the tent.

Three gray-clad healers, two men and a woman, moved among the moaning men. The woman wore an apron to protect her healer's robe from dried blood and gore. She'd pushed the loose sleeves of her robe to her shoulders and secured them with black ribbons.

Fatigue lined the faces of all three healers. They wore their hair cut short for convenience. Sweat dulled their faces and hair colors to a uniform dark gray. Clearly the healers had worked since the battle began. How long?

Myri began her work in the corner farthest from the healers. What use her defying the guiding voices if she were evicted as an untrained meddler before she began? Magretha had fostered her to an acknowledged magician, she might be one of these healers. But without that formal training she might resign herself to always being a mere witchwoman—maligned and feared by superstitious mundanes, regarded as incompetent by the trained healers.

A head wound on her left needed little more than a touch to remove the pressure and wake the man from deep unconsciousness. She sent him on his way with a fierce headache and orders to remain quiet a day or two.

She treated broken legs, gashes, and other nonmortal wounds. Those patients walked away and freed space for some of those waiting outside. Myri pulled a handful of dried nuts and berries from her pack to restore the energy she'd spent. Her stomach wouldn't tolerate the taste of meat in this bloody environment. She craved the nutrients in meat, though. If only she had some cheese.

Behind her, Amaranth prowled the shadows, seeking those who needed Myri the most.

His plaintive mew called her to the center of the tent.

Already two of the healers and a red-robed magician—she guessed he was a priest from the color he wore—stood over an unconscious man with his right arm dangling from a sliver of bone and tendril of white ligament. Magic hovered in the air around the healers who worked to save a life. Still the soldier's lifeblood pumped out of him.

Heedless of the censure that might come from the priest, Myri obeyed the persistent demands of her talent.

A *Song* of sweet healing sprang to her lips as a bundle of special herbs and moss came to her hand from her pack. She shouldered aside the older of the gray healers who stood helplessly at the patient's head.

Breathe in, hold, breathe out, hold. Her head cleared and magic simmered within her. A second deep breath and hold. Power tingled in her fingertips, focused and ready to fulfill its promise of healing.

"Hold his arm in place," she whispered to the female healer. She nodded, too tired and numb to do anything but obey.

"Magic isn't enough for a wound this severe," the elder of the two male healers countermanded. "The only way to save the arm is to stitch the blood vessels and the layers of muscle. But 'twill take too much time. We must amputate and cauterize to stop the bleeding."

"Please, let me try," Myri begged even as she made a poultice of her herbs in a bucket of clean water at the patient's feet.

"Ye'll not save him. I sense his spirit passing into the void already," the priest grabbed her hands in his own. Gnarled, scarred hands, meticulously clean, even under the neatly trimmed fingernails. A crescent scar that could have come from human teeth stood out from the knife-straight markings at the base of his right thumb.

"I can't allow you to interfere with the man's passing into his next existence." His voice was soft, caring. An unwary person could fall under the spell of that voice.

But Myri was wary. She noted the patches and threadbare spots where his elbows stuck through the faded red robe. She looked up into the priest's face, knowing she would encounter hate and fear in his black eyes. She'd seen that robe before. *She* had inflicted that scar on his thumb when he'd tried to interfere with her first serious healing—before she knew enough to fear him.

"Moncriith," she whispered. Not a priest. A Bloodmage who fueled his powers with blood and pain while he preached against demons only he could see. If he were here, then his followers wouldn't be far away. How many hundreds awaited his orders to burn those who interfered with the Bloodmage's wishes?

"Witchwoman Myrilandel." He jerked his hands away from her.

"Let me save this man. Please." She pressed her hands tighter against the severed arm, willing the blood vessels to mend and join before Moncriith could stop her. His campaign against witchwomen as the tools of demons was well known in every village where she and Magretha had sought sanctuary. Hundreds of women wandered Coronnan, homeless and maligned because Moncriith had labeled them witchwomen—whether they had magical talent or not.

"Because of you, a man walks soulless through life," Moncriith intoned. He lifted his hands in an appeal to the Stargods as he raised his voice to carry throughout the hospital tent. "Five years ago, you interfered with a man's destined passage into his next existence with your demon-spawn spells."

Off to the side, a soldier touched head, heart, and both shoulders, the Stargods' ward against evil. Then he crossed his wrists and fluttered his hands in a more ancient sign. Amaranth butted his head into the man's leg and purred reassurance. The soldier jumped away from the cat as if burned.

"Because you refused to use your magic to heal a simple cut, the man nearly lost his life," Myri reminded Moncriith. "Jessup would have died prematurely. His pregnant widow and two tiny children couldn't fell timber to earn a living and keep a roof over their heads and food in their bellies. Because I saved Jessup, the family thrives once more."

Myri continued her binding spell, praying she wouldn't have to go into a deep trance to restore her patient's vitality. Already Moncriith's fervor laid a taint of guilt upon her, weakening her power and control over the healing.

What did he see in her and other women that was so very evil? He never singled out the wives of powerful men, nor did he accuse men—only women who lived alone, without the protection of husband, father, or son.

"The timberman you cured limps painfully, clear evidence that he left his soul in the void when you dragged him back to this existence. Another soulless demon to aid you in your evil practices." Moncriith's voice took on tremors of righteousness.

Silence spread through the hospital tent. Even the screams of the dying fell off.

Myri ducked her head so the men wouldn't see her tears of doubt. Her talent sprang from deep inside her without her conscious control. Did it come from demons?

She had no arguments against Moncriith's accusations.

The three healers gazed suspiciously at Myri and Amaranth, who now circled the wounded man's pallet. Blue light glowed beneath her hands where the lifeless arm sought to rejoin with the body.

She had to stop Moncriith's interference before the blue light totally engulfed her mind and body.

"This witchwoman is possessed by demons. Burn her before she condemns this brave soldier to a soulless life!" Moncriith implored, reaching eager hands for Myri's shoulders. He jerked back, repelled by the barrier her talent erected even as it dragged her deeper into a trance.

Beneath her fingers, life pulsed into the dangling arm. The soldier moaned and clenched his fist. Then he fell back into unconsciousness.

"Stargods!" Men whispered around the tent. More wards against evil, modern and ancient.

The healers cleared the hovering crowd away to inspect Myri's work. Gently, the quiet woman who held the injured limb in place lifted her fingers from the injury. She saw with her eyes what Myri knew in her mind. Muscles mended and bones knitted. The bleeding had stopped.

" 'Tis a miracle from the Stargods," the healer whispered.

"Or a trick of Simurgh, king of all demons," Moncriith countered.

Myri took a deep breath, trying desperately to stay alert. If she lost consciousness and fell into a full trance, as her magic demanded, Moncriith would have her removed and condemned. He'd done it before. Only Magretha's good reputation in the village had saved her. But Magretha had died nearly two years ago.

Power flowed out of her. Her shaking joints became too heavy to support her body. She sagged to the floor, still holding the wounded arm in place. She tried to remove herself and her talent from the healing. Like a living being the spell enveloped her and fed from her strength.

"Look at the blackness in her aura!" Moncriith beseeched those around her. "Demons possess her. She taints us all with demons. Better to die blessed than live possessed!"

"I know nothing of demons," Myri whispered through numb lips as the void took her.

* * *

Nimbulan listened to the wind whipping around his pavilion. Saturated canvas walls bulged inward and sighed slackly with each blow. The candle flames of a dozen lanterns placed around the tent bowed almost flat within mica shields and then wavered upright again in rhythm with the howling of the skies.

Lord Kammeryl d'Astrismos and Lord Quinnault de Tanos argued almost as intensely inside. They paced and sat and shouted at each other while Nimbulan watched and ate his meal in near silence.

Nimbulan hunched his shoulders against the chill wind that crept along the carpeted tent floor. His woolen dressing gown, quilted with layers of silk wasn't adequate to warm him after the hours of magic battle. The first of the autumn storms had held off just long enough for Kammeryl and his enemy to finish the battle. Now the armies could hole up, rest, and resupply during the winter.

The brazier at Nimbulan's feet helped ward off the chill a little. Four hours of sleep and half a meal had barely restored his strength. But the two lords had awakened him to give them counsel almost as soon as his complaining stomach had roused him from deepest sleep. He left Rollett, Jaanus, and Gilby, his senior apprentices asleep in the back portion of the pavilion. They needed rest more than he did. He didn't know where Maalin and Bessel were. Maybe they slept in Ackerly's tent, adjacent to the large pavilion.

He fished another stringy piece of beef from the salty broth as he watched the warlord and the Peacemaker. The boys needed to eat, too. But they needed sleep more . . . unlike his years as Druulin's apprentice and journeyman when there was never enough food to fuel growing bodies.

"You must seek peace now, Lord Kammeryl. The weather has turned against you," Quinnault de Tanos said quietly. He sipped lightly at a mug of spiced wine.

Nimbulan looked for clues to Quinnault's mood and thoughts from the shift of his eyes and the bunching of muscles in his shoulders. His aura, his mind, and his face remained carefully schooled. Even the Peacemaker's grip on the cup handle remained steady and relaxed.

"Why should I sue for peace?" Kammeryl roared in his midrange of shouts. The hearty leader had a variety of bellowing tones and no soft ones. His aura showed a balance of colors as he paced the circumference of Nimbulan's tent. " 'Tis not me who started this feud with the Baron of Hanic. His grandfather kidnapped and raped my grandmother fifty years ago. I'll not have Hanic bastards set themselves up as rivals to *my* crown, when I am king. I'll be ready to pursue the fight at the first break in the storm."

"Fifty years is a long time. Wounds of honor should heal when the participants die a natural death." De Tanos raised one eyebrow and cocked his head. For a moment, the shadows from the dancing firelight cast a different image on Quinnault's bone structure. Something large and elongated, not quite human.

A whiff of Tambootie lingered in the air. The sweet smell of Tambootie flowers in Spring rather than the sharply musky odor of the oily leaves and aromatic bark.

An eerie chill passed over Nimbulan. He resisted the urge to cross himself in the ward against evil—against the unwarranted smell of Tambootie out of season or the bizarre shadows he didn't know. Instead, he turned his left palm upward, opening it to any stray power. An itch, unlike any known magic, irritated his palm. He twisted his wrist, seeking the source. The strange sensation evaporated.

"The bastards my grandmother bore Hanic now rule that clan and claim my lands." Kammeryl's roar rattled the cups on the wobbling camp table as he restated the ancient grievance.

"Bastards? More than one? Perhaps 'twas not a kidnap, but an elopement," De Tanos said quietly. Too quietly. The tug of a grin banished the mask of shadows. Nimbulan returned the grin. 'Twouldn't be the first or last time a noble bride foresook a political marriage for love. Quinnault sucked at his cheeks to control the smile. The mask of shadows returned.

Without the Tambootie in his system Nimbulan couldn't penetrate the secrets behind those shadows. But he'd had too much already. He didn't want to grow dependent upon the weed.

The void stripped away lies and delusions to lay bare a soul in the same manner. Nimbulan reviewed the vision of lords dancing in harmony he had experienced in the void. Had he seen the essence of de Tanos in the patterns and not recognized it? He shook his head clear of the puzzling vision. He had to concentrate on the present.

"You dishonor the memory of my grandmother, a queen descended from the Stargods!" Kammeryl's scream of rage drowned out the wind.

"The land you fought over yesterday was your grandmother's dowry. She bequeathed it to her son by Hanic, a symbol of her need to protect the boy. Her son by d'Astrismos claimed it by right of her lawful first marriage to your grandfather. Isn't it time you and your cousin sat down together and settled the issue?" Quinnault set aside his mug of wine. No grimace of distaste touched his face. Yet Nimbulan sensed the drink had gone sour. The drink or Kammeryl's company?

"The time is ripe, my lord," Nimbulan jumped into the conversation. The bread was gone, as well as the broth and the yampion pie. The sweetness lingered on his tongue. He craved more of the thick tuber baked in cream and eggs, laced liberally with sugar—a favorite treat that Druulin had always reserved for himself.

Nimbulan needed more fuel for his body. The two lords wouldn't give him enough peace to fetch more until they settled the argument or took it elsewhere.

"Consider," Nimbulan continued. He raised his hand, palm outward, as he talked. "Hanic retreated in disarray.

His army is broken, at great cost. He has no resources left to defend his stronghold. A blood oath from you not to pursue and destroy him in his moment of weakness would require a concession from him. What has he left to give you but the deed to the disputed land, signed in blood? He might also renounce all claim to the kingship and put you one step closer to ending this war forever." He finished his wine. It had indeed gone sour.

"Another magician already whispers in Hanic's ear of a way to wrest victory from this defeat," Kammeryl protested. "I'll not appear weak by offering peace when I can destroy Hanic and have all of his estates."

"Hanic retreated. Certainly that entitles you to claim victory. But at what cost? Your army is reduced to two battalions." Quinnault kicked his camp stool out from under him and began to pace. "This victory shed more blood than the last three battles combined. The healers are worn to the bone and have called in a local witchwoman to assist them—I shudder to think what her untrained talent will do to our patients. Did the dead and wounded win anything? What about the people who huddle in their ravaged homes wondering if they will have anything left to survive the winter with after two armies foraged through here for supplies? And let us not forget the taxes they owe you for a new pledge of loyalty.

"No one won this battle, Lord Kammeryl. No one truly wins any war," de Tanos ended on a sigh of grief. The sweet smell of Tambootie flowers sharpened into the more usual scent of oily leaves and aromatic bark.

A pang of longing for the taste of the Tambootie sent aches into Nimbulan's joints. He resisted the craving.

"My magician won." Kammeryl glared at the Peacemaker. His aura sprouted black spots, losing its recently restored balance.

Grief replaced Nimbulan's urge to indulge in Tambootie. "I won at the cost of murdering my most promising apprentice in order to end the carnage. That is not victory. If we have to kill each other to win your battles, soon there won't be any magicians left. New magicians are hard to find and we rarely beget children to inherit our talents."

He'd never have a son or daughter to replace Keegan,

only more apprentices. He had to hold close the boys who remained with him, love them and nurture them as well as train them.

"Nimbulan lost more than a traitorous pupil," Quinnault added. "Look at your magician, Kammeryl, really look at how gaunt and worn he is. In the last hour he's eaten three meals and still he hungers. His bones nearly poke through his skin. How long since he slept a night through? He cannot rest because the lords will beggar themselves to find a more powerful Battlemage. I beg of you Kammeryl, take this opportunity to treat with Hanic. Give your army, your people, your land, and your magician a respite."

"Peace is useless. Other lords see peace as weakness. They'll stab me in the back." Kammeryl dismissed Quinnault's suggestion with an impatient gesture.

"What is left for you to continue the fight with?" Quinnault continued to hound the warlord.

"My magician. The best magician in all of Kardia Hodos. He guarantees me victory at any cost. He'll have to conjure me the illusion of troops."

"If Nimbulan breaks his covenant with the Stargods to perform such an unnatural spell, Hanic will have to find an outland magician to defend himself—perhaps he'll recruit Moncriith, the Bloodmage whose talent demands he fuel his power with the death and pain of others." Sadness dragged Quinnault's shoulders down as all three men crossed themselves in the Stargods' ward against evil. "There will never be peace once blood powers are tapped."

"What if all magicians refused to fight your battles?" Nimbulan asked. A glimmer of hope beckoned to him like th red crystal in the void. Men moving in harmonious patterns until manipulated to violence by . . .

"You might as well wish for flywackets and dragons," Kammeryl snorted. "Magicians will never unite. They guard their secrets too well. Too jealously."

"That is the case now. But what if all the magicians banded together and refused to make war?" Nimbulan asked.

Quinnault looked up sharply. Ideas seemed to blossom in his eyes. Nimbulan nodded to him and tried to pass encouragement mind-to-mind. But the Peacemaker's solid mental barriers didn't allow such communication.

"Why I . . . I'd . . ." Kammeryl stammered, at a loss for words and bluster for the first time since Nimbulan had known him.

"You'd hasten to the treaty table," Quinnault prodded him. "You'd run with eagerness because war is too costly."

" 'Tisn't worth thinking about. Magicians can't prosper during peace. Of what use are they but to fight battles for lords such as me?"

Ackerly had asked the same question years ago when he'd first realized his talent would never match Nimbulan's. Neither of them could think of another magical profession Ackerly could pursue.

Nimbulan watched the canvas door flap behind Kammeryl's jerky exit. The lord's stiff spine and rigid knees helped him pretend that his dignity was intact. But his aura swung wildly from orange to purple with growing black spots in each layer. Nimbulan hoped Ackerly had access to more women for the warlord.

As if summoned by Nimbulan's thoughts, his assistant appeared in the doorway. "Nimbulan, please come. The hospital. Terrible. A stranger leads a virulent dispute in the *hospital.*" Ackerly wrung his hands together, looking over his shoulder toward the source of the disruption.

"The hospital?" Nimbulan pulled muddy boots over his house slippers. "Why would anyone disturb the hospital." His filthy formal robe, not cleaned yet from the battle, would have to do. In his weakened state he dared not trudge across the camp in the rain without protection. He checked the pockets for wand and glass and other arcane tools. A rustle of dry leaves reminded him that he'd stuffed some Tambootie in a pocket some time during the battle. He threw it onto the brazier rather than eat it now. He'd had too much already.

"I think it's the Bloodmage, sir. Moncriith. He's demanding that a witchwoman with the healing talent be brought to justice for dealing with demons."

Neither of them suggested they turn the matter over to Kammeryl. Disputes within the camp fell under the warlord's jurisdiction. But Kammeryl d'Astrismos might very well wade into this brawl, *in the hospital,* with fists flying.

"Please wait for my return, my Lord Quinnault. We'll continue this discussion over a meal. Many issues lie unresolved." Nimbulan plunged into the storm.

"*Stargods!* Hasn't there been enough death today?" Quinnault raised his hands in supplication. "That fanatic Moncriith won't be satisfied until he's the only living soul left in Coronnan."

CHAPTER 4

Witchlight glowed through the bubble of armor around the huge hospital tent. Nimbulan looked up through the armor. Raindrops sizzled and evaporated when they touched the magical shields. The wind circled, howled, and sought new targets when it couldn't attack the tent itself. He shuddered with a chill as several drops of cold rain penetrated the armor and his blue robe of oiled wool.

Something was weakening the armor.

Outside the tent, rows of wounded men waited beneath the bubble for their turn with a healer. Strangely, their comrades, battle-weary men who should be resting and eating, washed and cared for them. He'd never seen common soldiers tend the wounded before. That activity belonged solely to healer magicians.

Shouts of anger and dismay disturbed the aura of peace that should have surrounded the hospital, along with the armor. Lumbird bumps climbed Nimbulan's spine as the warmth faded and two more drops of rain worked through the magical armor to land on his head.

The brawl within the tent must be disrupting the protective spells.

Armed guards converged upon the tent door at the same time as Nimbulan.

"Let me try to calm them before you use force to end this." He waved the armed men to stand behind him.

A sergeant held the tent flaps open for him. Eerie blue light surrounded a litter at the center of the tent. The blue was paler than Nimbulan's robe which matched the signature color of his magic. Whoever was at the core of the light wasn't one of his magicians.

Wounded men filled row upon row of pallets, cots, and

litters around the core of blue light. Three gray-robed healers stood in a sentinel circle around the core of the blue light, their backs to it. They held scalpels, saws, and other surgical implements as weapons. They seemed prepared to use them against the shouting men pressing toward the blue light.

"Burning is the only cure for demon possession. We must take the girl to the funeral pyres and throw her into the purifying flames," Moncriith shouted. The Bloodmage just barely reached medium height, yet he dominated the crowd of taller men. His faded red robe took on the color of old blood—indicative of his perverted style of magic.

A shiver of disquiet snaked down Nimbulan's spine. Moncriith pitched his voice to draw listeners into his aura and meld with his opinions, right or wrong.

"Break her magic!" a wounded soldier called from a nearby pallet. "I saw her during the battle, her and her wicked familiar. They called the dragon what nearly killed me with its flames and talons." He held up a hand burned by magic and raked by long furrows. Probably his own fingers had made those cuts, seeking to shed a ball of magic thrown by Nimbulan or Keegan during the battle.

"I saw it, too," another man agreed. His wounds weren't evident.

"Dragon dung!" Nimbulan pitched his voice to penetrate the verbal fray. No one paid him any heed.

"She saved my life and three others that I know of." A man with a bloody bandage around his head joined the healers in defense of the blue-lit litter.

"Look what she's doing for Sergeant Kennyth! He lost that arm saving me." Another soldier limped to join the man with the head wound. "The witchwoman saved his life and she's givin' him back his arm, too. We owe her. Kennyth's the best sergeant in the whole *s'murghin'* army."

Moncriith advanced on the bubble of light. "Myrilandel wields the power of demons. No healer blessed by the Stargods can do the things she does. 'Tis unholy. 'Tis evil. The demons who possess her body will attack us all. Kennyth's soul has already moved into another plane of existence. Yet his body lives. He will become her undead servant."

"Enough!" Nimbulan shouted. The ridgepole vibrated with the power of his voice.

Silence reigned. All the participants turned to face the Senior Magician. Moncriith turned slowly, almost contemptuously, to confront a recognizable authority.

"So you finally crawled out of your lair, Nimbulan," Moncriith said without inflection.

"You are not welcome here, Moncriith." Nimbulan took two steps closer to the bubble of blue light, trying to see around Moncriith and the healers.

Not a bubble, an aura. He saw two forms within the glowing layers of energy. A kneeling woman lay collapsed over a supine male, her hands locked onto his upper arm at the source of the blue light.

"My mission is to halt the encroachment of demons into the very heart of Coronnan. My followers are prepared to take this witchwoman by force, if necessary. My people are fresh. Yours are battle-weary, Nimbulan. Will you throw them against my people for the sake of one demon-possessed witch?" Moncriith raised his voice again to preaching tones.

The thought of another battle exhausted Nimbulan. When would it stop?

When the harmony of dancing lords is no longer disrupted by self-serving magicians, he thought. Moncriith was the one breaking the harmony this time. Where were the Bloodmage's followers? Surely not in the hospital tent.

"You dare condemn any healer? You who take lives to fuel your magic, dare condemn healers! Do your followers know how you fuel your magic?" Nimbulan aimed his words at the wounded more than at Moncriith.

A wavering in the blue aura diverted Nimbulan's attention. Something important was transpiring and he needed to investigate and study the phenomenon. He needed Ackerly at his back, protecting him, warning him of intruders.

"I don't hide what I am behind platitudes. I draw blood only from myself and my enemies. I never feed upon innocent lives like you do!" An odd light gleamed in Moncriith's eyes as he turned his full attention on Nimbulan.

Fear of Moncriith's fanaticism swelled within him.

This one man might charm half of Coronnan to his distorted view of magic.

"Healers serve all who come to them in need. No matter which lord they serve." Nimbulan fought the urge to back away from Moncriith's fervent appeal.

"Every true healer in Coronnan is occupied solely with the armies, Nimbulan. The common people have no one to turn to but demon-possessed witchwomen. Your healers do nothing but patch up and mend enslaved soldiers so that Battlemages, like yourself, can throw the men back into the wars. Endless wars. *Needless* wars."

Nimbulan's vision of magicians manipulating lords flashed before him again.

"Without healers, the death and carnage would be much worse." Nimbulan ignored the idea that soldiers were slaves to the lords who recruited them—sometimes by force. "Men will fight with or without magicians to back them up. You threaten to renew the battle over one witchwoman. You are no different from any other Battlemage, Moncriith," he said, half believing his own words. The other half lingered in the void with the vision of symmetry and peace—magicians standing away from the balanced, political dance of the lords.

"With every true healer employed by the armies, you condemn the innocents of Coronnan to the mercy of demonic powers wielded by witchwomen," Moncriith said. "Dangerous powers that risk the immortal souls of all of us. The witchwoman here, Myrilandel by name, a demon by birth, leads her sisters in this evil work. Only I can protect you, the men of Coronnan, from her."

For the first time, Nimbulan caught a glimpse of the woman at the core of the blue light. The power she wielded reached out to touch his own, begging him to add his strength to her spell.

He coiled all traces of magic deep within him lest she taint it, or learn from it.

Suddenly he realized the truth of Kammeryl's accusation that magicians would never work together.

"There are no such things as demons. They are the product of your overvivid imagination." Nimbulan latched onto Moncriith's latest argument. All his other defenses of his profession and colleagues were shaken to the core by the events of the last few hours.

"You close your eyes to the evidence of demons because you have been bewitched by her. I see how your eyes linger on her false beauty. I see how your aura reaches out to join hers. If you, Nimbulan, and your ilk could do aught but lead innocent men into battle, you would oust the demons and keep them from destroying souls. You, Nimbulan. You are responsible for this carnage and the perversion of magic."

* * *

Myri awoke from her trance instantly alert to danger from Moncriith. No fire menaced her, and she lay on a soft mattress, not a pyre. She couldn't relax beneath the warm furs that kept off most of the chill wind leaking through the pavilion walls. She didn't trust the feeling of comfort or the sensation of protection shrouding her. She knew Moncriith would try to trick her into confessing her association with demons.

If only she could remember her childhood, or her parents, she might know if he spoke the truth about her. She rarely managed to keep images of her life for more than a day or two. Already Magretha and the village in the Western foothills where she died, were fading from her memory. Only Amaranth remained constant. The flywacket, in his purely cat form, purred gently where he rested, a heavy, secure weight on her chest.

Someone moved nearby. She turned toward the sound of footsteps shuffling on carpets. Through closed eyelids she sensed light around her; light that would stab and blind while her head ached with the aftermath of a healing. Yet she had to know who stood by her so protectively.

"Who are you, Myrilandel?" a man asked her gently. Not Moncriith.

If she knew the answer, she would tell him.

"Overworking magic will rob a person of their wits. Your sense of self will return as your talent and your body revive. Perhaps I should ask where do you come from?"

He lifted a cloth from Myri's forehead and replaced it

with a cool one. Blessedly cool. The throbbing in her head subsided a little.

"I come from nowhere," she replied. Her voice sounded hoarse.

"I have never heard of a drained talent taking memories with it. Perhaps you are in need of the ritual trial by Tambootie smoke."

Trial! Smoke! Surely this man was one of Moncriith's followers, sent to lull her into trust.

She had lived many places—none of them home. She had no memories of her parents to tell him. Magretha was the only parent she remembered. Her guardian had chosen a solitary life at the fringes of society when someone abandoned Myri in the woods with only Amaranth to care for her. The witchwoman needed a successor to her work and a healthy youngster to care for her in later years. Home had been a long series of shacks or caves. They'd fled to a new one very time local villagers began blaming an ugly old woman and her strange fosterling for every ill that life brought them.

Myri had few memories of her own about those early years, only the stories Magretha told over a winter fire. Indeed, most of her memories began with Magretha's death.

The comforting weight of her familiar disappeared. When? "Where is Amaranth?" He always helped her recover after a healing. He would warn her of danger—of Moncriith.

"Who is Amaranth?" The man sat down upon the bed where she rested. The rocking of the mattress sent her insides sloshing about and upset what little equilibrium she had attained.

"Merawk!" Amaranth growled and hissed at the man. His weight pressed against her side now.

"Yeow! You miserable animal. I'm not going to hurt her." The man jumped off the cot cursing. More movement, and a weight landed upon her chest.

Amaranth stretched his warm, furry body atop Myri. He butted his head into her chin. She found his ears with her fingers and scratched. She gritted her teeth against the pain in her head. Amaranth was back where he belonged;

nothing else mattered. His rumbling purr brought peace to her stomach.

With new courage, Myri opened one eye a tiny slit. A tall man, thin almost to gauntness, sucked on his hand where Amaranth had scratched him.

"You are a magician," she stated the obvious. Only the strange cult of men who controlled the forces of nature cut their hair so oddly, straight at the shoulders, with the back tightly braided. This man's dark auburn mane was shot with silver and slightly disheveled. Instead of tunic and trews, he wore formal blue robes, the kind usually reserved for audiences with noble personages. The length of blue cloth draping from his shoulders and loosely belted, added to his height and did nothing to hide his slenderness.

"And who are you, Myrilandel? You have a huge talent for healing, nothing short of miraculous. Kennyth's arm will be weak, but you gave it back to him and saved his life. And yet you are so poorly trained, you let the magic control you. We brought you back from the brink of death." He held his hand out, palm raised, fingers gradually curving so that his little finger almost touched his palm. A curious gesture that seemed a part of him.

"Moncriith allowed you to help me? Probably so he could enjoy the spectacle of watching me burn." He had crowed with delight as he watched another witchwoman burn. Myri had used his distraction to escape that village.

"I ordered armed guards to escort Moncriith and his motley cult from the camp. He won't trouble you again. Lord Kammeryl d'Astrismos agreed to my orders." He smiled slightly as his eyes held hers in a gentle gaze.

"You think me safe while I am under your protection. But what happens when I leave?" She broke the eye contact after a moment, uncertain of his intentions. The voices had promised her a home in the East. How much longer must she travel to find it?

She rolled to her side and tried to sit up, eager to be gone. Amaranth protested her movement with a squeak. Her stomach bounced and pain stabbed between her eyes.

"You aren't going anywhere for a while." The magician eased her back onto the mattress. His hand lingered on her shoulder. The strength in his fingers reassured her where his words hadn't. "I estimate at least a week for you to recover enough to get out of bed and move around a little. In a moon or more we will discuss your homeward journey—if the roads are still passable." His green eyes begged her to agree with him.

"No. I must leave before nightfall." She tried to sit up again but couldn't lift her head from the soft pillow. This time she didn't break the eye contact with him.

She'd heard much of this man's argument with Moncriith, though she'd been deep within her trance at the time and couldn't respond. Nimbulan, chief Battlemage for the lord. He and his ilk had directed the battle, determined who lived and who died. Many of the injuries in the hospital came from magic. She'd stayed away from those men, unsure how to help them. She knew only how to heal wounds inflicted by accident.

"I think you will stay, Myrilandel. I will train you to use your talent properly. Coronnan has need of healers." He stepped behind the shielded candle. His face and aura fell into shadow. "I have other duties of some urgency to attend to now. I've left you a little clear broth and a mug of wine. Don't drink too much too fast. I'll be back to check on you and bring you solid food when you have rested. Some yampion pie, perhaps?" He smiled with the charm of a little boy trying to wheedle sweets out of a stern parent.

Myri wanted to smile with him. Stewed yampion roots blended into a sweet custard of goat's milk and eggs was one of her favorite foods.

Dizziness attacked as she lifted her head to watch him leave. The same dizziness she'd felt as she ran from the village toward the battle. The sight of women dancing around the Equinox Pylon with only children as partners and a single drum for accompaniment haunted her.

"Magician," Myri called to him as he backed into the shadows. "You asked not *why* I came here, only where I came from."

"Why did you come to this particular battle scene when we have been at war for three generations?" He stepped into the light once more. He raised his palm again, almost as if he gathered information through it. His aura glowed blue with honest concern for her. She wanted to trust him. Didn't quite dare.

"I was sent." She had to deliver her message and leave. The voices would guide her to a home where she would be safe from Moncriith and others who needed to hurt her.

"Who sent you?" His hand jerked closed into a fist then opened again—as if caught in a spasm.

"I had a vision. I was sent to remind you of the cost of these battles. In the village three ridges South of here, the women must honor the Equinox in unbalanced numbers. There are no more men to partner them. No more men to father new lives, to plow and plant, to fish or hunt. *No more men.* They have all died in your battles."

"*Stargods!* The Stargods have sent you?" He crossed himself in the accepted manner and closed his eyes as if in prayer.

"I think that you as a magician, a man who needs rituals to perform magic, are the one I must tell of this terrible perversion of nature. You know rituals must be performed properly or not at all. The imbalance of dancers and drummers means the coming year will bring famine to all, including your precious army."

"This news troubles me. I must think on it." The magician turned without another word and faded into the darkness. A puff of wind from the doorway told her that he had left the pavilion.

Relief at his absence relaxed her clenched fists and tight neck muscles. Such a vibrant man. His aura filled the tent, with no room left for her own. And yet his departure left her with a curious sense of emptiness. Loneliness. She wanted to look into those vivid green eyes of his and read his secrets.

"I will sup and rest, but then we must leave, Amaranth." She stroked his fur, making certain his wings remained concealed. "You will have to hunt for me on the journey. I'm not strong enough yet to forage for myself. Moncriith may come back. Nimbulan and his Battlemages cannot tame my talent. They will demand I give up my life to heal the men they order into battle if I stay."

CHAPTER 5

Nimbulan paused outside his pavilion. The witchwoman's words troubled him. He needed time and privacy to meditate on all that had happened since Keegan's death.

"What will it cost me to retain you as my personal magician and adviser?" Quinnault de Tanos greeted him without preamble.

"I am not like other magicians, for sale to any lord with the right price." Nimbulan pulled his attention away from the problems of a demon-hunting Bloodmage and the mysterious witchwoman who commanded more magic than any three of his assistants combined.

Magic combined. If only . . . No. 'Twas impossible. Or was it? He stared past de Tanos at the water clock. His vision in the void beckoned him once more. The crystal all color/no color umbilicals of life reminded him of Myrilandel's white-blonde hair, visible only after he'd removed her kerchief. . . . He'd never encountered those particular umbilicals before. Both the pulsing symbols of life and Myrilandel's hair reminded him of Quinnault's coloring, but the lord's hair was darker and coarser. Impossible to tell for sure in the wavering candlelight.

"I swore loyalty to the clan of Astrismos eighteen years ago. My oath is important to me," Nimbulan replied instead of voicing his speculations. He sank into his comfortably padded folding chair. Someone, probably Ackerly, had placed hot flannels in the backrest. Just what his aching back needed. Now to ease his aching mind with meditation.

"I do not believe that Kammeryl d'Astrismos deserves your loyalty," Quinnault said.

"He's the best choice among many bad ones to lead a

united Coronnan. He is fair to his followers, unyielding to those who betray him. Strong in the face of enemies. People flock to his side . . ."

"For protection because he is strong," de Tanos interrupted. "Not because he is loved. What kind of leader will he be when there are no wars?"

"There are always wars." Nimbulan heaved a weary sigh. War had reigned throughout Coronnan for three generations. He'd never known life without war. "If we do not fight other armies, then we fight the weather, famine, disease."

When the numbers of dancers and drummers are unbalanced famine will follow, the girl had said. *No more men.* A headache pounded behind his eyes to the rhythm of the last phrase. *No more men.*

Would his remaining apprentices have the chance to grow up to be men?

"Speaking of hunger, I must finish my meal and sleep again."

The Peacemaker didn't seem to understand the broad hint. Nimbulan wondered if he'd have to risk rudeness and ask Lord Quinnault to leave. He desperately needed to think on today's events. He also needed to check the boys, make sure they were all safely tucked into bed.

"You proposed that all magicians band together and refuse to go to war." Quinnault de Tanos leaned forward. A jumping pulse in his neck betrayed eagerness to pursue the subject.

"An idea only, not thought through to a conclusion." Nimbulan's headache pounded. *No more men. Unbalanced rituals.*

"Think out loud, Nimbulan. Your reputation for wisdom is almost as legendary as your prowess with magic. Coronnan needs whatever small possibility of peace you can offer."

"I prefer to say no more until the idea has been thought through. Tomorrow I may have something to offer you." He watched the clock again. Involuntarily, his palms turned upward on the chair arms, opening to new thoughts and ideas. His awareness of reality vanished. He saw only the clock's symmetry and motion.

Symmetrical rituals. Lords pulled away from the perfectly balanced dances by magicians enticing them into chaotic patterns and violence. . . . Equinox dances falling out of symmetry without enough men to fill the places. . . .

"Twice in the last hour I have been accused of perpetuating the wars," he whispered. "By Moncriith and by the girl. Are they right?"

"I leave tonight. We need to talk now," Quinnault interrupted his meditation.

Nimbulan blinked rapidly, trying to grasp the present reality rather than his vision. "In the teeth of this storm? Your steed will be mired before you travel a league. I don't need to look into the fire through my glass to foresee a dangerous chill at the end of such a journey. If you complete it alive."

If you can leave, so can the lovely witchwoman. Before she answers all my questions.

"D'Astrismos won't discuss a treaty. Perhaps Hanic will, if I catch him before he walls himself into his fortress for the Winter."

Nimbulan peered at his companion. If only he could see something of the man's aura. . . . But he couldn't. Trust must build on other information. Reputation and tonight's brief acquaintance.

After a long moment he gave in to the impulse to confide in this austere man. The day's events had been too disturbing for him to sort through alone. "When you studied for the priesthood, before your family died and you assumed the lordship, did you have enough magic to access the void?"

"Only by clinging to my tutor's aura; never on my own."

A cautious answer. Every priest of the Stargods had to have a least a little magic talent to qualify for the revered calling. Few great magicians—those able to draw power from the ley lines welling up from the core of Kardia Hodos—stayed in the priesthood. Spiritual vows confined their power too much to satisfy them. On the other hand, minor magicians either became assistants to men with major talent, as Ackerly had to Nimbulan, or they became priests. Was Quinnault de Tanos a strong magician practicing in secret, or a very minor talent who had left his studies to assume lordship of his clan as he claimed?

The girl spoke the truth. We have wasted generations of men on these wars. If there is to be peace, I must grasp this opportunity while I have it. The girl and this lord are connected somehow. Is it their destinies or their pasts that mingle?

"Lord Quinnault, you have seen in the void how past, present, and future become one. You have known your soul stripped of masks so that every thought and plan is revealed, even those you did not realize you possessed."

Quinnault nodded. His mouth turned down, and his eyes took on a hard glint. De Tanos' experience with the symbolic life-path choices apparently had been unpleasant. Shadows played over his angular skull and once more took on the illusion of an otherworldly creature. Was his umbilical an iridescent crystal or some other more natural color?

Nimbulan wished for the strength to whisk Quinnault into the void and see for himself who and what the lord was. Until his body recovered, however, he'd have to rely on words and instinct. He couldn't help Myrilandel either until he replenished his reserves.

"While I liberated Keegan's ghost, I discovered some disturbing symbolism—which is the only way to view life while in the void. I believe Hanic was ready to negotiate a peace." The reluctant figure who was dragged out of the dance but kept trying to regain the symmetrical patterns wore Hanic's colors. The magician who pulled him away from harmony seemed young and over eager. "Keegan instigated this last battle in order to prove his superiority over me, his teacher."

Where had he gone wrong in training Keegan? Grief made the next words difficult. "Most of Hanic's troops were illusions. Very good illusions drawn from blood magic. Moncriith, the Bloodmage, wasn't present until later. Only Keegan could have conjured those troops. I trained my apprentice well in devising spells. But ethics, honor, and discipline meant nothing to him."

" 'Tis not unusual for a lord to listen to the advice of his magician over common sense. We have to make Hanic see sense now." De Tanos frowned again.

"Yes, we must." The civil war had lasted three generations and more. Magicians guided the lords every step of the way—first to find the best among the barons as a new king when the last one died without heirs. Later they managed the battles, tipping the balance of strength and resources unnaturally. The vision in the void became clearer; symbolism dropping away to reveal the truth beneath it.

"We must end the wars before Coronnan is destroyed completely and her people overrun by greedy neighbors," Lord Quinnault said as he stood to leave. His shoulders sagged as if his tall body no longer had the strength to support all of him.

"What if two or more magicians, who shared the same dream of peace as you, found a way to combine their magic to overcome another magician?"

"If such a thing could happen, and I know enough about magic to realize it can't, then the magicians could be controlled, the battles would depend solely on superiority of men and weapons and tactics. Lords would be more cautious about starting battles. They might even listen to talk of peace. A few of them have listened to me, but they are intimidated by stronger lords like Kammeryl and Hanic." Quinnault sighed heavily, then straighted with new resolve. "But magicians can't combine their powers. As lord Kammeryl said, we might as well wish for dragons and flywackets. Peace must be found in other ways."

"Some of the men think they saw a dragon on the field. I might very well find flywackets hiding in the clouds," Nimbulan chuckled.

"Have you experimented with combining magic?" Quinnault leaned over Nimbulan's chair. His excitement stripped years of care and worry from his face. He was younger than Nimbulan thought.

"The battles must end for the winter. I have five moons or more to experiment. I need a place of safety to work and train my apprentices, to recruit other magicians who are weary of war. . . ."

"Change your allegiance to me, Nimbulan, and I will give you one of my islands. An ancient monastery, abandoned before the beginning of these wars, stands fast against time and the elements. You'll have safety and privacy there."

"Isn't the peace of all of Coronnan worth lending that island without having me dishonor my previous vow?"

A smile lit Quinnault's eyes and banished the odd shadows. The candles blazed brighter and warmer.

"If you had given any other answer, Master Nimbulan, I would always doubt your loyalty. The island is yours for as long as you need it. Find your students and begin your experiments."

* * *

Moncriith watched Ackerly, the short assistant magician, through narrowed eyes. No aura of great power surrounded the square-built man, and yet he associated freely with the Battlemages.

"Take the provisions, Moncriith. I offer them freely, without obligations." Ackerly held out a bulging saddlebag. "It's not much but it should see all of you to the next stronghold or village."

"Thank you." Moncriith bowed his head. The humble gesture allowed him to watch Ackerly through his lowered eyelashes.

Ackerly squirmed a little. Moncriith bit back a smile at the magician's discomfort.

"I accept your gift of sustenance freely. But I do not understand why you give me aid when you serve Nimbulan, the man who exiled me from the hospital and my righteous quest."

"Harrumf," the guard tugging at Moncriith's elbow cleared his throat. He shuffled his feet, anxious to escort Moncriith and his followers two leagues beyond the camp perimeter. Five more heavily armed men encircled Moncriith's two dozen, very ragged followers.

Moncriith turned a warning gaze upon the impatient guards. They resumed staring into the distance. Watching elsewhere didn't close the men's ears though. In the army, every man must report to his superior officers. Many men stood in the chain of command between one sergeant and the chief Battlemage, Nimbulan. Moncriith wondered what the man would report and how soon.

"No man should be turned out into a storm without provisions. I don't care if the warlord and his mage disagree with your views. You're a magician and should be respected." Ackerly stopped shuffling and stood straight.

Moncriith stiffened in indignation. "The priests have rejected my vision from the Stargods. Demons have invaded even the hallowed temples. The priests and their puppet magicians have cast me out rather than face the demons who pervert their magic. According to them, you owe me nothing." Every time he thought of the humiliation heaped upon his head by the pompous elders of the temple, anger boiled up within him. His spine stretched taller. Blood swelled within his neck and face. His heart raced while his lungs panted and overfilled with air.

Ackerly stared him directly in the eye. "You and I have a lot in common, Moncriith. Neither one of us can weave the magic of the Kardia into our spells. Because of that we are relegated to minor positions serving those who can. No one is willing to give either of us credit for intelligence or other skills simply because we lack that one talent. Well, you've broken out of the mold this world cast for you and found a different way to work magic. I admire that. I'll never have the courage to do anything but what Nimbulan orders."

"In a perfect world, mundanes, who outnumber magicians one thousand to one, would rule. Magicians should be servants not commanders." Moncriith replied. "Our talent is a gift. But demons control Coronnan now, not mundanes. Demons led by Myrilandel." *Only magicians can root them out and turn the chaos that will follow into order. And I am the only magician who can see the problem.*

"Hanging around the army will only get you killed. Now take the food and seek more followers among those who aren't dazzle-blinded by magicians and their tricks."

"Thank you again. And courage, Ackerly. One day our other talents will be appreciated more than our failure to be great magicians."

"Where are you headed? Maybe I can send more provisions later."

"Money will be appreciated. We need winter clothes and shelter, things that are not easily bargained for or given in hospitality."

Ackerly squirmed at the mention of money. Moncriith smiled inwardly. He'd found this man's weakness.

"We head East. The source of evil that corrupts Coronnan lies in that direction. I will root out demons and their minions where they are born. I have heard reports of dragons flying over the eastern edge of the Southern Mountains. When I have seen to their destruction, I will be back."

* * *

Nimbulan raised his boots awkwardly out of the dirty water that always seemed to reside in the bottoms of boats. He and Quinnault de Tanos had just dumped the collection of rainwater out of the boat and set off on the final leg of their quick trip to the islands. Traveling downstream from the army camp with a swift current, they had been gone less than an hour. Walking, or riding fleet steeds would have compounded the time by four. Heavy, cloying mud clogged every track.

He rested his feet on the rocking sides of the rowboat, out of the water. At least the rain had eased from last night. They'd only had to empty the boat twice since leaving camp.

But debris from the storm moved down the river at the whim of nature, dark splotches of black-gray against the brownish gray river, beneath the yellow-gray of the misty sunrise. The dull light blurred outlines, magnifying the size of obstacles. Branches and tree trunks looked dangerous, even compensating for the distortions of light.

Quinnault de Tanos stretched his back and arm muscles against the oars. "The current is swift today. We'll reach the island soon, and you'll be back in your tent by sunset." He chuckled and continued to speed the craft toward the Great Bay, much too quickly for Nimbulan's stomach.

"I'll feel safer if you steer away from that bobbing

log." Nimbulan pointed at a floating tree with many of its raggedly broken limbs pointing directly at their fragile hull. "We could have waited another day for better weather and calmer water for this visit to your islands," he added.

If they'd waited, Nimbulan would have had a chance to visit with the pretty little witchwoman. His mind lingered on his plans for training the girl rather than on the boat.

"The sooner you start your experiments and gather recruits, the faster we can end the wars." De Tanos grunted and put more effort into his rowing.

"Who are you, Quinnault de Tanos? You are an enigma among your peers."

"I am the youngest son of a lord who never planned to accede to the title or the responsibilities of clan leadership. I had three brothers and two sisters. The wars and the plagues that follow battle took them all much too soon. Now I am the last of my immediate family. I can't go back to the priesthood. My people depend on me as their lord. I want my sons and daughters, when I have the time to marry and beget them, to have the choice I was denied."

"Magicians rarely have children of their own. But I have apprentices. Those boys and girls come to me as children, between the ages of ten and twelve usually. I feel like I am as much a father to them as their blood parents. I want choices for them as well. I want them to be allowed to use magic for peace and prosperity."

"Then we are allies on the same quest." Quinnault smiled at Nimbulan as he neatly fended off a tangle of vines and leaves with one oar.

"How far has this quest taken you, Quinnault de Tanos? You have been called 'the Peacemaker' for at least three years now."

"I have commitments from four other lords to refuse to join Kammeryl, Hanic, or Sauria in battle if—and it's a big if—I can keep those lords from attacking them in retaliation for that refusal."

"What about Baathalzan?" Nimbulan asked about his cousin, the lord of his home province.

"He refuses to talk to anyone. Can you persuade him?"

"Not likely. He fears his relatives will take his title and lands more than the other lords. My cousin is not a decisive leader. But five of thirteen lords is a good start. They command a lot of land and a fair number of troops. Banded together, they could mount a serious defense. Why have you not led them in that direction, Quinnault?"

"They want to make me king."

"And you fear that responsibility?"

"I am barely comfortable as lord of my own clan. I would make a very poor and weak king. Coronnan needs a better man than I. All I really want is to be a priest."

Silence hovered between them, like a living being, begging to be pushed aside. But neither had anything to say.

"Is this abandoned building large enough for a women's quarters? Almost as many girls seek apprenticeships in magic as boys," Nimbulan asked finally. Myrilandel must have a place there. He couldn't let her enormous talent go to waste.

"I think so. I haven't thoroughly inspected the building in several years. How many people are you planning on housing?"

"About a dozen to start. I'll bring in others as the need arises. At the moment, Ackerly and I are the only trained magicians I can trust." Keegan had run away and betrayed him.

An eddy caught the little craft and swung the bobbing tree dangerously close. De Tanos shifted the oars in a rapid maneuver Nimbulan couldn't interpret. The boat stabilized and nosed away from the entrapping branches.

"You've spent a lot of time on the water," Nimbulan said with a grunt as he pushed the tree farther away from them with his staff.

"I had my first boat almost before I could walk. Boats are necessary to people who live on islands. Boats are our livelihood. We don't have much arable land in the islands. We make our living by fishing and by transporting people and goods up and down this river. That livelihood has been seriously disrupted by these wars. I'm more comfortable with all kinds of watercraft than with steeds." De Tanos looked over his shoulder at the steep riverbank a quarter mile away. Waves lapped the red clay cliff with a ferocity reminiscent of the Great Bay.

"Neither you nor your father maintains an army." Nimbulan changed the subject rather than think about the wind-whipped water all around him and the next log aiming for their hull. "Yet your manors haven't been overrun. Unusual in these troubled times."

"The river provides a natural moat. We withstood a siege last Spring, mainly because my people retreated to the islands with every boat within ten leagues. They supplied the mainland manor in secret at night through the river gate. Lord Sauria bombarded us with boulders and nearly breached the walls in several places. He did overrun the stables and steal my best breeding steeds. We almost surrendered before he decided my small holdings couldn't give him the strategic advantage he sought. He threw away access to the Great Bay because he didn't plan ahead and bring his own boats."

"You've had to fortify your estates, then? Sauria is persistent. He'll return in the spring, with boats."

"Yes." De Tanos gritted his teeth and fought the oars once more as a snarl of tree roots and stumps loomed directly ahead of them. "I am making plans for that. Not a chore I like."

"How much farther?" Nimbulan dropped his feet back to the hull for better balance. He didn't like the way the current swept more and more debris up against that stump.

"We'll get around that menace." De Tanos put more effort into the oars.

Nimbulan crossed himself in prayer twice, the second time for the lord whose attention remained riveted on the snag that loomed closer, seeming to fill the entire river.

Wind gusts stirred the current into choppy circles. The boat aimed for the wall of debris.

"I haven't recovered enough magic to help much, but I might be able to send the wind elsewhere and divert the current around that snag." The stump and its collection of flotsam seemed too firmly anchored to budge with his exhausted talent.

"Tampering with the weather is forbidden. We can't upset the balance." Strain showed in Quinnault's neck and shoulders.

Nimbulan ducked as a huge branch bobbed up out of the water, aiming directly for his head. A wall of water followed the branch.

"I can't swim!"

CHAPTER 6

Myri crept beneath the outer wall of her tent as a sleepy bird chirped a question at the first signs of light in the sky. She stopped to listen for the waking chorus of birds. Notes of a wordless song sprang to her lips. A smiled stretched her weary cheek muscles. Every part of her body was tired. But she shouldn't linger, even to greet the rising sun with the birds.

Standing hunted-still, she tried blending into the muddy colored canvas walls. Her cloak should be the same color as the tent, effectively masking her presence.

Not much of a sunrise. The gradual spreading of light only hinted at the presence of a sun behind the clouds. Good. She'd cast no betraying shadow when she moved.

The guards at the front of the tent paced back and forth. She had heard Nimbulan give orders last night that she be kept secure inside the tent. Escaping them would be a merry game.

She had considered crawling beneath the tent around midnight. Muffled voices had betrayed the presence of Nimbulan's assistant and Moncriith. From the secure confines of the tent she had listened to Moncriith's plans. He was headed East. The same direction the voices urged her to flee. Therefore, she would wait until he was well gone. She would rather follow behind him than have to watch her back in constant fear of him catching up with her.

Pickets patrolled the edges of camp. Their shoulders sagged wearily. Men in bedrolls on the wet ground stirred and yawned. Some pulled their blankets higher while others sat and stretched. By the dim glow of false dawn, she scouted her escape route around them, picking out hiding places along the way. The back of a tent to her right, a stack of weapons beyond. She tugged the hood of her cloak lower over her face and moved toward the perimeter of the camp. She'd played this game before. But then she'd had trees to climb and no one ever thought to look *up*. They always looked straight ahead or down.

Amaranth mewed a protest at being carried beneath the folds of her cloak.

"Sorry," she whispered to him. "We have to stay hidden until we're beyond camp. Besides, you don't like wet on your feet."

The black flywacket settled into her supporting arm. His tail twitched, showing his reluctant acceptance of her wishes.

"Food first." Myri followed her nose to the cooking fires, slipping in and out of shadows, making faces at the men who passed her by without seeing her.

A sleepy-eyed cook stirred a gruel in a huge cauldron over a firepit carefully tended by a dozing teenager. They were protected from the rain by a red, green, and white striped awning. No canvas sides or shadows for Myri to hide within. Besides, she couldn't carry hot gruel. She needed jerked meat, journey bread, and dried fruit.

Carefully she scanned the camp for signs of a storage tent or covered sledge. Surely, the cook would need easy access to his supplies.

Ah. There, on the other side of the cooking pavilion—a low, square tent with alert guards front and back. No slackness showed in the fabric walls. Could she creep under the tent without rippling the canvas and signaling unlawful entry to the guards?

She skirted the cooking area with all the stealth she'd learned in the woodlands as a child. The far side of the awning offered a little concealment in the form of a sledge piled high with pots and other utensils. The harness end rested atop double crates for easier hitching to a steed. The triangular space beneath made a nice dark cave to hide in. A gust of wind, laden with fresh rain diverted the guard's attention long enough for her to slip beneath the vehicle.

"Stay here," Myri whispered to Amaranth as she shoved his muscular cat body into the shadow of the crates. Gently she slit the canvas wall of the tent with her belt knife. A moment later she crawled on her belly through the small opening.

She froze, waiting anxiously for the guards to betray their exact location. They were as loud and obvious as children thrashing through saber ferns. Slowly, very slowly, not making a sound, she stood, allowing her eyes to adjust to the dimness. Sharp-cornered boxes emerged from the shadows to her right. Lumpy sacks to her left. Grain? By feel, she found a corner of one of the sacks. She held her pouch beneath the corner as she slit it. Slowly the cereal siphoned into her container.

"What are you doing in here, soldier?" a male voice challenged Myri from the front of the tent. "There's plenty to eat outside for honest men. You planning on deserting?"

No time to argue. No time to search for more food. Myri dove for the opening. A hand grasped her ankle as she slithered toward the shadows beneath the sledge. She kicked back with her free foot.

"*S'murghit,* you little demon get!" the man grunted and let go.

Come! she commanded Amaranth, not daring spoken words. She crawled from the cover of the sledge and began running. Amaranth burst from his hiding place in a flurry of glistening black wings.

"A dragon. The dragon came back!" a guard cried.

"After them. The magicians will pay plenty for a real dragon."

"That's not a dragon. Too small. Maybe a flywacket."

"They'll pay more for one of those!"

Myri escaped while the men argued. Her heart beat loud and fast. The rolling hills and grasslands promised no concealment. Nothing to climb. Nowhere to hide. This wasn't a game any more. Myri willed her cloak to blend in with the morning mist. She locked her muscles.

Movement would betray her. She had no choice but to run. If she didn't, Nimbulan would keep her prisoner, make her a slave to the hospital. She had delivered her message and done what she could for the wounded. Now she must continue her own quest for a home—a safe haven.

Help me, please! she pleaded with the mysterious voices.

No answer.

She prayed she hadn't offended them by diverting her path to help a few of the wounded.

Amaranth circled above her, mewling his concern.

"Stop! Thief!" Heavy feet pounded the ground behind her.

"Who cares about the thief. Catch the flywacket," one of the guards yelled.

She ran, clutching the precious pouch of grains to her breast. She wished she could spread her arms and fly like Amaranth. But she had to protect the food. Above her, Amaranth flew higher into the clouds and safety.

Please, save me from the magicians who would enslave me, and Moncriith who would burn me. I'm going East now, as you commanded.

No answer.

"Where's the blasted flywacket?"

"Can't see it. But it will follow the thief. Catch him, catch the flywacket." Her pursuers came closer.

She ran faster. Up to the first ridge. Down the steep escarpment on the other side. Her bare feet slipped on the wet grass. The men slipped, too. First one man fell, knocking into another, then a third. Together all three guards tumbled down the long hillside.

Myri collected her wits and balance before the others. She ran. She dodged hummocks that appeared in her path, jumped across a stream, and rolled behind a boulder that spread across the hillside with a tumble of other rocks.

"Hey, where'd she go? No one could just disappear like that," the youngest of the men asked.

"She's a witchwoman. What do you expect?"

"That flying thing was probably just a crow," said the tallest of the men as he stood, brushing himself off.

"Them nasty birds are a nuisance, always snatching at any food left untended," replied another.

"Think we could catch a crow and dress it up to look like a flywacket?" asked the third.

The men wandered around the hillside more slowly, reluctant to move too far from camp. They looked directly at Myri and didn't see her. As soon as they turned their backs to retreat to the protection of their fellows, Myri ran on.

Uphill again, over the second ridge, and onto the third. A trade road wandered through the next valley. Where there was a road, there would also be villages.

Two armies had marched through here a few days ago. The warlords probably recruited men as they traveled. Any village on this road would have been deprived of all its men. The few people who remained might welcome her where they would shun more soldiers.

She slowed her pace and steadied her breathing.

Amaranth, where are you? A dark shadow within a shadow circled above her head.

"We're safe now, Amaranth. Come. Come to me." She patted her shoulder in invitation.

The shadow dropped lower, took on form and resolved into a flying creature. The sunlight rippled purple lights along his black fur and wing feathers.

Myri held out her arm. Amaranth dropped lower, wings raised, claws extended. Fanning the air with backward sweeps he slowed and landed lightly on his accustomed perch. Quickly he folded his wings beneath their protective flaps and wrapped his tail around Myri's neck for balance.

"Ready?"

(*Yes.*)

Myri marched around the next bend in the trade road and into a quiet village.

A woman emerged from the first hut carrying a bucket. Another woman stepped from the next home with a basket for gathering eggs. Together they turned and watched Myri's approach.

"Have you shelter for a weary traveler?" Myri asked with ritual humility.

"Ye're out a might early. Or you been traveling all night?" the Bucket Woman asked. " 'Taint right for a woman to be traveling alone at night—or any other time."

"Makes no difference. We owe her hospitality, like any other traveler," Basket Woman replied.

"She could be a spy for the army. They'll steal what little we have left. We won't survive the Winter if they claim our harvest."

"If you can call it a harvest," Basket Woman snorted.

"I have a little grain to share." Myri offered her half-full pouch.

"The red-robe told us to beware of spies with gifts."

"One good breakfast will prolong starvation a little. And that preacher doesn't know everything. You're welcome, stranger." Basket Woman gestured with her free hand for Myri to enter her humble home. "The flusterhens are still laying, and there's sausage."

Myri's mouth watered and her stomach rumbled. "What preacher?" She clamped down on her hunger. Amaranth dug his claws deeper into her cloak in warning.

The women looked to each other without answering.

Myri set Amaranth on the ground, ready to run again. "What preacher?" she asked.

"Moncriith," Basket Woman said quietly.

"*Sieur* Moncriith warned us about witchwomen and their demon familiars." Bucket Woman gave the man a priestly title. She backed away from Amaranth. "Sieur says we aren't to give hospitality to any traveler. I respect the words of a priest. Only demons stray from their homes these days." She dropped her bucket and crossed her wrists with a flapping motion. The flapping hands symbolized the ancient demon god Simurgh. The crossing acted as a ward against him.

The sun pushed aside the thinning clouds, sending a shaft of light into the center of the village. The Equinox Pylon, its harvest decorations slightly wilted, glowed as if on fire. Myri backed up at the omen of fire.

"I knew the Stargods would lead you back to me, Myrilandel." Moncriith emerged from the first hut. His patched red robe seemed to glow in the growing light. Red for priestly orders or red for the blood he shed to fuel his magic? " 'Tis time for you to face justice! My people are camped nearby. I will summon them to join the village elders. They will judge you for your demonic crimes."

Amaranth darted into the shelter of a woodpile beside the house. Myri dropped her pouch of grain and ran.

Moncriith grabbed her around the waist before she had gone two steps. "You'll not escape me again, Myrilandel, daughter of demons."

CHAPTER 7

Myri clawed at Moncriith's restraining hands with her fingernails.

He latched onto both her wrists with one strong, scarred hand.

Desperate to escape the images of fire that leaked from his mind, she kicked at his booted shins with her bare feet. Sharp pain shot through her toes, hot and intense.

She had to break free before his followers joined them and imprisoned her.

Moncriith laughed. His thoughts broadcast into Myri's receptive mind. She cringed away from the images of herself, naked, writhing within a bonfire.

Myri's imagination added details of pain in her own limbs. Green flame boiled around the edges of her vision. Her lungs gasped and labored with suffocating smoke that existed only in Moncriith's mind.

Or her memory?

She remembered dragging Magretha from a burning hut. Flames had licked at her hands and singed her fine hair as she put all of her childish strength into escaping the fire with her unconscious guardian.

The memory cleared the panic from her mind. Her strength pooled into her hands and feet. She focused on Moncriith's posture and muscular tension for clues to his next action. Though she stood nearly as tall as he, he had the advantage of weight and breadth.

With one last jolt of strength she slammed her elbow backward into her captor's well-muscled belly.

"Oomph." Air whooshed from his lungs into her ear. He didn't relax his grasp of her hands or her body.

"Moncriith, let her go," Basket Woman commanded. "I've offered her hospitality, and I'll not have you bringing curses upon this village for abusing her rights as our invited guest."

"She has no rights. This woman isn't human. Not like us. She was born of demons and stole this body from a human child. She's a changeling seeking to steal your souls and claim your bodies for her own vile purposes. Yesterday she worked her evil magic on a brave soldier, leaving his soul trapped in the void between the planes of existence while she cured his body. Perhaps he was one of the men missing from this village. One of the men who will follow her rather than return home."

"How . . . how do you know this, Moncriith?" Basket Woman wavered. Moncriith could have offered no more damning evidence than the threat to deprive this village of yet more men.

"I have been blessed by the Stargods with a vision of this woman in her true form. I wear the red robes of a priest. Dare you doubt me?"

"I am not a demon. I swear to you, I'm not," Myri pleaded with the woman.

"Meerawck!" Amaranth swooped from the sky, claws extended, teeth bared, aiming directly for Moncriith's eyes.

"Ayii!" Moncriith screamed. He thrust Myri away, raising his arms to protect his vulnerable face and neck from the flywacket.

"Stargods preserve us!" Bucket Woman crossed her wrists and flapped them. Then she touched her forehead, chest, and each shoulder in the more accepted blessing. "I renounce this evil with my mind, my heart, and the strength of my shoulders."

"Demons. Demons from the sky!" Basket Woman buried her face in her apron and fled.

Amaranth swooped and tore at Moncriith's hair with his claws. The Bloodmage beat at the winged cat with his hands. He tried to duck his head within his robes. Amaranth reached again to claw at the man's scalp.

Myri dashed behind the woodpile, out of sight of her persecutor. Her bruised toes complained with each step. She ignored them, running along a trail that guided her East and South, toward the mountains. East toward something that called her. The wind swirled up and pushed her in that direction. She spread her arms, letting the air catch her cloak like a sail, speeding her on her way.

But Moncriith was headed East, too, in search of demon lairs. She fought the wind, turning West and North toward the village where Magretha had raised her. The cold bite of circling air thrust her harder toward the East.

(East.) Voices filled her mind, crowding out every other thought. *(East. Home. Safety.)*

Myri gave in to the driving force of the wind. Before she had traveled a league, a grove of oak trees south of the trail beckoned her. Oak with protective mistletoe hanging heavy in the upper branches. A hiding place. She could watch the pathways for Moncriith, let him go ahead of her. Safer to follow unseen than flee ahead.

(Yes. Hide now.)

Silently she stepped off the established path, blurring her passage with magic as she went. Amaranth would find her. Moncriith wouldn't. She prayed to the Stargods and the guiding voices that Moncriith wouldn't find her.

* * *

Nimbulan coughed and spluttered through muddy water, crawling up a soggy embankment. He dragged his staff along with his heavy body, as much a part of him as his arms and legs. Each breath took a concentrated effort and ended in another cough. He expelled more water from his laboring lungs and collapsed, face-down in more mud.

Some force he couldn't understand propelled him onto solid ground. Water ran from his hair, his clothes, from the sky. . . . Everything was as wet as the river. Why didn't he just give up and let himself drown?

"The first lesson you give to your apprentices had better be how to swim," Quinnault de Tanos said. "I'll not have my people risking their necks rescuing every land-hugger who throws himself into the river. Thank goodness you wore a tunic and trews and not those long robes you magicians favor. I'd never have gotten you out of the river with the weight of all that sodden wool dragging you down."

"I didn't throw myself into the river. The river threw itself all over me," Nimbulan said between hacking coughs.

Quinnault grabbed the back of Nimbulan's shirt and lifted him. Nimbulan scrambled to get his feet under him, balancing on his staff. He needed to regain some semblance of control.

"Breathe, Nimbulan. You've got to get your lungs working again." Quinnault slapped the magician on the back, hard. Almost too hard. Something seemed to snap between Nimbulan's ribs.

Deep coughs racked his body. He spewed more fluid, from his belly this time. When the spasms tapered off, each breath seemed less painful than the one before.

Instantly he was back in his memories of Druulin's tower. Boojlin and Caasser opened their mouths in protest as the cold water from Nimbulan's booby trap hit them from above. Both bullies breathed in too quickly, taking water into their throats and up their noses. They coughed and choked. Caasser's face took on a funny gray-and-pink tinge.

Instantly remorseful, Nimbulan jumped to slap Caasser on the back, forcing him to expel the water.

"Not so hard, Lan. If you break his ribs with your pounding, you'll only make it worse," Ackerly had waned him, only half seriously. He and Nimbulan had suffered much at the hands of the larger bullies. Returning some of the pain and humiliation brought satisfaction to Ackerly's grim smile.

Nimbulan shifted his attention from hitting Caasser's back to forcing the boy's arms over his head with a firm grip on both elbows. The shift in posture seemed to open the taller boy's air passages. His convulsive coughs tapered off. Nimbulan waited for Caasser's gasping to ease into long sobbing breaths. Part of him wanted to pull Caasser's arms back, hard; to prolong the boy's pain in retribution for all the nasty tricks he'd played on Nimbulan and Ackerly.

The part of him that was growing up and assuming more responsibility knew that if he did, he risked making a lifelong enemy.

He released Caasser and rubbed his back and shoulders to ease his breathing more. The pranks and tricks might not stop, but Nimbulan had earned Caasser's trust.

They had eventually become friends and battle comrades.

Until that fateful day when Nimbulan and Ackerly hadn't joined Druulin and his assistants in their last battle.

An older and more experienced Nimbulan recognized his vulnerability while he gasped and choked. Quinnault's rough handling emphasized his determination to get Nimbulan upright and breathing again. Nimbulan shifted his back and ribs, assessing any damage. Nothing permanent, maybe a bruise or two.

"My thanks," Nimbulan wiped his streaming eyes on his sleeve. Caasser hadn't been so generous.

"Come along now, Nimbulan. We have an entire island to survey." De Tanos marched forward. He strode easily through the high underbrush, long legs stretching over small shrubs and hummocks.

"We need to build a fire and dry out before we catch the lung rot." Nimbulan hastened to catch up. The slight effort started a tickle in his chest again. He swallowed it and kept moving.

"Nothing dry enough to burn, except maybe some old furniture inside the monastery. Did you bring a flint?"

"I'm a magician. I don't need a flint to start a fire. Even exhausted and half-drowned, I can start a fire just by thinking flames into the wood."

"Then we'd best get under cover and dry off. The sun is coming out, but it's too weak and too late in the year to be much help. You need a drink? You sound a little hoarse."

"No I do not need a drink. I've already drunk half of the river."

"There's a well in the monastery. We'll have to test the water to make sure it's still sweet."

"Well, I won't test it by drinking it, that's for sure."

"Stop complaining, old man. this is the start of a truly great adventure that could change the history of Coronnan." Quinnault fairly bounced over the rough ground.

"I'm an aging magician, not an old man. That gives me the right to be as crotchety as I want."

Quinnault stopped short and stared at his companion. "Crotchety, yes. Interfering and stagnant, no. I hope you have something solid to experiment with. Coronnan needs innovation. Soon."

"Hmph," Nimbulan snorted as he passed the lord on the narrow trail. He glimpsed stone buildings within the dense overgrowth. Eagerness replaced his preoccupation with small ailments. He forged ahead faster than his abused lungs could manage.

He paused to catch his breath just as a ray of sunshine broke through the cloud cover. Brilliant blue beams of magical light reflected off glistening paving stones in front of the old monastery.

"Stargods preserve us! What is that?" Quinnault crossed himself, paused, then crossed himself again.

"Something special. Something very powerful," Nimbulan gasped. "Only ley lines glow that shade of blue." He forged ahead, anxious to discover the source of the strange light.

"Hold on, old man. This could be dangerous. There are rumors of ghosts and demons haunting his island." Quinnault grabbed Nimbulan's sleeve.

"I'll protect us with magic, boy." Power began tingling through Nimbulan's boots into his feet. Eagerness lifted his spirits and urged him to run. Energy coursed upward through his legs, into his belly and chest. The staff vibrated and stood upright on its own. His heart beat strong and true. All lingering coughs faded from his lungs. His eyes focused sharply.

He watched sap draining from leaves into tree trunks; saw individual drops of moisture in the air; knew every different rock that had crumbled to form the dirt at his feet.

New sounds entered his ears. Distant birdsong, the whoosh and sigh of the river lapping its banks, worms crawling beneath the surface of Kardia Hodos. The moon and stars danced through the universe, beckoning him to join their balanced movements.

His vision in the void took shape before his eyes. This time the magicians stepped back and watched rather than distorting the patterns. The lords danced in harmony with the Great Wheel of sun and moon and stars. . . .

"This is better than an overdose of Tambootie," he whispered in awe.

"What do you see?" Quinnault remained behind him looking anxiously right and left.

"I see the source of all magic. Come, boy, let's find out what other miracles this abandoned monastery shelters."

"Slowly, Nimbulan. We don't know what kind of traps lie hidden, nor what drove the last inhabitants away."

Nimbulan shrugged his agreement. "You go left, I'll go right, but stay within sight." He pointed directions with his staff, but the tool jerked back to the pool of blue between each gesture.

"We stay together, or we don't go."

"Oh, all right." Nimbulan stepped onto a fat ley line to his right and followed it toward the pool of glowing blue. With each step, he sensed the power in the ley line increasing. The line itself grew wider until he placed his feet side by side and still saw blue around the edges. "*Stargods!* I've seen smaller parapets in Castle Krej where Kammeryl d'Astrismos holes up every Winter. Ley lines are supposed to be as fine as spider silk."

"I've never truly seen a ley line before." Quinnault turned in a circle, gaping at the lovely blue glowing beneath the Kardia's surface.

"Can you draw the power into you, de Tanos?" Nimbulan's skin began to itch with the magic he hadn't unleashed yet. His staff glowed with power. There was so much of it!

"My feet and fingers tingle. Is that the magic?"

"Yes. Yes. Try something, Quinnault. A simple spell. Anything. See if the massive amounts of power fuel your talent where small ley lines can't."

"I can't think of anything to do."

"Something useful. Shift some of these shrubs to the side and make a path."

Quinnault closed his eyes and screwed his face up in concentration.

Nimbulan watched the plants in front of them. None moved. "Open your eyes, de Tanos. Stare at the fibers of each plant and think them in a different place."

"I . . . I've never been able to move anything before. Not even a simple transport."

"Have you always closed your eyes to try the spell?"

"Yes. It's easier to concentrate."

"Then try it with your eyes open!"

The young lord stared at a small tuft of grass. He clenched and opened his fists rhythmically. The blades of greenery wiggled and waved to the right but didn't move.

"Again. You've got the essence of the plant listening to you. Now be more persuasive. Draw the power up through your body and out your hand. Point at the grass."

Quinnault lifted his left hand slowly, index finger extended toward the tuft in question. Again the blades wiggled and straightened.

Nimbulan resisted the urge to help the lord. He needed to know if the vast reserves of power on this island could turn minor talents into major ones. Quite possibly, after having experienced a large ley line, de Tanos would be able to find and use lesser ones in other places.

And once awakened, could he learn to combine his power with another's?

"I don't think I can do this." Quinnault bent over, bracing himself on his knees and panting.

"Maybe you think too much."

"It's like a wall grows between me and the grass."

"I've heard better excuses from first-year apprentices. We'll try again later. After we've seen the source of these ley lines and the monastery. I do hope the roof is sound." But it didn't have to be. With all this power surging through his body, he could repair any damage with a thought.

Together they walked onward. Youthful vigor put a bounce in Nimbulan's steps. He wanted to dance with joy and energy. He felt as young as Quinnault. Younger. As young as Myrilandel.

"I'm suddenly quite hungry. Do you suppose there are any late brambleberries left?" Quinnault stopped to inspect the thorny vines. Two overripe berries fell into his hand. Both splattered against his palm, too swollen with rainwater to hold their shape.

"You are hungry because you spent a great deal of energy while trying to transport that tuft of grass. Walk on the ley line. It will replenish you."

"I can't see it anymore. The blue is gone."

"No, it's not. It's fatter and stronger than ever!"

"I can't see it . . . or sense the power anymore."

A shadow passed over the watery sun. Both men looked up. The clouds parted, revealing a bright rainbow. The arcing prism drifted until it ended directly in the center of the pool of blue ley lines. A shower of sparks rose to greet the colored light.

"I've never seen a rainbow move while I'm standing still." Nimbulan raced forward to inspect the phenomenon. Large boulders and small creeks diverted his path to the East. The low stone building built around three sides of the pool blocked his view.

A path of sorts seemed to lead him to a doorway in the center of the south wall of the building. His next step sent him flying backward into a bed of thistles. The plants stung his hands and neck and poked through his clothes. His staff lay ten feet in front of him.

What kind of force was strong enough to separate him from his staff?

"Nimbulan!" Quinnault helped him up with strong hands beneath Nimbulan's shoulders. He brushed some of the excess mud from Nimbulan's already filthy clothes. "What happened?"

"I don't . . . don't know." Nimbulan clutched his temple to keep the world from spinning away from him. His free hand came up, palm open and receptive to power of any sort. "One minute I was on solid ground, the next I was flying through the air."

(You trespassed where your kind are not welcome.) A shadowy mist rose up between the two men and the monastery.

"Who are you?" Quinnault addressed the air. "I am Lord of this island. This is my land, and I may walk where I will! Show yourself to your rightful lord."

(I recognize no lord. I am the guardian of the beginning place.) The mist, crowded with gray and purple shadows, shaped itself into the vague outline of a man, twice the height of a normal man. *(I guard these hallowed grounds against all who would misuse the power that begins and ends here. The Stargods gifted this power to the peoples of Kardia Hodos for the good of all. I guard against misuse—intentional or accidental. Be gone!)*

A circling wind wrapped around and around Nimbulan and Quinnault de Tanos, driving them back the way they had come. Back toward the raging river that would drown them.

Nimbulan fought the wind with an image of calm within his mind. The tornado battered his defenses. He dug in his heels. The shadowy spirit threw slates from the roof at him. He enclosed himself and de Tanos in his strongest magical armor.

Gradually the assault lessened. Nimbulan sensed that the guardian of the monastery merely gathered his energy for his next attempt to rid the island of the magician and the lord.

Nimbulan pulled bits of verse together for his plea, as if they were a spell. Since this creature seemed to be made of magic, he'd address him as magic.

"Peace we seek,
here and now,
for strong or meek.
Peace we wish,
for all to kiss."

The spirit paused. The shape shifted enough to suggest a man tilting his head in consideration. Did he recognize the human tradition of a kiss of peace to seal a treaty and forgive past battles?

"We come in peace. I seek a way to bring honor and good back into the use of magic," he shouted to the four cardinal directions and four elements. In his mind he saw them bound in harmony with all humanity, mage and mundane alike. His staff returned to his hand, passing through the guardian.

The wind slackened. *(How can I believe you?)* The spirit drifted and reformed directly in front of Nimbulan. Some of the shadows lightened, no longer carrying the menace of darkness. *(You directed this honorable lord to clear a path by magic when he need only look with his eyes for an existing path.)*

"I sought only to test his powers, as I must test many things before I find a way to end the wars that destroy Coronnan."

(You seek peace when all around you know nothing but war?)

"We seek peace. We mean no harm to you or the power you guard so diligently. We ask only for time to experiment with the power—to find a way for magicians to band together in neutrality. Only then can we make honor, ethics, and education our priority rather than war."

"Mewlppp! Mewlppp!" A winged form circled their heads.

"What a strange cry. Too large and bulky to be a bird. So black it seems to absorb light." Quinnault shaded his eyes with one hand as he looked up. "What creature have you sent to us, Spirit?"

(You will be tested first. Only those found worthy may use the beginning place.)

The beast and the mist collided and burst into a column of fire. The flames spun in place, then sped directly toward Nimbulan.

CHAPTER 8

The column of flame engulfed Nimbulan in an explosion of magical energy. Blue sparks invaded his eyes. Each one carried a memory of minor misdeeds, lies, and careless words that had wounded another.

He remembered a time when he and Ackerly had ventured into a village marketplace. Druulin had forbidden them to leave the tower until they had finished a long and boring series of chores. But they had slipped away early anyway.

A band of Rovers was reputed to be entertaining the farmers and shepherds. The Rovers had brought their racing steeds as well. Every man with a steed had met the challenge of a series of races. Betting ran heavily on the local steeds, known winners.

"We can make some money, Lan. Then we can buy some real food at the market," Ackerly urged his friend.

"I don't know, Acker. Betting an illusory coin on a race that we fix . . ." Nimbulan hesitated.

"What's the harm in making a plow steed feel heavy and weary so he won't run? I tell you it's a sure thing."

Just then, Nimbulan's stomach had growled, reminding them both that Druulin had forgotten to buy flour for bread. None of the apprentices had had breakfast.

"We might make enough to buy a warm cloak or an extra blanket, too," Ackerly said. "It will be easy, Lan. No one will know."

"If it's so easy, why don't you do it, Acker?" Nimbulan wanted the reassurance of his friend's participation. He was only ten and Ackerly was two years older, two years wiser and more experienced, though they were both new to Druulin's tower. Ackerly should be able to carry out his own plans and take the consequences if anything went awry. "What if we get caught?"

"We won't be caught. Who can tell that you used magic? None of these mundanes have enough imagination to think we'd interfere."

In the middle of the race, the plow steed suddenly lifted his tail and relieved the heaviness in his gut. The smelly addition to the smooth meadow brought laughter and jeers from the onlookers. The farmer beat on his steed with fists and boot heels to no avail. The steed added a long hot stream of urine to the growing pile of manure.

The farmer spotted the two magician apprentices cheering on the Rover steed as it crossed the finish line, barely winded. He also saw the large number of coins the boys collected from disgruntled locals. He grabbed a whip from a drover and ran after the two boys. Men who had lost good money on the bet took up the hue and cry. Ackerly pocketed the coins and dodged into the brothel tent where a series of semi-outraged squeals followed the passage of intruders.

Nimbulan didn't have the courage to peek into the tent let alone lead a parade of angry farmers through it. He ducked behind a huge pile of jacko squash. A little orange tint to a delusion disguised him as just another ball in the display. Until the vendor tried to lift his head off his shoulders and sell him to Druulin. . . .

He cringed inwardly with the remembrance. Other misdeeds flashed through his memory. Guilt brought tears to his eyes. But regret over Keegan's death outweighed all of his other indiscretions combined.

The sparks turned healing green. His onerous self-blame faded. Druulin's inattention and cruelty had driven his apprentices to seek food and warm clothing elsewhere, any way they could. Nimbulan's grief for his lost apprentice remained at the front of his regrets. He was responsible for the boy's upbringing. He should have seen Keegan's unbridled ambition and burning impatience.

The tiny bits of flame swirled around him faster and faster, fed by his guilt. He became the center of a massive vortex of burning flame. The tremendous circular wind threatened to rend him limb from limb.

He cried out in psychic agony.

A wall of power slammed into his jaw and sent him flying backward.

The vortex died as rapidly as it sprang up.

He landed flat on his back. Pain jarred his bones the full length of his spine. His lungs expelled air in a sharp *whoosh,* leaving him stunned and unable to breathe.

The flames dissolved into a pile of ash. No sign of the flying black creature or the shadowed spirit remained. Was it only yesterday he had watched Keegan die in the same manner? He choked back a lump that lodged in his throat.

"What happened?" Quinnault shook his head spasmodically as if clearing his vision. "Are you all right?" He reached a hand down to assist Nimbulan to his feet.

"I don't know. What was that creature?"

"The guardian or the flywacket?"

"Flywacket?" A smile tried to break through Nimbulan's shock and discomfort.

"A flying black cat. What else should I call it? It sounded as if it were crying for help. 'Mwelp.' Help?" Quinnault looked up in the direction the creature had come from.

"Who knows what strange cries such a creature would make." Nimbulan weighed the sounds in his mind. "Mwelp, mwelp." Just sounds.

"I'm certain that the creature was crying for help, Nimbulan. The look in its eyes, just before it crashed into the guardian, was a plea for help."

"Of course it needed help. It had lost control of its flight path. If every joint in my body didn't hurt, I'd laugh. Just yesterday Lord Kammeryl said that magicians cooperating was like wishing for flywackets and dragons. The men on the battlefield said they saw a dragon. You saw a flywacket here. What other miracles await us?"

Probably just a fledgling eagle. Maybe a Khamsin eagle strayed from the desert and its parents, he told himself. Others could indulge in superstitions and omens. He had a kingdom to save and a system of magic to rewrite.

"I don't know if 'twas a miracle or not. I'm still dizzy from the whirlwind the guardian kicked up." Quinnault shook his head again, pressing fingers to temples. Gradually his eyes cleared of disorientation.

"So am I." Nimbulan stretched each muscle, testing for injury. He prodded a few tender spots and rotated his shoulders seeking more specific information. "Nothing broken. I'm just shaken and sore. How do you fare, boy?"

"I believe I'm unharmed—a little sore in places. But my feet are curiously numb."

"Mine, too, now that I think about it." Nimbulan looked at his boots. A miasma of ash seemed to float a hand's span above the ground in a perfect circle. Two tall men could stretch out in a line across the diameter. He scuffed at the ash. A bitter smell rose around him. He wrinkled his nose against the unnatural scent. None of the ash moved. He lifted his left foot through the ash with some effort. There residue reformed in a thick covering beneath his raised foot, almost the texture of drying clay.

For a brief moment he caught a glimpse of bright silvery blue as his foot cleared the ash. He set his foot down again. It did not penetrate the covering. The blue winked out. He shifted his weight and lifted the other foot. Again that brief hint of many ley lines coming together. The lovely sight withdrew into hiding again as soon as his foot cleared the ash.

As he set his second foot back down, full feeling returned to his extremities.

Nimbulan looked around before darting out of the now gray circle. "Step clear, Quinnault. Quickly." The ash rapidly solidified beneath him. The young lord leaped free just as the residue hardened into a thick mortar.

"How'd we get into the courtyard of the monastery?" Nimbulan watched for any imperfection in the hardening ash. It looked like a giant piece of slate set as a single paving stone over the courtyard.

"I think the explosion threw you here. I followed as soon as the flames let me pass."

Low stone buildings with sharply pitched roofs of slate surrounded them on three sides. The fourth side of the square looked upon a narrow causeway connecting the island to a larger landmass about three hundred paces distant. The River Coronnan churned through the passage, eating away at the natural bridge.

"I must meditate on these events, my lord. But first let's examine the buildings. The guardian seems to have left us passage to them while denying us access to the pool of ley lines." Only then did he realize the power no longer flooded his body. He couldn't see a trace of the spiderweb of ley lines normal to the rest of Coronnan.

(You must find a different source of magic before peace is possible,) the guardian said deep inside Nimbulan's mind. No other trace of the spirit remained.

* * *

Ackerly watched a knot of common soldiers moving toward Magician's Square within the army camp. Three uniformed men seemed to lead the growing procession of excited soldiers, officers, and camp followers. Male voices undulated upward from normal bass tones to cracking boyish squeaks. The sound beat at his ears. He pulled his magical armor around him. He might not be able to weave major battle spells, but armor was essential to anyone serving a Battlemage.

Breathing carefully to maintain protection, he sought another spell that honed and defined the words flying around the volatile group of people. While Nimbulan and Lord Quinnault explored the river islands on some private quest, he, Ackerly, must deal with these petitioners.

"I saw it. I swear!" A fair-haired young private raised his voice above the babble. 'Twas his voice that squeaked as it gained in volume. He probably wasn't old enough to have his vocal cords truly settled.

"You three been sneaking extra rations of ale from the cook's supplies again?" a grizzled sergeant bellowed. "Heard there was a break-in at the kitchen tent this morning."

"We investigated the break-in! *We* chased the thief." Fists on hips, a black-haired giant stopped in front of the sergeant, daring the man to doubt his word. Few men would question the man who stood head and shoulders above average soldiers. The breadth of his shoulders and diameter of his upper arms proclaimed his strength. Ackerly wondered if his mind was as muscle-bound as his body.

The crowd flowed around the tall man and the sergeant until they met the boundary of the magicians' enclave.

They stopped between the hospital and the supply tent, unwilling to enter the area without invitation.

Ackerly waited to see if they would go any further.

Some of the men, more curious than brave, nudged the squeaky-voiced youngster and his slightly older companion forward. The two privates stumbled across the invisible boundary. They looked anxiously right and left. The giant joined them. All the others remained firmly on their side of the imaginary line of separation.

For a brief moment, pride swelled in Ackerly's chest. The other magicians might look down upon his minor talent, but these people respected him for having any talent at all!

"What did you see that brings so many to the private enclave of magicians?" Ackerly pitched his voice to carry across the compound and into the ears of all those who babbled as well as the few who had spotted him standing beside the large blue pavilion.

Silence descended as the crowd stood shocked by his words. Many crossed themselves as they stared at him with gaping jaws and wide eyes.

I may not be a great magician, but I am far above these mundanes.

"Step forward, my sons." He beckoned to the trio of privates at the front of the group. "Tell me your tale. The truth never hurt anyone."

"We found the witchwoman stealing supplies," the middle soldier said. He lifted his head proudly, almost defiantly.

"Theft is a matter for your sergeant."

"But she's a witch, one of you."

"So she is. What did you do when you found her stealing supplies?"

"We chased her."' The middle private continued to speak. Clearly, the boyish one and the giant looked to him for leadership.

"And . . . ?" Ackerly allowed a little kindly pink to tinge his aura. He schooled his posture and expression to radiate trust.

"That black cat, her . . . ah, her familiar was with her. It spread wings and flew."

"I saw it, too," the boy chimed in.

The giant nodded vigorously.

"Cats cannot fly," Ackerly said.

"This one did."

"Flywackets are creatures out of legend." A *flywacket!* A mighty portent of strange events to follow. Ackerly began thinking in terms of the money to be made from a flywacket. He nearly bounced in his excitement. The old books he studied to help Nimbulan create spells spoke frequently of flywackets and other winged creatures thought to be extinct. *A flywacket!* Three men had a confirmed sighting.

If Moncriith heard about this portent of demons, he'd stir up a lot of unrest. Mundanes always paid well for a magician to settle chaos.

"Dragons are mythical, too, but we saw one on the battlefield yesterday." The crowd shouted unanimous agreement with the boyish private.

"We shall see if you speak the truth. Sighting a magical creature can only be verified by magic." Ackerly fought to maintain his dignified, slightly disapproving demeanor.

Dramatically he spread his arms wide and slightly above shoulder level. With a blink of his eyes and fierce concentration he transported his staff into his right hand. The crowd gasped in awe.

Good. Let them think he had as much magic as Nimbulan and was more than just an errand boy. They'd treat him with respect next time he requested a service or bumped into them in camp.

"Let those who claim this magical sighting step forward, clear of all the others." He swelled his voice and lifted it to reach far beyond normal human limitations. The crowd flowed backward. The three privates each took two hesitant steps forward. Ackerly nodded his acceptance of the increased separation.

He took a deep breath to clear his lungs. A second breath cleansed his brain. The third put him in touch with the void, the deepest trance he could achieve on his own. None of the onlookers needed to know the strain on his back and thigh muscles to remain upright. Trances weren't easy for him.

Nimbulan wouldn't have wasted the magic to perform this task. A few tricks of crossed eyes and decisive questions by the Battlemage would set the three to babbling uncontrollably.

Ackerly wanted the magic to prove the men honest or tricksters. He didn't have enough magic to *not* use it whenever possible.

Within the trance, Ackerly gathered power in his belly until it expanded throughout his chest and flowed down his arm into the staff. The flowing grain of the wood glowed blue with brilliant green sparks all along the length. He pushed more power into the staff until it rose of its own accord and pointed at the three men.

Sweat broke out on his brow. His shoulders trembled with the strain of maintaining the flow of power. He didn't have the ability or skill to tap a ley line to fuel the magic. Only his own stamina produced the energy for this spell. He'd have to finish soon or drain himself of all strength.

He almost wished the Tambootie worked for him. He could use some enhancement right now.

More power into the staff. The wood glowed with heat, burning his hand. More power still and the blue light shot from the end of the magical tool into a cloud of sparkling dust that settled upon the soldiers. Blue truth glowed around their heads in a brilliant aura for all to see.

"Ooo!" a camp follower in a patched green dress cooed. She reached a hesitant hand to capture some of the glowing dust. "So pretty." She sprinkled the dust in her hair and pranced in front of her customers.

Ackerly lowered his staff to the ground and leaned heavily upon it. His arms and legs trembled with fatigue.

"If any of you had lied, the truth spell would have turned red and burned right through you, leaving only a skeleton," he said. An exaggeration to be sure, but such demonstrations kept the crowd honest. None of them would ever dare lie to Ackerly again. They might even pay him to find out if a comrade lied. That was worth the fatigue and hunger that gnawed at his belly and brought stabbing pains behind his eyes.

"What should we do about the flywacket?" The sergeant stepped forward, ready to stand by his men now that they were proved truthful.

"Did you capture it or the girl?" Ackerly asked.

"No. They disappeared without leaving a trail."

"Which direction?"

"East."

Moncriith was headed East. If the girl and her familiar could be found, the Bloodmage would be the one to root them out of their hiding place. How could he make Moncriith pay for this information?

"Send a small patrol with tracking dogs that way. Report back here if you find anything. Anything at all. If you find nothing, return here at this hour tomorrow. I must discuss this with the other magicians." He bowed deeply and stepped back toward the tent. He wished he could fade into the shadows and disappear like Nimbulan could. Like the witchwoman seemed to have done.

But he couldn't. He could only retreat like an ordinary man.

CHAPTER 9

"Why don't we wait for torches and assistants?" Quinnault de Tanos remained three steps behind Nimbulan as the magician measured the long corridor with his paces. Pale yellow sunlight pierced the interior gloom in long streaks through the narrow windows.

"I can see fine," Nimbulan replied. "Sixty-seven . . . sixty-eight . . . sixty-nine. I want to find the kitchens. Maybe someone left some food. Seventy . . . seventy-one . . . seventy-two paces," he said.

They'd found a motheaten blanket, probably threadbare before the priests left, upon a stone bed carved into one of the small cells. Nimbulan had stumbled over a broken sandal in the bathing chamber. Nothing else remained. No furniture, no clothing or linens or decorations. Nothing.

"How long has this place been empty?" Nimbulan asked as he tried the door handle in the middle of the long passageway. He couldn't move the latch with brute strength. Briefly he wondered if magic would remove the weight of years and rust on the mechanism.

"My father explored the place as a teenager. My grandfather mentioned once that he might remember someone living here during his childhood. Caretaker, squatter, or priest, I have no idea." De Tanos turned in circles as he walked, surveying the masonry and the view from narrow arched windows. Even the storm shutters had been removed.

"Help me with this door, please." Nimbulan stood straight and rubbed his shoulder where he had shoved against the wooden panels.

Together they leaned their combined weight into the door while Nimbulan wiggled the latch with a releasing spell. The handle lifted, but the door remained firmly closed.

"We can come back later with tools and more men, Nimbulan," Quinnault said. "The kitchens should be in one of the wings, near an end, not in the center. No sense in burning the entire structure if a cooking fire blazed out of control."

"Yes. Logical. But this secured door puzzles me. Every other door is wide open to the wind and the elements. The stone beneath each window is heavily damaged by repeated rain and sunlight. What is so special behind this door that it alone is locked and protected?" He stared at the door one more time, trying to pry its secrets free of the closed panels.

No images stirred his imagination.

He paced to the other end of the corridor. Seventy-two steps. The closed room sat in the exact center of the monastery.

"Did anyone ever offer a reason for the priests leaving this place?" He hastened to catch up with Quinnault who had turned into the eastern wing of the one-story structure. Only the central portion of the U-shaped building rose to a second story. They hadn't discovered access to basements. On these islands, the water table might be too high to allow digging a deep foundation.

"I have heard only rumors of the haunting. Was the guardian spirit a ghost?" Quinnault poked his head into another empty room, this one larger than the individual cells of the residential wing—a refectory perhaps?

"It didn't act like a ghost. Most spirits of the dead are rather lost and bewildered, seeking guidance to the void between the planes of existence."

Keegan would have been a ghost without Nimbulan's help. *Why, Keegan? Why did you make me kill you?* The pain was still too new and raw to dismiss. The guardian had relieved his other annoying little guilts, but not that one. He must have done something wrong in bringing up the boy.

"The kitchen is through here." De Tanos led the way through a low doorway at the end of the corridor.

Nimbulan added up his mental count of the length of the corridor. Forty-eight paces. The east and west wings were the same size. The south-facing central wing was almost twice that length as well as double in height.

Three narrow stairs brought him down into a room that took up half the wing. Two massive fireplaces, one on each outside wall showed sooty stains around and above the hearth. They'd been swept clean of ashes, but no amount of scrubbing would remove the smoky stains. Kindling and firewood lay neatly prepared for the touch of a flame. Long worktables stretched down the center of the room, clean and clear of equipment or debris. The scrub sinks were equally clean and empty.

Someone had taken time to clean and tidy up—as if they didn't want to leave a mess for the next cook.

Quinnault's footsteps echoed eerily across the stone flooring. Nimbulan tried to walk more silently. The extreme emptiness of the entire building suddenly struck him. Noise of any kind seemed out-of-place.

Nimbulan forced himself to speak in normal tones rather than whisper. The vast emptiness made the fine hairs on the back of his neck stand up.

Had the guardian spirit come back?

He looked around. No writhing mist awaited them.

"The last inhabitants weren't attacked and driven out. Not if they took time to clean the kitchen. Perhaps a plague decimated their numbers and they combined with another facility." Quinnault opened cupboards to reveal more emptiness.

"Perhaps. A hot, wet summer could breed any number of diseases in stagnant pools among these islands." Nimbulan drifted toward the pantries and storerooms at the west end of the room.

"My people have never suffered any plagues living on the islands or nearby shoreline. Summers are either hot and dry or cool and wet. But the river is constant. The tides from the Great Bay keep the level fairly regular, regardless of rainfall or snowmelt."

"We must search further for answers. Perhaps another monastery has records. De Tanos, can you light the fire someone so kindly left us? I'm still rather damp and chilled."

"Not without a firestone and tinder. Is there a firebox around? My magic is too minimal to generate flames."

"What can you do? That's the first spell I learned." Nimbulan stomped back to the hearth. An image of flames dancing merrily among the kindling brightened his mind. With a snap of his fingers and two words to trigger the spell, he transferred the image from his mind to the reality of the hearth.

Flames licked eagerly at the dry wood.

"I never wanted to be a magician. I only wanted to be a priest. When I try very hard, I can pick up people's thoughts. It's so much work though, I haven't tried since I passed the preliminary examinations." Quinnault didn't drop his head in shame at his paltry talent.

Ackerly would have.

Nimbulan smiled at the comparison. Successful magic was as much a matter of attitude as talent. De Tanos would have been a very good priest, and his magic—the ability to help people confide their troubles so he could find ways to help them—would have grown. Ackerly's talent, though stronger than the lord's, hadn't improved one bit in thirty years of constant practice, because he wanted to have more rather than work to improve what he had.

Too bad Ackerly had no respect for his wonderful talent as an administrator. Nimbulan and his apprentices depended upon Ackerly every day.

"At least you can build up the fire while I poke around the pantry, Quinnault. There might be more wood in the firebox by the back door."

The pantry door opened as easily as all of the others, except the center room. Again, Nimbulan found shelves and cupboards swept clean. "Do you know what's really missing? Cobwebs and mice droppings. It's almost as if someone cleans this place from top to bottom frequently."

"Maybe the guardian kept the vermin out as well as people." De Tanos leaned against the pantry door, blocking what little light filtered in from the kitchen. The three high windows in the outside wall offered little illumination.

"Possibly, or . . ." Nimbulan sniffed the air and stamped his feet. "I wish that pool of ley lines hadn't been barricaded. I sense magic of some sort, but I can't tell the nature or source. Maybe there's a stasis spell on the monastery. Nothing changes until someone breaks the spell."

"In which case, our coming here, and the guardian's disappearance may have disrupted the magic field enough to erode the spell. Will the walls come tumbling down once the magic dissolves?" Quinnault looked anxiously at the thick stone walls surrounding them.

"I doubt the mortar will crumble so quickly. How's your fire?"

"Fine. Did you find anything in here?"

Nimbulan peered into the pantry. He held his left palm up and brought a hint of magic into his vision. The shadows took on definite lines, still black on gray, but with outlines and texture.

A single journey pack sat in the center of the middle wall of shelves. He approached the bundle with care.

"What do you see?" De Tanos moved into the room, one hand extended into the gloom to find obstacles before he tripped over them.

"A trap perhaps. I don't know. I am suspicious of something so conspicuous in an otherwise empty building." Nimbulan spread his hand above the pack. Tendrils of magic shot from his fingertips into the heavy leather seeking answers.

He shifted his vision to InterSight. Radiant shades of green surrounded the pack, indicating heat. The temperature beneath his fingertips did not change.

Something within the pack quivered in answer to his magic probe. Nimbulan traced the outline of the minute vibrations. A thin "string" of power drifted away from the core. When he touched it, an image of a closed door rose in his mind. A door very like the one in the center of the abandoned monastery.

"A trap or a clue, I'm not sure." He followed the now-glowing, green "string" around the pantry to the door, one finger extended just above it, maintaining the sensation of a long-dormant being rousing from sleep.

Quinnault walked behind him, two paces back. The lord kept one hand on the hilt of his short sword.

The magic led them through the kitchen, up the three steps to the corridor and along the passageway to the intersection of the main hall. The image of a locked door grew stronger, more vivid.

"Curious. I've never seen a spell constructed so subtly."

"Is the guardian present in the spell?" Quinnault asked, looking around for the column of fire or mist.

"I can't determine the signature in the weaving. Only the presence of something that has waited a long time." Nimbulan paused at the locked door. The magic led through the keyhole. He touched the lock with his questing finger.

Again the pack flashed through his mind. This time the image hovered beside the lock.

The metal latch grew warm under Nimbulan's finger. "If I'm following the clues properly, we need to bring the pack here."

"It could be a trap."

"It could, but I don't think so. There is no hint of malice in this magic."

"But you said it was a subtle spell. The violent intent could be buried beneath layers of innuendo and diverting spells."

"You learned your magic theory well, Quinnault de Tanos," Nimbulan said. "But I am a Battlemage. I am well-versed in all forms of destructive magic. No. This spell has the feel of curiosity, intelligence, and a quest for knowledge."

"Why don't we leave this for another day when you have the backup of your assistants and apprentices?" de Tanos asked. "The day grows late. If we are to get off the island, we should start now."

"How? Our boat sank."

"The causeway is clear at low tide. There are farms and the family keep on the next island. I have other boats to take you back to camp."

"Why didn't you say so? Here I've been thinking we were stranded and would have to signal a fisherman with a fire after dark."

"Like as not, the fisherman would see the signal as evidence of haunting spirits and stay away."

"How long will the causeway be clear? I want to investigate this puzzle while we're here."

"Several hours. When the moon is full in Spring and Autumn and the tides run high, the passage can be dangerous, but not today."

"Good. Come with me. We need to bring the pack to the door. But it must not stray from the path of the magic I followed here."

Moments later, Nimbulan held the slight bulk of the pack beside the lock. Slowly, testing for undue warmth or stabs of light, he pressed the old leather to the latch. A faint hum filled the corridor.

"What? Where?" Quinnault spun, belt dagger extended, seeking the source of the increasing noise.

Bouncing balls of green, blue, and unholy red witchfire joined the hum reverberating around the passageway.

Nimbulan dropped the pack, pressing his hands against his ears. He didn't quite dare close his eyes against the bright witchfire. He had the sense that while he watched them dart around, they wouldn't attack him.

Quinnault ducked a buzzing blue ball, slashing at it with the flat of his blade. The noise grew to an intolerable level. He dropped the dagger to press his hands against his ears. The clatter of metal against stone barely registered against the incredible whine of sound.

Suddenly the witchfire flashed and died. The hum ceased.

Nimbulan's ears rang in the silence.

The latch clicked open quietly.

He looked from the latch to the crumpled leather on the floor. Jerked meat and dried fruit spilled from the pack. He bent to touch the journey provisions. They seemed real.

The door opened a tiny crack. He pushed gently against the panels. The hinges didn't creak. No dust met his nose.

He looked closer. Light spilled into a vast room around the edges of many closed shutters. A sense of warmth and welcome surrounded him. He sniffed for magic and found only the special scent of vellum and leather.

"Books? Lots and lots of books!" He raced to the nearest window, throwing open the shutters. These, too, opened without protest or signs of age.

He turned slowly, holding his breath with anticipation. Walls and walls of books awaited him.

CHAPTER 10

"You've returned at last." Ackerly scowled at Nimbulan. He had said he'd return before sunset, and so he had, barely. Ackerly's anxious waiting hadn't made the time pass faster, adding to his irritation.

"You won't believe the adventures I've had today, Ackerly. Lord Quinnault and I found the most amazing treasures." The Battlemage brushed past his assistant in the doorway to the large pavilion. The glowing aura of the setting sun behind Nimbulan's back followed him into the tent.

Ackerly shied away from the energy his friend radiated. That yellow-gold aura effectively barred Ackerly from sharing Nimbulan's thoughts and enthusiasms.

"Lord Kammeryl has been looking for you most of the day. Some amazing things have happened here as well." Annoyance bristled the hair on the back of Ackerly's neck. Nimbulan positively bounced as he walked. "Will you stop for a moment and listen, Lan? Maybe you need some Tambootie to settle you."

"I've never felt better, Acker. Send a page for Lord Kammeryl now. I need to tell him that you and I and the boys will be spending the winter away from his fortress. We leave as soon after dawn as Lord Quinnault can send a barge for our books and equipment. Books—" He trailed off in a kind of dazed reverie. His aura increased in size, if that was possible.

"We can't leave Lord Kammeryl d'Astrismos! He depends upon you for protection. We depend upon him for employment." Ackerly's supper formed a lump in his belly. What would he do for food and shelter away from the lord's stronghold. The thought of weathering the Winter storms outside the snug warmth of his room near the kitchen filled him with dread. No more tasty tidbits pressed upon him by the scullery maid. No more stolen kisses and frantic fumblings with the wenches in the armory. No more gold paid out every moon.

"I'm taking a leave of absence from Lord Kammeryl to study and experiment, Ackerly. Lord Quinnault showed me an abandoned monastery today. The most amazing place. Intact. Good roof. No signs of wear or decay. Not even any cobwebs." Nimbulan started throwing books and pieces of arcane equipment into a pack without regard to efficiency or breakability. "Rollett, have you seen my oak wand with the river agate?" he called into the interior of the great pavilion.

"Your attention is needed here. Nimbulan. Three men reported seeing a flywacket. Three *confirmed* sightings. Do you realize the significance of that?"

"Yes, yes. I saw it, too. A wonderful omen that I belong in that monastery. It's perfect for my experiments. We'll need to recruit some new apprentices, and send an open invitation to trained magicians who genuinely desire peace. We're going to find a way to end these wars, Ackerly. I can feel it in my bones." He scratched his left palm, the one he held up to weave his spells, then moved to another collection of paraphernalia, stuffing it into a large sack.

"The men swear the flywacket was also the witch-woman's familiar." Ackerly dropped his voice, curious to see how his comrade reacted to that bit of news.

Nimbulan looked up from his frantic sorting of mirrors and powders and mathematical charts of the stars. "Impossible. Myrilandel keeps a black cat. I saw the beast—she called it Amaranth. It bore no signs of wings or beak or talons. Unlike the creature we saw today. What we saw was truly an omen from the Stargods."

"What if they saw a true flywacket? What if the shadows the men reported yesterday came from a dragon?" Ackerly asked.

"Illusions. The men were exhausted from the battle. Now where did I put that Khamsin eagle quill. It's my favorite pen."

Ackerly dropped his head in disappointment. Usually Nimbulan listened to him. Tonight he was too full of his own plans to heed anything but the direst shocks. Ackerly vowed to use a heavier dose than usual of the Tambootie on Nimbulan's supper. Maybe then the Battlemage would listen.

"Maalin," Ackerly called to the dark-haired young man loitering near a small two-man tent beside the large pavilion. "Maalin, inform my lord Kammeryl that Nimbulan and I will attend him shortly." The apprentice nodded as he hastened to the other side of the camp.

"We haven't time to waste discussing Kammeryl's latest female companion. And you know he won't hear anything else we say until he gives us a blow-by-blow description of his latest bedding." Nimbulan shuddered slightly with distaste.

Ackerly refused to flinch. They both knew the lord's tastes. Distastes was a more accurate word. But feeding the man's addiction to pretty virgins gave Kammeryl d'Astrismos a feeling of godlike power and thus blinded him to manipulation by the magicians. Ackerly needed Kammeryl in a fog of sexual satiation to keep his treasury open.

"Just send a message to Lord Kammeryl. Compose it for me, will you? Are all of the books on history and moon phases in the trunk?" Nimbulan turned back to his sorting without waiting for an answer.

"What am I supposed to tell *our* lord?" Ackerly gritted his teeth. Nimbulan wasn't listening to him at all—wasn't paying attention to anything but his own thoughts spinning in a mad whirl.

"Tell him anything. You're better at diplomatic notes than I am. Oh, and tell Myrilandel to be ready to travel with us. I'm looking forward to training her. She has the most amazing talent."

"The witchwoman escaped."

"What do you mean, escaped? She couldn't escape. She wasn't a prisoner."

"She left, then. Secretly. Without notice. And she tried to steal supplies. That's when the guards saw her flywacket. That's when she ran Westward in the same direction as Moncriith." He smiled to himself at the misdirection. Nimbulan wouldn't find either Moncriith or Myrilandel if he sought them. Moncriith would be free to act upon any information Ackerly chose to feed him, and Nimbulan wouldn't lose himself in his infatuation with the girl.

"I've got to stop her. She needs my help." Nimbulan dashed toward the door.

Ackerly stood firmly in his path. "No. We need to speak to Lord Kammeryl about his plans to follow Lord Hanic's army. We need to help spread the rumor that the flywacket was a message from the Stargods that the House d'Astrismos is their favorite to rule all of Coronnan."

"Get out of my way, Ackerly. I've much more important things to do than cater to Kammeryl's delusions of godhood."

"What is more important than catering to the whims of the man who provides you with food and clothing and a place to work as well as a generous salary? What is more important than his plans for Coronnan?"

"Peace." Nimbulan pushed past Ackerly.

"Peace will be the end of our kind," Ackerly whispered to himself. "And the end of our money." Nimbulan hadn't heard a word he said. No one ever did. No one had listened to him since he was thirteen and had failed his journeyman trials for the second time. . . .

"Fumble fingers!" Boojlin taunted Ackerly as they emerged from Master Druulin's private study. Boojlin had passed the first test set for them. He'd successfully lobbed a ball of witchfire out the window to ignite the scarecrow in a nearby field.

Druulin and Boojlin had laughed at the farmer's frantic attempts to extinquish the fire before it burned the entire field of corn.

Ackerly had failed the test. He couldn't "throw" anything with magic. He could retrieve personal items that he knew well, like his staff. But throwing eluded him.

"How can you expect to be a Battlemage if you can't throw something as simple as witchfire?" Boojlin continued his teasing. "You're a clumsy half-mundane and you'll never be anything more."

"You didn't do much better, Boojlin. You failed the second half of the test," Ackerly retorted. Boojlin hadn't been able to extinquish the witchfire he'd set. The farmer had lost almost half an acre to witchfire before Druulin stepped in and doused the flames with a counterspell.

"I'll be a better Battlemage than you will. When I

master the spell, I'll master the *whole* spell, not just the fun part," Ackerly retorted, not knowing what else to say.

"Will not!" Boojlin launched a torch at Ackerly. He ducked that missile and the books that followed him as he ran away.

Boojlin continued to pelt him with whatever objects came handy to his magic. Ackerly didn't stop running until he reached the kitchen in the ground level of the tall tower. His tormentor pelted down the spiral stairs, laughing at Ackerly's cowardice.

Until he ran into a yampion pie hovering at face level just inside the door to the kitchen.

"I might not be able to throw, but I can think ahead, Boojie." Ackerly wiped a pile of sweet pie filling from Boojlin's face with his index finger. He smiled as he licked his hand clean of the sweet treat. "Looks like no dessert for you tonight, Boojie. You ruined it for all of us. I'll have to tell Druulin precisely why he won't get his favorite pie tonight."

Caasser and Lan had laughed at the trick as Ackerly was forced by Druulin to clean the entire kitchen for wasting the pie. But Ackerly never forgot that he'd had to hold the pie in place with his hands until the last moment before Boojlin slammed into it because he didn't have enough magic to levitate it for long. He never forgot how all the others had passed their tests eventually, leaving Ackerly to clean up the messes they made.

"You don't appreciate me anymore than Druulin did, Nimbulan. I'm still cleaning up your messes."

* * *

"Excuse me." A short, wizened man of indeterminate years blocked Nimbulan's exit from his pavilion. "I understand you are looking for colleagues to join you in a new venture." The man bowed from the waist. A sign of respect for an equal.

He wore ordinary black trews and tunic and carried a black cloak or robe over his arm. His skin had yellowed with age, was seamed by a million wrinkles, some of them smile lines around his mouth and laugh lines near his eyes. Even now a mischievous twinkle glistened in his pale blue eyes, so pale they seemed almost colorless.

Like Myrilandel's eyes and hair.

The witchwoman was gone, fled of her own will. Nimbulan needed to go after her. . . .

He didn't have time to waste worrying about her.

Or regretting her absence.

"How did you know about this venture?" Nimbulan asked the old man warily.

"News travels fast among magicians." His smile quirked up enigmatically.

"Excuse me, Master Nimbulan, I have errands to run and chores to perform." Ackerly shouldered his way past the intruder. "I'll meet you in Lord Kammeryl's pavilion in a few moments."

"Yes, I'll join you there, Ackerly." Nimbulan didn't take his eyes off the stranger. "News must travel very fast among some magicians. I didn't decide to pursue this venture until a few hours ago and only announced it to my assistant now."

"Ah, but your delight in the project broadcast a psychic shout of glee across the heavens. I heard and sought you out." The old man bowed again.

"You must have been very close."

"Closer than you think."

"Do you have a name?"

"Yes. I am called Lyman in this existence."

"A strange way of giving your name. Do you, perchance, possess the unique ability to remember your previous existences or know the future ones?" Suspicion crawled over Nimbulan's skin. His need to scratch and worry at the itch was like his need for the Tambootie.

"Anything can be found in the void if only you know where and how to look, Nimbulan. Would you take me there to see if I am what I seem?"

"And what do you seem to be?" Maybe he should have asked what the old man pretended to be.

"I am merely an old magician, tired of war, as you are. I would use my remaining years in this life to seek peace. I choose to join you in the same quest, for I believe you have the answers, though you do not know it yet."

Nimbulan's suspicions dissolved, as if he'd poured

water laced with oatmeal over his itchy skin. "Why do I trust you, Lyman?"

"Because I tell the truth. Finish your errands. I will join you on your island tomorrow morning." Lyman bowed again.

Nimbulan felt compelled to give the same gesture of respect.

Then Old Lyman backed up and dissolved into the mist.

"That's my trick, old man! Where'd you learn it?"

A soft chuckle in the distance was his only answer.

* * *

Dust motes drifting on a soft beam of sunlight penetrated Myri's awareness. She blinked rapidly several times, trying to remember.

"Where am I?" she asked the sunbeam. "Why did I come here?" She remembered running. Running from . . . something terrible but important. Why couldn't she remember what had happened to her? She wasn't home. That she knew. A vague image of Old Magretha crossed her mind. Home was a shack in the woods or the vague promise of the voices on the wind. This shelter . . . what was this shelter?

Behind the ray of light, she saw rock walls. Not the dressed stone of a man-made fortress, but the undulating flow of natural stone patterns. Yellow and gray layered upon each other in irregular widths. Light to the left. Dark to the right. A glow in the center.

She looked down to discover a neat fire ring and a fresh fish spitted over the coals. Her stomach growled, reminding her that she had caught the fish earlier. She had settled into this cave above a sheltered cove for the Winter. The cave was nearly invisible from the sandy beach below, nestled into the shadow of the curving headland. She had run from something to this coastal refuge.

The sound of waves shushing against a sandy shore added itself to her growing picture of her campsite.

Campfires? Dozens of fires serving hundreds of men. An army. The face of a Battlemage who tried to be gentle with her. His green eyes promised protection.

She had run away from the camp. Run to . . . danger.

Danger that was past now.

"How long have I been here?" The sound of her voice echoing slightly within the cave reassured her that she still lived and wasn't lost in some void-induced dream.

No memory responded to her question. Only a sense of fear and running. Quickly she checked the cave for others. She seemed to be alone.

Someone was missing. An emptiness yawned in her chest behind her heart.

"Who?"

She stretched her arms to her side, expecting to feel wings catch on the slight breeze coming in from the opening. The lift and surge of flight did not follow.

"Not me. I am Kardia-bound. Amaranth. Amaranth flies. Where is he?"

Shadows danced across the sunlight. Myri scrambled to her feet and looked out the mouth of the ancient sea cave. Gulls swooped and soared. A large bird dove into the waves and sprang free of the water with a fish in its beak.

The flying shapes were all too small and white. Myri searched the fluffy clouds and pale autumnal sky for signs of a bulkier black form. Nothing. She stretched her listening senses for Amaranth's mewling cry.

"Merwack." In the far distance. Faint and excited. *(We have tested him and found him worthy!)*

"Who? Who did you test and find worthy of what?" Myri almost laughed at Amaranth's excitement. His mental pictures of towering columns of mist and blue sparks didn't make sense. "Where have you been, Amaranth?"

She dug her toes into the flaking sandstone, stretched her arms as if for flight, and sent her mind on a straight line to Amaranth. Her mind blended with his and she found the freedom of flight she dreamed of so often. Up through the clouds. Up toward the blessed sun. The wind buffeted her. It smelled of salt and cold dampness. A storm gathered beneath her, preparing to assault the Great Bay. She rose above it. Seeking. Always seeking.

She reached out for him with her mind and her love. *We are together now. Come to me, Amaranth. I miss you. I need you, Amaranth.* Awareness of her Kardia-bound body layered on top of her illusion of flight. Finally a black spot appeared to her physical eyes far to the North and West.

Come, my precious Amaranth. Come and tell me all about your adventures, the test, and who you found worthy.

Gradually the black spot grew and took on the distinctive shape of a falcon. The bird broadened. Its tail lengthened and fluffed. Instead of a wickedly curved beak, she sensed a flatter cat's muzzle and whiskers.

"Amaranth." Myri sighed with relief. The one constant in her life. No matter what she forgot, how many days she lost in the void, Amaranth always returned to her.

"Meereek!" The flywacket faltered and lost elevation. Through his eyes, Myri saw a fish glittering in the waves below. Extreme hunger overcame them both. Together they dove to catch the enticing meal.

The vision of the fish vanished, replaced by the symmetrical grid of a fisherman's net. "Pull up, Amaranth." Fear lanced through her. She sent him strength along the line of her mind. "Release your wings, Amaranth. Catch the wind and fly upward, quickly." Her arms stiffened and rose in sympathy with the attitude he needed to assume.

Amaranth reached with his back claws to grasp the fish that wasn't there. His wings stretched and he rose with his prize. The dark strands of netting tangled around his hind legs, trailing backward into the waves. The weight of the saturated strands dragged him back.

"Drop it, Amaranth! Drop it before it pulls you beneath the water and drowns you."

As Myri watched, the net moved in the air currents to ensnare his front paws as well.

He fought the net, beating at it with his teeth and wingtips as he strove for elevation.

"Come ashore, quickly." Myri caught her breath again, praying he had enough strength to fly the last little bit.

"Merwack," he chirped in a more normal tone. He stretched his neck forward, toward the sandy beach, still fighting the net.

Myri scrambled down the cliff face below the cave entrance.

Amaranth extended his talons and backwinged for

landing. The net flew upward catching a wingtip and dragging it down.

Myri caught her breath, praying that Amaranth could land safely under his own strength.

The flywacket's left wing collapsed under the weight of the net. He plummeted to the beach below him.

CHAPTER 11

"Amaranth!" Myri ran toward the tide line where saltwater lapped at the flywacket flailing about in the sand. The net tangled tighter with each flap of wing and thrash of foot.

He whimpered in growing frustration. The pain from the net tightening around his legs like a noose lashed her mind as well as his body.

"Stay still, Amaranth. I'm coming." She skidded the last few feet, landing on her knees.

At last she reached out with a single finger to touch his wing.

"Hisscht!" He warned her how much he hurt. His claws extended into full talons.

"Why did you go after that fish, my precious? You could have waited and shared mine," she said softly.

(I had to. The hunger would not wait.) The flywacket relaxed a little at the sound of her voice, retracting his claws. His eyes remained fearful and glazed with pain.

Memory of the hunger that had assaulted her at the moment of his dive puzzled her. She hadn't sensed the need for food in him a moment before that, only his excitement.

"You know I won't hurt you Amaranth." She spread her palm over his injury. Blue light glowed beneath her palm. Her talent pulled her toward the source of pain and repelled her at the same time. Energy drained from her arm into the flywacket with no apparent healing.

With a strong effort of will, Myri reined in her talent before she drained herself. The blue light dimmed. "That has never happened before. Why won't you accept the healing?"

(Your healing is grounded in the Kardia. I am a creature

of the air. The power of the healing must come from those who fly.)

Myri untangled the net. It relaxed at her touch where a moment before it had seemed almost alive as it wound around and around Amaranth in ever tightening loops.

"You're only bruised and tired." She smiled at Amaranth. "Time and rest will do more for you than I can. But you must not use that wing until it is completely healed. I think your pride is damaged more than you are."

Amararnth sniffed with indignity. He gathered his feet beneath him and sat with his back to her, tail twitching. Keeping his damaged wing half-furled, he began his bath, carefully ignoring her.

"When in doubt, wash," Myri chuckled. "You'll feel better after a bath." She would, too. She couldn't remember when she'd last had the opportunity. "I wonder if the bay is warm enough to swim in."

"Not at this time of year," a deep male voice replied.

"Who are you?" Myri stood hastily. She searched the crescent beach for potential enemies, wishing she was higher to get a better view.

A solitary man stood about ten arm-lengths away. His smooth skin beneath a black, scraggly beard made him look to be about her own age. The squint lines around his dark eyes and weathered skin suggested a decade more in years.

"You're a Rover," she stated the obvious. Only the nomadic traders wore the garish color combinations of black trews and embroidered vast, red shirt, green neckerchief, and a purple head scarf beneath a broad-brimmed, black felt hat that shadowed his eyes. No man native to Coronnan would be caught dead with a large hoop earring piercing his left ear and a belt full of dangling coins from many countries.

"You don't know me. Surely every beautiful woman in these parts knows Televarn, by reputation if not in fact." He swept his hat off and held it across his heart. Every movement he made showed an enticing ripple of muscle beneath his shirt and trews. His limbs perfectly balanced the proportions of his torso. He moved with an easy grace.

Even when standing still, he seemed about to step into a beautiful dance.

She wanted simply to stare at him.

Her fingers felt incomplete. She needed to reach out and caress his marvelous face, feel the smooth movement of his muscles beneath his flawless skin in order to become whole.

(He knows not how to tell the truth if a lie is more interesting.) Amaranth's voice broke through her mental fog.

No memory of this man stirred in her. Not unusual. Most of her memories of recent months had fled. An ache of loneliness formed in the center of her chest. If she had ever known this beautiful man, she didn't remember.

Distrust replaced the lonely ache. Only Amaranth remained a constant in her life and her memory. She trusted only Amaranth.

"Where did you come from, Master Televarn?" Myri stepped forward to stand between Amaranth and the stranger.

"The cove beyond that headland." He pointed over his shoulder, never taking his sight away from her. Every movement he made compelled her to watch him. "We always winter there."

"We?" she squeaked. "How many?" Her heart pounded loudly in her ears. Thoughts of spending the Winter in her own snug cave halfway up the cliff vanished. A tribe of Rovers so close. . . . Her lungs labored at the thought of so many people invading her privacy. They would demand cures for endless small ailments. Her talent would compel her to help them time and time again until one of them met with a fatal accident or died of old age, or a disease she couldn't cure. Then they'd accuse her of murder and threaten her until she was forced to flee for her own life.

The pattern of life for witchwomen was always the same. Over the years, she and Magretha had met many such women, always on the move. "The next village will be kinder," they said. "If not that village, then the next one beyond that." Rarely did any of them spend more than a few seasons in each village.

She and Magretha had lingered in their last village for

nearly two years. Two years of goodwill and mutual dependence before the villagers turned on her.

"Only my family winters in a cave in the next cove. A dozen or so." Televarn flicked his fingers in dismissal of the paltry number. "May I see your pet's injuries, witchwoman?" He stepped closer. His legs were long enough and strong enough to bring him dangerously close in three strides. His aura glowed with warm charm.

"Why do you call me that?" Suspicion flared within her. He was *too* beautiful. She remained where she stood, protecting Amaranth. She fluffed her skirts nervously, hoping the inquisitive flywacket would remain out of sight until he hid his wing.

"Who else keeps a flywacket *familiar.* Both of you seem to be faded from view, or blending with the morning shadows. Is something wrong, witchwoman?"

"I think you are mistaken. My cat is just a cat. He was curious and became entangled in a fishnet. Your net, perhaps?" A quick glance confirmed that Amaranth had his bruised wing safely folded beneath its protective fold of skin.

"Only old women and untried boys use nets. I have skills that charm fish onto my hooks and I reel them in by the dozen. Is he truly only a cat?" He stepped closer again.

"Stay where you are." She erected a little armor around herself and Amaranth.

"A witchwoman's duties include providing relief from all sorts of ills. I have an itch that needs to be scratched." He touched his crotch suggestively.

"Only a witchwoman of little power buys the loyalty of men with her body." She fought her instinct to run. Amaranth was still too tired and sore to follow.

"But I love all women. How could I betray any one of them." Televarn held his hands out away from his body as if reassuring her he carried no snares or hidden weapons.

"Your women will always be jealous of your whores. They will poison the minds of other men against one they fear or dislike. Their whispers will make her a witch even though she isn't one. The men have the authority to order a burning of a witch in order to please their women." Myri nearly spat on his shiny black boot to keep him away.

Another man wished her death by burning. She knew that. Vague memories of a man in a faded red robe with a compelling gaze and charming voice flitted through her mind in ragged wisps. If that man happened to enter the district, the Rovers would sell him information. Rovers would sell anything. They'd also steal anything.

She strengthened the magic protection around Amaranth and herself. A flywacket would fetch a high price in the right circles.

Which circles? She had encountered someone who would pay a fortune for her flywacket. They had tried to capture Amaranth. Who? Fruitlessly she searched her faulty memory. No other images sprang to mind. Her feet and arms ached to run and climb as far and as fast as she could.

She couldn't run. Amaranth needed her protection. He couldn't fly yet. Not with the bone-deep bruises he'd earned in his struggle with the net.

"Rovers value witchwomen for all of their talents. You needn't be jealous because you've heard I fathered a bastard or two in my wanderings. That just proves I could give you children as well. You look ripe for motherhood, witchwoman." Televarn continued to assess her attributes with knowing eyes. He reached out a hand, palm upward in entreaty. His slightly curved fingers silently begged her to join him.

She'd seen another man use a similar gesture to weave magic. A man in blue.

"I do not value the company of people, especially Rovers. I claim this cove. Go back to your own camp at once and do not return." She scooped up Amaranth and placed him on her shoulder. The need to stay in a place she knew would provide her with food and shelter for the Winter vied with her need to keep people away from her.

She was so tired of running.

"The tide has turned, my exit around the headland is cut off." Televarn stepped closer yet. His eyelids drooped in sultry speculation. "You've fascinated me and kept me talking beyond the time of safe return."

"Then climb the hill." Myri strengthened her magical armor to repel him if he dared touch her.

"A steep cliff. 'Twill be a dirty and treacherous climb. I will stay with you until the tide turns again. You really want me to stay. Only your jealousy wants to send me away." He looked up, then flashed his dark eyes at her, delight and mischief glowing in their depths as if this were a familiar game with him.

She longed to reach out and touch his beckoning fingers. What would the crisp curls peeking out from beneath his head scarf feel like as she ran her fingers through them.

His eyes continued to hold her in place when she knew she should run. A curious numbness spread to her feet.

A woman could get lost in his eyes, with their thick fringe of black lashes. His voice slid over her senses like warm honey. Why had he wished him gone? He was so beautiful.

She'd been alone so long.

She'd known a man's touch. Four years now she'd danced the ritual around the Equinox Pylon at the beginning of Spring. Each year she'd mated with a different man, three clumsy and hasty youths. One older, gentler widower seeking a new mate. But never had she conceived, so her Equinox partners hadn't invited her to share their lives or their beds again.

She might never know a man again if she sent Televarn away.

Magretha scorned her for enjoying the Vernal Equinox festival and the men. The old witchwoman claimed a man's loyalty was firmly rooted in scratching his itch, not in remaining faithful to any one woman. Magretha had been betrayed by a man before her face and back became scarred by a fire.

Filling a few hours with this man's company while exploring his beautiful body would result in no harm. She wouldn't conceive. Witchwomen never did. Televarn wouldn't own her despite his desire.

There had been another man who desired to own her. Tall, slender, older, wearing a blue magician's robe. He'd wanted her talent, not her body.

The man in the red robe wanted to possess her soul

while he cast her body in the fire. She shuddered away from that memory.

This Rover wanted to possess her flywacket, and enjoy her body at the same time.

Who wanted her or valued her for herself?

She recognized the compulsion to love him for what it was, magic imposed by him rather than desire from within herself. Once she recognized it, she broke the spell by closing her eyes and turning her back on him.

"You should have considered your retreat before you ventured this far. Leave my beach any way you can. I care not if you fall or ruin your clothing. I care only to be alone." She started walking toward the cliff and her high cave as fast as the soft sand clutching her feet allowed.

With Amaranth still draped limply over her left shoulder, she reached for tiny finger and toeholds. Stretch, brace, cling. She mounted the sheer wall of sandstone smoothly. She forced her concentration away from the Rover's pretty eyes and into her climb. She forced her thoughts onto the fish that cooked slowly over the coals. She dared not lose herself in contemplation of weak sunlight glinting off layers of yellow and gray rock. Watching how her blood rose close to the skin beneath her fingernails, turning them lavender, wouldn't gain her the protection and solitude of the small cave she had claimed.

The sound of small stones tumbling in the far curve of the cliff made her pause. Balancing on tiny knobs of rock, she risked a look down and to the far right. Televarn mounted the cliff near where a volcanic headland jutted into the bay. The jagged rocks and slopes offered an easier climb than straight up the smooth sandstone where Myri sought the shelter of her cave.

The Rover glanced her way. A big grin split his face. His white teeth showed clearly against his tanned face and dark clothing. His hat lay against his back at a rakish angle, slung in place by a thong around his neck.

S'murghit, he was beautiful.

"I'll be back, pretty witchwoman. When you need a man, call my name into the wind." He raised a hand in salute.

The unstable rock beneath his other hand crumbled in

his grip. He lost his precarious balance, windmilling his arms as he fell into mixed sand and gravel.

The incoming tide rushed at his unmoving head.

"Now I have to go rescue him." Myri sighed. "I'll never be rid of him." She knew she couldn't leave him. Her talent wouldn't allow her to ignore anyone who needed healing.

CHAPTER 12

"Why do I have to sweep a clean floor?" Powwell, the newest apprentice, pouted at Nimbulan.

"Because we can't afford servants," Nimbulan replied. No need to tell the twelve-year-old boy that sweeping their new home was a test. He needed to know how long before the three recruits figured out how to manipulate the brooms with magic. They could all light fires with a concentrated effort. That ability had proved their inborn talent and gained them places as apprentices. None of them could yet move an object with his mind.

Their minds seemed equally closed to the concept of reading and ciphering. Only magicians were allowed, by law and by tradition, to use the arcane knowledge contained within letters and numbers. The newest boys refused to believe themselves worthy of this secret skill.

Nimbulan spent nearly all of his time coaxing the boys into learning. Not for the first time in the last few weeks, Nimbulan regretted his haste in seeking new apprentices and withdrawing to the monastery. He needed more help than Ackerly, Lyman, and his older apprentices offered. If he had other teachers to work with the boys, he could spend more time experimenting and cataloging the massive library.

"But why does the floor need to be swept at all. It's clean?" The boy stared up at Nimbulan. A need to know poured forth from his gray eyes. Determination rode firmly on his shoulders.

Sunlight streaming in through the narrow windows added a glint of auburn to his muddy brown hair. More often than not, any trace of red hair accompanied magical talent.

Buried deep inside the boy's stubborn brain there must

be the intelligence, or he'd not have figured out how to start fires upon command rather than at random. Nimbulan had to draw it forth by devising ways to stimulate Powwell's curiosity rather than answering every question.

Powwell assumed Ackerly's posture when demanding an answer from Nimbulan when Nimbulan was lost in thought or distracted. He almost chuckled at the one thing the boy had learned as an apprentice.

Nimbulan bit his lower lip, resisting the urge to say, "Because I said so." Too often that had happened during his own training, and he'd wasted valuable lessons because he defied the statement and his tutor. He'd never given up defying Druulin in the all the years he had served the irascible old magician. Right up until the day he had died on the field of battle along with Boojlin and Caasser and two full armies. All of them reduced to ashes by magic gone awry. Nimbulan and Ackerly had fled the impending battle the night before in order to seek employment elsewhere. They'd finally managed to break Druulin's binding spells upon Ackerly and had slipped away from the old man's tyranny.

"The floors must be swept every day, Powwell. We need to make certain they stay clean so that the dust from our shoes and clothes does not mar delicate instruments or interfere with our experiments," he explained patiently.

Experiments that couldn't begin until the three new apprentices had enough training to guard magicians in deep trance and reawaken them if necessary. Sometimes the Tambootie drugs used to heighten magic awareness tempted a magician to remain in the void. Only a trained magician who had achieved at least the second level of apprenticeship could bring a lost master back from the void, body and soul intact. Jaanus and Rollett could almost do it. They were the most advanced and needed to be involved in the experiments. Gilby, Bessel, and Herremann weren't far behind them in skill and control.

The new boys had a long way to go before Nimbulan could begin to work on his grand scheme of combining magic for peace.

Nimbulan sorely wished he could spend more time in the library, searching for magic clues with Lyman and his older boys instead of supervising the youngsters. Just last night he'd scanned a text on Rover culture with a tantalizing hint about rituals and joining magic. But he didn't have time to read further. Libraries and Rover legends had to wait.

"Water works better at keeping down dust," Powwell said with careful thought. "We should douse the stones and then sweep. Everyone should brush their clothing each morning too. That way we'd only have to sweep every few days instead of every afternoon after lessons. If dust is your only concern." He lifted his eyes to challenge his master.

Nimbulan suppressed a chuckle. The boy was quick, if only to find ways to avoid working. Hopefully, his talent would catch up with his brain shortly. In his experience, the best magicians were also the most intelligent.

"Then do it, Powwell. And inform your classmates." Three boys. They'd only been able to recruit three boys on the short notice of the move to this island. No women. No pretty witchwoman with moonlight woven into her hair.

Nimbulan wondered if Myrilandel's eyes always wore deep violet shadows beneath the skin or if that lovely shading was a result of fatigue and an improperly worked talent.

He gave himself a mental slap. He didn't have time to dwell on Myrilandel and why she ran away from the opportunity to train with a senior Battlemage.

"They'll beat me up if I tell them to do more menial chores, sir!" Powwell sulked. His mouth turned down prettily. Too prettily for a boy verging on manhood.

I'll have to keep this one out of Kammeryl's sight, he thought. Not that the lord had set foot on the island since Nimbulan had informed him of his Winter plans. Kammeryl d'Astrismos had raged for two days when he heard the news. He'd dismissed the entire enclave of magicians, including healers, from his army, vowing to replace them all.

Nimbulan wondered how soon Kammeryl would need to send emissaries requesting his return. Seasoned Battlemages were few and far between these days. Especially since Keegan's death.

Never again! he vowed. He clenched his fist in rage and grief.

Powwell backed away from him, eyes wide with distrust.

"I'll not thrash you, Powwell. Nor will Zane and Haakkon if you figure out what the lesson is in your chores. Remember that every task I assign, no matter how trivial or distasteful, will teach you something. Now run along and finish sweeping." He shooed the boy back to the dormitory wing, keeping his temper carefully under control. No need to frighten the boy with the master's private demons.

Briefly he peeked along the kitchen wing to check on Zane. The oldest of the new recruits, a few days shy of his fourteenth birthday, sat with his back against the outside wall, legs thrust out before him. A fierce scowl marred his freckled face. His broom stood propped against the wall.

Nimbulan guessed Zane was trying to make the broom work for him. He quickly noted that the apprentice had instinctively placed himself against the wall closest to the pool of ley lines in the central courtyard. How much power could he feel?

The guardian had effectively masked the massive well of magical energy so that even masters like Nimbulan could draw only normal amounts of power from the radiating ley lines.

He watched the boy for a few moments, praying that he was one of the few magicians who could learn to weave the Kardia into his spells.

The broom wobbled. Zane leaped to his feet with a whoop of triumph. He scowled at the broom again. He closed his eyes. His fists clenched at his sides. His shoulders rose nearly to his ears as he fought the inertia of the broom.

With a small smacking sound, the broom dropped to the floor, refusing to move.

Zane rubbed his temples, clear evidence of the headache beginning to form. He'd be craving sweets, too. Nimbulan's mouth watered at the thought of the candied coneroot Quinnault's cook had sent them this morning. When the boys took a break before the evening meal, he'd make sure he shared the treats with them.

One day soon, the boys would learn that magic took more effort than sweeping. But most adolescents, with their bodies growing and maturing so rapidly their minds and emotions couldn't keep up, exhibited a weird mixture of curiosity and laziness. The two made Zane ripe to discover many things about magic. Powwell was not far behind him in age and discovery.

Nimbulan turned back to the library wing to watch Haakkon perform his chores. The dark-haired lad leaned against the library doors, his ear pressed close to the wood panels. His broom lay forgotten on the floor beside him.

A faint murmur of voices drifted down the corridor. From the library. Nimbulan drew a little power from beneath his feet up into his ears to catch the words.

"You're supposed to list and sort the books by author and title, not stop and read every *s'murghing* one of them!" Ackerly's affronted tones rose almost loud enough to hear through normal senses.

Why was Ackerly in the library and not at the market searching for a permanent cook?

"This text distinctly contradicts accepted magic theory. It claims that Rover rituals give a single magician the combined powers of all those involved in the ceremony," Quinnault de Tanos replied. "I think it's important we set it aside for closer study."

Ah, so the lord had discovered the same text Nimbulan scanned last night.

Quinnault de Tanos had taken to spending part of each day helping about Nimbulan's school, however he could. He couldn't perform the smallest of spells, so he couldn't demonstrate magic lessons for the boys. He knew nothing of cooking or cleaning. But he knew ancient languages and magic theory flowed from him in precise detail, even if he couldn't work a spell.

Nimbulan wished he could spend his afternoon hours poring over the books and discussing ancient and modern practices with de Tanos. In a few moons perhaps, when everything was set up and other magicians taught and observed the apprentices, he'd have the time to indulge in long afternoons in the library.

Lyman and the five older boys were qualified to tackle the monstrous job of sorting and cataloging the books. Only Nimbulan knew how to watch the new boys for signs of major talent. The ability to weave the Kardia into their spells wouldn't settle in the boys until they passed through puberty and the trial by Tambootie smoke. Until then, their magic would be erratic.

"Hear anything interesting?" Nimbulan whispered to Haakkon.

The boy squeaked and jumped away from the door in surprise.

"You won't have to be so obvious in your eavesdropping, Haakkon, once you learn to do it with magic. However, magic takes more effort and the normal way works just as well . . . as long as the door remains closed." Nimbulan pressed his own ear to the door panels.

The voices came through muffled, but he could still discern Ackerly's words. "Time enough for study *after* we know what is here and we've sorted the junk from true work." The sound of a book being slapped against a table echoed through the door panel.

Nimbulan could almost see his assistant's tight-lipped control of his face. Ackerly would never lose his temper in the presence of an anointed lord, but Nimbulan heard his vexation. Time to intervene.

"Ackerly, I need you a moment." Nimbulan opened the door just enough to poke his head through.

Behind him, he felt Haakkon withdrawing. If the apprentice could melt into the shadows, he would. Nimbulan risked a quick glance over his shoulder. A concealing shadow crept up from the floor, wrapping itself around Haakkon.

Good. He'd found a way to use magic for a simple thing. Later, the magic would obey his will as easily as his instincts. Nimbulan turned his attention back to separating clashing personalities in the library.

"Ackerly, I am almost ready to begin experiments. But I am concerned about our Tambootie supplies."

"Can't gather the leaves this time of year. But now is the time to collect and dry the wood for burning."

"My personal supply of dried leaves is dangerously low and the time has come to begin lacing the boys' cider with small bits. Breathing Tambootie smoke is too intense until they've learned to handle smaller amounts first. We have to find a new supply soon." An edge of anxiety crept into Nimbulan's voice. He tried to hide it with a judicious cough.

"You had five pounds of dried leaves, Nimbulan. The foliage of nearly a whole tree, sun-dried to perfection. You can't have used it all up so soon."

"I . . . I don't know." But he did know. He'd used it all, in ever larger doses that worked with less effectiveness in inducing the proper sensitivity to magic. He wondered why. He didn't remember using so much Tambootie since settling on the islands. Maybe Lyman had been dipping into the supply. Ackerly never used it.

"We'll have to find more. Soon." Ackerly pulled at his lower lip in thought. "Lord Kammeryl d'Astrismos has a stand of Tambootie two leagues from his fortress in a sheltered glen. Perhaps we can salvage some of the leaves still clinging to the trees and the recently fallen ones."

"But Kammeryl has forbidden us to return to his lands. He calls us deserters. He does not forgive disloyalty easily."

"You have to have the Tambootie, Nimbulan. I'll make sure you get some."

* * *

Myri ran her sensitive fingertips over the Rover's skull. His thick dark hair tangled in her fingertips. The temptation to linger with a caress kept her from trailing her hand down his throat to his nape to check his spine for injury. In repose, he was even more beautiful than when animated.

She settled her eyes on the long fringe of eyelashes brushing against his cheek. Beneath a dark tan, his skin showed an unnatural pallor.

A cold wave rushed around her feet and Televarn's head. He groaned as the shock of the chill water brought him to partial consciousness.

Quickly, Myri scanned his neck with all of her healing talent. The soft sand had cushioned his fall. No broken bones. She could drag him safely away from the encroaching tide. With a hand around each of his ankles she tugged his body back toward dry sand.

Another wave sucked at his weight. She pulled harder, digging in her heels. The quagmire of drenched sand released him. Myri pulled him clear of the next wave.

"I . . . can . . . walk." Televarn's words came out slurred and slow.

Myri released his ankles and moved behind him to help him up. "You won't drown in the next two minutes. But you will get wet and cold." She placed one hand under each arm and heaved while he flailed his feet to gain some leverage.

His legs seemed unconnected to his body, sliding in all directions. He had no balance.

Myri heaved him upward, using the strong muscles of her thighs for leverage.

At last he stood with his arm draped around her shoulders. He was only slightly taller than she and the bend of his arm must have been awkward. His knees visibly trembled. He placed his free hand to his right temple. "Wh . . . what happened?" He swayed, not moving forward.

Another wave slapped against Myri's ankles.

"You fell. Now walk."

"Fell? When? Why?"

"Move your feet, Televarn. You can flap your mouth later, when I know you won't drown."

"Who's Televarn?'

"You must have hit your head harder than I thought." What would she do with him? He couldn't climb to her cave in his present condition. "I'll settle you in the curve of the cliff, away from the wind, and build a fire. Once you've rested and supped, your thoughts will straighten out."

She hoped. He'd never manage to climb to her cave for shelter. Until then, she'd keep him close to this headland and away from the other where her cave nestled.

"I think I know you." Televarn paused in his shuffle toward the cliff. Gently he traced the curve of her cheek with his fingertip. He hesitated as he caressed the outline of her lips. "I sense that we belong together. Are we mates?"

Myri gasped, more from the sensuous appeal of his touch than the audacity of his question. "No, we are not mates."

"Then we are meant to be. Soon." He lifted her chin with his caressing finger. Slowly, he bent his head to touch her mouth with his own.

Heat exploded in Myri's breast. Her lips grew soft and moist under his kiss. She parted them, eager for his questing tongue as she longed to open her thighs for a more intimate thrust.

Televarn enclosed her in his strong arms, pressing her tightly against his body. She rose on tiptoe and tangled her fingers in the springy curls of his dark hair. He'd lost his kerchief in the fall. She didn't remember when hers had blown away. His hands reached down to cup her bottom, caress her back, pull her closer yet to his wonderful body.

Her dreams of a home and family took firmer shape in her mind as she molded her body to his.

(You must come East to find a home and safety.)

Her knees melted with the fire of his kiss. *I'll stay with him for a while. Until he's healed.*

A cold wave shocked them both back to reality.

"You will be my mate as soon as I can arrange it, *cherbein,*" Televarn whispered, nuzzling her ear. "We are meant to be together forever."

The foreign endearment grated harshly in Myri's ear. "I never met you until today. We cannot wed until next Vernal Equinox. After we have been paired at the Festival Dance. 'Tis custom so old it has become law."

"I cannot wait that long, *cherbein.* Tonight you will be mine. Tonight and forever." He kissed her again, claiming her mouth harshly, as if to brand her his possession.

The fierceness of his desire awakened new sensations in Myri's womb. Her instincts clamored for her to join him in a ritual far older than law, right here on the sand. Right now, with the cold tide creeping up on them.

(Forget him. He lies. Come East. Now.)

He is injured. I must build him a shelter and light a fire. I cannot leave him.

CHAPTER 13

Moncriith shivered within the meager shelter of his lean-to. The first autumnal storm had given way to clear skies and chilling frosts. He dared not light a fire to ease the ache in his bones. The witchwoman would flee at the first hint of his presence.

She had escaped him at the village. He couldn't let her go free again. Her kind were poison to Coronnan. Only when she and all her demon-possessed magicians had been purged from Coronnan, would he be safe.

She must come here. Demons and their magicians fed upon the Tambootie. This sprawling grove of the toxic trees was the only stand left between the River Coronnan and the foothills of the Southern Mountains. Moncriith and his followers purged the land of the evil trees as they progressed across Coronnan each spring and summer. If they deprived demons of the food, they would be weaker, more vulnerable.

Myrilandel had to come here to feed her demonic powers.

He stared at his small ritual knife. Cleansed by fire and guarded by a silk sheath, the instrument offered the means to draw Myrilandel and her demon consorts to this exact spot. Briefly, he contemplated his choices. If he used the knife to slit the throat of a small animal, the death of the creature would attract Myrilandel more quickly. If he drew blood from himself, the spell of attraction would be stronger and more focused.

Before he could change his mind, he slashed the sharp blade across his cheek. He welcomed the familiar burning pain. The initial flush of power that always followed the pain tingled through his body. His eyes lost focus, then abruptly cleared to sharper, narrower vision. He squeezed the wound with his fingertips until he felt the warm flow of blood dripping from his jaw. Cautiously he caught the drops on a fresh Tambootie leaf he had ready. Then he leaned over a nest of specially prepared herbs and magical powders.

His blood mingled with the ingredients for the spell. Pungent fumes rose to fill his head with clear images of what he needed the spell to accomplish.

"Bring Myrilandel, obedient and docile, to stand before me for judgment."

When cold sweat dotted his brow and the pain swelled into his left eye and ear, he staunched the flow of blood with a square of white linen dipped in a special powder. Then he dropped the bloodied Tambootie leaf and the cloth on top of the nest.

With a stick cut from a Tambootie tree he drew circles around the mixture, each one smaller and closer to the center than the previous one. As he completed each circle, he drew a special rune of enticement. He knew the spell would only work after she started her journey toward the grove. But she had to come here to feed.

Energy streamed up the vibrating stick into his hand and arm. Each of his senses came into sharper focus. He saw the distinct outline of every tree, branch, and leaf within the grove. The scent of wet dirt and decaying leaves permeated his nose. He heard the small rustlings of nocturnal animals below the louder stirring of the wind in the high branches.

A spark of witchfire ignited his mixture into one brilliant flash. The circles came to life with writhing flames running around and around the perimeter, working ever closer to the core of his spell. The runes glowed into fire-green sigils.

As suddenly as the flames sprang from his fingers, they died. All was still. He looked up, expecting to see Myrilandel standing inside the outermost circle.

"*S'murghit!* Where is she?" he cursed. His eyesight still hummed with super-sharp vision. No one but himself waited inside this grove.

He'd wait another hour, then light a fire and curl up in

his blankets for the night. Perhaps tomorrow she would come. Tomorrow, when the moon was dark, his spell would be stronger. She wouldn't be able to resist him tomorrow night.

Mist and shadows drifted through the wild trees. He shivered again. Ghosts ran icy fingers up his spine. He dismissed them. The lost spirits of the dead couldn't hurt him.

He concentrated on his vision of Coronnan free of the witchwoman and magicians who provided host bodies for demons. The fire of his resolve replaced the blaze he longed to light at his rapidly chilling feet. As the power drained out of him, the cold night air attacked him anew.

None of his followers had ventured away from the barns and village pubs where they sought shelter for the winter to join in his ritual. Glumly, he realized their zeal for a demon-free Coronnan, united under one priest-king wasn't as strong as his own.

The thin slice of the moon rose higher in the night sky. He waited until chills numbed the burning pain of the cut on his cheek and set his teeth chattering. When he could stand the discomfort no longer, he stood to prepare his bed and a small fire.

The faint slurping sound of people walking among the fallen leaves sent his attention off to his left. He stilled every muscle in his body.

The spell had worked after all!

Patiently, he calmed his wandering mind and erratic heartbeat as he reached for his larger knife. He must kill the witchwoman quickly, before she could summon her demons to shred his soul and take over his body. No one else was near enough to distract the demons. He'd have gladly sacrificed one of his people for the opportunity to end Myrilandel's tyranny once and for all.

"S'murghit," a man cursed.

A man? Which man had Myrilandel seduced into following her blindly to feed from the poisonous trees? He had no doubt that she corrupted innocent men. Magretha had betrayed lover after lover until she eventually died for her crimes against men.

Something heavy plopped onto the ground, followed by a squirt of moisture hitting a tree trunk.

Thick, oily Tambootie leaves rotted into a sludgy mess that inhibited undergrowth and made for treacherous footing. Only Tambootie seeds could grow beneath a Tambootie tree, unlike honest trees whose leaves decayed into fertile dirt.

The footsteps came closer and amid muffled profanities. Several people wearing heavy boots, not a solitary witchwoman who ran barefoot until deep Winter. He enhanced his TrueSight, looking for traces of Myrilandel. He sensed only males in the grove. Two men. Lord Kammeryl's men?

No. They would carry torches or shielded lanterns. These intruders must be magicians who needed no light to steal the Tambootie. Magicians Lord Kammeryl did not control, or they wouldn't need to steal.

Moncriith shifted position, ready to attack. The death of one of Myrilandel's consorts would bring her in a hurry.

A smile crept into one corner of his mouth. Perhaps he should hurry to the nearest village and send messengers to Lord Kammeryl. The warlord would want to know who invaded his land in the dead of night. Kammeryl d'Astrismos guarded closely all that was his. The captured magicians would die, but only after confessing all under torture. Moncriith would derive much power from the men's pain and blood.

Lord Kammeryl might even be grateful for the information and grant Moncriith the right to winter in the fortress or one of the villages.

"There are a few late leaves here, sir. And some Timboor. The berries have almost as much of the essential oils as the leaves." A quiet, authoritative voice broke the silence of the night.

"Only the leaves carry enough untainted power for my experiments. We must fill the baskets with leaves and come back for the Timboor." That voice took on an edge of impatience. Or was it desperation?

Glee lightened Moncriith's heart. He recognized the two men now. Nimbulan and Ackerly. Nimbulan, who had had him exiled from the army camp in order to protect Myrilandel. Ackerly, who had defied orders and given him provisions.

Where was Myrilandel now? Why was Nimbulan stealing from his own lord?

He'd get answers later. This opportunity to rid Coronnan of one more of Myrilandel's consorts was too good to waste. Nimbulan's death would decrease her power and make her vulnerable when she finally came to this grove of the Tambootie to feed.

Moncriith rose to his full height. His knife fit his hand perfectly. He reversed his grip to strike with the heavy hilt.

Blood would attract a horde of demons. He could draw power from Nimbulan's pain and death, but he wasn't certain it would be enough to overcome more than one demon at a time until Myrilandel was dead.

He wouldn't have to kill Nimbulan here and now, merely rob him of his senses with a single mighty blow to his head, then deliver him to Lord Kammeryl.

"Run, Ackerly. It's that crazed Bloodmage again. He has a knife!" Nimbulan screamed.

Moncriith followed the sounds of running feet. Nimbulan's fear fed Moncriith's magic and trued his aim.

* * *

Ackerly dodged right, off the narrow path. He crouched beside a massive trunk, hoping his dark cloak would shield him from view.

"You can't escape me, Nimbulan!" Moncriith dashed past him, knife raised high, hilt forward.

Surprise destroyed Ackerly's caution. With the knife reversed, Moncriith must intend to merely stun his victim. Would he then consign Nimbulan's partially conscious body to the flames? The hideous, painful death made Ackerly shudder.

"I know the demon that leads you. I know all of her tricks," Moncriith bellowed. His rage burned sparks at the end of his fingers where they were clenched around the knife, and on the heels of his feet when they struck the ground.

Ackerly examined the details of his glimpse of Moncriith, committing them to memory. The Bloodmage let his temper cloud his judgment. He was also too fond of announcing his intentions and motives to the entire world before acting. Over the years Ackerly had stored a great deal of information within his capacious memory. The right information was as good as gold. Who would pay to know Moncriith's weakness?

He never had enough gold.

The sound of the knife shattering against a tree trunk reverberated through the grove of Tambootie. Ackerly looked toward the source of the sound, bringing as much magic as he could to his vision.

Moncriith stood trembling a dozen paces away. His knife had indeed shattered and lay in pieces around his feet. He crossed and massaged his arms with kneading fingers, probably from the shock of his blow. He shook his head as if clearing it of the rage that gripped him. Reason returned to his eyes and posture. Quickly he picked up a fallen branch and tested the weight in his hand.

Where was Nimbulan? Ackerly hunted the night with anxious eyes. Another crouched figure shifted in the gloom three trees to the left and slightly behind Moncriith.

Ackerly adjusted his magic vision to survey his oldest friend. No visible signs of injury, merely the trembling of fear and Tambootie deprivation. Nimbulan needed a fresh dose of the drug soon. His magic grew more dependent on the artificial enhancement every day. Ackerly made sure he had ever increasing daily doses to feed that addiction. Even when Nimbulan forgot to ask for it.

Thank the Stargods, he, Ackerly, had never succumbed to the temptations of the Tambootie. After his trial by smoke at the age of thirteen, he'd known he couldn't weave the Kardia into his spells and Tambootie did nothing to increase his powers.

Nimbulan had grown to depend upon the drug for more than just magic. In the desperation of battles that taxed his endurance beyond safe limits, the Tambootie was the only thing that kept his magic alive, and therefore ensured his own safety during and after the battle.

The drug also kept Nimbulan oblivious to mundane matters like the cost of provisions. If he didn't count his coins carefully, Ackerly wasn't about to tell the Battlemage how many coins he skimmed from the budget.

Ackerly could tell by the way Nimbulan cowered beside the tree rather than facing his enemy with spells and guile that a lack of the Tambootie in his system left him vulnerable, defenseless.

"Sir, are you all right? Where are you, sir? I can't find you." Ackerly shuffled his feet and threw his voice ten paces ahead of Moncriith. A trick that looked like magic but wasn't.

Moncriith followed the diversion away from Nimbulan's crouched form. Ackerly crept silently over to Nimbulan's side.

Nimbulan stood and stepped toward Moncriith. He raised his left palm in preparation for a spell. Ackerly grasped the Senior Magician's shoulders. Nimbulan stared at him with wide, questioning eyes. Ackerly pressed a finger to his lips, signaling silence. Keeping one hand on Nimbulan's shoulder, he guided the taller man away from Moncriith and his heavy club.

Nimbulan stumbled on some unseen obstacle. Ackerly smiled to himself as he slipped his arm around Nimbulan's waist in support. Better to make the Senior Magician think himself weaker than he was. Together they slipped back into the forest darkness, toward their waiting steeds.

The sound of running feet brought them up short.

"Come back here, you cowardly magician! I must cleanse you of demon possession!" Moncriith yelled. "Face the wrath of the Stargods and know the truth. Demons lead you into battle. Demons guide your every step. Demons rule Coronnan." His words echoed against the trunks of the Tambootie trees.

Firelight glimmered in the near distance as men ran toward Moncriith.

"What's this? Who are you?" Men wearing half armor in the dark green and maroon of Lord Kammeryl d'Astrismos' colors moved into view. They held their torches high, seeking the source of the disturbance.

"Come back here, Nimbulan. We haven't finished this!" Moncriith's cry broke off. "Let go of me, you imbecile.

He's getting away. He's stealing Tambootie from your lord."

"There's no one there, you crazy preacher. You're chasing shadows. Come with us to report to Lord Kammeryl."

"We haven't time. Demons are shielding Nimbulan. They're helping him get away."

"You're crazier than I thought. Now will you come quiet or do we tie you up and drag you to Lord Kammeryl's dungeons?"

The sound of a struggle, grunts and moans, slaps, and a heavy body hitting the ground, urged Ackerly to move faster toward the steeds.

He counted an officer and ten men. Enough men and weapons to contain Moncriith. Unless Moncriith had become so crazed he ignored his own safety.

"We'll be safe now, Nimbulan," Ackerly said when they had silently led their steeds nearly a league away before mounting.

No reply. Nimbulan stood beside his mount, swaying—with indecision, fatigue, or reaction?

"I'll find you Tambootie, sir. We can buy it at the market in Sambol. Then you can finish your experiments." He offered his friend cupped hands to help him mount.

"Buy it? I used most of my gold to buy furniture and supplies for the school." Nimbulan stared at Ackerly's offered hands as if uncertain what to do with the gift.

"I'll find a way to get some. Just leave everything to me."

* * *

"I thought you condemned conventional magic, Moncriith. And yet you trespassed into my Tambootie grove—the trees that feed magicians," Lord Kammeryl d'Astrismos said in weary tones that barely reached the seven people standing around his chair of office. "My men found your camp. You have been there for some time. Since you condemn the Tambootie as demon food, I thought you would try to fell the trees, not live amongst them."

The guards who had arrested Moncriith had roused the lord from his bed to deal with the crime of trespass and resisting arrest.

Moncriith stood before the lord, unbowed by the heavy, and totally unnecessary, chains on his wrists, ankles, and neck. He had no intention of leaving Castle Krej, the ancestral fortress of Kammeryl d'Astrismos, until Spring.

The lord glared at him from beneath heavy eyelids. Clad only in an ornate dressing gown of red-gold brocade that matched his hair to perfection—too perfectly—Kammeryl lounged against his chair of office, one ankle crossed over the opposite knee. His bare leg was revealed to his upper thigh. He wore no undergarments.

A pretty boy of about twelve stood to Kammeryl's right, his arm resting casually on the arm of the chair. His blond curls dangled delicately around his shoulders. He appeared to wear only an oversized shirt that hung below his knees and well past his wrists, as if he'd grabbed Kammeryl's garment instead of his own. The lord caressed the smooth skin of the boy's hand and arm as he waited for an explanation.

Moncriith didn't feel like explaining himself. Let the guards who had arrested him speak if they must. He needed all his energy to contain his shivers and the fiery ache on his left cheek that now spread from the top of his head to his collarbone. The first sharp intensity was gone. He couldn't use this aching aftermath to fuel a spell of compulsion.

"There were others in the grove, my lord," the eldest of the guards, a man of no more than seventeen summers, said. "I believe they were demons in search of the Tambootie. They disappeared in a puff of smoke, as if they'd never been there." The guard crossed and flapped his wrists. His smooth cheeks flared with heightened color.

Moncriith hid a smile. The guard didn't know the truth. No one, demon or magician, could transport a living being safely. Only inanimate objects survived the trauma of such a spell. Let the guard's fears and superstitious awe work for Moncriith. He could feed their imaginations with horror stories of what demons really did to a man's soul. Given a Winter in their company, he'd have them organizing his followers for him next Spring.

Moncriith stared at Kammeryl until the lord's gaze locked with his own. "I find it strange that your own Battlemage must steal Tambootie from you, sire." He added the royal title as a bonus to the lord's ambitions. "If you are not giving the weed to Nimbulan and his assistant, perhaps you, too, recognize the evil inherent in the tree that feeds only demons and their ilk."

Lord Kammeryl threw back his head and laughed long and loud. "So Nimbulan is reduced to theft of the Tambootie to feed his powers. I seem to have gotten rid of him at the right time. He is getting old. His abilities as a mage are declining. If the Tambootie kills him, I won't have to have his replacement assassinate him."

"If I replace him as your chief mage, I can purge your army and your household of the same demons who infest Nimbulan. You cannot rule a united Coronnan until all the demons are removed." Moncriith pitched his voice to soothe and calm. Given enough time, he'd have the lord believing a witchhunt for Myrilandel and her demon consorts was his own idea and had not come from Moncriith.

"You may stay the winter and throw the few spells I need for communication and preventing plagues. Time enough to find a better magician in the Spring. I intend to rule a united Coronnan with or without demons." Kammeryl yawned and rose from his chair. He placed an affectionate hand on his companion's feminine locks, then let it fall to the boy's shoulder and hip, caressing at each stage of exploration. Kammeryl wandered out the back door of the audience room, preoccupied with the boy.

"A meal and a bed would be welcome, brothers." Moncriith slouched as the guards unlocked his chains. He allowed his fatigue and hunger to show in his face as he looked at the threadbare patches on his red robe—the same cut and color as a priest's.

His followers didn't need to know that he had been exiled from the temple because he would only fuel his magic with blood. The respect people gave him upon first glance of his vestments opened their ears to his persuasions. His followers turned away from the temple as soon as they learned how the priests and magicians harbored demons like Myrilandel.

"There's always a pot of soup and bread in the kitchen."

The young soldier gestured toward the low doorway that led to the stone kitchen addition attached to the keep.

These guards were no different from the peasants Moncriith usually dealt with. Tomorrow he'd ingratiate himself into the good graces of the steward who supervised the servants. Tonight he would meditate on how Nimbulan might be killed without casting blame on anyone Moncriith found valuable.

CHAPTER 14

Timboor sang through Nimbulan's blood. The fruit of the Tambootie tree gave a crystalline sparkle to the auras of each piece of wooden furniture in his room. The simple lines of cot, chest, and table glowed with new elegance.

The nerve endings in his fingers and toes burned with new sensitivity. He drew power from the energy of wood, fabric, and stone. Different power from what the Tambootie leaves allowed him to tap, but power all the same.

He reached out to caress the aura above his worktable. The yellow-white energy fed him in ways food neglected.

He needed nothing more. Thank the Stargods Ackerly had thought to collect some timboor in his pockets the other night. Perhaps this kind of magic energy that allowed him to see everything so clearly was the key to combining magic. If he could see the individual components of an aura or, better yet, mesh his thoughts precisely with another man's, they could join and magnify their powers.

Carefully, Nimbulan folded the power around him in a spell of listening. The thoughts of Haakkon, Powwell, and Zane whipped through his mind with the lightning speed of their youth. Thoughts of lessons and chores, of the mysteries of women, and mixed resentment and awe of their masters. They asked themselves questions about magic and about life.

Too unformed and unskilled. The boys couldn't help him now.

Nimbulan sent his spell deeper into the old monastery, seeking Maalin and Jaanus, the two apprentices in the library. Their thoughts lingered on the smell of baking bread and the stacks of books yet to be cataloged.

For once, Quinnault de Tanos had not joined them.

Nimbulan found himself missing the lord's enthusiasm and his company. He reached out with his spell, seeking the brightly colored thoughts of the man whose patronage made the school possible.

He'd never managed to penetrate de Tanos' thoughts in his presence. If he could break through the lord's natural armor with the help of timboor, then he could read any man. That reading—rather a blending of thoughts and auras—now seemed essential to joining magic. Quinnault's thoughts remained elusive.

He needed familiarity. Ackerly. His oldest friend. They'd studied and worked together since Nimbulan was ten and Ackerly was twelve. Ackerly's mind and actions were almost as familiar to Nimbulan as his own.

Out of the stone buildings, across the wide courtyard to the beaten path and the causeway between two islands. The tide was full and the chain of boulders and land covered with water. The physical obstacles did not stop Nimbulan's questing magic. He flew across to the big island with its farmhouse and fields and the squat stone keep where de Tanos made his home now.

From the big island he wandered up the River Coronnan, seeing every twist and cove with his mind as if his body truly floated above the surging river. Past the battlefield where he'd had to kill Keegan to save two armies. That wound still pained him, more so than his guilt for deserting Druulin, Boojlin, and Caasser the night before they died in battle on the same field eighteen years ago. If he and Ackerly had stayed, would they have found a way to control the awful spell that destroyed everything in its path? Or would they, too, have died in screaming, burning agony?

No answers came to him from generations of ghosts that haunted the battlefield. He traveled on, upriver.

Many leagues distant, Nimbulan paused his seeking magic at the river gate of Sambol. Perched at the head of navigable waters on the river, at the base of a mountain pass and juncture of several trade roads, Sambol played host to merchants from throughout the known world. Anything could be purchased in the market stalls of the city, be it legal, moral, or not.

This was where Ackerly had come to purchase a new supply of Tambootie for Nimbulan and his students.

From his distant listening post, Nimbulan scanned the myriad minds of the city for a familiar syntax, inflection, and accent. He heard jewelers from Jehab, lace traders from SeLenicca, captains of mercenaries from Rossemeyer, and spice brokers from Varnicia. At last he picked up the educated tones of a magician haggling with a pottery maker in a small booth next to a shadowy alley. Any number of substances could be secreted in one of those utilitarian pots. Including the precious Tambootie.

Ackerly finished his bargaining. He withdrew five gold coins from the pouch Nimbulan had given him, one at a time as if counting and regretting every coin. The last of Nimbulan's savings.

Nimbulan watched as his assistant brushed his hand across the side of his face as if swatting a fly between placing each coin into the merchant's hand. As the last coin exchanged hands, Ackerly slapped his pockets as if searching for something. An expression of alarm spread across his features.

Nimbulan chuckled inwardly. Ackerly was probably presenting some ploy to recover one or more of the coins. Money and bargaining had always been a mystery to Nimbulan. Ackerly, however, excelled, keeping the two of them and their apprentices fed and sheltered on the meager allowance Nimbulan paid. The coins Ackerly had earned when he and Nimbulan fixed the horse race so many years ago had lasted them both for several years. They'd used the money for extra food and warmer clothes in the markets Druulin passed through once the boys started traveling with him.

Confident of Ackerly's miserly instincts to cut the best bargain possible, Nimbulan returned to the river and a lazy mind trip back to the islands at the mouth of the River Coronnan.

Briefly he circled the buildings on the big island. If he could find Ackerly in so distant a place, surely he could sense Quinnault. The lord's mental armor might be unconscious, but it also had a pattern of light and dark that swirled in a confusing whirlpool.

Only people with the placid concerns of farm chores and

housekeeping met his soaring mind. Into the keep and up the single stairwell his otherself flew. At the top of the stairs, he hesitated. Would the lord be in the public reception room to the right or in his private chambers to the left?

Mentally shrugging his shoulders, Nimbulan listened to the left. Quinnault's quiet breathing betrayed his presence. Quickly, the magician slid into the mind of his patron. A thin barrier blocked his entry. He pushed gently. A little harder.

A worn parchment scrawled with numbers swam before his vision. Smudged and worn spots that had been scraped free of ink blurred the new ink. Column after column of entries tangled and straightened to make some sense. Nimbulan saw the ledger through Quinnault's eyes!

He felt the lord's quill pen in *their* hand. Heard the sound of the pen scratching across the parchment. Knew the rhythmic intake and expulsion of air through lungs younger and stronger than his own.

Black swirling numbness rose up before him, blocking the sight of the ledger. Physical sensation ceased.

Where was he? Who was he? Endless darkness stretched before him. No light. No sound. No body to feel with.

* * *

Ackerly swatted in annoyance at the soft buzzing beside his head. *S'murghin'* flies. The city was full of the filthy pests today. He'd never been bothered by them like this on his previous visits to Sambol.

The soft flutter near his right temple brushed past him again. He tried to ignore it. His business in Sambol was more important than the annoyance of an insect.

He fished the fifth gold coin out of his purse reluctantly and placed it in the outstretched palm of the pottery vendor before swatting at the persistent fly.

Silently he gloated at the number of coins left in the purse. Nimbulan had given him twenty pieces of gold with instructions to use it all if necessary to purchase the necessary Tambootie. Overuse of the drug had rotted the Battlemage's mind. Tambootie rarely cost over three coins and never more than eight. Even when the wars and trade embargo inflated prices, and the only sources were in the black market, he could always bargain to a reasonable level. Who else would want it but the decreasing number of great mages?

Nimbulan didn't think logically anymore because of the drug. What he didn't know about prices helped Ackerly. His employer would never miss the remaining fifteen coins.

Well, he might miss fifteen coins, but not another five or eight. Maybe ten.

If Nimbulan had wanted to save money, he should have given him copper and lead. Base metals were for spending. Gold was for saving. Gold was for hoarding. Gold was for polishing and counting.

Ackerly always collected stipend from Kammeryl d'Astrismos in gold and he never spent it. He spent Nimbulan's money, adding a few of those coins to his hoard as a commission for making good bargains. He never spent his own money.

A wave of resentment washed over him at returning any of the leftover coins. He argued with himself that some, at least, had to be returned to avoid suspicion and keep Nimbulan believing in his bargaining ability.

The fly buzzed again. Only this time, Ackerly recognized the pattern of the sound as a summons spell, not a disease-ridden insect. He touched his glass in his pocket. It remained quiet. Then he touched each of his other pockets to make sure he hadn't tucked a crystal or other arcane equipment there that could attract a stray spell. Nothing.

The wizened old pottery seller lifted a medium-sized, handleless jug from the back of his stall and placed it carefully into Ackerly's hands. The old man acted as if the jug weighed more than he did, so Ackerly was surprised at the lightness of his purchase.

Cautiously he lifted the lid. The crisp-sweet fragrance of dried Tambootie leaves caressed his senses. The old man hadn't cheated him. These were prime leaves kiln-dried while still fresh and full of the essential oils. This jug with its contents was worth much more than five coins to a magician who was addicted to the drug. He chuckled to himself as he felt the heavy purse safely resting in the pocket inside his tunic.

His senses tingled once more, as if a summons had gone astray and brushed against every magician, seeking a recipient. But the buzzing ceased. Had Nimbulan's magic decayed to the point he couldn't send a simple summons?

With one arm wrapped tightly around the expensive jug of Tambootie, Ackerly fished in his trews pocket for his glass. The smooth edges of a journeyman's oval mirror fit neatly into his palm. He hesitated to bring it out in public. Clear glass was so rare and hard to come by, only magicians owned it. The appearance of the piece in his hands would mark him—either as a target for abuse from war-weary citizens or as a magician to be kidnapped by mercenaries for sale to the highest bidder. Not that the buyer would gain much from Ackerly. He was only an assistant, destined never to throw battle spells, only to hold them together and assist a true master like Nimbulan.

He almost showed the glass openly in perverse defiance of his fate. Anyone who kidnapped him was in for a big disappointment.

Reality reasserted itself, and he sought the closest open flame to receive and channel the summons through his glass. The young woman selling chestnuts roasted her wares over a small brazier. He smiled up at her. Her mouth curved up in invitation as she offered him a peeled nut from her gloved hand. Maybe when he finished the summons, he could persuade the young woman to roast his nuts in bed.

He liked provincial women better than the jaded camp followers in an army camp. Provincial women brought an innocent delight to bed. Ackerly grew warm in anticipation of unlacing the girl's bodice. She laced it from top to bottom with the ties at her waist, as did any properly modest woman. He licked his lips in anticipation of coaxing her out of the bodice. Only whores placed the ties at top for easy access.

He had to answer the summons first. Crouching down as if warming his hands at her brazier, he held the glass before him. The glass magnified one tiny flame licking the hot coals.

He emptied his mind to receive the message from the sender, expecting Nimbulan's face to flash into the clear surface. The precious piece of glass remained empty. No vibration thrummed through his fingertips.

Had the summoning magician given up? Nimbulan knew he was engaged in business and might not be able to answer immediately. Who else would call him?

He looked around furtively. What if Kammeryl d'Astrismos had hired a new Battlemage who sought to neutralize Nimbulan? More likely the new mage would try to lure his predecessor's assistants and apprentices away, with the hope of learning some of Nimbulan's tricks and spells.

Abandoning his plans to seduce the chestnut seller, Ackerly scuttled back through the winding streets of Sambol to his inn. Someone watched him with magic. He had to hide his gold before the watcher spied on him again.

* * *

Myri paused a moment in her dash through the rain to the lean-to she and Televarn had built against the cliff. Thoughts of the meal she would make vanished. She forgot the three fish tucked into her basket.

Instead, she watched a dark squall line dance across the roaring surf. Iron gray clouds played shadow games with the green-gray of the water. Highlights of creamy surf swirled in an intricate mosaic over the top. Waves rose, crested, and crashed in rounded undefinable shapes and sent a bubble of poetic magic through her soul. She wanted to *Sing* the images into an indelible memory.

(Come up to the dry cave before you catch a chill,) Amaranth said from the lip of the high opening in the cliff. *(Autumn is full upon us. The rain is cold.)*

She danced in a circle for the sheer joy of being alive, of bonding with a precious flywacket, of knowing Televarn's love.

Maybe she should climb up to the cave and spend some time with Amaranth before returning to Televarn in the lean-to. Amaranth couldn't fly yet. His wing was still bruised bone deep. One of the fish in her basket was for him.

I must return to Televarn. The thought inserted itself

into her mind, blocking the idea of climbing up to the cave where Amaranth waited for her.

(He lies to you. He is not worthy of you,) Amaranth reminded her.

"Come to me, Amaranth. We'll dance in the rain together. I'll take you to Televarn." She held out her arm to the flywacket, not certain why it suddenly seemed important that Amaranth be in Televarn's arms.

(I do not trust him.) The flywacket turned his back on her, retreating deeper into the cave.

Myri held out one of the fish as an enticement, suddenly anxious for her familiar to come to her. *Come to Televarn.*

Amaranth ignored her and the fish.

A blast of cold air against her face told Myri of the rapidly advancing squall. She resumed her run for the shelter of the lean-to before the rain drenched her.

Amaranth's continued rejection of her lover darkened her mood. Televarn promised her a home and family. The voices that had sent her East promised only a home. Couldn't Amaranth see how important the beautiful man was to her? To them both.

I have to love Televarn. She couldn't question the need deep inside her to love him without hesitation.

Her stomach growled, and she laughed at the ridiculous noise.

"Come in out of the rain, *cherbein.*" Televarn tugged at her arm from beneath the driftwood angled against the cliff where it curved into the headland. Amaranth's cave was well above them and closer to the opposite headland, commanding a full view of the curved beach.

Their bed of moss and grass sprawled across the center of the shelter, inviting her to stretch out there with Televarn at her side. A small fire burned brightly against the cliff at the back of the lean-to.

She laughed again at the pleasure his touch gave her. As his arms folded around her, she traced the shiny embroidery on his vest, delighting in the symmetrical design. She continued laughing in delight at the beautiful contrast of the silver and gold against stark black.

"I don't understand you, Myri. You laugh at everything. I thought witchwomen were supposed to be solemn, predicting doom and gloom." He dropped her hand and retreated to the warmth of the fire.

Some of Myri's joy deflated with the separation he put between them. If she had climbed up to the cave, Amaranth would have warmed her and showed his contentment with his purr.

Don't think about leaving Televarn, ever.

"Witchwomen are women first. We laugh. We cry. And we love like any other woman." She placed her basket of fish beside the entrance and knelt on the bed next to him. "Mostly we love life and the men who give it meaning." She kissed the side of his neck.

He enfolded her in his arms. The fierceness of his grip startled her. Usually he was more gentle and teasing in his passion.

"What would I do without you, Myrilandel? My life began the moment I opened my eyes and saw you bending over me, your black cat cradled against your shoulder." He continued to hold her close. "All my life before that, my family, my travels, my other lovers, are all meaningless without you."

Myri's muscles twitched with the unaccustomed stillness of remaining in one position so long. Gently she wedged her hands between them.

"I need to cook the fish. Did you find any of the wavebulbs to go with them?" She squirmed for release.

Televarn dropped his arms from her body slowly as if he were reluctant to let go.

"I'm getting tired of fish and wavebulbs. We've eaten nothing else for weeks." He sighed heavily as he reached for his own rush basket. "My mouth waters for bread and meat and yampion roots."

Myri examined the five wavebulbs inside the basket, looking for soft spots where rot would make them inedible. The green globes were all fresh and ripe. They had dense skins that would roast to a delicious tenderness. The thick liquid inside, bitingly bitter when raw, became sweeter with cooking. Dried or fresh, the long flat leaves of the seabed plant prevented many ills and gave an interesting, salty flavor to their food. She longed for heartier fare also but dissmissed the notion. Her life was here, on this beach with Televarn.

"We've nothing else to eat, but what the sea gives us, love. The tides have been so high, we can't go around the headland in search of paths inland," she reminded him. Not that she wanted to meet his tribe of Rovers camped in the next cove. She could climb the steep cliff near the cave where Amaranth sulked, but she didn't want to without Televarn. He hadn't the sense of balance or extra length in his toes and fingers to climb with her.

"You'll feel better after we've eaten." She busied herself spitting the gutted fish and wrapping the bulbs in wet leaves before placing them in the coals.

"As much as I love you, Myrilandel, I'm lonely. Even your cat won't come out of his cave to break the monotony. I have always been around other people. I need to know my people are safe." He slammed his fist into a support beam. A shower of aromatic bark drifted into the fire.

Myri watched the small pieces flare and coil into smoking tendrils. Her mind drifted with the smoke.

"Are you listening to me, Myrilandel? Why doesn't your cat like me? He won't let me touch him. It's almost as if he's afraid of me."

"Amaranth became tangled in a fishnet and hurt himself just before we met. He doesn't want anyone touching his back and side until he's fully healed." Her three attempts at healing had slid right over Amaranth without penetrating to the core of his pain. He needed a different kind of healing that she couldn't offer. Otherwise the bruise might take all Winter to fade.

The dangerous fishnet must have come from one of the Rovers. But why had it tangled so insistently?

Televarn had never mentioned that first meeting. He claimed his memory of it had been knocked out of his brain when he fell from the cliff. He remembered only climbing over the headland into her cove and nothing more until he awoke after the fall. If so, he didn't know that Amaranth flew.

"The cat's healing seems to be taking a very long time." He looked at the knife slashes in the beam he had just slapped. One for each day they'd been together. Myri's ten fingers filled a slot three times over plus an additional three. "You may be a witchwoman, but I'd like another healer to look at him. We need to find a better shelter before Winter settles in."

"Amaranth doesn't need another healer. All he needs is time and me." Something close to panic clutched at her throat.

Trust Televarn. Myri looked sharply to her lover, wondering if he inserted that idea in her head or if her own instincts did.

"You can't see that Amaranth needs someone else because you love him so much you won't let yourself believe he might be damaged. The moon will be dark tonight. Tomorrow's morning tide should be low enough to get around the headland. We might not have another chance to find another healer for him. To find my family in the next cove. Don't you see, Myrilandel, we have to go now. We have to take Amaranth to my family."

You have to love me, now and forever. Trust me without question, Myrilandel.

CHAPTER 15

"Master!"

Nimbulan heard the voice in the distance. The directionless, sense-robbing blackness jerked and righted. A feeling of up and down blasted him into the realization that he lay prone upon a hard surface.

"Master, what happened?" The voice—voices?—echoed around him, still defying specific direction.

Pain assaulted him next. More an ache than pain. Above him. That must be his back and neck. Longer. His knees and feet where he made contact with . . . with stone.

"Master, wake up."

Rough movement irritated the discomfort in his back. The ache throbbed and spread outward to his arms and hands.

"Arrrrgh." Was that his voice?

"Thank the Stargods he's alive. Help me turn him over."

Several hands lifted and supported him. More than one person. As many as three. A sensation of floating robbed him of his precious sense of up and down.

"Uughhh." This time he knew the inarticulate sound came from his own throat. The throbbing in his head increased.

"Open your eyes, Master. Please."

So that was why he couldn't see. He willed his eyes open a tiny slit. The effort almost sent him reeling back into the void.

"Light the lantern. It's too dark in here to see if he's injured."

Light filtered around the edges of his perception.

The voice sounded familiar. He didn't dare open his

eyes again. He should know the speaker. Youthful, peasant tones. Ah. Haakkon.

A giggle followed the onslaught of light. Two more young people. Powwell and Zane. None of the new apprentices' voices had changed yet.

"Whisst your nonsense," Haakkon ordered his classmates.

What was so funny about the master passed out cold on the floor of his room? Why were they laughing at all of the aches and pains left over from his astral flight with the aid of Timboor?

Ah, the flight! He'd found a way to merge his thoughts and aura with another's. But at a terrible cost. No magician would willingly endure this aftermath for the sake of joining magic with another.

All the aches centered in his groin. He needed to empty his bladder. Desperately. A bigger itch plagued him. He needed a woman. Any woman. Camp follower, noblewoman, or peasant. He didn't care. Just so the pressure in his groin found an outlet.

No women resided on the island. The only women on the island were Quinnault's servants, most of them married. Even in this anxious state he wouldn't stoop to forcing another man's mate.

An image of Myrilandel's fair skin and pale hair flashed before him. He longed to reach out and caress the lavender shadows around her eyes, to feel her gentle, healing touch on the most intimate part of his body.

Myrilandel had run away. She'd never be his mistress or his apprentice.

Nimbulan tried opening his eyes again. Three concerned adolescent faces stared at him.

"Uuughhh," he groaned again.

"Quick get the chamber pot. He's going to heave." Haakkon lifted his master's head and shoulders so he wouldn't gag on his own vomit.

"Cold," Nimbulan ground out between clenched teeth.

"I know you're cold, sir. You'll feel better as soon as you get rid of whatever's making you sick."

"Cold water. Towels. Need cold." What he really needed was to get rid of the aching pressure in his groin. Lacking a woman, a cold plunge in the river might work.

Powwell scuttled out of the room and returned in moments with several thick towels. He left a trail of small puddles in his wake.

Blessed chill engulfed Nimbulan's face. The throbbing in his head subsided. He held a second soggy cloth against his chest and neck. His hands felt as if he'd plunged them into a snowbank. The cold crept down his body, reducing the swelling.

He sighed in partial relief and turned his gaze to his cold hands. More than just his penis had become engorged by the overdose of Timboor. His fingers were double their normal size. Red splotches ran up his arms, and he guessed they ran onto his chest and face.

"Thank you, boys," Nimbulan said as he pressed the cold towel over his eyes again. "Your quick thinking may have saved my life. I ask two easy chores of you, then leave me to rest and recover on my own." And get rid of the last of the uncomfortable swelling without their curious eyes watching his every move.

"Anything, sir," Zane said. The other two nodded their agreement.

"First, ask cook to prepare a sweet yampion pie for our supper. The sugar in the root restores much of what magic depletes. Remember that as you progress with your magic lessons. Candied coneroot for dessert will help too."

"And the second chore, Master?" Powwell asked, licking his lips with an eager tongue.

"The second lesson is much more important. The basket in the corner is filled with berries. Green-and-yellow-striped, oily berries of the Tambootie tree. Study them carefully so you will know them in any form. Then throw them into the river and never ever touch one again." The essence of Tambootie was too strong in berry form. Too alien in its affects on the body. Power lay within the oils. Power so strong it couldn't be managed by mortals. He had to find a different method for joining thoughts and powers. At least he now knew the first steps toward joining magic.

"But Tambootie is supposed to help magic," Powwell protested, rolling one of the berries between his fingertips.

"When I was a little boy, younger than you three, my

father's great aunt told me that only dragons can eat Timboor and survive."

"Then you must be part dragon, Nimbulan, if you ate the berries and lived to warn the boys about them." Old Lyman stood in the doorway, arms crossed, face frowning in disapproval. "Off with you three. Your master needs rest and privacy." He shooed the apprentices out of the room.

"Part dragon, indeed," Nimbulan snorted as he dragged himself to his knees by clinging to his chair. He must have fallen off of it at some point.

"Do you have a better explanation for surviving a lethal dose? I didn't think you stupid enough to try those berries at all. Perhaps I should have taken you into the void to discover your past existences." Lyman cocked his head as if listening to a voice in the far distance. Then he scratched his neck with fingers longer than normal with purple shadows on the tips.

"Get into the privy, even if you have to crawl. Then we'll discuss your experience." Lyman grasped Nimbulan's arm with the long, long fingers that looked more like talons than human digits.

* * *

Myri eyed the rapidly rising waves with skepticism. Amaranth struggled in her arms to be free of the encroaching wet. She held him closer to keep him from escaping. The moon had pulled the tide to its lowest point in many weeks. A storm hovered just over the horizon, sending large erratic waves.

If she and Televarn didn't dawdle in crossing the slippery, broken rocks of the lowest point of the headland they might make it to the next cove unscathed.

Might. Each time a wave rushed to the shore, a deep boom warned her of the dangers. She counted the waves, edging across the sharp rocks, one step for each wave. A ninth wave, bigger than its fellows sprayed water above their heads.

The ninth such wave would signal the turning of the tide. They hadn't much time.

Amaranth mewled plaintively, burrowing his head beneath her arm. His damp tail lashed at her side.

She risked this trip to the next cove and the Rovers only so she could consult a different healer about his bruised back. Myri had given the flywacket strict telepathic instructions to keep his wings hidden. Despite her misgivings about meeting the Rovers, she knew Amaranth needed help. He should have healed by now, with or without her aid.

(You draw your magic from the Kardia. I need healing magic that floats in the air,) Amaranth told her again. He'd been saying that for over a moon. Myri didn't understand what he meant.

If she'd spent more time with her familiar, rather than in Televarn's arms, maybe she'd know how to help him. She caressed the flywacket's fur, feeling guilty for neglecting him. But . . .

Why did Amaranth mistrust Televarn so? The Rover promised her everything she wanted most out of life—a home and a family, people to love and be loved by.

Memory of Televarn's extreme interest in Amaranth and his wings, before his fall haunted her for the first time in the moon she'd been with him.

How much of their meeting and his subsequent fall did he really remember?

She banished the thought. *I love Televarn.*

(You love his body and his tender lovemaking,) the voices in the back of her mind reminded her. They had been silent since she'd found the cave—letting her remain there for the Winter. Why did they plague her now with doubts?

"Silly cat. Hiding your head won't keep you dry." Televarn brushed his hand along Amaranth's back.

"Hssst!" Amaranth lashed at the Rover with unsheathed claws.

"Dragon's spawn!" Televarn raised his scratched hand to strike back.

Myri reared back in surprise and loathing, pressing her body against a jagged outcropping. The waves continued to pound the land just below them.

At the height of its arc, Televarn stopped his hand. He narrowed his eyes in speculation, then lowered his wrist to his mouth. He sucked on the bloody scratches a moment, never taking his eyes off Amaranth.

"He's in pain. Of course he's temperamental. Watch your step, Myrilandel. That strand of wavebulb will be slippery." A calculating smile lit his face, but not his eyes.

Myri's unthinking count of the waves registered eight. They needed to move or be overcome by the tide. Amaranth needed another healer. She needed to understand Televarn's true motives. She'd never trusted her own judgment before, always relying on the guiding voices.

I need to be strong enough to think for myself.

Did Televarn truly long to return to his own kind for Amaranth's sake? Or had he tricked her with his vulnerability and charm to steal her familiar?

Those couldn't be her own thoughts. They had be echoes of the voices.

Amaranth mewled again, reminding her of the encroaching waves.

Televarn blocked her retreat back to her cove. She'd never survive a swim to freedom among the rocks and vicious surf of this headland. She had to move forward.

A ninth wave crashed two finger-lengths from her already cold and wet feet. She turned her eyes away from the fascinating pulse of pale purple blood through the dominant veins of her instep. She'd slung her Winter boots around her neck, so her bare feet could find the best toeholds across the broken rocks. She tasted salt and felt the sting of the icy water on her face. The next ninth wave would cover them with enough force to drag them into the churning water. The next ninth after that could crush them against the headland.

She threaded her way through the first low boulders beside the sand and swirling waves. The wind slackened as she rounded the prominence of the headland. A drop in the elevation of the rocks and a stretch of wet sand came into view. The end of the trek was in sight.

Sharp spines of volcanic rock lacerated the soles of her feet as she hurried toward safety. She barely felt the pain due to the cold. Her gray-green cloak flapped in a rising wind. The wet hem of the long garment tangled with her ankles. Televarn pressed his hands against her back, urging her to hurry.

Hurry away from the tide. Hurry toward a camp of

Rovers. Rovers who never worked at honest labor; who stole and cheated to make their living.

Amaranth represented a rare prize. How many gold pieces would a magician like Nimbulan pay for a real flywacket?

(Nimbulan would cherish a flywacket as a wonder. The Rovers will only sell Amaranth.) The familiar voices echoed hollowly around her mind.

Tears started in Myri's eyes. She turned to face her lover, desperately needing to know the truth of his motives before she met his people. Why hadn't she listened to her doubts before venturing onto this dangerous headland?

She opened her empathic talent to him, making his emotions her own—something she never allowed herself to do except during a healing.

A flood of greed washed over her, colder than any storm-tossed wave the Great Bay could throw at her. She shivered the full length of her spine down to her toes.

Move, s'murghit. *I don't want to get killed before I have a chance to spend the gold.*

His thoughts came to her as clearly as if he'd spoken aloud.

Pressing her balance forward, her shoulders lifted and her free arm spread away from her body. Her cloak caught the wind like a wing.

Amaranth leaped from her embrace to the cliffside, scrambling up the rocks with agility beyond a normal feline's.

"You lied to me, Televarn," Myri said quietly.

"Not now, *cherbein.* The tide will catch us. Tell me all your doubts when we're safe and dry." He placed a hand on her shoulder in an effort to turn her around and move her closer to the end of their treacherous journey.

"You did not armor your thoughts against me, Televarn. I know your scheme. I know your lies. You compelled me to love you so that you could capture and then sell my familiar. The fishnet that snared him was yours!" She thrust his hand off her.

"Myrilandel, this is not the time. I know you are shy about meeting strangers. But we must get away from the tide. Now." He grasped her arm in a fierce grip. His fingers crushed her skin through the protection of her cloak and clothes.

"Let go of me." She pulled her arm away from him.

His grip tightened. Blood rushed to the bruises already forming on her arm, swelling them painfully.

A wave sloshed their feet. She counted it as the sixth.

Myri pried at his fingers with her free hand. "I said, 'Let go.' "

"When we safely reach the next cove. Now call the flywacket and move!" He pushed her toward his goal.

"I will not go with you." She raked her fingernails across the bloody scratches Amaranth had given him earlier.

He jerked his hand away in pain.

The eighth wave wet them to their knees.

Myri reached over her head for the nearest handhold.

"You've come back at last, Televarn. We wondered how much longer you'd allow your new companion to distract you," a man said from behind her. Strange hands clasped her shoulders.

Startled, Myri paused in her instinctive seeking of a high place to hide.

"Come now, we'll carry you to safety. We've a fire and dry blankets in the caves to warm you. Our healer will take care of those rock cuts on your feet." The speaker lifted her free of the rocks.

Myri's hood folded over her eyes, preventing her from seeing who carried her away from the waves.

Or aided Televarn's betrayal?

She batted the cloak away from her face to see who laid hands upon her. An older man with Televarn's intense dark gaze and thin straight nose smiled at her. She squirmed to be set free. His grasp on her tightened and his stride across the sand lengthened.

"Come, now. No need to be shy, pretty lady. We'll take care of you."

His voice washed over her in soothing cadences. Her body relaxed in his grip. Her mind urged her to fight the compulsion to be still.

"Never mind her," Televarn shouted behind them. "Get the flywacket!"

"The creature will come to her when it is ready. We have all Winter to wait."

"Let go of me!" Myri struggled to be free of the man who carried her. "I'll not stay with thieves and liars."

"I promised you a home and family, Myrilandel. You belong to us now, and we keep those we claim. Forever, *cherbein.* You and your flywacket belong to *my* clan of Rovers now."

CHAPTER 16

Nimbulan listened to the rising wind as it whipped around his new School for Magicians. That's what the locals called the old monastery now. The same locals were much more accepting of the school than the people he remembered living around Druulin's tower. But then Nimbulan and his students aided the locals in building and repairing homes. They also helped with minor healing. None of his boys would consider setting fire to fields and homes as part of a lesson or experiment.

His shivers were as much part of his memories as the chill air. Each gust found new cracks and crevices to invade the shelter. Old cold had deeply penetrated the stone walls over generations of abandonment and now dominated every corner of the ancient building. Fires in the large hearths did little to dissipate the frigid air.

"I think it's colder in here than in a campaign tent in midwinter," Nimbulan said to the assembled apprentices without expecting an answer. They were all huddled in the kitchen area, cradling mugs of hot cider between their palms and wrapped in whatever quilts and blankets they had scrounged from the farmers who hid out among the islands. More refugees moved to Lord Quinnault's lands every day, seeking relief from the famine and plague left behind by generations of war.

The islands had a reputation for being sheltered and relatively untouched by the wars. Lord Quinnault de Tanos had earned a reputation for dealing fairly with his people and not conscripting them to serve in any army.

A lot of the settlers had served in one lord's army or another. They were prepared to defend their new homes. Nimbulan wondered if the influx of settlers wasn't really part of Quinnault's plans to unite the lords in a mutual defense pact against the aggressions of the warlords.

Whatever Quinnault's plans, Nimbulan and his boys were part of the island community now. They were as much a family as any of the more traditional hearth groupings. Old Druulin had never sat with his apprentices around a warm fire with an extra mug of cider before bedtime. Nimbulan cherished these gatherings. The boys shared their little triumphs and frustrating defeats with him. They shared their hopes and dreams as well. He talked of peace and his own dreams of a community of magicians.

If he should die tomorrow, one or more of his apprentices—probably led by Rollett—would pick up that dream and carry it forward. He couldn't wish for more if they were sons of his body.

Lyman had chosen to remain in the library tonight, gaining warmth from his own love of the myriad books still uncataloged. The other war-weary magicians who had come here to teach had retired to their rooms early. They were more than tired of war, they were tired of life and slept away much of their remaining years. The sense of community Nimbulan built with his boys was as alien to these Master Magicians as it would have been to Druulin.

Nimbulan blew steam from the top of his mug, as interested in keeping chilblains from his fingers as drinking the spicy brew.

He'd laced the batch of cider with the last of the dried Tambootie leaves he'd scraped from the folds of a pouch. The boys needed to become used to the effects the tree of magic had on their bodies and minds before they began taking concentrated doses to increase their magic.

He had to find the right dosage and combinations to duplicate the meshing of thoughts he'd attained with the Timboor.

One taste of the brew had set Nimbulan's craving for Tambootie afire. Ackerly had better return soon.

"It's the damp that makes you feel colder." Rollett, the eldest of all nine apprentices and nearly ready for promotion to journeyman, stirred the fire in the small baking hearth with an iron poker. The big roasting hearth had been blocked to prevent further heat loss.

"My da was born not too far from here. He used to say that the river mists chilled his bones so deep it took an entire Summer to get warm." An old sadness clouded his eyes. "Da always said the damp would kill him. He was wrong. The wars killed him."

Nimbulan remembered Rollett's father, stoop-shouldered with the joint disease while still fairly young. He had reluctantly handed his youngest son to a magician for training seven years ago. Nimbulan had taken the boy with marginal talent more to give the impoverished farmer one less mouth to feed than because he needed another apprentice. But Rollett had proved his worth time and time again. Eager to please and more eager to learn, he'd mastered all his lessons and improved his talent tenfold. The young man had begun tapping ley lines only a few weeks before the guardian spirit sealed the well.

Nimbulan had expected him to become no more adept than Ackerly, who could hold a spell together and feed Nimbulan strength, but couldn't levitate anything heavier than a small parchment, nor conjure more than a whisper of flame.

Last Spring, Rollett had taken a brief respite from his studies to return home for a much anticipated reunion. He'd hoped to help with some of the heavy plowing and planting, maybe use some of his magic to repair the family hut. He could lift a new roof tree by himself with magic, something ten men would have found onerous.

But foraging scouts for one army or another had stripped the farm, burned the buildings and left the family's bodies to rot in the rain.

Nimbulan grieved with Rollett, then and now. In this case he had truly replaced the boy's birth father. In the moons since that terrible time, Nimbulan had spent many evenings comforting Rollett, sharing memories of his father. Reliving the events of Rollett's loss was the first time Nimbulan had allowed the endless wars to touch him personally. His long road to a quest for peace had really begun there. Keegan's death had been the final catalyst that had brought him to Lord Quinnault de Tanos and this ancient building with Ackerly, Lyman, a few tired Battlemages, and eight apprentices.

"Someone comes." Zane lifted his head, sniffing the air for changes.

"A man. Walking with heavy steps, as if very weary," Powwell added, cocking his ear toward the door. "Two men, one younger and stronger than the other."

"Ackerly." Haakkon closed his eyes and furrowed his brow in concentration. "He's thinking of food and ale and gold. The boatman walks behind with heavy luggage."

He'd expected Ackerly two days ago, before this latest Winter storm had made the river a churning cauldron of eddies and wicked currents.

"Together, you three would make one powerful magician," Nimbulan acknowledged the young apprentices' various talents. "Now which of you will be able to open the door for Ackerly at the moment he reaches for the latch?"

The three youngsters looked to each other as if consulting. A grin of mischief crossed Zane's face as he shook free of his blanket and walked to the kitchen door.

"I meant, open it with magic!"

"But you told us just yesterday not to waste our energy with frivolous uses of magic," Haakkon reminded his master.

"Since none of you has mastered levitation with any precision, this is a test and not a waste. Back to your chair, Zane. And no help from you other apprentices." Nimbulan glared at the five older boys who looked as if they wanted to open the door with an easy magical gesture.

Lyman wandered into the kitchen from the interior of the building without a word and moved to warm his hands over the fire, watching the boys with curiosity and amusement.

Zane settled into his blankets once more. The three new boys stared at the door with intense concentration. A blue aura burst forth from each apprentice. The wavering sapphire glows hovered separately. Haakkon's aura took on a hint of red and purple, the colors that would eventually become his magic signature. Zane's yellow and dark red were not as strong, but definitely present.

Nimbulan looked deeper into Powwell's aura for signs of another color. The initial blue swirled and faded. It lost shape, sending out tendrils. Like a river mist, the questing scraps of energy drifted with the air currents, probing this way and that without direction.

Suddenly Powwell's vague blue flared white and engulfed the other two auras. The colors whirled in a bright circle, blending into one riotous rainbow of energy. The book in the library about Rovers said they joined their auras in order to combine their magic!

The door flew open with a flash of eldritch light and wind that smothered the fire in the hearth.

Ackerly stood framed in the doorway, his hand lifted as if to raise the latch. The boatman dropped the small trunk he carried on his shoulder, staring wide-eyed, gape-mouthed at the locked door opening without the aid of a human hand.

* * *

Myri huddled in the shadows at the back of the Rovers' sea cave where Televarn's uncle had dumped her without comfort or ceremony. His eyes had glittered with greed as he turned his back on her. No one had offered her any of the communal meal, or a blanket, or a change of dry clothes. All those niceties had been reserved for Televarn, who also ignored her.

She'd tried once to run past them, only to find five brawny young men blocking the opening of the cave. Desperate to be free, she had flashed compulsion spells, sleep spells, invisibility spells at the men. Every attempt had bounced back at her tenfold. She'd crumpled into the soft sand on the floor of the cave, exhausted and humiliated. How could she have been so naive as to fall under Televarn's compulsion to love him?

She fell into dreamless sleep, only to awake, unrefreshed, hours later on the bundle of blankets that retained Televarn's distinctive scent. Would he expect her to continue as his lover after his betrayal?

Hungry and cold, she watched twenty members of Televarn's clan standing in a tight ring around the flickering warmth of a cheery fire, hands linked, bodies swaying, minds in tune with an old woman's chant.

Televarn stood next to the old woman who led the clan in invocation and response. Myri sensed that the strange words they half-sang were in thanksgiving for the man's return. And something more.

A well of power rose with the flames toward the high ceiling of the cave. Each word and sway intensified the spell they wove.

The chant grew in volume. The circle of people dropped hands and shifted into an intricate dance pattern, still going round and round the fire. In and out. Around. Turn back the way they had come.

Myri inched closer to the Rovers, drawn to the magic they worked in unison. She needed to see what they did and how, needed to become a part of it. Memories of other dances performed around Equinox Pylons overlaid the current ritual. Which was she seeing?

Shivering in the darkness beyond the light and warmth of the spell, her feet and hands twitched, eager to join the dance, become a piece of that mighty spell. She reached out to touch Televarn as he passed her. Energy repulsed her hand. Televarn ignored her, intent on some inner beauty she couldn't yet see. His eyes glazed over with the trance induced by the dance—the chant.

Threads of energy bound the entire clan to each other. The intricate web seemed to begin and end with Televarn. Because he had been absent and they welcomed him back? Myri shook her head, trying to clear it of the need to entwine her own life's energy with the Rovers. Her need to join them only intensified.

The web of energy combined with moonlight streaming into the cave and became a dome encasing the Rovers, shutting Myri out.

A flash of movement near the mouth of the cave became a part of the compelling rhythms and dancing energy.

Amaranth skulked near the cave mouth in search of her.

Fear for her familiar sizzled through Myri's mind and body. The spell pulled at her, as if a strong wind dragged her toward the heart of the Rover clan. She resisted the magic, recognizing it for an artificial attraction similar to Televarn's love spell. The compelling need to join the Rover ritual burned out of her system.

Sand, shells, and bits of waveweeds swirled around the edges of the magic. The spell pulled all toward its heart.

The Rovers danced *widdershins,* along the path of the moon. Myri resisted the urge to join the debris of life circling *deosil,* the path of the sun.

Amaranth stalked closer to the dancing Rovers, nearly dragging his belly on the ground. He mewled and prodded the invisible wall around the Rovers with nose and paw.

Colored lights sparkled across the spell's armor along a serpentine line. Amaranth's paw marked the beginning and end of the rainbow flashes. Shades of purple and lavender dominated the sparks. The barrier tore open in a ragged hole just big enough to admit the flywacket into the inner circle.

Myri pushed at the armor with her own hand and magic. Burning energy pushed her hand away with a painful jolt. Whirling sand crashed against the shimmering wall and burned in a beautiful array of red, green, and blue sparks.

Only Amaranth was admitted. The spell called him specifically. Amaranth, the rare flywacket who would bring the Rover clan gold, prestige, and honor.

She had to separate her familiar from the ritual and escape with him without disturbing the Rovers. Mind and eyes clear, she stepped away from the magic's influence.

Amaranth took a step closer to the doorway, into the circle.

"No!" Myri screamed. The sound bounced against the barrier of magical armor and echoed about the cave.

Amaranth took another step forward, oblivious to her cry.

Myri opened her mouth again. All of her inborn magic demanded release in defense of Amaranth, her familiar, her only friend, her family. Magretha had warned her against Rovers and their compelling rituals.

She unleashed a wordless *Song* in notes so highly pitched human ears could barely hear them. She *Sang* her love for the pesky black cat. She *Sang* of the freedom of the open skies he so enjoyed. She *Sang* of their life together, the two of them alone and separate from the rest of the world. Then she added notes of powerful love reminding him of how they had never been apart, and never should be.

Amaranth stopped in mid-stride, one front paw lifted to take the next step. The hole in the Rover barrier began to close. The dance inside the magic circle froze; the dancers caught in whatever pose the notes of her *Song* penetrated.

Still *Singing,* Myri grabbed Amaranth and pulled. The magic tugged him back toward the inner circle. Myri pulled harder, grasping her familiar firmly around his ribs, just behind the delicate fold of his wings.

The old Rover women who led the chant and dance broke free of Myri's *Song*. Her black eyes, so like Televarn's in shape, color, and greedy treachery, locked with Myri's own. The magic compulsion to enter the circle began again.

Amaranth and the magic resisted her grasp.

Myri closed her eyes and *Sang* again, in quieter tones, lulling Amaranth to accept her will as best for them both.

The flywacket collapsed beneath her hands. Myri scooped him up and ran from the cave.

"Stop her!" screamed the old woman.

"She's got the flywacket," Televarn said.

Outside the cave, wind and rain lashed at Myri's face and hands. Cold numbed her fingers around Amaranth. Waves crawled forward, nearly to the mouth of the cave. Escape across the headland was truly blocked. The only way out of this cove was up.

A rude staircase had been cut into the cliffside to her right. That escape route led to a grassy plateau where the Rovers could chase and catch her and Amaranth.

"Can you fly?" she asked the now squirming familiar.

(No.) His entire body shook with reaction to the abrupt release of the compulsion spell.

"Hold tight," she told him as she slung him over her shoulder. Blindly she let her hands and feet find purchase among the jagged rocks. Up she climbed. Up where she could see and survey the terrain. Up where the Rovers couldn't follow.

"Myri, come down from there. You'll fall!" Televarn called. Charming persuasion oozed from his voice. But she was immune to him now. He had betrayed her.

He followed her. He was close. Too close.

She climbed higher, faster, using fingernails and toes to cling to the rocks. Amaranth mewed an encouragement.

"Myri!" Televarn's voice contained a note of desperation. "Myri, I love you. Come back to me."

"You only love the gold my familiar will bring to you," she retorted. Tears for a lost dream and the shattering of her love for Televarn blinded her in her quest for a new purchase among the rocks.

"I love you, too, Myri. We are meant to be together," Televarn pleaded.

"You used me. You used magic to compel me to love you so you could kidnap Amaranth. You don't know how to love for real." She reached higher, found a handhold, and pulled herself up.

"I love you, Myri. I won't ever let you go. Never. You belong to *me* now. Me and only me." Televarn grunted as he pulled himself up the rock face. He seemed to be an adept climber, following her rapidly.

Behind her and to the right she heard other feet scrambling on the staircase. She angled her climb to the next rock outcropping. She'd come out above the plateau, above the Rovers and their treachery.

"Myri, help me. I can't hold on!" Televarn's words trailed off to end on a scream.

Briefly she looked below her. A dark form lay sprawled on his back at the edge of the waves. Frothy water lapped at his feet, rose and covered him.

Her empathy reached out to him, needing to drag him to safety, needing to heal him.

She fought the powers within her. A compulsion stronger than the Rovers' ritual pulled her back to the cove. Pulled her back to betrayal and danger.

"No," she told herself. "I can't risk Amaranth to heal a lying, cheating, thieving Rover." She climbed on, easily outdistancing the men who climbed the staircase.

"Will I ever be allowed to stop running from those I want to love?" Tears fell freely from her face. A home and family seemed further away than ever.

Only the wind answered her with a lonely howl.

CHAPTER 17

Ackerly stared at the assembly in the kitchen. The five older apprentices stood, chairs overturned behind them, jaws hanging open and expressions of sheer amazement on their faces. The three younger boys, stared at each other in puzzlement, their mugs of cider hanging idle in their hands. They looked as if they hadn't the strength of will or steadiness in their legs to stand.

Nimbulan leaped from his comfortable armchair, splashing cider down the front of his robe. Another stain for Ackerly to sponge out.

"You did it, boys! You opened the door with magic." The Senior Magician patted each of them on the back so enthusiastically the apprentices stumbled out of their chairs.

Ackerly paused, assessing the room before entering. Opening a door and latch with magic shouldn't have elicited so much excitement. A matter of a series of simple levitations opened any lock. Ackerly could do it, with effort. So why all the fuss over the apprentices? And why all three of them instead of one?

"Come in, Ackerly. Don't just stand there. We have cause for celebration. Did you bring the Tambootie? Of course you did. Which pack is it in? We've got to try a new experiment." Nimbulan searched all the bags before the boatman could set them on the floor. "This is amazing. I wonder if it was the combination of Tambootie and cider or something special about the friendship among the boys. They did all come from the same region."

Unerringly, Nimbulan found the parcel wrapped in Ackerly's dirty shirts. Ackerly wondered briefly how his master knew where to find the pottery jug of dried Tambootie leaves.

"Maybe it was the age of the Tambootie. All of the essential oils permeated the pouch and seeped back into the leaves, giving the dose unusual potency," Nimbulan rattled on, heedless of the nonsense of his words.

"What happened, Nimbulan? What makes you so excited?" Ackerly placed a soothing hand on his friend's shoulder. He'd never seen him like this, even when they were boys in training. Even when they sold their first viable fertility spell to a middle-aged couple who had lost their only child and despaired of having another. Nimbulan had been so jubilant when he heard the spell worked he hadn't paid attention to the coins Ackerly had collected and pocketed.

Ackerly prayed Nimbulan would be equally forgetful of the gold left over from buying the Tambootie. The gold was the only triumph left to Ackerly. Nimbulan had all the magic. Why shouldn't his miserable assistant get to keep the gold?

"They did it." The three of them combined their magic to open the door. I saw it in their auras. Is this all the Tambootie you bought for five gold pieces? I had no idea the weed had become so dear." Nimbulan held up the now unwrapped crock.

How had Nimbulan known the exact price of the Tambootie?

Nimbulan had been the magician spying on him in Sambol. Nimbulan had somehow watched him pay over the five gold pieces. They both knew how many were left and should be returned.

A pain stabbed Ackerly in the gut. He wouldn't give up the extra three gold pieces he'd secreted in the sole of his boot. Nor the other five he'd hidden in the lining of his cloak. They were his. He'd earned them! Nimbulan would have paid over the entire twenty coins and more to get the Tambootie. Any price to feed his addiction to the weed. Surely he wouldn't begrudge Ackerly a small commission for saving him so much.

"This crock of Tambootie won't last very long. You should have gotten more. We have a lot of experimenting to do, boys. Come, let's get started." Nimbulan turned toward the stove. "We'll need more cider and a brighter fire. Nothing like a strong flame to focus on while heading into a trance. Will you fix the cider, please, Lyman. You seem to have a special touch with the spices."

For the first time since entering, Ackerly became aware of the old man standing by the hearth. He could have sworn that Lyman wasn't there when he entered. And Nimbulan had asked him politely to make the cider. Not an order. A request. He'd said "please." Nimbulan never said "please," to Ackerly anymore.

"Wait a minute, Nimbulan." Ackerly grabbed the Senior Magician's sleeve. "You mean you've already been giving the boys Tambootie in their cider?"

"Of course. They need to become used to the side effects before they face the trial by smoke."

"But you can't. It's too dangerous. They're too young." Ackerly frantically sought a way to stall the new experiments. He had to find out how much Nimbulan knew about his gold before a deep drug-induced trance took the magician into the void where all knowledge was available to those who knew where to look and what to look for.

Concern for the boys was the only thing that would keep Nimbulan away from the drug tonight. Ackerly didn't care if they all became addicted and stunted their growth. He needed time to hide his gold more securely. Perhaps a tale of bandits. The country was rife with them.

"You are right, of course, Ackerly. I was too excited by the way the boys combined their magic. We are all cold and tired. Time enough in the morning to examine the ramifications of this spell. Off to bed, boys. We all need a good night's sleep."

The three youngsters looked dead on their feet already. The spell they had worked dragged their shoulders down and made them shuffle. They could hardly keep their eyes open.

"Rollett," Ackerly called to the oldest of the apprentices. "See that they wash up and take their clothes and boots off before they fall into bed. We'll need all of you in the morning. Who's on kitchen duty?"

Powwell held up a weary hand.

"Forget it, Powwell. I'll take care of it." Briskly, Ackerly instructed the boatman to bring extra scullions with him at dawn when he brought the cook over from the keep on the big island. In a few moments he'd cleaned up the shambles Nimbulan left behind him with increasing frequency. When they'd both been apprentices, Nimbulan was known for his fastidiousness. This mess was worse than ever, clear evidence that the Tambootie Ackerly always added to Nimbulan's food had impaired his judgment.

Something needed to be done before Nimbulan figured out what had happened to his gold. Something drastic.

"May I help you clean up, Ackerly?" Lyman raised one white eyebrow with his query. "You seem troubled. Perhaps you'd like to talk?"

Not bloody likely, old man. You have a way of ferreting out secrets that I don't want told, he thought. Then he smiled and said, "Not tonight. I have much to think on. Take a hot brick to bed with you, Lyman. You'll sleep better with warm feet."

* * *

Nimbulan slumped in his cross-legged position, his shoulders nearly touching his knees. The fatigue of a long session in the void with the boys made him dizzy and nauseous. The elation of one small success sent his heart leaping into his throat.

Combining magic was possible. He'd witnessed it last night with a simple door opening. Today he'd participated in a similar spell to move a chair two hand's widths away from its original position.

I could have done it myself with only minor effort, he thought. *So why this tremendous fatigue?* Rovers wouldn't combine magic if the process were always so tiring. Maybe something in their rituals?

The deliberate vagueness of the book in the library irritated and intrigued him.

He sat up to assess the boys' condition. If they were in as bad shape as he after such a small achievement, he'd have to let them eat and rest. He needed a full meal himself, though they'd all partaken of a hearty breakfast at dawn. The water clock showed only an hour had passed since then.

The workroom spun. Each of his three young apprentices wavered and became three overlapping images. Hastily, he put his head back down. His brief glimpse of the boys had shown them collapsed on the floor in a similar condition.

"Food, Ackerly. We need food," he murmured, never doubting that the ever faithful Ackerly was nearby and ready to supply his needs.

A bowl of warm broth and a mug of cool cider appeared beneath his nose. Shoved there by Ackerly, no doubt. He sipped cautiously until his stomach stopped rebelling.

He peeked at the boys. They, too, were reviving, but still kept their heads down.

"Here, Master. I think you're ready for this now." Rollett handed him a plate of thick bread, meat, and cheese, and a jug of cool fresh water.

"Where's Ackerly?" Nimbulan asked between gulps of water. Using Tambootie always left him thirsty and needing to empty his bladder. As if the drug drained all liquid from his body.

"He said he had an errand to run on the big island, sir. He and Lyman crossed the causeway just after the morning meal. He left strict instructions for you to finish the water and all of the food. Lord Quinnault was here while you were in the trance. He'll be back later. Oh, and a messenger from Lord Kammeryl arrived. He's waiting for you in the courtyard, wouldn't enter the buildings, said they were haunted."

Nimbulan chuckled. The shadowed guardian spirit of the monastery hadn't been seen or heard from since he covered the well of ley lines two moons ago. If he reappeared again, he'd come through the courtyard where the messenger waited.

"Anything else, son?" he asked between mouthfuls. The food had a strange taste to it today. Probably an aftertaste from the Tambootie. He'd used a large dose this morning. He gulped more water to wash his mouth clean. The bitter taste lingered.

"A different messenger from Lord Kammeryl came earlier and left this for you." Rollett placed a rolled parchment into Nimbulan's hand. "He said it was urgent but didn't wait for a reply. He said you'd know what to do when you read it."

Nimbulan unrolled the message. His palms started sweating and itching. He rubbed them on his trews and looked at the sprawling handwriting he didn't recognize. Not Kammeryl's. The lord couldn't read or write for all his brilliance with maps and strategy. Some new clerk probably wrote the missive.

The written symbols blurred and danced all over the parchment, refusing to form words. Nimbulan closed his eyes and shook his head to clear it. He reached for the water again. His system should have cleared itself of the after affects of the Tambootie by now. He'd never had the legendary hangovers some magicians suffered.

He put down the parchment and rubbed his eyes clear. When he opened them, he could focus. The pale faces of his three apprentices greeted him. A little color tinged Powwell's cheeks, but blue veins pulsed wildly beneath the skin of his hands and neck. The other two were in no better shape.

"You boys aren't used to the void." The problem with the spell finally hit Nimbulan like a sandbag between the eyes. "I was dragging you through the void by myself as well as holding the spell together. Rollett, put the boys to bed for a few hours, then bring your classmates and Ackerly here, and Lyman, too, if he'll come. You all have some experience in the void. If any of you can get there on your own, beside me, I'll promote you to journeyman immediately."

"About time," Rollett muttered as he led the young apprentices out of the windowless workroom.

A few moments later, Rollett directed Maalin, Bessel, Jaanus, and Gilby to sit on the floor in a circle close enough to hold hands. He assumed the place to Nimbulan's right. A big grin creased his face. "I'll be journeyman before the hour passes," he said smugly.

"Me, too," Bessel chimed in. "I've been practicing and Tambootie doesn't make me sick like it does Maalin and Jaanus."

"Shouldn't I observe?" Gilby looked nervously toward the door. "Master Ackerly and Old Lyman aren't back from the big island yet. There's no one to guide your return if something should go wrong. You always told us, Master Nimbulan, never to go into the void without an anchor to pull us home."

"Correct, Gilby." Nimbulan gulped down a fresh pitcher of water. His tongue felt thick and clumsy. Yet he felt refreshed and fired by his eagerness to complete this experiment successfully. "Step out of the circle and monitor the fire. Try to maintain a light trance without any Tambootie. At the first sign of trouble, grab Rollett and me first. We're the strongest and should be able to help you pull the others back. Not that I'm expecting trouble. This same spell worked this morning. Only the inexperience of the apprentices held us back."

He snapped his fingers. An infusion of Tambootie leaves in hot water brewing in large mugs appeared before each of the six experimenters.

"Drink up, boys. I'm anxious to see how this procedure works."

They all hoisted the dose of Tambootie to their lips and drank deeply of the bitter brew.

"Breathe in, one, two, three," Gilby guided them.

Reality blurred around Nimbulan. People and furniture grew fuzzy around the edges. His heart rate increased with excitement. He was finally going to prove that magic could be combined and thus control any solitary magician. No single Battlemage could defeat the combined might of Nimbulan and his helpers. Only then could magic and magicians remove themselves from war and politics and become neutral servants of all the people of Coronnan.

"Breathe in, one, two, three," Gilby chanted a second time.

The void beckoned Nimbulan, crowding out the lantern light in the workroom. He'd never climbed into the black nothingness so easily. His elation didn't keep him from checking on the boys. All four were still seated in a circle holding hands, but each aura reached for the void individually.

"Breathe. . . ."

Nimbulan lost track of Gilby's chant as blackness enclosed him. He looked around for the others.

Nothing. No one.

The blackness robbed him of sight, hearing, smell, touch. Only the bitter aftertaste of timboor lingered.

Timboor! Poison Timboor, not useful Tambootie.

CHAPTER 18

Ackerly bent over Nimbulan's crumpled body. He listened carefully with ears and magic for signs of breath or heartbeat.

Nothing.

He pulled his glass from his trews pocket and held it beneath the master magician's nose. No cloud obscured the pristine clarity.

Tall and thin in life, the man he had served since they had both been boys, seemed diminished, shrunken in death.

"In the end we all are reduced to this, regardless of talent," he whispered to himself. "How much Tambootie did he have?" he asked the assembled apprentices. All eight of them who now looked to him for leadership and training.

His heart beat a little faster with excitement.

Grief, he told himself. *Only grief. But now I can make something of this ragtag school. Something important. Something profitable.*

"He took a standard dose with the younglings right after we broke our fast at dawn," Rollett said through the tears he choked back.

"That spell succeeded, but he was greatly fatigued. Once he'd eaten and drunk deeply, he took another standard dose with the older boys," Gilby finished. White-faced with shock and guilt, the young man's hands shook and his shoulders trembled. "I tried to pull him out of the void. Him and Rollett first, like he said, but his soul wouldn't return to his body."

"We followed him into the trance just like always. But when we got to the void, he wasn't there. I saw the others but not him!" Jaanus added. "He wasn't there."

The others nodded their agreement. Something had gone terribly wrong between the first and second dosage. Or perhaps all the years of accumulated addiction had finally taken him.

Ackerly looked at Nimbulan's body once more for obvious signs of why he had died. Beside him lay a wrinkled piece of parchment, partially unrolled and flattened. The writing wiggled and bounced around as he watched. He reached for it then quickly withdrew his hand.

"The guilt is not yours, boys," he said still staring at the parchment. "Where did this come from?" He pointed at the written message.

"A courier from Lord Kammeryl d'Astrismos," Rollett replied, also staring at the parchment. "He didn't wait for a reply but said it was urgent." His mouth remained slightly open, eyes wide, as the implication of the spell contained within the message penetrated his grief.

"Maalin, you are good with fire. Burn the thing, without touching it, as soon as we leave the room. It is tainted with magic and poison. I sense blood in the ink—the work of a Bloodmage!" Ackerly bowed his head and closed his eyes until the gasps and murmurs of the apprentices died away. "I should have been here to guide the spells. I could have intercepted the message and kept Nimbulan from going into the void so soon after the first spell. If he'd waited, the poison in that parchment might not have affected him so strongly."

Powwell sobbed openly. Zane and Haakkon sniffed.

Suddenly their love for Nimbulan irritated Ackerly. *They don't love me!* But he was the one who made sure they were fed and had blankets and firewood to keep out the Winter chills. He was the one who did all the work around here.

He suppressed his anger. After Nimbulan was safely buried, he could show these ungrateful boys where their loyalty should lie.

His thoughts kept returning to the possibilities for the future, now that Nimbulan and his ideals no longer hindered him.

"We must dress him in his ceremonial robes for burial. Delay will serve no purpose. There is a crypt beneath the chapel. I can think of no more fitting place for him to take his final rest. We will bury him at sunset." Abruptly, he turned on his heel and exited the room before he broke out in shouts of glee.

Free, I'm free at last! He'd just slip Nimbulan's formal robes over his everyday clothes. That way he wouldn't have to pay the village women to wash and prepare the body. A little delusion spell would make the boys think he'd wrapped the body tightly in expensive shroud cloths, but he'd only use strips from an old sheet. No use spending any more money on the dead than necessary. They certainly weren't in a position to appreciate it.

Only briefly did he wonder at the warmth and suppleness of the body that had supposedly been dead for some five hours.

* * *

A tangle of bright umbilical cords knotted and dragged Nimbulan across the void so fast he couldn't comprehend the colors or his destination. He sensed, more than saw, a purpose or design in the symbolic life forces. All seemed to be shimmering crystal tinged with a primary hue. Except the center one. The one driving the others flashed all colors of the spectrum so fast it appeared to be no color at all.

A thought struggled to be born in his consciousness, for he had no body or brain left to house such things. These strange life forces must be guiding him to his next existence. An existence free of his addiction to Tambootie. The drug was necessary to enhance the inborn talent of magic. Too bad it also hastened his next existence. An existence he couldn't yet imagine, but wanted to reach. Now. Without delay, before he regretted leaving Coronnan and his work unfinished.

(The time is not yet ripe for you to leave your destiny behind.) The bright life forces wrapped tighter around him, propelling him deeper into the void, or out of it. He couldn't tell which without a body to sense direction.

Once before that voice had sent him out of the void. Who? What?

His questions and concerns dissipated. The effort to remember was too much. Better to drift with the bright life forces. Red and blue, green and yellow. Red for

Keegan. Blue for himself. Yellow for Ackerly. Green for the combined auras of his apprentices. Iridescent crystal all color/no color reminded him of Myrilandel with her pale blonde hair and skin so thin her blood veins shone through it, pulsing purple shadows like bruises. . . .

(Go back, Nimbulan.)

Why?

(Impudence in a human will not be tolerated!)

Was that a chuckle behind the demanding voice? Nimbulan fought the lethargy of the sense-robbing void. Laughter. Humor. Irony. These were the qualities of Life. Qualities he missed greatly, had known too little of these last years. So many of his friends and acquaintances had died. *We should have explored the world with laughter rather than fight each other to the death,* he mentally addressed the spirits of all his fallen comrades.

He appreciated the quirk of fate that he found laughter in the infinite darkness but not in his corporeal life. He laughed with the voices who loved Life and wanted to make the most of it.

What was his life? All he'd known for many years was a driving need to find new magic, better magic to protect his lord. The only lord capable of holding together the volatile factions of Coronnan and ending the wars.

He'd supported that lord—what was his name?—and his father for nigh on twenty years. Neither man had accomplished much in that time.

No lord had.

(Lord Quinnault de Tanos dares to dream of peace when the others are too shortsighted to think farther ahead than the next battle.)

Or the next lover, Nimbulan added, remembering Kammeryl d'Astrismos and his string of younger and younger bedmates. A wave of revulsion flooded his consciousness.

(Does your reaction to that man tell you the value of your loyalty to him?)

Too heavy a question. The tangle of bright life forces danced around him with sparkles of joy, of life, love, and laughter.

Laughter. He'd miss laughter if his next existence proved as full of war and responsibility as the last one.

(Your latest life doesn't have to end. You can fill it with

love and laughter, with family and friends. You don't have to be grim and sad all of the time, if you place your loyalty correctly this time. If your loyalty belongs to peace and not to one man who will betray you, you will know Life to its fullest. Peace. Love peace. Love life. Love the one who draws you back to Coronnan. . . .)

A sinking sensation. Tendrils of pain. Cold. Hands and feet that trembled with weakness and chills. A hard bier pressing against his aching back.

"I'm alive. I have a body," Nimbulan whispered through stiff and parched lips. "I'm thirsty and hungry." Sound echoed in his ears. The kind of sound that bounced against stone walls.

He tried to open his eyes. He thought they were open. Blackness still surrounded him. A different blackness from the sense-robbing void. Sense-cleansing as well. All traces of a Tambootie hangover had disappeared.

The sound of dripping water, steady and rhythmic, awakened his other senses. Mold and something rotten assaulted his nose.

Feebly he snapped his fingers on his right hand, too tired to lift it more than a finger-length above his chest. A tiny flicker of witchlight sat on the end of his index finger. Not much. Enough. He lay on a stone slab in a stone niche—open blackness to his right, solid, damp stone to his left, above and below.

The witchlight vanished, leaving false flashes before his eyes. He'd seen enough. Only the walls of a crypt were lined with open niches the perfect size of a man's body.

He pressed his feet hard against the end of his bier trying to straighten his cramped knees. This burial chamber had been intended for a shorter man.

Men were shorter in centuries gone by.

An old crypt. A very damp and untended one. Where would Ackerly and the boys bury him but beneath the chapel in the old monastery? They must have believed him dead. Perhaps he had been dead for a time. During the time he'd wandered the void with the pretty crystal umbilicals.

For a moment he wanted nothing more than to be a part of the intricate dance of life-that-was-not-Life.

Some force beyond his ken had given him back his life.

The destiny planned for him by the Stargods had not yet been fulfilled.

And yet the void was so beautiful, so peaceful. . . .

"Snap out of it!" he admonished himself. The Stargods had returned him to his body for a reason.

Carefully, he turned his head to the open side and flicked another ball of witchlight ahead of him. Crumbling skeletons filled a few of the other niches. Most people avoided these older crypts because of the sight of so many generations of the dead. No one would think to bring flowers to his tomb and rescue him.

He had to find his own way out. Only one niche lay between him and the stone floor. He drew up his stiff knees as far as the ceiling of his tomb allowed and inched closer to the edge. He tried to swing one long leg out, only to discover both legs bound together by a shroud. The same shroud, hastily and scantily wound about his body kept his hands crossed on his chest. He could wiggle his fingers but not move very far. Whoever prepared him for burial used just enough winding cloths to keep him in place, and no more.

He couldn't break the hold the few cloths had on his limbs. Very well, he'd have to roll out of the niche all at once and hope he didn't break any bones during his fall.

As he squirmed and wriggled free of his tomb, the shroud tore and loosened across his chest. He'd been bound in a threadbare old sheet rather than sturdy new linen. He worked his right arm free and felt for the edge. His hand measured the distance and found a small ledge to grasp and ease his fall. Ready to swing his legs out, he paused and wondered why the shroud hadn't completely covered his body and head in tight wraps of linen soaked in preservatives. Surely Ackerly had access to necessary funerary regalia. Lord Quinnault de Tanos would have provided a shroud and servants to wash and prepare the body for burial.

If Ackerly had bothered to ask for them. If Ackerly had informed anyone of Nimbulan's "death." Surely lords and peasants alike would have noticed the lack of proper burial clothes and herbs.

"I thought you my friend, Ackerly. Couldn't you spend a little money for the old women who tend the dead?

Didn't you have enough respect for me to provide a proper funeral with shroud and priest and mourners?" Anger heated Nimbulan's cheeks. He allowed his emotions to fuel his cramped muscles and propel him outward.

With one hand braced on the ledge, he landed safely on his side a few feet below his "final" resting place.

"Why the haste?" he kept asking himself as he stripped off the winding cloths and discovered he was still wearing his everyday tunic and trews beneath his formal robe—not the newest or cleanest one at that.

Why?

(Who?)

Nimbulan looked around, seeking the source of the voice in the far corners of the crypt. Had he truly heard it or was it an echo of his spirit journey in the void? No answers came to him. He aimed the witchlight toward the shaky ladder carved into the wall that led to the trapdoor entrance.

(Hasten not from one death into another.)

This time Nimbulan used the last of his reserves to fill the subterranean crypt with light.

"Are you a ghost? Perhaps the guardian spirit returned?"

No answer. Only the echoes of his own whispers and the lingering memory of the warning bounced in his head. *Hasten not from one death into another,* the voice still echoed in his mind.

Who wanted him dead? Who could have arranged it?

The aftertaste of Timboor returned to his mouth. *Timboor.* An overdose of the poison fruit on top of the extra doses of Tambootie he had ingested for his experiments.

He'd destroyed all of the remaining bits of Timboor after his bad experience with it while Ackerly was in Sambol. None of the apprentices would have had the boldness to contradict his orders and give it to him.

Keegan had deserted him when Nimbulan thought the boy well-loved and loyal.

No. Rollett and the others weren't as cynical, nor as ambitious as Keegan. They trusted him.

Didn't they?

Who? Who had been around that day? He had no way of telling how long ago that was. A few hours perhaps or several days? Possibly a week. He was hungry enough for that amount of time to have passed. A murderer could have slipped the Timboor into the Tambootie dosage and left the island before Nimbulan was pronounced dead.

Someone with a boat. Two messengers had arrived from Lord Kammeryl d'Astrismos. One had waited, one had left a parchment. The words written on the parchment had bounced and wavered as if written in magic code. He did remember the pattern of the writing had fallen into verse, like a spell. Could the Timboor have been rubbed into the parchment and combined with a spell? He had just come out of a Tambootie trance. His system was sensitive to all forms of the tree at that point. Perhaps his skin had absorbed the poison.

Or the poison had already been in his system causing his vision to blur.

He had no way of knowing now. If someone had tried to kill him once, they would try again.

He needed more information.

He needed a plan, a place to hide until he knew who had poisoned him and could guard against him.

Who? Who? Who? The question ricocheted around his skull with no answers.

A place to hide. Nowhere on the island.

How to escape from this tomb? He'd lift the trapdoor and find out what time of day awaited him. At night, when all slept unguarded, he'd leave.

He had to get off the island unobserved.

CHAPTER 19

Nimbulan dragged the little rowboat onto dry land beyond the sucking mudflats of the Great Bay. Winter dormancy made the beach grasses brittle and sparse. A stiff offshore wind smelled of salt and a new storm hovering on the eastern horizon. He needed to find shelter soon.

The night was clear and icy cold. Starlight and a crescent moon lighted his way. He pulled a thick winter cloak tight across his chest and shouldered a pack of provisions.

His raid of the pantry and storeroom had been surprisingly easy. Almost as if someone expected him to wake from the dead and flee the old monastery. He hadn't dared pilfer his private quarters for his staff and glass. Perhaps he should transport them here. No. Someone might witness the disappearance and trace the transport.

He would cut a new staff for his new life and career. What about the glass, expensive and difficult to replace? So many spells depended upon the qualities of perfectly clear glass to work. He'd just have to improvise with a clear pool of water.

He spared a moment to regret leaving his boys. But he had confidence in them. He'd trained them well, taught them honor and respect. He could imagine Rollett gathering all of the apprentices in the dormitory late at night, telling them stories and passing on the message of peace through community. Nimbulan's dream would live a little longer. At least until he came back with Rover secrets and new spells to implement the dream.

Which direction?

(East,) the frigid South wind seemed to sigh.

Rovers lived in the South more often than not. A Rover

spell might give him the clue to combining magic. Because of the curve of the Great Bay, East was the fastest way to the lands South of Coronnan. Once he had information about how Rovers worked their magic together, he'd return to the school and his work to remove magic from battles and politics. And find the man who had tried to murder him.

(East.) As good a direction as any. He centered his magic, concentrating on South, the closest magnetic pole. With his left hand up, palm outward and fingers slightly curved, he turned in a slow circle. A slight stab of awareness pierced his palm. South lay up that dune and to the right about twenty degrees. He must have drifted into the great curve of the Bay. If he kept a true course, halfway between East and South, he'd run into the trade road within a mile or two. Rovers traveled the highway.

The well-trod road wandered from village to village offering Rovers many opportunities to sell their distinctive metalwork and earn coins by entertaining the locals with music and dance. Eventually the road crossed the Southern Mountains at a point almost due East from Quinnault de Tanos' islands, and then into Rossemeyer. He had no desire to explore the high desert plateau of that impoverished kingdom. The road went many places before it reached the mountain pass.

Many places. Many choices. The sudden freedom of his situation swamped his senses. His friends and students and patrons thought him dead. He had no obligations. No responsibilities. No expectations.

For the first time in his forty-nine years he could go anywhere, do anything, and not keep a schedule. Giddy laughter sent him to his knees.

"I am free!" he yelled into the wind. Was that a laugh he heard in reply?

Nimbulan stared at the tree on the bluff above the beach. Just an ordinary tree. He tried remembering the last time he stared at a tree for no reason other than to stare at a tree, and failed. For the past thirty years, at least, he'd had to weigh the location of the tree, its height, how much wood it could provide campfires, would it become a rallying point to turn the tide of battle, how many men could hide in it for ambush. . . ?

"You are the most beautiful tree I have ever seen!" he yelled as loudly as he could, throwing out his arms as if to embrace the world. "You are beautiful because you are just a tree."

He drank in the tranquillity of the moment until the Winter air reminded him to move on.

A pang of guilt almost sent him back toward the islands. He'd set up the School for Magicians in an attempt to force peace on the lords of Coronnan. The lords didn't want peace. He'd tried. What more could they ask of him?

(Success.)

His only clue to success lay with the Rovers, along the trade road that wound its way East. He set his steps toward his journey. He'd find answers in the East. Maybe he'd find his life there, too.

* * *

"Have you hospitality for a lost traveler?" Myri asked the stout woman who hovered in the mouth of an old sea cave. The ocean had changed levels many generations before and left the cave on a plateau a hundred feet or more above the beach. A village had grown up around the mouth of the cave. A fishing village judging by the nets strung out to dry and the boats hauled up for winter repairs.

"A mite young to be out on your own, girl. Where you hail from?" The woman placed her beefy hands on her hips. Her girth and the double doors framed and hung in the mouth of the cave clearly blocked Myri's passage into the domicile behind her. The raucous songs and the smell of spilled ale coming from behind the woman told her a tavern filled the cave.

"I ran away from a great battle. The wars took everything from me, my home, my family. . . ." Myri cuddled Amaranth closer to her face as if hiding tears. In all the places she'd asked hospitality in the past weeks since fleeing Televarn and his searching Rovers, she'd learned to stretch the truth and portray emotions she didn't always feel. Villagers empathized with those who'd been displaced by the war, a fear they all shared. Few trusted aimless travelers. Rovers, thieves, and marauding soldiers made them cautious.

So Myri told them what they wanted to hear. The voices and the circling wind that kept pushing Myri East didn't object to her half-truths and playacting. She couldn't travel East any farther without running into the ocean.

If only she could forget Televarn and the pain he'd left in her heart. She forgot so many things, why not the treacherous Rover?

"Like as not, we'll see more of your kind. Had a whole family through here last week. Thought they'd try their luck in Hanassa rather than put up with the wars here. Living with outlaws and thieves in that hole in the mountain can't be worse than living with armies constantly tearing up fields and scavenging all they can cart away." The woman dropped her arms bud didn't move aside.

"I'm very hungry." Myri's stomach growled loudly of its own volition.

"Bet that cat is, too. Can't afford to give everyone food. You'll have to work for it. You don't look strong enough to fetch and carry here in the pub."

"I know herbs and healing. I can sweeten the stale ale and make your bread so light it doesn't need to be dipped in beer to chew."

"Healing? You a magician?" Suspicion darkened the woman's eyes. Healers belonged with the armies that plagued them all. "We got no use for those bastards. Stealing out harvest and our young women. And if we don't give 'em up fast and willing, they burn us out." The woman crossed her arms across her ample bosom and stared hard at Myri, daring her to claim the extensive training required to turn a person of talent into a magician.

"I'm only a witchwoman. I've never been trained in magic, and I wouldn't accept it if offered. But I know what phases of the moon to gather witchwort." Myri stared back, letting her own fear of magicians shine through her eyes.

"If you want to hasten a birth. . . ?"

"Pluck the freshest leaves of witchwort at the full moon and make an infusion of them immediately," Myri replied to the testing question.

"Every woman knows that. What else can you do with witchwort?"

"Gather the blossoms at the dark of the moon and dry them until they crumble. Sprinkle them on porridge three mornings in a row and your courses will come regular again." Or abort an unwanted baby.

"I heard you had to use them five days in a row."

"Only if you are more than a moon late."

The woman nodded her acceptance of the prescription. "Got me a great, honking boil under my arm. Won't let me raise my arm or lift anything heavier than my drawers. Can't sleep 'cause of it. All Granny Katia's poultices didn't help at all. Reckon you can't hurt nothing if you lance and drain it. Do it proper so's the infection don't spread, then you've got a place to stay, girl. I'm Karry, short for Katareena. You got a name?" Finally, the woman stepped aside, clearing the doorway for Myri to enter.

Warmth and noise blasted Myri's senses the moment she crossed the threshold. The smell of unwashed male bodies nearly overwhelmed the aroma of baking bread and fermenting brews. Amaranth buried his head beneath her arm rather than face the men who halted their songs and stopped eating to stare at her.

"She's a healer, boys, not a whore. Go back to your drinks," Karry said loud enough for all to hear, even in the back corners of the tavern.

"What's the difference between a healer and whore?" yelled a man with broken teeth and long ropy scars on his arms.

"How much she charges!" replied a man from across the room. "Whores are cheaper."

"Ask your wife the difference when she needs a midwife, Timmon. She'll bash your head in for looking at another woman after knocking her up for the ninth time," said a man across the room as he shook his finger at the man with broken teeth.

"Maybe she'll welcome another woman to keep him away from her after the ninth babe gets here." Timmon's drinking companion slapped him on the back laughing.

"Never mind them, girl. It's Winter, and they're bored 'cause they can't get the boats out. If the wind dies down by dawn, they'll be out all day and too tired tomorrow night to know their names, let alone bother you. Though with that pale hair and clear skin of yours, you'd best keep your distance from some of them. The quiet ones are the ones you gotta watch. The loud ones are more interested in hearing their own words than doing anything about it. You got a name, girl?"

"Myrilandel, and my cat is Amaranth." Myri followed her hostess along a winding path through the crowded trestle tables toward a curtain draped across the back of the chamber. No man touched her, though she passed quite close to some. Apparently the tavern mistress' word was law here.

"Karry they call me, though I was born Katareena, like my Ma and her Ma before her. Did I tell you that a'ready? Name goes back almost as old as this cave and the pub in it. Always been Katareenas here. Probably always will be. My own daughter has the name and the babe she carries will, too, if this one's a girl. She's got three boys already. But she's carrying this one different. Hope it's a girl. Need another Katareena to carry on the tradition."

"Is she having trouble with the babe?" Myri's healing instincts awakened after weeks of dormancy. She hadn't allowed herself to "feel" anything for the people she treated with herbs and simples along her journey.

Suddenly this little village felt like home. They needed her. They'd welcomed her—after a fashion. Some villages begrudged her the bread and cheese they handed her and made her eat outside for fear of a stranger in their midst. Karry had invited her in. Granted she'd be expected to earn her keep. That was better than being denied admittance just because she was a stranger.

She must have traveled far enough East and South for

the wars to have remained a distant threat rather than an imminent peril.

Is this the home you promised me? she asked the voices.

No one answered, but the warm and comfortable feeling didn't leave her.

"Nothing much wrong with my Katey, but she's carrying high and all in front. From the back she don't look eight moons along. She's tired all the time and her feet swell, but that isn't unusual so close to her time, especially chasing three boys with more energy than sense." Karry chuckled as she thrust aside a wall curtain to reveal a larger inner chamber that served as home and warehouse for the tavern.

"Has the boil troubled you long?" Myri set Amaranth down on a barrel of ale. He sniffed the rim with grudging curiosity. When he was satisfied the barrel posed no threat, he jumped down and investigated the one beside it. He kept his wings safely hidden. He hadn't flown since he tangled with Televarn's fishing net. She hoped he'd healed, but she didn't know for sure yet.

"This boil started up as a little spot of rash going on two weeks ago. What you going to need, girl. Hot water? Mustard? Cobwebs for a bandage?"

"Lie down and let me look at it first. Two weeks is a long time. I hope I don't have to treat you for more than just the boil."

Karry heaved her bulk facedown on the pallet off to the right. She fumbled with the ties of her gown until she freed her left arm and breast. Her firmly muscled arm showed pale pink in the dim light. An angry red lump the size of Myri's thumbnail glared at her from beneath the arm near the back. Red streaks were beginning to spread outward in a spiderweb of infection.

Deftly, Myri prepared what she needed for the simple procedure. She cleaned her knife and the boil. Then a quick slash of her smallest, sharpest knife across the top and a second cut across it.

Using the side of the knife to press against the eruption, she drained it, catching the pus in a clean cloth, until it bled freely, cleanly red and free of infection.

Should she add a little of her own healing to keep it healthy? Not a full trance; that would make her lose control and drain her of too much energy. Just a touch to make sure all of the infection was gone.

"Mbrtt," Amaranth rubbed against her ankles. *(Trust her. Help her with magic.)*

With her familiar leaning against her, she channeled a little energy through her hand and into the open sore.

"You finished yet?" Karry squirmed restlessly on the pallet. "I've got to get back to my customers before they sneak out without paying up. Reckon you've earned a good meal and place to rest. Stay here. No one will bother you."

"I'm finished, Karry." Myri applied a quick poultice of warmed herbs and pressed it firmly against the wound to keep it open and draining into the absorbent moss. "You'll need to keep this compress on for a few hours. Do you have a bandage?"

"My shift is tight enough to keep it in place." Karry stood, righting her clothes and checking the poultice. "Stargods help me, I get stouter faster than I can make new clothes."

"But you work hard. Your body is healthy." Otherwise the boil wouldn't have cleaned up so easily. A frailer person would have been riddled with the poison.

"Well, the men don't mind a little extra of me when the need is on them and I've got the time. And I'm strong enough to heave barrels around when I need to. Don't have to depend on a man like most women. The Katareenas have always been independent. 'Bitches' some of the men call us when we don't act meek and helpless. They learn to respect us, though."

"Um, Karry, ah . . . I don't think you should sleep with the men for a while. Not until the wound closes."

"You volunteering to take my place, girl? Men get angry when there isn't a woman around to take care of them. A lot of their wives are carrying too heavy to safely lie with their men this time of year. We had a bountiful Equinox festival last Spring."

Televarn's beautiful body flashed through Myri's memory. She'd found great pleasure and satisfaction in their lovemaking. None of the men she'd seen in the pub could compare with the handsome Rover. They would be more honest in their faithlessness.

She couldn't enjoy quick, temporary joinings. She wanted a husband or nothing.

"I'm thinking maybe one of them gave you the infection that started the boil. I've known men to pass all sorts of ailments on to their women."

"Not my men." Karry threw back her head and laughed. "They're clean, and I don't take on strangers. Not that we get many. Moncriith's the only visitor we get. He wouldn't let himself pick up some nasty disease."

"Moncriith?" Myri stilled, all senses alert. Her balance shifted to her toes automatically, ready to flee.

"So you know him?" Karry's eyes narrowed in speculation. "You the witchwoman he's hunting?"

Myri grabbed for Amaranth rather than answer. The pesky flywacket eluded her hands. He stared at her, annoyed and indignant, as only a cat can be.

"Don't worry about Moncriith. He's got a honeyed tongue, but folks around here don't care for him much. He wants them to uproot and follow him to the ends of the Kardia in search of demons. No one in this village has the time or money to leave hearth and home to follow him on some wild lumbird chase. Who cares if magicians are causing all kinds of trouble with the armies up North? Doesn't mean they have demons living inside them. None of them ever comes here to trouble us. Only magic we ever see is an occasional witchwoman seeking a new home. And maybe a Rover or two. But we ain't big enough or important enough to warrant much else."

"You get Rovers here, too?" Myri gulped, trying hard not to dash out the door and keep running until she . . . until she . . . What? *This is the closest place to a home I've found. I have to stay a while to know for sure.*

"Oh, don't worry none about Moncriith. He won't come again until high Summer. By then we'll figure out a way to hide you or disguise you. If you're as good a midwife and healer as I think you are, this village needs you. We won't let some crazy Bloodmage take you. Who's to say but him if he's really a priest like he pretends. Yoshi!" She raised her voice on the last word.

A moon-faced young man with light, almost colorless eyes and dark hair peeked from behind the curtain. "Yes'm?"

"Yoshi, get Myri something hot to eat and find her an extra blanket and pallet. Give the cat some milk and a little of last night's fish. They're staying with me a while."

CHAPTER 20

Nimbulan shivered slightly as rain once more penetrated his cloak and hood. Tonight he'd beg hospitality in a village. If he found one. For several weeks he'd shied away from other people lest they recognize him. His aimless wandering in a generally southeasterly direction had taken him well beyond the usual battlefields and recruiting regions.

As if his thoughts of warm huts and cheerful fires with tasty dinners roasting over them had conjured the aroma, he caught the scent of bread baking. The warm yeasty smell roused his stomach and set his mouth watering. Food. Warmth. People to share the food and the fire with. A place to sleep out of the rain. Magic and lords, battles and schools had no place in his life now.

Following close upon the aroma of baking bread came the clip-clop of steed hooves against the hard-packed dirt road. The light rain was persistent but not intense enough to turn the road to mud. Nimbulan counted the sounds. He heard several steeds plodding along at a slow but steady pace. He guessed they pulled heavy loads rather than bearing riders.

A whisper of caution wiggled into his mind. He stepped off the road, behind a tree and waited.

Voices. Gibberish. Either they were farther away than he thought, or the other travelers spoke a foreign tongue. Curiosity vied with caution.

Down the road, four sledges came into view. Brightly painted cabins perched atop the conveyances. A thin coil of smoke rose from a metal chimney in the last cabin—the source of the baking bread. A team of two small draft steeds, perhaps half the size of the huge sledge steeds used to haul heavy trade loads or army supplies, pulled each of the strange vehicles. Dark-haired men walked beside the teams. None of them carried the long whips customarily used by caravan wranglers. Following the sledges came a host of people, old and young, male and female. All of them dark-haired with olive-toned skin. They wore black accented with bright colors in kerchiefs, vests, sashes, and petticoats. Scrolling embroidery decorated each layer of clothing.

He'd found a clan of Rovers. Old legends and fearful gossip raced through his memory. *Can't trust a thieving Rover. No one crafts metal better than a Rover. Rovers will steal your children. Wild animals love Rovers and obey with little or no training. Rover women have no morals and will steal your soul. Rover women know tricks that will delight you in bed and leave you smiling for days.*

The old whispers lingered, especially the last one.

An elderly man lifted his voice in song.

The lyrics slid over Nimbulan's understanding. Definitely a foreign language. But the tune made his feet itch to walk in rhythm and harmony with these people.

The women picked up the chorus, children chanted the refrain and men hummed a harmony in three parts, unlike anything Nimbulan had ever heard. The haunting rhythm reached out and grabbed him, setting his feet tapping and begging him to join his voice with the others.

He resisted, unsure if he should betray his presence yet. Instead he hummed along, letting the music vibrate from the back of his throat down to warm his belly. A hint of magic drifted in that song. The entire clan sang a spell of joy.

Nimbulan chuckled. Though he didn't recognize the words, he knew their intent: avoid trouble they didn't initiate by robbing troublemakers of their anger.

"You might as well join us, stranger," the lead wrangler said without stopping the caravan.

Nimbulan stepped out of the shadows. He knew the song had robbed him of caution and alarm. He didn't care. "Which way do you travel?" he asked, falling into step beside the man. His face seemed young, though squint lines around his black eyes suggested years and maturity.

"We travel where the road leads us, unless we find a better direction along the way." The wrangler whistled sharply at the steeds who had slowed their pace. The animals picked up their feet with brisk purpose immediately.

"This road looks good to me for now. I'd welcome companionship for a time." Nimbulan scanned the clan spread out behind him. A vague similarity of the shapes of nose and chin told him they were truly a clan and not a motley gathering of outcasts. Who knew what crimes such a group would be capable of if they were immoral enough for Rovers to throw them out.

"Rovers are never lonely and rarely alone. Do you have a name, stranger?"

"Lan," Nimbulan offered the childhood shortening of his name. Rovers traveled everywhere; they probably had heard of Nimbulan the Battlemage.

"Lan." The Rover rolled the name around his tongue as if tasting it. "A good, simple name. Easy to say and remember. You are wise not to reveal your true name."

Nimbulan almost checked his stride in shock. A measure of self-preservation kept him beside the shorter, younger man, matching him pace for pace. "I've heard of that tradition. Some people believe possession of a true name gives one power over another."

"Possession of a true name gives a *magician* power over another." The Rover looked him up and down. "If you have magic, you keep it hidden, Lan."

For the first time, Nimbulan noticed the embroidery on the man's vest. Tiny stitches in silver and gold outlined symbols in ancient writing. The spoken language had died out centuries ago. Some magicians still used the pictorial writing to hide spells. Each glyph became a sigil of power.

"If I had magic, I'd run away from it. Few love magicians in Coronnan these days. They blame . . ." he almost said "us." "Magicians take the blame for winning and losing battles. Whoever wins, the common soldiers and their families lose."

"Aye." The Rover whistled again to the small steeds.

"Do you have a name, fellow traveler?" Nimbulan asked.

A comely woman in her twenties, with a babe on her hip moved up beside them before the Rover could speak. An intriguing mole rested near the right corner of her mouth, inviting his gaze to linger on her full lips. She lowered her lashed flirtatiously over luminous dark eyes, watching Nimbulan as she did so. Her breasts nearly spilled out of her bodice when she walked. She'd reversed the lacing so that the garment opened from the top. Probably to nurse the child more easily.

In most societies, most women laced their bodices from top to bottom to indicate their lack of availability.

"The children are cold and hungry. Can we stop for a meal and a rest?" she addressed the leader of the clan while smiling speculatively at Nimbulan.

Nimbulan couldn't take his eyes off her mouth except to peer longingly at her breasts.

"Aye," the Rover chieftain replied. "At the next bend in the road. There is a clean-flowing creek there." He didn't look at the woman's blatant sensuality.

She twitched her hips in invitation as she moved back to the mass of Rovers behind the sledges. Nimbulan licked his suddenly dry lips. He hadn't had a woman in many, many moons. Perhaps more than a year. Women robbed a man of the energy needed for magic. Battle-mages habitually made use of the occasional camp follower when they required a quick release of pent up frustrations. That kind of woman didn't expect courtship or lasting relationships. They didn't demand attention that could be put toward the work of saving an army from defeat.

He'd never understood Ackerly's preference for peasant women who clung to him, begging him to return and settle in their villages.

He wasn't a Battlemage anymore. If he succeeded in his quest, there would be no more Battlemages. He could take the time and expend the energy to woo a woman, get to know her, take time making love to her. . . .

"Tell me, leader of this clan of Rovers—I assume you lead, since the woman asked your permission to stop rather than relaying the orders of another—is pursuit of that woman forbidden to me?" Nimbulan continued to watch the woman, hoping he'd read her invitation correctly.

"Maia's man died last Spring. He made the mistake of seeking shelter from a brief storm beneath a tree. Lightning killed him and the tree. I trust you'll be smarter."

"Is that permission to accept her advances?"

"She's free. I trust you are as well, or you wouldn't be wandering Coronnan alone." The Rover shrugged.

"I have no woman to bind me to hearth and home." An image of Myrilandel's moon blonde hair and lavender-shadowed skin flashed before his mind's eye. More images of his apprentices tugged his heart back to the river islands and the school.

"I have never let a woman bind me." The Rover looked away as if embarrassed. "I find my taste running to fairer women than Maia. My instincts are telling me to spread my seed outside the clan. We become inbred too easily. For that reason, we'll welcome your seed. Take your pick of those who seek you out."

Nimbulan decided not to press the matter. The emotions filling the Rover's eyes could as easily lash out in punishing anger as they could dissolve into tears.

"If I am to rove with you for a time, I must know what to call you."

"Televarn. I am king of this clan and don't fear giving my true name to one and all."

"Televarn." Nimbulan tasted the name in open mimicry of the Rover's reaction to his own name. "An unusual name. Televarn, the one who talks to the Varns—mysterious beings who trade only in diamonds for vast quantities of grain and appear in our ports once a century. They never reveal face or hands or even the shape of their bodies, keeping all veiled and gloved in swathes of rainbow-colored cloths that appear filmy and transparent but hide more than they reveal. You must be a very powerful man if you are privileged to speak to these entities."

"I have more power than you can dream of, Lan. You may be a wandering magician, or a man who has lost all to the wars, though you have not the bearing of grief for such a man. I don't care what you are as long as you tell a good story over the campfire and break none of our laws."

* * *

"I have only a few beds left." Ackerly put a sorrowful expression on his face, trying not to look at the few coins the displaced family held out to him. "Alas, many families seek a place of safety for their children. I can only accept those who are truly talented." He allowed a sigh of regret to leave his lungs. The coins were base. Easily ignored.

"But . . . but Kalen has very powerful magic. We haven't had to use firestone to light the rushes since she lost her milk teeth." The mother, a wasted woman worn out by childbirth and hunger, held out her hand in entreaty. A single gold coin glinted against her palm. Her husband closed his fist around the five base coins, removing them from the bargain.

"Fire is an early sign of talent. Tell me, what else does the girl do?" Ackerly tried not to lick his lips in anticipation of handling that single piece of gold. He'd acquired twenty new pieces in the weeks since Nimbulan died. He'd made it known throughout the land that the School for Magicians was offering new apprentices a safe place to learn the one profession that could give a peasant family a guaranteed income and a measure of security against marauders.

The old monastery was fair to overflowing with adolescents and five more weary Battlemages seeking a quiet retirement from the wars.

"Show him, Kalen," the father ordered. He pocketed the lead and copper coins but let his wife keep dangling the gold before Ackerly.

He had been a merchant in Baria on the North coast until Lord Hanic had burned the town. From the ragged and threadbare state of their once finely tailored clothing, the family had been on the road for some time. The gold was probably the last of their former wealth. They must be desperate to be willing to part with it.

Kalen shook her head and tried to hide behind her mother's skirts, being careful not to let any part of her touch the father on the other side of her. Not quite ten, she looked to be a year or more from reaching puberty. If her talent proved true before her body matured, she would be one of the great magicians. Most apprentices didn't show any sign of talent until they were within a few moons of the change. Only the great ones, the men and women who could tap the ley lines and become as powerful as Nimbulan showed talent earlier.

Of course some of the great magicians refused to acknowledge their talents until raging growth sent their emotions awry and they couldn't keep it secret any longer. Minor magicians, like himself, only exhibited talent at or after puberty.

"What is it that you can show me, Kalen?" Ackerly squatted in front of her, making sure his head was level with her own. No use intimidating her into losing control or hiding her talent altogether. He'd learned that much in his recruiting these past moons.

From his crouched position he raised his eyes slightly to look the mother directly in the eye, tacitly asking approval to approach the child. So far, the woman had kept her head down, face in shadow.

As their eyes met, the woman's mouth opened in a silent gasp. "You?" she asked soundlessly. She moistened her lips with a flick of her tongue. Then she firmed her expression into meek subserviance. Whatever flicker of recognition had passed across her face was gone, as quickly as it came.

Ackerly shrugged and turned his attention back to the little girl. The mother looked vaguely familiar. Maybe he'd met her in his long years of traveling with Druulin and then Nimbulan.

"It's a special secret." Kalen lisped the esses, not badly, but enough to hint at why she shied away from others.

"Special, yes. I can make fire, too. Does that make me as special as you?" Ackerly snapped his fingers and blinked. A tiny flame appeared on the end of his finger. Quickly he damped it and shook his hand as if the witch-light had burned him. Then he sucked the finger, making a rueful face.

Kalen giggled. "I don't burn myssself," she announced proudly and imitated the trick, holding the flame much longer than Ackerly did.

He watched her face for signs of fatigue. Her gray eyes remained calm and shining long after he would have collapsed from sustaining the spell.

"That's a very nice fire, Kalen. Can you do anything else?"

"Sieur Moncriith says I mustn't. He says the Stargods won't like it if demons find me cause I can work magic."

Curse the wandering misfit. This wasn't the first potential apprentice who'd had magic scared out of them by the wandering preacher. Ackerly had sympathized with Moncriith when it cost him nothing and gained him an ally. But now the Bloodmage stood between him and gold.

"The Stargods only get angry if you use your magic for bad things, like hurting a pet cat or making your brothers look like fools. Surely it wouldn't hurt if you showed me your special secret." Ackerly opened his eyes wide, willing the child to trust him.

"But it's a secret," she protested, looking up at her mother. The woman caressed the girl's hair soothingly. The father glared hard at her, lifting his upper lip in an almost sneer.

"Then perhaps you can show me if we go out into the corridor where no one else can see?" Ackerly held out his hand to her.

Her mother prodded the girl's back with an open hand. "It's all right, Kalen. He won't hurt you, and we won't tell Sieur Moncriith when we see him."

Shyly, Kalen put her tiny hand into Ackerly's pudgy one. Ackerly stood up stiffly and walked her through the open doorway of his office. A few weeks ago this large room had been Nimbulan's private study. Only one of many things Ackerly had claimed as his inheritance from his former master.

Now he was Master of the School for Magicians. He knew how to run a school that earned money instead of draining it from Nimbulan's purse. Acquiring a truly talented child could fill his coffers faster.

In the long echoing hallway, Ackerly sat on the empty bench where supplicants usually waited for him. Kalen's family was the last of the day's applicants. No one else lingered within sight.

Kalen climbed up beside him. She sat with her hands in her lap and her feet swinging above the floor. She looked out the narrow window to the central courtyard rather than at Ackerly.

"Now will you show me what you can do, Kalen?"

Every door along the corridor slammed shut, loudly and without the aid of human hands.

Ackerly jumped at the sudden noise. "Very good, Kalen. Can you open them, too?"

She nodded as each door in turn creaked open, one right after the other, starting at the far end and progressing to his own office. A tiny smile twitched at the corner of her mouth. "Want to see what else?" She didn't lisp now.

Ackerly nodded, trying not to show how impressed he was by the strength of her talent, nor question the sudden confidence in her demeanor. Telekinesis and fire before the age of ten! She'd match Nimbulan in power, if she took to disciplined training.

Kalen closed her eyes in concentration. Ackerly watched her small face scrunch up. Her skin turned pale beneath her muddy brown braids and the spray of freckles across her nose. Was that a touch of auburn in her hair? Red hair usually accompanied a magical talent inherited from the Stargods. Neither of her parents showed a trace of red in their hair.

Suddenly he lost touch with the Kardia. Vertigo sent his vision whirling. His stomach dropped into his feet. The distress passed quickly and he looked down. The bench floated an arm's length above the stone floor. Slowly, Kalen turned the bench, with them on it, around and gently set them back down.

"Very good, Kalen. I think we've found a place for you here in the school." Ackerly jumped off the bench before she sent him flying again.

If her communication spells developed as easily, she could keep him in contact with the far corners of Coronnan and beyond.

Visions of gold piling up as he controlled a network of Battlemages from the school almost sent him into sexual ecstasy. Lords would have to come to him for access to any magician!

"With talent like hers, you shouldn't need quite so much money," her father stated, standing in the doorway. His brown eyes turned cold and calculating. "You'll be able to sell her services earlier than most apprentices. You should pay us for the privilege of training her."

No sign of gold winked at Ackerly from the mother's hands where she stood beside her husband. She refused to look at anything but the floor. Her posture reminded him of someone. . . . The name "Guiilia" jumped into Ackerly's mind. He wondered how he knew that.

Ackerly swallowed, trying to think. He needed that gold, not half memories of a quick tumble in the hay somewhere on his journeys. "Training is very expensive. Kalen must have books, equipment, and a variety of teachers, who must be paid. There is rent and food and firewood to be purchased."

Kalen's father held up a hand to stop Ackerly's protests before he uttered them. "Perhaps we can strike a bargain. You need a steward, someone to deal with suppliers. Someone who can travel and find your books and special equipment, as well as recruit new students who have gold to pay in tuition. Parents will pay more if you provide someone to oversee the raising of your students in matters other than magic. They are, after all, children in need of parents. My wife is an excellent cook. Our other children can run errands. Take in the entire family and you won't need to rely upon Lord Quinnault for servants and supplies. You will be beholden to no one and can sell the services of magicians to the highest bidder rather than give them away to the lord to whom you owe your livelihood."

"I can pay little. The school is not yet large and profitable." Ackerly stalled.

"For now, food and shelter will suffice. In a few moons, when we are all settled we can discuss my salary. A percentage of the profits, perhaps."

CHAPTER 21

Nimbulan watched Erda, the ancient witchwoman of the Rover clan, strum a lute lightly. The soft notes drifted around the large single-roomed lodge where the extended family had settled for the Winter. Beside the central hearth, Maia complemented the quiet melody with a lilting descant on a wooden flute. Her green bodice and yellow headscarf played games with the colors of the flames. Highlights of bronze and gold flushed her face with intriguing shadows and planes.

Ah, Maia. He smiled at the thoughts of her nimble fingers stroking fiery music through his veins as they lay together beneath piles of warm furs each night.

At first he'd been hesitant to indulge himself in her softly rounded body, but privacy was an implied thing in this close-knit clan. Living so close together they simply ignored each other when appropriate. Drifting to sleep with the sounds of other couples making love had quickly dispelled his shyness.

The tune shifted to a more intense rhythm. The melody bounced into a compelling variation that set his toes twitching. Across the fire, a middle-aged woman and her man began a dance. They stamped their feet in counterpoint to the flute. She flipped her skirts, showing off shapely calves and knees. He bumped her hips with his own and clapped his hands over his head. In another quick gesture, his fingers tangled with the ties of her bodice, loosening them. Someone beat a new cadence against a skin drum. Others joined the suggestive bumping dance.

Nimbulan straightened from his recline against a makeshift backrest of packs. Maia grinned and winked at him around the flute. Her eyes twinkled mischievously. The mole at the side of her mouth taunted him as she puckered her lips to blow into the flute rather than into his ear. He winked back, knowing the delights she promised later.

How could he have believed himself content with his semicelibate life before joining the Rovers? To them sex was a open and joyous affirmation of life, not some furtive fumbling in the dark—paid for and quickly forgotten.

He leaned back again, watching the dancers. This clan made their own amusements. Night after night they found something new to while away the long hours of Winter darkness. Music dominated their evenings and their days. They all worked hard at assigned tasks, then spent the rest of their time in pursuit of pleasure. He was amazed at the number of hours he had each day for contemplation, and enjoyment.

No bickering and passing off of responsibility among these people. Nor any question of authority. They all knew who led them and what their role in the clan was. Sometimes, Nimbulan wondered if their minds were all connected, passing thoughts and commands back and forth.

What an interesting idea. If he could figure out how to do that, then his school could train magicians to truly work as a team, even if they never learned to properly join their magic.

An ache of regret formed a knot in his throat. He missed his boys. But he couldn't return to them yet. He had secrets to learn.

Someone had tried to murder him to keep him from pursuing his quest for unity among magicians. He had to be careful.

An image of Powwell's freckles turning darker against his pale skin as he concentrated on a spell, invaded his mind along with an intense wave of loneliness. He pictured Powwell turning his wide gray eyes up to him, begging for an easy answer.

And Rollett, the orphaned apprentice who stood by his side in battle. Without his keen observations of all that happened during the battle, many of Nimbulan's spells might be misdirected. Rollett, who looked to him as a father. . . .

He gulped and pushed the emotions aside. This lazy routine of wandering was his life for now. The Rovers had accepted him as one of their own—mostly. He needed their complete trust before they'd show him the secrets of their rituals.

"My family works together very well, does it not, Lan?" Televarn sat beside him.

"You move as quietly as a cat. You should announce yourself." Nimbulan breathed deeply, trying to quiet his racing heart. People had never startled him before he met the clan. His magic hummed a warning whenever someone approached. How did Televarn avoid his natural alarms? He couldn't detect any countermagic.

How had the Rover known the precise angle of his thoughts?

"Why should we announce ourselves? Enemies could be warned as easily as family."

Without that sense of awareness, Nimbulan would never truly belong to them. Some of the warmth went out of the lodge and his life. His longing to return to his boys and the school intensified. He belonged there.

"There are ways for you to participate in our *Kardiagenea,* friend," Televarn said casually, watching the dancers rather than Nimbulan.

"*Kardiagenea,*" Nimbulan murmured and stroked his new beard. "You make your own Kardia? Impossible." While his words denied the process, his heart leaped into his throat with eager anticipation. Televarn offered him a chance to share in the clan's unique bonding. Perhaps they'd finally reveal some of their magic.

"No, we seek to become the Kardia. All the elements and the cardinal directions combined. We merge with the blue lines that lace the surface of the land, connected by energy to the source of all knowledge, all magic, all life. Think of it, Lan. You could share the most intimate relationship of all. Better than joining your body to Maia's. You would join yourself to all life in your thoughts, your emotions, your very being." Excitement tinged Televarn's voice, infecting Nimbulan with the possibilities.

"How is this done?"

"With magic. Special magic."

"How can you know that I am capable of this magic?"

"You are a powerful magician. I sensed it the first moment we met. I knew it when you refused to give your true name."

"You have not asked for proof of my magic."

"Rovers know when they are in the presence of one who can work our magic. It is part of the *Kardiagenea*. We need no proof that you have Rover blood in you."

"If I have Rover blood in me, then why am I not part of the *Kardiagenea* already?" Part of him screamed a denial that any of his ancestors had stooped so low as to introduce Rover blood into the aristocratic family. He might be only the second son of a second son with no chance to inherit land or title, but he was proud of the lineage traceable back to the time of the Stargods. His dark auburn hair—before gray had faded much of it—proclaimed his pure ancestry.

"You need to be awakened if you are not born among us and exposed to the *Kardiagenea* from the moment of conception. Maia wants another child. Our clan needs more children. Children are the only true wealth of Rovers. You must be truly one of us before the child is conceived."

"You have too many mouths to feed now, Televarn." Nimbulan wasn't about to dash the man's hopes and deny himself access to this new magic. True magicians rarely sired children, and females with magic never carried a child to term. That was a fact of life he'd tried to compensate for with his numerous apprentices over the years, seeking a son or daughter in each one who came to him for training.

He'd lost them all to disease, accident, betrayal. Keegan's death had been the worst loss of all. The emptiness in him yearned to be filled. Televarn offered him the chance. . . .

"Our children are often born sickly. We mate too closely within the clan. Soon we must invoke the ancient laws against incest and banish all the young men to other clans as soon as they mature."

Nimbulan winced at the sense of loss each parent must feel if the boys were sent elsewhere, never to return.

"Your child will be healthy and wouldn't have to be banished," Televarn whispered.

"I would like a child of my own."

"As would I, but all the women of my family are too

close to me. Many of the clans who might offer me a bride are also too close, or feuding with us. I must seek a mate elsewhere." A wistful look came over Televarn's face as he looked into the distance.

Nimbulan sensed his mind floating to a different time and place. A woman who eluded him? "How does this magic work?"

Televarn shook himself lightly, as if to banish his far away thoughts. "We have rituals that must be performed precisely. Any variation breaks our contact with the Kardia, and we must begin again. Interrupting a ritual, once we have begun is death. A horrible death as the forces of sun, moon, and Kardia align and crush the one who interferes with the harmony. Are you willing to risk joining us tonight, as the full moon reaches its highest arc? We must begin soon for the ritual to climax at the proper moment. Timing is as essential as form."

"If the ritual is so dangerous, why do you risk it?" Once he learned it, would he dare teach it to apprentices?

"For the reward of unity. Will you join us tonight, Lan?"

Across the fire, Maia stood up. As she bent to place her flute on the floor beside her stool, her bodice gaped open to reveal the full globes of her breasts. She lifted her head and smiled invitingly to Nimbulan.

"You will join with her afterward, and her thoughts will be yours. You will feel what she feels, know what she knows, and never lose the awareness of her presence again," Televarn whispered.

"What must I do?" Nimbulan swallowed deeply, trying to restrain his desire for the woman and his need to belong to someone. This ritual might prove the beginning of a whole new system of magic that would allow magicians to join their powers. Then, and only then, could they impose ethics and honor on all magicians. He could remove magic from the wars and politics allowing a natural balance of power to bring peace to Coronnan at last.

But once he learned this magic, he'd have to leave the clan and Maia.

* * *

"Forget the cold, soon the magic will take you," Maia breathed in Nimbulan's ear. She squeezed his hand and let it drop. Her scent lingered in the frosty air as she moved into her place in the ring of people outside the lodge.

Every adult in the clan gathered in a circle around their Winter home. They alternated male and female in even numbers. Televarn was the only unmatched person. He walked around the outside perimeter of people, lost in his own thoughts, mumbling to himself and breathing deeply.

Nimbulan recognized his exercises as the beginning of a trance. The form of magic might be different, but a trance was a universal ingredient, essential for the magic to work with a body.

He, too, inhaled on a ritual three counts, held it another three counts, and exhaled on the same rhythm. The women on either side of him did the same. Visibly their muscles relaxed and so did his. The chill Winter night, the hand's span of packed snow, the glittering stars in the clear sky, all receded from his consciousness.

A second deep breath in three counts, hold three, release three, gave him access to the void. The blackness beckoned, urging him to take that third deep breath and release his body.

"Not yet, Lan. Wait for the rest of us," a voice reminded him.

Televarn? Possible. He didn't care. Only the trance and the void tugging at him in opposite directions mattered. He felt stretched almost to the point of dissipating into mist.

The circle of people began moving to his right, widdershins, along the path of the moon. Each left hand held a candle. Every right hand circled in a complicated gesture, fingers weaving. He followed them, imitating every movement.

Televarn wove in and out among them, odd man out and the binding force of the whole.

Erda, who had strummed the lute, uttered the first phrase of a chant in an ancient language Nimbulan didn't understand: the ancient pictorial language represented in the embroidery they all wore. The next person to her right repeated the phrase, then the next, and the next around the circle. By the time the words had reached Nimbulan, they had become a one-note song, sung to the peculiar rhythm of stamping feet and twisting hands.

A web of energy, sparkling white, like snow crystals, followed Televarn's progress through the clan. In and out, around and around.

A thrumming sound rose through Nimbulan's feet, into his body and out his hands along the growing intricacy of the magic. The pulsing energy shifted to match the vibrations of the Kardia beneath him. He looked up to the clear sky and the cold white stars beyond. The web extended up and through their patterns as if the ley lines of Kardia Hodos wound their way through the universe and he was at their center. All of it hummed and danced in tune.

He was caught up in the wonder of the music of life, all connected, all in tune, all one.

The magic spread inward, as well as outward, engulfing the lodge. A dome of shimmering white enveloped the clan and their home. The lodge became a piece of the magnificent web, so much in tune with the clan and the magic that it ceased to stand out as a man-made structure in the midst of the wild creation of the Stargods.

The energy dome magnified before his vision. He saw each filament of magic, woven into the intricate protection. The web began and ended with Televarn's heart, stretching out to each person in the clan, binding them all together. Nimbulan saw the common element in their blood that allowed them to work this wonderful magic. A tiny amount of it showed clearly in his own life force.

Suddenly knowledge of the great-great, multi-great grandmother who took a Rover as a lover awoke in him. Unhappy in her marriage, she cherished her fifth child sired by her lover rather than her husband. Four children stood between the child and inheritance. She had been certain the exotic heritage of the boy would never taint the lords of Baathalzan's pure line of descent from the Stargods. Fate had eliminated all other heirs, war and disease taking them one after another. The Rover's secret child had inherited and survived to sire more children. Much diluted, the *Kardiagenea,* the ability to tap the magic of all life in concert with others of his kind, had come down to Nimbulan.

A wobble in the web of magic filaments revealed imperfections in the inborn talents of many of these people. The ones with the purest Rover blood, the ones who showed signs of diminished intelligence and bone deformations due to inbreeding, had weak and warped talents.

The clan needed the strength of outside blood to strengthen the magical talent inbreeding destroyed.

Nimbulan reached out and traced a filament of this web of life extending from his own body to that of Maia. No weakness showed in her.

His mind melded with hers. He saw through her eyes, sensed the powerful unity of the spell, felt the cold ground beneath her bare feet, knew the longing in her body for the joy of sex tinged with the need to conceive another child now that her first baby was weaned. Her feminine longing, bordering on an ache, returned to him, enhancing his own desire. He explored the sensations with wonder.

Tentatively, he reached beyond Maia to Televarn's uncle and knew the satisfaction of completing the protective ritual properly with exact numbers of male and female. Nimbulan's presence in the clan was welcome if for no other reason.

On and on around the circle, Nimbulan touched briefly each member of the clan. Their personalities opened to him as they never had before. And he knew they would never again be able to creep up behind him in surprise.

Finally he touched the last person in the circle and centered his consciousness on Televarn. The man's thoughts did not open. Nimbulan could not share the sensations of the Rover king's body. Yet he sensed Televarn was totally connected to every person in the circle by a one-way path of communication. Televarn dominated every personality in the clan.

The Rover king completed the ritual by turning three times deosil, sunwise, before the only door of the lodge. The web snapped inward, collapsing into the Rover's body as if he had pulled a flexible string.

The Winter lodge was now protected from discovery by outsiders. Would the same protection prevent Nimbulan from escaping with the secret of Rover ritual magic?

The connections to the others in the clan dissolved. Nimbulan's entire body tingled with reserve vibrations.

He could increase that humming music of life and recapture the unity within the spell. If the others helped. If they wished. The absence of their minds in his mind left him curiously empty and refreshed at the same time.

He concentrated on his hand, willing the magic to reach out and connect him to Maia once more. Wispy tendrils of magic shot from his fingertips but stretched toward Televarn, not his lover. He retracted the probe and moved closer and closer to Maia until his hand rested on her shoulder. She did not respond to his tentative touch. All her attention was on Televarn.

Televarn, whose mind and intentions had remained closed to Nimbulan's probe. Televarn, who commanded this clan and had ordered Maia to lie with Nimbulan. New blood in the clan was more important than any of their personal desires and emotions. Televarn directed Maia's love affair with Nimbulan as he directed everyone within the clan with direct mind-to-mind control.

Nimbulan shuddered in the cold. If he took this system of magic to his apprentices, would they, too, become totally dependent upon one dictatorial mind? Would the absence of Rover blood in their heritage prevent them from performing this ritual?

A more shattering thought shot ice through his blood. Televarn might have inserted the seeds of mind-to-mind control in Nimbulan's brain without him knowing it. If he had, there was a good chance Nimbulan might not be able to break it, or escape it.

CHAPTER 22

"I don't like you very much, Moncriith." Lord Kammeryl d'Astrismos paced his Great Hall. His fingers twitched as he fussed with the alignment of a bench against the trestle table, then moved on to kick at the fresh rushes and finger a tapestry. "Give me one good reason why I should put up with your preaching and the stench of old blood that surrounds you one more day."

Stargods, can't you stand still one moment! Moncriith clenched his teeth rather than blurt out his thoughts. The lord's constant prowl around the room made him dizzy. Thank the Stargods none of the lord's toadies were present to rush in a new bed partner. The denizens of this dark castle seemed willing to sacrifice anything to avoid one of Kammeryl d'Astrismos' rages. This restlessness was always the first warning sign of an imbalance in his temper. An imbalance caused by his own self-doubt. Only deflowering a virgin returned his self-confidence.

Otherwise, he'd been known to set out on a lightning raid, burning, pillaging, and raping every village he encountered—including some of his own.

Just last week Kammeryl had informed his valet, who informed the sergeant of the guard who informed Moncriith that he "felt like a god," when he claimed a girl's, or boy's virginity and initiated them into the joys—and pains—of sex. Moncriith wondered if Kammeryl had invented his descent from the Stargods and suffered major self-doubt when he remembered his lies.

The lord's red hair, the visible symbol of his Stargod heritage, was definitely the result of dyes. He'd cropped his hair short to fit under a war helm today. A new, more-vibrant-than-usual shade of red colored it.

"You will tolerate me, Lord Kammeryl, because your

retainers would rebel if you threw me out." Moncriith remained serenely still and calm in the face of Kammeryl's increasing restlessness. He had no self-doubts to plague him into rash actions.

Kammeryl stopped in his tracks. He stared a long moment into Moncriith's eyes. Amazement and possibly a little fear colored his expression. Then he threw back his head and laughed, loud and long.

"Do you think my people will honor your prattling warnings of demon possession over their oath of loyalty to me?" Kammeryl asked, wiping tears of mirth from his eyes with his sleeve. The moment he recovered, he resumed his pacing. "No one will renounce their oath to me because they know I will exact a swift and terrible vengeance."

"No, Lord Kammeryl, I don't believe they will follow me rather than you. I *know* they will. Preservation of their souls is more important than any temporal power. They know I may slaughter a goat or sheep in performance of my rituals. I do not lie about what I do, nor do I hide behind threats. One animal is a small price compared to losing an entire village to one of your raids. Are you certain a demon does not possess you? The Stargods desert those who succumb to the lure of demon power." Moncriith sat easily into the chair beside the lord's demi-throne. He leaned back into the depths of the pillows meant to cushion the delicate bones of the lady of the manor.

The chair had been empty for many years and was not likely to be filled by a "lady" ever again. Kammeryl d'Astrismos had an heir by his long-dead wife. He needed no other consort as long as the constant parade of virginal bed partners satisfied him.

"Why? Why would anyone accept you as a leader, Moncriith? You own no land or gold. You have no trading empire. The temple threw you out years ago. The magicians scoff at you. What can you offer the rabble? Not protection, not food, no *tangible* power of any kind," Kammeryl barked, leaning over Moncriith's chair, hands resting on the padded arms. The knuckles on his hands showed white.

"I have shown them the demons who feed upon war—

demons who inhabit the bodies of magicians and witches—and possibly lords—and force them to perpetuate wars. The people want relief from war. I have shown them a way to get it. We must kill all of the magicians." Moncriith relaxed into the chair, more certain than ever of his control over Kammeryl d'Astrismos and his followers. "Support of me would prove to one and all that demons do not possess you."

"Relief from war? Bah! Peace is an archaic concept, a myth as unreal as dragons and flywackets." Kammeryl resumed his pacing, glaring at any servant who dared enter the Great Hall to prepare it for the evening meal.

"And yet, at your last battle many hardened soldiers reported seeing both a dragon and a flywacket—evil demons though they are." Moncriith crossed himself. He'd suffered several serious scratches from Myrilandel's flywacket—clear proof of her association with demons. "Think about it, Lord Kammeryl. Think of the power you would wield if you brought peace to Coronnan. Tax revenues. Trade profits. Ambassadors from all over the world bringing you gifts of gold, silk, and slaves."

"Slaves are illegal in Coronnan." Kammeryl paused in his pacing, right hand rubbing his chin in consideration. The florid color in his cheeks intensified and his eyes glowed. Some poor child would end up beaten and bruised when the lord released his emotions in bed.

Moncriith felt a reaching out of his magic talent in anticipation of the unknown child's pain. He preferred fueling his magic with the blood of his enemies. His spells had a sharper focus when combined with anger and hatred. For now he'd settle for absorbing the power of pain inflicted by another.

"As the ruler of a united Coronnan, you would make your own laws. Think of the exotic treasures that could be yours for the asking. Nubile young slaves taught from childhood to please a man of your appetites, without having been touched, waiting for you to tap their erotic knowledge." Moncriith held back a smirk. No sense in letting this lord know he was being manipulated. He had no intention of allowing the likes of Kammeryl d'Astrismos to survive long enough to reap the benefits of peace. His temporal power was necessary now as a catalyst for the populace. As soon as the mission had been accomplished, all of the demon-possessed lords and their evil magicians would perish in the flames. Just like Myrilandel and her familiar.

"Coronnan can't know peace until it is united. Conquering the other lords is the only way to do that. Quinnault de Tanos and his band of minor landholders can't stand against me in battle." Kammeryl resumed his pacing, deep in thought rather than restlessly seeking a diversion. He clasped his hands behind his back, a sure signal that his restlessness was appeased by serious thought for the moment.

"What if every peasant in the land acknowledged you as their lord, including those who follow de Tanos?" Moncriith dangled the possibility like bait.

"The other lords still have armies to force their tithes and loyalty."

"But if every soldier was occupied enforcing taxes and loyalty, they wouldn't be available to battle you and your armies."

"Some of the lesser lords would have to offer me alliances to maintain order. *Me,* instead of de Tanos," Kammeryl mused, counting on his fingers. He stopped at eight—Quinnault's four and four others who wavered back and forth with their loyalty. The exact number of lords Moncriith figured would flock to Kammeryl's side for protection.

"Alliances lead to unity. Six small lords command more troops and land than any one of the major lords. Begin now, before the campaign season and by the time the fields are planted, no one lord could stand against you."

"What if they band together against me, like de Tanos is trying?"

"They can't if all their peasants desert them for you. Only I can make certain they do."

"Why should I trust you to convert these people to me?"

"You must learn to trust someone, or your reign will never be easy. Trust the Stargods, Kammeryl d'Astrismos. Your family name means 'son of the three stars.' You are the only *legal* descendant of the Stargods. Trust me. Trust the vision the Stargods have given me." Moncriith followed the lord, whispering seductively in his ear. Power, after all, was as much an aphrodisiac as all the virgins in the world.

"You can't carry the true word of the Stargods. The priests threw you out for working blood magic."

"They exiled me from their ranks because they are afraid of me. Afraid that I alone was granted a true vision of the demons that truly rule Coronnan. If they accepted me, they'd have to acknowledge the demons that possess them and kill themselves to be rid of them."

No sense in letting Kammeryl know that the priests had removed Moncriith from the temple because he refused traditional methods of magic. He could use those methods but chose not to. He'd seen how traditional magic caused death and destruction while promising life and healing. He preferred the honesty of drawing blood to fuel magic rather than inflicting murder as a result of magic gone awry.

Priests of the temple were now so sheltered from life that their only contact with magic included meaningless rituals and passing apprentices through the trial by Tambootie smoke.

Moncriith shuddered in memory of his own trial.

"You pursue only a vision born of your imagination, Moncriith." Kammeryl resumed his restless wanderings.

"My vision was born of the Stargods and their desire for peace in Coronnan. When all of Kardia Hodos fell victim to the plague so many generations ago, the Stargods came here, to Coronnan. They gave our people the cure for the plague. We are their chosen people. Think how they must grieve at the way we ravage the land and each other with these endless wars. Think with your heart and your head; not your dick, Kammeryl. Think and know what destiny of greatness the Stargods offer you through me."

"What do you suggest as a first step?"

"First, we destroy the magicians. Lord Quinnault's School for Magicians is a good place to start. Nimbulan is dead. They no longer have a strong leader to rally them against you. And if you kill Quinnault at the same time, his alliance of minor lords will fall apart. Then, we offer a marriage alliance with Lord Sauria. His lands border

Quinnault's. He longs for access to the Great Bay. You can divide the islands and the trade profits between you."

* * *

"Magic isn't fun anymore," Kalen complained to Powwell.

Ackerly leaned closer to the door that separated him from his two most promising students. The tone in the girl's voice and the absence of her lisp alerted him to trouble. He heightened his senses a little with magic so he could hear the entire conversation.

"Magic isn't supposed to be fun. It's work. Hard work," Powwell returned.

The children were supposed to be sweeping the floors of the bedrooms in this wing. Powwell had already discovered that brooms pushed by muscles didn't tire him as easily as brooms pushed by magic.

"Well, I don't want to do it anymore. I'm tired, and I ache, and my head spins when *he* gives us those drugs." A thump followed that pronouncement as if Kalen plunked herself down on the floor, arms crossed in her usual pouting position. Ackerly had come to dread the times Kalen resorted to a pout. Underneath the innocent charm, the little girl hid a stubborn streak that taxed the patience of all fifty inhabitants of the school. Not even her doting mother or her coldly calculating father could coax her out of a good pout.

"The Tambootie is necessary to working magic," Powwell said thoughtfully.

Ackerly could almost see the boy biting his lip in indecision. A terrible habit he'd have to make Powwell break. Paying clients wouldn't rent the services of a magician who appeared indecisive.

"I never needed doses of the weed before I came here, and I did a lot more magic than *he* thinks I do now. Besides the drugs make me sick to my stomach. I can't concentrate when I'm about to heave," Kalen said.

"Magic's a lot easier for me when I take the drugs. But it nauseates me, too. What did you mean you worked more magic than Ackerly thinks you do now? Aren't you doing everything he asks?" A clatter of a dropped broom followed Powwell's words.

"Of course not. I never let anyone know precisely how much I can do. Sieur Moncriith used to preach against me and make people throw mud at me for summoning witch-light. Sometimes they threw stones to keep us out of the village before we could ask for food and a place to stay. If Moncriith had known I could levitate things, he'd have demanded people burn me. They would have, too." A touch of fear colored Kalen's voice. Ackerly made a note of it.

He hadn't summoned the Bloodmage in many moons. Perhaps now was the time. He could let drop a few hints about the girl in exchange for a small payment. Moncriith paid well for all information. If Moncriith came back, seeking her, maybe Kalen's fear of him would drive her to throw the destructive battle spells she resisted.

"Master Nimbulan trusted Ackerly with everything before he died. We can trust him, too," Powwell said.

Silence followed that statement. Ackerly wondered what was going on in the girl's head. He didn't have enough magic to break through her natural armor.

"I can't trust a man who gives me drugs that make me sick. I'll just pretend I'm a slow learner."

Aha! so that was why Kalen didn't pick up the principles of distant communication as readily as she had fire and telekinesis. Ackerly smiled as he listened. He wondered what would happen if he reduced the doses of Tambootie and turned the lessons into games. Would Kalen be tricked into stretching her magic for the fun of a game?

He pictured himself crawling around on the floor with a bunch of toddlers.

No. These children were too old for such infantile amusements. He hadn't been around children at all since he left home at the age of twelve to become an apprentice magician. None of Druulin's apprentices had had time or energy for play, unless you considered practical jokes and stealing extra blankets play.

What games had he played at ten and twelve? He remembered vaguely boisterous contests with balls and sticks, of hide-and-go seek, of follow my leader. Yes, he could still play those games—but with a magic twist.

Where? Not outdoors where such rambunctious games were meant to be played. Winter's last storms still raged around their ears with snow and howling winds. When the thaw came, the island would be a sea of mud. He hoped that day was not far off. He'd had enough of chilblains and runny noses. Perhaps he could organize games in the refectory. The trestle tables and benches could be pushed aside after each meal. The center of that long hall would make an adequate ball field. The children would have to learn control to keep witchballs confined and not knock over rushlights and candles. The rest of the school provided infinite hiding places and obstacles to overcome. Yes, he'd start the games tonight.

But he wouldn't eliminate the Tambootie from the curriculum. He needed the apprentices to become dependent on it. Just as Nimbulan had. Then, gifts of the drug—or withholding of it—became tools. Tools to keep his pet magicians performing while he collected enormous rental fees for their services.

He almost tasted the gold as if he were already biting into the coins to test their purity. The weight of them filled his hands and pockets with satisfaction.

Soon. Soon the school would begin to pay. He just had to be patient a little longer.

Ackerly turned away from his eavesdropping, satisfied he had outsmarted two very bright children.

Kalen's voice rose once more, but he didn't pay attention to her complaints. He'd learned what he needed.

* * *

"He's gone now, Powwell." Kalen pressed her ear to the door.

"Are you sure?"

"Of course I'm sure. His aura left an imprint on the door. Now it's fading."

"I can't see it."

"Look with your magic, not your eyes."

"You sound just like Nimbulan." Tears filled Powwell's eyes. "I wish you could have known him."

"He sounds like he was more honest than anyone else at this *s'murghing* school."

"We're not supposed to curse, Kalen," Powwell gasped.

"There's no better word to describe this place. I wish Papa had never brought me here." She stamped her foot and plopped down on the floor again, arms crossed over her skinny chest. She scrunched up her face as if trying not to cry. "I want to go home to our house in Baria. It was the most beautiful house ever. I want to go back to the time before Lord Hanic burned the town, before Moncriith discovered me. Before magic was more than a bright, shiny toy."

"You haven't gone hungry since you came here. And you haven't had to sleep in the fields, cold and wet," Powwell reminded her.

"That's true. But before we came, I wasn't sick all the time from the drugs, and if I got tired, it was from walking and carrying my baby brother, not from forcing strange magic. Magic that could hurt someone if I lose control. *He* can't work real magic, so he doesn't know how bad I feel all the time."

"Master Ackerly is a good teacher. He explains things ever so simply."

"Have you ever seen *him* work any magic?"

"N . . . no."

"That's 'cause he's got precious little talent for magic. What he does is mostly illusion. He makes you think he's doing magic. Like he made you think Nimbulan was dead."

"But he was! I saw him die." Powwell's eyes went wide with disbelief and hope at the same time. "What makes you think the master lived?"

"His niche in the crypt is empty. The body's gone, but his formal robes are there, neatly folded."

"Master always was obsessed with neatness and order when he wasn't too deep in a drug trance. He'd never leave anything untidy after a good sleep and a full day without a dose. Do you suppose the Stargods took him to heaven in their cloud of silver fire?"

"No. I think he woke up from a deep trance and walked away. That's what I'd do. That's what I want to do."

"You're making this up. I saw Master Nimbulan die. I helped lay him in the niche." Powwell jumped up from where he sat on the floor. Suddenly the room was too small, the air too close. He couldn't believe what this little girl . . . this troublemaker, said. If she was right, he couldn't stay here. He'd have to go in search of his true master, Nimbulan. He'd have to leave the security of the school. This was the first place he'd ever lived where the taint of bastardy didn't follow him. Every village his mother moved to, even when she claimed to be widowed—a common enough occurrence these days—someone always found out that his father was a wandering misfit who hadn't bothered to return and marry the daughter of his host. He'd promised to come back. But promises were easily broken.

"I'll show you the empty crypt, Powwell," Kalen whispered as if afraid Ackerly might return and overhear.

Powwell stared at the floor, wondering if he had the courage to follow her and discover the truth.

CHAPTER 23

Myri poured another bucket of water over the hot rocks in the brazier. Aromatic steam gushed upward, filling the tiny hut with the scent of crushed herbs and a little of the essential oil of the Tambootie. The old woman lying on the thin pallet coughed heavily in the onslaught of steam.

The coughing spasm continued, racking her frail old body with shudders, robbing her of air, slowly choking life from her.

Each time Karry's grandmother gasped for air or clutched her chest in pain, Myri endured the same. Her strength faded almost as rapidly as the old woman's.

(Resist the need to Heal with magic,) the voices whispered to her as they had guided her all night.

"I can't let her die," Myri sobbed. She'd tried every mundane remedy she could think of. Granny Katia's fever and cough only worsened.

(Hold back. Don't waste your strength on her. She will die anyway.)

Myri gritted her teeth and sought the courage to ignore the voices. Resolutely, she placed her hand on the old woman's chest. Blue sparks shot into the air the moment she made contact. She poured her energy deep into Granny Katia, pulling fluid away from her lungs and attacking the fever.

She wished for Amaranth's comforting presence, but knew the superstitious villagers feared that cats sucked breath out of babies and ailing old people. They'd forbidden her to bring her familiar into Granny Katia's home.

Another great spasm of coughs racked the old woman's body. Shudders ran the length of her wasted frame. Myri helped her patient bend over and expel the fluid in her lungs.

"Drink some water now, Granny Katia." She held a small cup to the old woman's lips, still keeping one hand on her back. Strength continued to drain out of Myri into her patient.

Granny Katia tried to push the cup away. Her hands were so feeble she barely touched the cup.

(You can't help her. She's too ill, too weak. Save yourself. Your strength is needed elsewhere.)

An uneasiness in the back of Myri's neck, like an itch that got worse with scratching, followed the whisper in the back of her mind. She knew a sudden urge to pack her few possessions and move Southward. She could travel no farther East.

She pushed the compulsion aside. She'd had enough of being manipulated by magic when she was with Televarn.

"Please, Granny. You have to drink." *Karry and the other villagers will never forgive me if you die. They'll blame me, threaten me, drive me away.*

Or burn me. The villagers had heard Moncriith preach. If Granny Katia died, they would blame her.

"I want to stay here. This village feels like home." *You promised me a home,* she accused the voices.

The old woman passed into uneasy sleep before Myri could force more than a few drops past her thin lips. Myri's talent reached out. She poured more magic into Granny Katia, trying once more to draw fluid out of her lungs.

Dizziness scattered Myri's senses. She had trouble concentrating on the healing. Her lungs felt heavy and her breath rattled when she exhaled. Her eyes refused to focus. The walls of the tiny hut spun around her. She dropped her head and scrunched her eyes closed.

"If you don't take the medicine, you'll die, Granny. You have to drink," she said when the room righted itself and she could concentrate once more.

The old woman roused slightly and took two small sips before losing consciousness again.

Myri bathed Granny's fevered brow with a cool cloth. The old woman's skin felt too dry and thin, like a fragile leaf ready to fall in Autumn. The fever burned her vitality like fuel in a hearth. Every ragged breath stole air from Myri's lungs as well.

"The cure isn't working, Myri." Karry stood in the low doorway of the hut, arms crossed, grief already dragging down the corners of her mouth.

"I'm sorry. I don't know what else to do for her." Myri bowed her head.

"I can see that you have tried all within your power." Karry looked pointedly at the blue glow of energy surrounding Myri's hand where it lay against Granny's shrunken chest.

Myri resisted the instinct to jerk her hand away and hide the evidence of magic. She tried distracting Karry's gaze by pressing the cup of medicine on Granny once more.

"Leave off with your smelly cures, child," Granny Katia whispered weakly. "Let me die. I'm too old to endure another Festival. 'Tis the Equinox Festival today. A good time to die. Make room for the new lives beginning tonight." She chuckled dryly and coughed again.

This time Myri had to lift her body to a sitting position, so she wouldn't gag. Her lungs gasped in sympathy with the old woman.

Karry rushed to wipe the bloody spittle from her grandmother's mouth. "She's coughing blood now." Fear widened her eyes.

"She's been coughing blood all night," Myri said. She wiped a few drops of blood from her own lips with the back of her hand. Her empathy with her patient had brought the disease into her body already. Would she have the strength to cure herself?

(Leave the woman. Her death is killing you!)

Tremendous heat pushed her hand away from Granny Katia's chest. This time, Myri let the power separate her from her patient.

Karry sat back on her heels. Her face paled, and her hands shook. Amaranth pushed open the door Karry hadn't closed completely and climbed into the pubkeeper's lap. He rubbed his head against her chest, offering his sympathy. She wrapped her arms around the cat, clinging to his body as if he were the spirit of her beloved grandmother.

Granny Katia gasped again as another coughing spasm gripped her. Myri tried to lift her inert shoulders. A curious rattle replaced the old woman's ragged breathing. Air and phlegm tangled in Myri's lungs, too. Katia's eyes glazed and rolled. Her entire body shuddered once and went limp.

A vital part of Myri's talent wrenched away from her body, trying desperately to follow the dying woman into the void. No amount of willpower could control the need to grab her patient's essence and bring it back to the body that was too weak to support it.

Utter blackness closed around Myri.

With a nauseating lurch she found herself back in her own body. She closed her eyes as the hut spun around her, upsetting her tenuous balance.

Silence filled the too-warm room. Gradually, Myri came back to herself, weak and shaking.

Karry clutched her grandmother's hand to her ample breast.

"I'm sorry, Karry. I have nothing left to try." Gently, she closed the sightless eyes.

"Pass easily to your next existence, Granny," Karry murmured.

They sat in silence a moment. Karry rocked on her heels, still clutching Katia's hand. Amaranth purred gentle comfort in her lap.

"I guess I should leave. This village won't look to kindly upon the healer who lost a favorite patient." Myri bowed her head in regret. She liked the people in this little fishing village. She had almost dared hope they would welcome her, let her stay. Maybe even hide her when Moncriith came looking for her.

Magretha had warned her how often villagers preferred to blame healers for every problem and forget the good they had achieved. Most of Myri's childhood had been spent fleeing one village or another—often with Moncriith hot on her heels.

"You don't have to leave, Myri.' Karry reached across her grandmother's failing body to hold Myri's hand. "You saved my Katey and her baby, Katareena. No one else thought to reach in and pull the baby out, ass-backward. If you hadn't, they'd have died and the Katareenas would end with me. And don't forget Yoshi's fever. You cured him last Solstice. We're grateful for those of us you have saved."

"But I couldn't increase the fishing catch. How many of the men blame me for that? They've been drinking heavily for two days, anticipating festival tonight. Some of them get very mean when they are in their cups. We have both broken up a dozen fights a day this Winter. Will they turn on me when drink fires their courage?"

After a long and barren winter, the fish had returned to the bay in the last day or two. But many of the men didn't want to believe in the fish. They'd rather drink and complain and fight among themselves.

More and more frequently, Myri heard the men mutter that the village resided under a curse. If Moncriith arrived and pointed to Myri as the cause, the men were ripe to believe.

She forced herself to think about the pretty flowers and the lilting music nine women practiced by the Equinox Pylons. This village could have been home.

(We will give you a safe home.)

"We want you to stay, Myri." Karry pressed her hand reassuringly. You are welcome to join in the Festival dance tonight."

A moment of longing pressed deep inside Myri. She remembered other Festivals. Lilting music guided her steps widdershins around an Equinox Pylon. Men danced deosil in the same pattern. Each pass brought the men and women closer together, brushing suggestively against each other. A hand reached out and loosened the laces of her bodice—all the girls had painstakingly reversed the order of lacing so the simple garment opened from the top. By the end of the dance, several hands had tugged at her clothing, exposing her breasts, heightening the sexual anticipation of the night.

She clamped down on her desire to join the village in the ancient fertility rites.

Amaranth leaped from Karry's lap to prowl restlessly around Myri's ankles.

(Betrayal!) The voices came sharp and insistent. *(You must leave. Now!)*

"Merow," Amaranth agreed with the voices. He twitched his ears as if listening.

Myri walked to the door, looking out at the preparations for tonight's Festival. She sought a glimpse of something out of the ordinary that might reveal who betrayed her.

From the safety of the cliff edge, children watched mandelphs sporting in the warm currents just beyond the Dragon's Teeth, the wickedly sharp rock formation in the center of the cove. Birds danced in the air above them, dipping down to feed among the rich schools of fish. Winter storms no longer drove them into the depths of the bay beyond the reach of men's nets.

Children, flowers, and wildlife burst with energy on this first day of the new season. The entire planet seemed poised for Spring with abundant life.

She needed to belong to the joyous celebration tonight, perhaps find a permanent mate among the fishermen. Instead she would have to run away again.

(Betrayal.)

She stood rigidly staring at the three times three Equinox Pylon, not seeing it or the floral decorations. Awareness of Karry, the dead woman, the village, faded as she listened only to the voices that had guided her so often.

(Go. Now.) Urgency to be out of the village pressed on her.

(Now.) A circling wind began to whip the tops of nearby trees. Her feet needed to follow the wind.

"I can't stay." Disappointment tugged her toward the Pylon. The voices pulled her in the opposite direction.

(Hurry!)

"The men will be disappointed you won't stay to lift your skirts for your partner in the dance." Karry crossed her grandmother's arms upon her sunken chest and brushed her thin gray hair away from her face.

Myri listened for the voices again, ignoring Karry's persuasion. Did she have time to pack some provisions? The sense of urgency lifted. A little. Not much time. Food and extra clothing were necessary. She wouldn't be coming back here soon.

* * *

"Look with your FarSight, Lan. Look into the storehouses, look into the fishing nets, look at the fertile fields ripe for the first touch of plow and seed," Televarn whispered seductively.

Nimbulan looked down from their hidden perch on the cliffside above the village plateau. To the West of the village, the fields spread wide, ready for tilling. To the East lay the ocean and a cove pierced by a spreading rock formation. Just beyond the jagged spires of rock, screeching gulls dipped often and plucked squirming fish from the warm currents.

"Look at the Equinox Pylon the women decorate. Three times three poles erected over the place where three ley lines meet. Three is a powerful number. It represents the three Stargods. This village is rich in fertility as well as magic." Televarn pointed at the proud collection of stout poles presiding over the center of the village. Weddings, funerals, and judgments all took place at the base. Three times three granted extra blessings to those events.

"Our people are hungry, Lan. These people deny us sustenance."

"We haven't asked them for hospitality yet. Why do you believe they will deny it to us?"

The Rover chieftain irritated Nimbulan with his broad assumptions. Not just on the issue of prejudice against all Rovers, his clan in particular. Every topic of conversation brought a statement of half-truth that Televarn demanded be accepted as words of profound wisdom. The magical control Televarn maintained over the minds of each of his clan ensured they all agreed with him.

Only Nimbulan remained aloof and untouched by that control. Often, though, he sensed the Rover eavesdropping on his thoughts.

Nimbulan knew that not all women were faithless. Not all children were incapable of behaving, not all steeds were stupid, and not every man lost potency with age. He bristled with indignation every time he heard the last accusation. Just because Maia hadn't conceived yet. . . .

"The lords and magicians teach the stupid villagers to distrust us."

"They have good reason if you plan to steal from them without even asking for food or offering to buy it first."

"Rovers do not *buy* what the Stargods should provide them. Food, sledges, steeds . . . these are ours by right. The Stargods decreed we must rove. Therefore, they must provide for us."

"Then we should remind these folk of their obligation to offer us hospitality."

"The teachings of the Stargods have been corrupted." Televarn spat on the sloping ground. "I know from experience they will give us nothing."

"We could offer to work for the food, trade for it, even sing and dance for it."

"Tonight is Festival. They make their own entertainment. At Festival, all villages refuse outsiders so that no foreign seed spreads to their women." The Rover grinned lasciviously. He had remarked often of late that he fancied finding a woman with fair hair and eyes. One woman in particular who had run away from him.

Myrilandel had pale hair and nearly colorless eyes that reflected whatever color was near.

Strange, he hadn't thought of the mysterious witchwoman in many moons. Maia was the only woman who occupied his thoughts. Myrilandel pricked his curiosity with her wild talent and curious visions. Maia satisfied only his lust. He couldn't converse with her beyond where they would make their bed each night now that Spring had arrived and the Rover clan was wandering again.

"Tonight, when the moon is full and the drink flows freely, we can sneak into the village and make off with as much food as we need. Our people won't go to bed with empty bellies for many weeks."

"I still think we should offer to buy the food."

"Coward! No Rover would think such a thing. You can never truly be one of us until you put such craven thoughts aside. You are not worthy of Maia. No wonder her womb has rejected your seed." Televarn backed away. A disgusted sneer spread across his handsome face. His hand reached instinctively for the long dagger he wore on his hip.

"Don't be a prejudiced fool, Televarn." Nimbulan held his hands away from his side to indicate his reluctance to engage in violence. "The safety of the clan should be your first priority. Breaking into that storehouse should be a last resort, after we've tried fishing, or hunting, or asking. What if your men are discovered, and the village turns on them? They have tools and knives that are just as deadly as the pikes and lances of any army." At the end of Winter, not much was left in field and forest to glean or gather, or Nimbulan would have suggested that as well. If the Winter storms that had ravaged all of Coronnan had driven away the fish, this village could be as hungry as the Rovers.

"If they see us in the vicinity, they will guard the storehouse. Any attempt to liberate the food will end in violence, perhaps death." Televarn's eyes narrowed as if he expected Nimbulan to lead the raid and be the first to die.

Nimbulan had no intention of taking part in the theft from innocent, possibly hungry people.

"Do what you must, Televarn. I will go hunting. I will feed our people honestly." Nimbulan turned his back on the village and Televarn.

He took three steps into the depths of the forested hillside and stopped abruptly. He directed his feet to move, but they remained firmly in place.

"Do not walk away from me, magician. I am king of this clan. My word is law."

"Then perhaps I should no longer be a part of your clan." That thought had a strangely liberating feel to it. He hadn't realized how uncomfortable he had become with the lack of privacy, the constant wandering, the uncertainty of each day. Avid curiosity for a different way of life had turned to boredom. No, disgust. He didn't *like* any of the people in the clan, especially Televarn.

He knew a few of the secret rituals now. He could take that information back to school.

His feet refused to move forward. Instead, he found himself turning to face Televarn.

"You cannot leave after you have shared in our rituals, slept with one of our women, broken bread with us." Televarn seemed genuinely confused.

"You said yourself, I was not born to your way of life. I

tried to fit in, to learn your customs. But I do not belong. The time has come for us to part." He wore all the clothing he owned, and his knife. He hadn't become used to his new staff yet and could easily cut another. He had no possessions to retrieve. Best if he just walked away, here and now. He couldn't move.

"I cannot allow that. We taught you our secrets." Televarn shifted his balance, eyes searching the surroundings. For observers, help, a place to run?

"Release me from your control. I will not betray you." But he would. He'd use the secrets to bring unity to magicians all over Coronnan.

"No one outside the clan may share our knowledge. You must stay with us, be truly one with us, or die. You defied me every day when you wouldn't let me into your mind. You deserve to die for that crime alone." Televarn's hand flicked and the long dagger flew out.

Acid sharp pain exploded in Nimbulan's gut. A beautifully decorated knife hilt seemed to be growing from his rib cage. Thick warm blood stained his hand. His blood.

CHAPTER 24

"Do we have to go down there?" Powwell eyed the trapdoor to the crypt with loathing and . . . and fear.

"Yes." Kalen placed her fists on her hips and glared at him.

"I believe you that his body is gone. So you don't have to prove it to me." Powwell mimicked her pose to hide the shaking of his hands. The last time he'd gone into the crypt had been to place the master's limp body into a niche. The darkness and the weight of the Kardia above him had pressed on his lungs until he couldn't breathe. The apprentices and Master Ackerly had formed a semicircle in front of the burial place to say the funeral prayers. Powwell hadn't closed his eyes. He'd been too afraid that the act of diverting his sight from the walls and ceiling would cause them to collapse. As he scanned the other niches, most occupied by decaying skeletons, he'd seen the ghosts of all the other occupants of the crypt rise up to greet Nimbulan and invite him to join them in haunting the ancient monastery.

Powwell hadn't slept well the entire winter, waiting for the ghosts to come for him, too.

Kalen bent to lift the trapdoor hidden behind the altar in the chapel. "You need proof, or you won't run away with me." She grunted under the weight of the door.

Ingrained manners made Powwell rush to help her. "What made you go crawling around down there in the first place?" he asked as she made ready to climb down the ladder carved into the stone wall. He admired her bravery, but he was coming to dread her stubbornness.

She wasn't aggressive and talkative with the others. For them she put on a mask of starry-eyed innocence and awe, lisping sweetly like a child much younger than her ten years. Maybe he was the only person in all of Coronnan she trusted. His chest swelled with pride and protectiveness. He had to follow her into the crypt to prove to himself he'd earned that trust.

Maybe if he left the door open, the Kardia wouldn't weigh so heavily on him. Still he hesitated descending after her until she sent three balls of witchlight circling her head like a crown of glowing fire.

The directionless light illuminated the small crypt better than a hundred torches. It revealed a small square room lined with shelves, much like a library—only the information stored in those shelves was beyond interpretation. Powwell wondered briefly if learning to read the memories of the dead was like learning a new language. He already knew three. His name meant bright in the oldest tongue known to Coronnan. Perhaps he had the intelligence and intuition to decipher the memories of the men who had lived in the monastery long ago.

He shook his head to rid it of the fanciful thoughts. *Snap out of it,* he admonished himself. *I'm just giddy from the closeness of the walls and the low ceiling.*

Kalen beckoned him to follow her into the far corner. The corner where he and the other apprentices had laid Nimbulan's still-warm body so many moons ago.

The body had remained warm though eight hours had passed between the time of Nimbulan's death and his funeral. Why the haste? Eight hours. Not enough time for decent mourning before putting a beloved friend and teacher to rest. Were Rollett and the other apprentices so grief-stricken they didn't question the premature funeral? Perhaps they were all so used to obeying the orders of a master without question they had obeyed blindly—too blindly.

The wrongness of the situation sent his balance awry. He stumbled over a crack in the paving stones. Ackerly had directed the funeral. What did he have to hide?

Suddenly, Powwell believed Kalen's story from the depth of his heart. Though seeming not to breathe, or have a heartbeat, Nimbulan hadn't been dead, but so deep in a trance ordinary means could not revive him.

Given time, the master magician could have awakened

into darkness, hungry, depleted of magic and strength. The winding cloths soaked in preservatives would have bound him so tightly he might not have been able to break free. What terrors had he known? What ghosts haunted him?

Powwell searched the far corners of the crypt for evidence of the spirits of the dead. They had all fled from Kalen's witchlight. Nimbulan might not have had the energy to summon light. Had he gone insane from the haunting?

He looked where Kalen pointed, hoping he wouldn't see what he knew must be. Nimbulan's body, huddled in agonizing terror as he died a second time, alone and friendless in a crypt as a dark as the void.

Powwell swallowed deeply and forced his eyes open.

The second niche above the floor, last row on the southern side, was empty.

* * *

"Which way?" Myri asked the voices as she cuddled Amaranth in her arms. He hadn't flown since his injury and she had no idea if he had healed. His wings remained tightly folded and hidden.

The wind pushed her South, around the pub and up a narrow trail toward the top of the cliff. Thick loam of half-decayed leaves and everblue needles muffled her footsteps. No one could hear her passage. If someone sought to betray her, they would have to seek with other senses than sound.

She walked rapidly, not looking back at the gathered faces that watched her. Faces that could betray her as easily as welcome her. She might see Karry's face in the crowd. Karry who had just lost a beloved grandmother.

"Stargods, comfort her," she prayed. "Give Granny an easy passage to the next existence."

No reply, only the shifting wind guiding her away from the village, uphill toward the mountains that formed a near impenetrable border between Coronnan and Rossemeyer. Somewhere in these mountains lay the hidden city of Hanassa, home of outlaws, Rovers, exiles, anyone who didn't belong in the three civilized kingdoms.

"Maybe that's where we must go, Amaranth. I don't belong anywhere within the borders of this kingdom." The relentless wind increased and pushed her uphill. She set Amaranth down to walk beside her or fly if he chose. He walked.

Their path circled around: West, then South again and finally back to the East until she heard the pounding surf in the cove below the village. She paused as soon as the wind let her, looking around. An opening in the trees beckoned to her. She looked out over the village from a perch well above the milling people.

The bright colors on the Equinox Pylon drew her eye.

(Careful,) Amaranth warned her. He half-spread his wings, ready to launch into flight if danger threatened.

"So you've had enough time to heal?" She touched the place where he had been badly bruised.

(Time enough and love enough.) He ruffled his wing feathers and stretched wide with an almost visible sigh of satisfaction.

Myri stepped back into the shelter of the trees, but no one looked up from the daily activities to espy her or the flywacket.

"Why here? What am I supposed to find?"

"Oooooh. . . ." A moaning sound greeted her.

Was that the wind sighing in the treetops or. . .

Her talent leaped to awareness.

Pain. Blood. Darkness.

She started the long slide into full rapport with the injured one. *Not yet. Don't let me lose consciousness yet. Not until I find him.*

Amaranth nipped her ankle. The tiny pain kept a part of her awareness inside her own body. Part of her continued to blend with the one who lay wounded and bleeding. The encroaching darkness slowed. Certainty that the victim was male increased as she gained control of the rapport.

Slashing pain, sharp, intense across her midsection. Difficulty breathing. She reached her right hand out, questing for the source of the agony that ripped her patient and herself in two.

Not again. Not so soon after losing Granny Katia!

There, stronger to her left, farther uphill. Not far.

One slow step after another she pushed herself closer to

the pain, knowing that running away from it was as impossible for her as for him.

She nearly stumbled over a huddled form collapsed on knees and forehead. His threadbare cloak of mud brown with hints of dark green in the weave blended with the forest floor, making him nearly invisible.

Her hand still reaching out, she scanned his body. Blue sparks of magic arced from her fingertips to him. A vague sense of familiarity touched her. Had she met this man somewhere before?

"Oooooh . . ." he moaned again. His arms convulsed as they clutched his middle.

A desperate need to keep his life's blood from draining into the soft blanket of leaves filled her mind and emotions. She'd just drained herself of strength and stamina in a desperate and futile attempt to heal Granny Katia. What did she have left to give this new patient?

(His destiny is not yet fulfilled. You must Heal him. We will give you what strength we can. Too much of you passed into the void with the old one.)

She touched the man's shoulder. A vision of two men bound together by a nearly tangible bond leaped into her mind. They argued. One threw a knife, then retrieved it and left. Myri tried desperately to see faces. The wound filled her vision. Blood. Too much blood.

She'd treated knife injuries before, but never one inflicted purposely by a friend.

Was this the betrayal the voices had warned her of? Or had the villagers planned some treachery toward her? She'd never know now. She had no future until she healed this man or they both died.

She aimed the magic in her fingertips toward the wound, willing the blood to thicken and slow. She sensed his fading life stall in its progress toward the void. Half a heartbeat later, sensation-robbing blackness swept over her.

(Stay!) Amaranth commanded. His mental voice was backed by the authority of the anonymous ones who guided her, but the love and familiarity of his mental touch broke through her desire to flee outward into the void.

She stayed, half in her body, aware of the magic

healing that tied her to the wounded man. The other part of her mind hovered over them both ready to flee into the void with his soul. Another entity lingered, watching, faceless and yet familiar in stature and poise. She examined it. Blackness shrouded its aura. The man's soul, not ready to slide back into the body until she healed it or released it to death.

Memories of Moncriith's preaching filled her with dread. What if she failed at both and condemned this man to a soulless life?

"I can't let that happen. You won't escape my healing so easily," Myri said through gritted teeth, tears streaming down her face. Numbness weakened her limbs. "I won't lose you without a fight." She rolled him gently onto his back and settled comfortably beside him to conserve as much of her strength as possible. Concentrating on the wound, she placed her hands on top of his at the center of the ugly gash. She didn't bother to look at his face. Time enough later to explore the familiarity—if he lived.

In her mind she saw muscles pulling together, blood vessels closing. She plugged a nick to the left lung and stopped the leaking air.

She ignored the bones. If any were broken, they could wait. She had to stop the bleeding.

Strength drained from her life into his. The opening to the void grew wider. The tie between them grew stronger, pulling the last vestiges of her life into his wound.

Desperate to save herself, she wrenched her hands away from contact with him. The force of her release sent her rolling downhill. The healing magic snapped and recoiled into her hands. Her palms burned. She looked for physical evidence of the pain snaking up her arms to her shoulders. Red and swollen, her hands sparked inside and out. Her magic sought to reestablish contact against her will.

"Forgive me. I have nothing left to give you but my own life!" she cried, burying her hands in the thick loam of rotting leaves and everblue needles. Contact with the Kardia soothed the burning but not her churning talent. The magic demanded she stay with her patient until he recovered. Her sense of self-preservation kept her anchored out of reach.

"I can't give anymore." Tears poured down her cheeks.

Relentlessly, she kept her raging talent within her, refusing to check the man and see if he lived or not. Even the hovering shade of his soul was no longer visible to her.

"Ahhck!" the man groaned again, almost coughing. Ripples of the muscles along his body told her of the pain that came with the effort to make even that little noise.

"Do you live, stranger?"

"I'm afraid so." He choked out the words, rolling to his side, hands still clutched to his middle.

Myri looked at him as a person and not as a patient for the first time. An auburn beard shot with silver covered most of his face. His hair, dark auburn streaked with gray, hung in limp tendrils about his shoulders. Tentatively, he brushed a lock out of his eyes. He clenched his eyelids closed as another spasm of pain crossed his face. Finally, he opened them. He took a moment to focus on her. Deep green, the color of Tambootie leaves in spring, before they turned almost black in midsummer.

She'd seen those eyes before. Ages ago, last Autumn. That time, the lines radiating out his eyes had shown fatigue, but the eyes themselves had been bright with intelligence and curiosity. Now they were clouded with pain.

"Hello, Myrilandel," Nimbulan said. "I knew we'd meet again someday. But I didn't dream *you* would rescue *me*."

"I had no choice. I don't like you, Nimbulan. I wouldn't have chosen to help you because when you are well you will try to enslave me and my talent. But I have no choice. Until you are healed, I must stay with you." A shiny silver tendril of magic ran from her heart to his. Her talent refused to sever the connection. As long as that cord existed, he had control over her mind and her talent.

* * *

Nimbulan awoke gradually to the realization he was no longer cold or lost in darkness. Nightmares of a freezing hell lingered long after he knew he had survived Televarn's knife thrust. He shivered in memory of the ice that had invaded his gut. That slight movement sent sharp pain in a broad band across his belly just below the ribs.

Myrilandel's healing had not been as complete as the miracle she had worked on Sergeant Kennyth last Autumn. She'd stopped the bleeding and saved his life, but hadn't done much more to the wound.

He stilled his muscles with conscious effort. The pain receded to a constant but tolerable level. Very carefully, with sensitized fingertips he explored the region. He discovered a bandage wound tightly around him. From the way his skin felt stretched and pierced, he guessed the witchwoman had resorted to fine stitches to close his wound.

Such barbarity! Only the untamed tribes of the northern most regions of Kardia Hodos resorted to such primitive methods of healing. Or a young woman without enough training to control her healing trances. She must have withdrawn from the spells before the work was done in order to save herself.

Where was she now? Had she deserted him again?

Loneliness washed over him, bringing a momentary tear to his eye. Clear evidence of his weakness. Without magic to speed the process Myrilandel had begun, his recovery could take weeks, moons.

Slowly, lest he jar the wound again and bring a new wave of pain, dizziness, and nausea, he turned his head. A small campfire, burned down to coals, gave off a soft glow of warmth to his right. On the other side of the fire Myrilandel's strange cat blinked at him. Its dark eyes looked almost purple in the growing light of early morning.

The creature blinked at Nimbulan several times, then heaved itself up, as if incredibly weary or bored, and sauntered over to him. Without asking permission, it climbed onto his upper chest and settled into a doze. Its paws kneaded gently into the cloak that covered Nimbulan's body from neck to toe. The cat's gentle purr spread instant warmth and calm through Nimbulan's body and soul. The tiny desire he'd entertained of getting up or moving left him.

"If you are here to nurse me, Cat, then your mistress can't be far away."

Then he saw the silver tendril of magic running from his heart and remembered briefly that it had remained after she removed herself from the healing. Had she left him weak and vulnerable so he couldn't break the cord? She'd have almost total control over his mind and body through it.

A moment of panic skittered through him. Moncriith had warned them all about her demons controlling the souls of those she yanked back from their next existence.

"I'm here. Are you hungry or thirsty?" Myrilandel was beside him, sounding incredibly weary.

He turned his head to find her lying with her back against his side. His cloak covered them both. Her cloak seemed to be beneath them.

The panic receded. He'd watched her heal Sergeant Kennyth. No evidence of a magical connection remained after that powerful spell.

"I'm thirsty, and I need . . . I would like . . . um. . . ." How did he broach the delicate subject of needing a privy? Some things were more important than demons controlling his soul.

"Can you wait until you've had a little broth to strengthen you?" She heaved herself up with more effort than the cat had exhibited.

Upon closer examination, her skin looked so pale it was almost transparent.

"Are you all right, Myrilandel?" Concern for her well-being overrode his pain and he rolled to his other side in preparation of rising. The movement drove spasms of agony from his chest to his gut and back along his spine.

"Merow!" the cat protested, climbing onto his side rather than be displaced. Or was the cat keeping him in place? Nimbulan didn't care anymore. He wasn't going to be moving again soon.

"No, I'm not all right," Myrilandel spat at him. "All my strength is in you right now."

"Thank you for saving me. But my life isn't worth the loss of yours. Why didn't you let me die?"

"I couldn't." She turned her back on him to rummage in a pack. "I'll be back in a moment with water and kindling." She set off into the thick woods, her feet dragging and her shoulders drooping.

When she came back carrying a pot full of water, bright color splotched her pale skin, as if she'd dashed icy water on her face to revive herself. Perhaps fever burned her cheeks. Her eyes looked dull, and she still shuffled as she walked. She poked the fire listlessly. Finally, she set the pot on a rock next to the blaze and sat back on her heels to rest.

"All I have is some jerked meat and dried fruit. I'll boil the meat for a broth for you. I'll eat the meat."

"The fire isn't hot enough to boil the water. We'll need more wood."

Her shoulders drooped further and she dropped her gaze to the few branches beside her. Clearly the effort to gather more was too much for her. If they were to survive and recover, he had to help.

Bracing himself to endure the pain he gathered his knees beneath him and rose to all fours, back arched to keep his abdominal muscles moving as little as possible. "I can't wait any longer. I'll bring a few sticks on my way back." He gritted his teeth and crawled into the underbrush.

CHAPTER 25

"I suppose it's too late to warn the village," Nimbulan mumbled into the horn cup Myri had fished from her pack.

"Warn them of what?" Myri couldn't muster much enthusiasm for the trek back down the hill to the village she had left . . . was it only yesterday? She'd be content to sit and watch the birds flitting through the branches of the everblue trees. A flock of a hundred or more tiny kinglets had gathered to serenade the world.

"Rovers. They planned to raid the storehouse last night during Festival," Nimbulan said.

"They won't find much but torn fishing nets and broken bay crawler pots. The winter stores have been exhausted and the fishing sparse. The villagers probably didn't notice the raid until this morning. They were quite intent on making a good Festival in hopes of a bountiful Summer." They needed a fertile Festival. Nearly half of last year's Festival babies had died within a few days of birth. Several of the mothers had also died despite Myri's best efforts to save them. All of them might have succumbed had she not been there to midwife them. Experience and hard work often worked better at birthings than magic. Not always. She could not save all of them. She hadn't been able to save Granny Katia, beloved by the entire village.

Mourning families tended to remember only the losses. How many of them blamed her for the deaths?

If the villagers followed her, Nimbulan would be in danger, too. She looked at the slender silver cord of magic that connected her heart to his. He'd only crawled a few yards into the woods before the cord stretched thin and tried to yank him back. Her trip to the creek hadn't been much farther away. They were bound together, probably for a long time. Whatever fate followed one, would involve the other. Concern for him overrode her resentment at the implied control he had over her through that cord.

"Televarn seemed to think this village rich, with adequate stores left over."

"Televarn! *Stargods,* we have to get out of here." Frantically, she gathered together her few possessions. The cooking pot, the water jug, her knife . . . Amaranth!

"Neither of us is in any condition to move, Myrilandel."

"And less prepared to defend ourselves when he comes looking for me and . . ." she almost said "my flywacket."

"He thinks I'm dead. And I would be if you hadn't come when you did. Televarn has no reason to return."

"Unless he questioned the villagers or overheard them talking about me. We have to leave. Now!" This time she stood and kicked dirt over their little fire. Should she scatter the remnants and obscure all evidence of their presence?

"How do you know Televarn?" He grabbed a fistful of her skirt, the only part of her he could reach.

"He covets something of mine he can never have." She wrenched her skirt free of his grasp.

"What?" He stared at the few possessions she crammed into her pack.

Just then a dark, winged shadow fluttered into the little clear space of their camp. Amaranth landed between them, near the remnants of the fire, a gray scurry clamped firmly in his jaws. He left his wings half-furled.

Nimbulan stared, gape-jawed at the legendary flywacket.

"Amaranth!" Myrilandel gasped. "You shouldn't reveal yourself to strangers."

(He's not a stranger. We trust him.) Her familiar dropped the dead rodent near the fire. He fluffed his wings and tail as he paced circles around the two of them, growling and mewling with every step.

"He says I must trust you," Myrilandel said.

(Televarn is in the village. He questions people in the pub. He knows you were there yesterday.)

Myri related that bit of information to Nimbulan. "We have to go. We have to hide."

"I see why Televarn pursues you so relentlessly. Amaranth is a rare prize. Where do you propose we go?" Nimbulan struggled to his feet. His skin paled as pain and dizziness overwhelmed him.

She watched him struggle against the impulse to collapse again. Intelligently, he gathered their cloaks as he righted himself rather than risk bending down again.

"Anywhere away from here. Where do you suggest?" she replied, accepting her cloak from his outstretched hand. She helped him settle his mud-caked outer garment about his shoulders.

The silver cord strengthened. They must flee together or die together. That *s'murghing* connection wouldn't break until he was healed and strong. She couldn't do anything about that now. She hadn't the strength or the time.

"Not back to the road if you are intent on hiding from the Rovers. Though I don't believe he's stupid enough to return to the scene of a murder."

"No, he's not stupid. He's obsessed. If he suspects we are anywhere in the vicinity, he'll hunt me down. I ran away from him once. He can't let that happen again. And if he discovers you still live, he won't rest until he's completed his quest."

"Obsessive. Yes, that describes Televarn well. We'd best rake the leaves and such to remove traces of our camp."

"I'll do it, you start walking. Amaranth, stay with him," she ordered the flywacket.

(Of course.)

"Which way?" Nimbulan cocked one eyebrow up, removing worry lines and lending him an illusion of youth and strength.

Myri remembered his boyish grin touched with mischief last autumn and longed to see it again.

She paused to listen to the wind for a suggestion. A gentle "push" from behind. "Uphill, due South. I'll be right behind you." As if she had a choice with that magical bond holding their fates together.

* * *

"Where is Kalen?" Ackerly asked her father.

Stuuvart looked up from counting the sacks of grain in the storeroom. "I have no idea. She's supposed to be in class." He returned to inspecting a ragged corner of one of the sacks. Evidence of mice?

"She is supposed to be with me, practicing communication spells. But she isn't. I thought she might have joined her *family* for some reason." Ackerly took a sudden dislike to the man. Stuuvart managed the school's resources with efficiency and struck bargains with a brilliant flair for conservation of money. But since the day he had arrived, he'd ignored his own daughter, as if she no longer existed—or wasn't his.

"Then ask her mother where she is." Stuuvart moved into the still room filled with crocks of pickled vegetables and salted meat.

"I did ask Guillia. She hasn't seen Kalen since breakfast and she's worried sick for the girl."

All of the children and adults ended up in the kitchen with Guillia at some point during each day. Kalen's mother proved to be a wonderful cook. She was generous with treats and lent a sympathetic ear to one and all. Her homey domain radiated warmth and love along with the wonderful aromas of baking sweets and savory pies. How could such a warmhearted woman have married this cold and unfeeling man?

"You seem to have lost Kalen, Ackerly. A very valuable child." Stuuvart finally straightened from his inventory. He didn't call Kalen "Daughter." Ever. "You have also failed to keep the wards around my stores to prevent vermin from stealing us blind. I will require compensation for the damage to my reputation for this. Allowing vermin in *my* storeroom!"

Was the storeroom more important than his daughter? If she was his daughter. Kalen's younger siblings all had blue eyes and blond hair like their mother. Only Kalen had a touch of red in her hair. Stuuvart's hair was dark brown, as were his eyes. Kalen's eyes were gray—like Powwell's and Ackerly's.

His thoughts paused a moment with that realization. A secret smile touched his mouth. Possible. Yes, it was possible. How could he use his blood link to the children, if indeed the relationship existed?

"You are the one who is blind, Stuuvart. The holes in the corners of the sacks have been cut with a knife, not chewed by mice. Only a magician could slip around the wards. One of our own has been stealing. Have you and your wife been keeping *my* students and faculty so hungry they must steal?" He turned the accusation back onto Stuuvart, the only overt way to maintain control of the man. Would Stuuvart succumb to coercion? His honor would be marred much deeper should it become publicly known that he had not sired Kalen—a very valuable witchchild.

Ackerly hid his revulsion of a man who suddenly seemed as mean and small-spirited as Druulin. His inventories were more important than feeding the apprentices. Ackerly had vowed never to go hungry again.

"Excuse me, Master Ackerly," Rollett said, knocking politely on the doorjamb. His hand went immediately to an open crock of dried fruit and nuts. He popped a handful into his mouth before continuing. "I can't find Powwell, Master. I'm supposed to team up with him today for practice in summoning. Haakon thought he might be with you."

Ackerly looked pointedly from the journeyman's hand plunging into the crock a second time, to Stuuvart. The steward stood his ground, refusing the accusation of short rations. Druulin had done the same thing.

Ackerly didn't have time for this battle of wills.

"Powwell is not with me as you can see. Nor is Kalen. Take Gilby and two others and start searching for them." One gifted child playing hooky from lessons spelled mischief. Two gifted children missing, along with dried fruit, nuts, and grains, and possibly a ham—he'd spotted an empty spot in the orderly rows of smoked meat hanging from the ceiling—smelled of trouble.

"We will discuss this later, Stuuvart, when the children and missing stores are accounted for." Ackerly turned sharply on his heel and left the room before his steward could increase his demands of blackmail.

S'murghit! if Stuuvart weren't so valuable as a manager

and accountant, Ackerly would dismiss him, his wife, and the other children as well. *I'm in charge of this school, not him. The profits are mine and I can't afford to share them with another.* As soon as he found Kalen and knew the child and her enormous talent to be safe, he just might turn the rest of the family out. The girl and her talent were all that truly mattered. Couldn't her father see that? If he was truly her father. He didn't think Guillia the kind of woman to stray from her marriage bed. But he knew from experience that any woman could be seduced with the right promises.

Maybe that was why she looked so familiar! He'd visited Baria a number of times over the years and remembered an innkeeper's daughter on the verge of a convenient marriage to a rich merchant she didn't like. . . .

Ackerly didn't need Guillia and her family to make a profit from Kalen. A blood link could be made to keep the child close at hand. Moncriith would know how to do that.

Maybe Stuuvart was hiding both children so that he could demand ransom, a tidy sum of gold for them.

If he was, then Stuuvart had best watch his back. Ackerly had an entire school of magicians to force the truth out of him, very painfully. He'd summon Moncriith to be on the lookout for the children.

He couldn't allow anything to harm those children. They were too important an investment.

* * *

"We need help, Myrilandel," Nimbulan gasped as he sank to his knees for the third time. Ruefully he looked back along the path they had come. The crooked rowan growing beside the double everblue that marked the beginning of their trek was still in sight.

"I know." She clung to the trunk of a stout tree as she dropped her meager pack to the ground. Her knuckles were white where she grasped a branch level with her shoulder.

"Perhaps if we went downhill?" He looked hopefully at the easier path.

Myrilandel cocked her head as if listening. "No," she said righting her head and gathering her strength.

That curious habit of listening to the wind bothered him. She reminded him of someone when she did that. What did Amaranth tell her?

"They . . . I said no. We can't take the risk."

"Televarn?"

"He's still in the village." She bit her trembling lip, looking longingly at the downhill path. "I hope he doesn't hurt anyone there." She blinked back a tear, then resolutely shouldered the pack again. She didn't let go of the branch that supported her.

"I don't believe he'd risk hanging around after he raided the storehouse."

Nimbulan thought about rising from his knees and decided to wait a moment more. He'd not lose track of Myrilandel. Not with that pretty silver cord stretching from his heart to hers. What kind of magic had she worked on him? He'd never heard of such a thing.

He should resent the tie she'd established. Strangely, the connection pleased him. He'd wanted her to stay with him last Autumn. Now she couldn't run away from him. He had the chance to . . . To what?

"What would Televarn do if he found the storehouse as empty as I know it to be?" Myrilandel looked back at him, as reluctant to move as he. "He'd believe the villagers tricked him, and he can't allow anyone to trick the great trickster. So he'd watch and wait for another chance. He'd ask questions that would lead him to another storehouse. Only there isn't another storehouse. Drinking in the pub is the best place to observe the entire village." She shoved herself away from the tree and took two steps uphill.

"You know him well."

"Too well. Take a drink. You need fluid to replace the blood you lost, then we must move on."

Much later Nimbulan could no longer see the crooked rowan. Blindly he set one foot in front of the other—he was no longer sure which foot moved and which was right or left—and bumped into Myrilandel's back. The silver cord swelled and tugged at his heart when he didn't move away from the warm sensation of her back pressed against the length of him.

"We can stop here." Her teeth chattered as she spoke. "He won't see our fire from the place where he left you. Amaranth says he'll bring us more fresh meat. I think he spotted another gray scurry nearby."

Nimbulan didn't care. If his enemy found him now and killed him again, he didn't have the strength or the will to protest. Anything to end this endless journey.

(No, you must fight for yourself.)

"Who said that?"

Silence.

He looked at Myrilandel. She stood with her head cocked to the left. Amaranth pointed his nose uphill, to the South, ears alert, tail straight up.

"You heard them, too?" she asked. Curious shadows elongated her face and fingers. Where had he seen that otherworldly image before.

"Yes." He continued to search the small open space for evidence of another being.

"You won't see them. They have guided me my entire life. I have learned to trust them, but I have never known who or what they are." She dropped the pack and began gathering firewood.

"Did they say it's safe to stop here?" He reached to his hip where he should carry a knife, but Televarn had stolen it from him.

"They don't push me forward now."

"I wonder who they are." He sank down and collected the few dead branches he could reach. Her relaxation of her vigilant attention to her surroundings told him that these mysterious voices were trustworthy more than her words had. He'd never seen this strange witchwomen other than wary, almost feral in her desire to remain unconfined by people or places.

"I don't know. But they told me of betrayal and sent me to you. I don't know if they meant I would be betrayed or you would. Now they push me to climb this hill. There is something up there. . . ." She paused and looked in the direction they had been traveling. Her nose twitched and her eyes brightened. "I think I'm going home. But I've never been there before."

Three days passed, three days of struggling uphill along a path only Myrilandel could see. Amaranth brought them gray scurries and an occasional striped lapin. On the second day, Myrilandel had enough strength to dig a few roots. Both of them drank deeply from the numerous streams they crossed.

Finally, at the end of the third day, when Nimbulan was sure he could walk no farther, and could barely lift a hand to push away branches that slapped his face, they both stumbled at the same time, landing flat on their faces. Had the magical cord that bound them together tripped them?

When he had enough strength to raise his head, a wonderful sight greeted him.

"An old woodsman's hut," he murmured. "The roof is intact." Shelter at last.

"A flusterhen coop!" Myrilandel crawled to her feet.

"We'd best check for people." He searched the clearing with his normal senses. He hadn't the strength to look with magic. The place smelled abandoned. But he couldn't be sure.

"Hello!" Myri called.

A flustercock strutted out from the coop in response. He stretched his neck and crowed loudly at them.

Myri laughed and lunged for the brightly feathered bird. He ducked back into the small shelter. She followed and emerged a moment later with two white globes held triumphantly in her hands. "Laying hens. No one has collected the eggs in moons and moons. The hens obligingly laid these two a moment ago just for us. Tonight, we eat properly."

Something snapped behind Nimbulan. With the last of his strength he looked in the general direction of the sound. His eyes saw nothing. A tendril of magic stirred within him for the first time since Televarn had stabbed him. He hadn't the energy or the will to push the magic outward and explore the unusual sound. Yet he had the distinct sensation of something closing, almost as if someone had closed a door with a sigh of relief.

"Did you hear something, Myrilandel?"

She paused in her progress toward the hut. She turned in a complete circle, sniffing the air and cocking her head to listen. A smile lit her face. Joy danced in her eyes. "I'm home. I'm *home!* This is where they need me to be. This is where *I* need to be. We're safe here." She turned another circle, arms outstretched in welcome, head thrown back in laughter.

He'd never seen a more beautiful woman.

His magic stirred again, pulling his hand toward the center of the clearing where Myrilandel continued her delighted capering. Curious to know what power tugged at him, he allowed the little magic stirring within him to sharpen his sight.

Blue! Ley line blue spread before him. Not the intense well of blue hidden beneath the courtyard of the old monastery, but still strong and pulsing with energy. He fine-tuned his focus to follow individual lines. Four, five, six. *Six.* Unprecedented except for the well. Six lines equally spaced, coming together at the exact point where Myrilandel danced. There the lines crossed and radiated out again.

A nexus. He'd heard old Master Magicians speak of the legendary points as places of unusual power. Most scholars dismissed the idea as improbable. Ley lines occurred randomly, at irregular intervals. Only rarely did two or three lines cross. No one had recorded more at any time in recent history.

Nimbulan remembered an essay on the subject in one of the books in the library at the school. A major nexus. Six of the phenomena had been recorded in ancient times, one on each continent of Kardia Hodos. No one mentioned the well. The locations of all six of the nexi had been lost to modern magicians shortly after the departure of the Stargods. After a brief skimming of the essay, he'd seen no mention about the well of ley lines as the source of all power. He'd put it aside to read carefully later, but later never came.

Gratefully, he positioned himself directly over one of the lines. Energy filled him with enough strength to crawl to Myrilandel and the nexus. His heart pounded stronger and more regularly, pushing blood to all parts of his body. Warmth filled him to the tips of his very cold fingers and toes. Tingles played with the angry wound across his gut, hastening the healing process and restoring some of his lost strength.

He stood up with only minor dizziness and a raging hunger for food and for Myri.

A smile grew from his belly and spread outward to every corner of his being. He was not satisfied until he held her tightly against his chest, kissing her soft mouth. They continued their spiral dance together, embracing the clearing and each other. The silver cord connecting their hearts swelled and wrapped them closer together.

(We have brought you home. Soon we will meet with you and teach you what you need to know.)

CHAPTER 26

"What are we to do with you?" Moncriith asked no one in particular. He stared at the two grubby children from the height of the throne in the great hall of Castle Krej, the ancestral home of Kammeryl d'Astrismos. A conscientious farmer had brought the children to the court after finding them hiding in his barn, stealing milk from his goat.

The lord himself was busy elsewhere and so Moncriith listened to the farmer's tale of woe, as he listened to most petitioners for the lord's justice. Kammeryl d'Astrismos didn't like to sit still and found dispensing justice tedious. He'd almost blubbered in delight when Moncriith showed him the merits of allowing an educated magician to sit in his stead.

"You stole food from an honest man's barn. You milked his goat and stuffed his eggs into your pockets." He looked at the boy, the older of the two, straight in the eye. Most people blinked and stammered when he challenged them with direct eye contact. Not this child. The boy returned the stare and kept his mouth shut. His arm stole about the shoulders of his sister in a protective gesture that said much about them.

Moncriith presumed they were brother and sister. They possessed the same mud-brown hair and gray eyes with incredibly long lashes. The spay of freckles across their noses fell into almost identical patterns. He'd seen those gray eyes before. Where?

The girl kept her eyes lowered. She darted shy glances to right and left. Her mouth opened slightly in awe. Her innocence tugged at Moncriith's heart.

He vaguely remembered meeting her somewhere in his travels. Probably the boy, too. That was why the eyes looked so familiar. Why hadn't they heeded his sermon and become too frightened of demons to ever work magic again?

"This honest farmer also tells me that you frightened his plow steed with witchlight. I have forbidden all witchcraft within Lord d'Astrismos' land." He had to remain stern, make an example of all witches. Their magic would attract demons. He would not tolerate rival magicians in his province, no matter how beguiling the children could seem.

"We didn't know that, Sssieur. We were hungry and cold. We only did what we had to do to thurvive," the girl said quietly, very meekly.

A solitary tear moistened her beautiful eyelashes, threatening to spill over onto her cheek. Moncriith wanted nothing more than to rush forward with a clean handkerchief to brush the tear aside so she could look up at him with thanks. He adjusted his estimate of her age downward.

"Hush, Kalen. He won't listen. He's like all the other witchhunters. He doesn't care about us. Only about his laws." The boy pulled her closer, still protecting her.

"Master Magician Ackerly sent word that two of his students had run away." Moncriith shook his shoulders to rid himself of his foolish emotions. He had to maintain control here. "Witchchildren run away from the witch school, only using enough magic to survive. Perhaps Myrlandel's demons haven't found you yet. I may be able to redeem your souls after all."

Among the d'Astrismos soldiers and retainers he already had commitments from two hundred people—he'd worked hard all Winter recruiting those commitments. Soon the weather would allow him to take his crusade farther afield. By the time the fields were plowed and planted and the men could leave home, he'd have control of the lord's army. Control of all Coronnan would soon follow.

The children exchanged a glance. Communication without words.

"Speak with words, not magic!" Moncriith roared.

The farmer backed out of the room with undue haste. Moncriith ignored him, though he should have taken the time to reassure the man he had nothing to fear from Moncriith, being an innocent mundane. Only the abominations who used demon magic had reason to fear Moncriith and Lord d'Astrismos' justice.

"Sieur?" The boy leveled his gaze on Moncriith once more. He used the respectful title reserved for honored priests, but his eyes were more seeking than respectful.

Moncriith had the eerie feeling this child could read him to the depths of his soul. No one could do that anymore. No traditional magician could penetrate the armor he'd erected when . . . when he realized how vulnerable to demons he'd become. Not even the priests in the temple with their coercive methods could force their way into his mind.

"Speak freely, child. I'll not harm you." Moncriith added another layer of armor to his mind.

"Sieur, we don't think we want to stay with you. We're on a quest. An urgent quest."

"Now that Nimbulan is dead, the cult of Battlemages will die out, child. And without the Battlemages, the wars will cease. You need not worry about quests anymore. Soon I will return you to your parents and we will all live in peace."

The children exchanged another of their deep glances. Moncriith drummed his fingers on the arm of his throne in frustration. Why did everyone question and doubt the truth?

"But Master Nimbulan ithn't dead, Sssieur. And we have to find him. It's important. Very important," Kalen said. Finally, she raised her eyes to him. Determination overshadowed the innocence and beauty he had seen in her, leaving only a willful child who must be disciplined. After she had outlived her usefulness.

"Yes, finding Nimbulan is very important, if he is indeed still alive." Moncriith leaned forward. His knuckles turned white under the force of his grip of the chair arms. He forced himself to remain calm. How could that man still live to plague him? Nimbulan had to be dead, as reported. Ackerly wouldn't lie to him, not after Moncriith had paid out three gold pieces for information. His plans to eliminate all magicians along with the demons would blow away as dust if Nimbulan still lived. No other

Battlemage commanded the respect of both magician and mundane armies. As long as Nimbulan lived to direct battles and train other magicians to do the same, Moncriith would remain an outcast.

The kingship of Coronnan eluded him as long as Nimbulan lived to oppose Moncriith.

"I will help you find Master Nimbulan, children. But first you must bathe and have a hot meal. Some new, warm clothing and boots, too." He clapped his hands for servants to see to the children. "We will begin our journey at dawn."

* * *

Myri explored the boundary of the clearing with her hands and magic senses. Yesterday, when she and Nimbulan had collapsed into the clearing, she thought she heard a popping sound, as if a door had closed behind them. Now she sought that door again.

Inch by inch, she traced the perimeter of the area around her new home. An invisible wall resisted the pressure of her hand. The thought of being trapped here forever didn't bother her. Within the magic enclosure of several acres, she had about an acre for a garden, access to a creek for water, and a secluded pool fed by hot springs for bathing and laundry. Nimbulan was there now, washing away the blood and dust of his adventures.

A long soak in the warm water would aid the internal healing she hadn't been able to complete. She had probed the wound last night and realized she could do little more for him with magic. Only time and rest and good food would finish the job she had begun.

She hoped he shaved his beard as well. She liked being able to watch his facial expressions. She wanted to see that boyish grin light his eyes again.

It was curious that the silver tendril of magic still bound her to him. She had thought the connection born solely of the incomplete healing and his need to keep her close and controlled until he no longer required her talent. Something else must be maintaining it. She tugged gently on the cord and sent him the message to scrape the beard from his face.

A sense of well-being crept over her at the realization

she didn't resent the silver cord or Nimbulan anymore. "We belong together. We belong here. This is home," she whispered, utterly amazed.

Briefly she gave up her examination of the wall to touch her lips where he had kissed her yesterday. The sensations he roused in her still puzzled her. He wasn't as beautiful or as skilled as Televarn, but the raw honesty of his embrace had touched a portion of her heart she thought closed and locked away forever.

Televarn had roused her lust but not her love. What kind of emotions would grow between herself and Nimbulan if she allowed him to stay in her life?

When Old Magretha had died three years ago, Myri had grieved for her lost mentor and companion. If she lost Nimbulan now, she thought she might feel the same kind of loneliness and regret. Or worse.

"You feel it, too?" Nimbulan came up behind her, almost as if she had conjured him with her speculations.

"Feel what?" She was lost in the wonder of examining his bare cheeks and upper lip. Would his kiss delight her as much without the beard tickling her?

He'd pulled his long hair back into a single braid, without the distinctive shorter sides hanging loose, as most magicians did. Now he looked like an ordinary country gentleman, the kind of man who might be willing to linger with her in this remote clearing.

"Feel the wall. I managed to step beyond it and back through it down by the creek, but it took a major effort of will. My magic won't return fully until my body is completely healed. I doubt that anyone else will be able to penetrate the wall without our permission."

"A kind of armor?" She visualized a small opening in the wall and pushed her hand against it. The wall resisted the way a feather pillow compressed under the weight of a head, shaping around it, but not splitting. She opened the image of the door. Her hand slid right through. "Oh, my!" She pulled her hand back in surprise and stared at her palm. Somehow she expected it to burn or at least tingle from the magic. Nothing. Her hand seemed perfectly normal and undamaged.

"Do you think your voices guided you here? Perhaps your guardian spirits prepared this place for us, a place where we are safe from Rovers and witchhunters." He took her hand in his own larger ones, examining it, kissing it, tracing the crease of her heart line across the palm.

Bending over her hand didn't disguise the slight stoop in his posture. The wound must still pain him.

"We are safe from those who would betray us. I know it with the same certainty that tells me the sun will rise in the East tomorrow." Her breathing seemed strangely uneven as his hands moved up her arm to her shoulders, then moved to cradle her face.

"You needn't force me to stay with you, Myrilandel. I want to be with you. This silver cord isn't necessary." He slowly lowered his mouth to cover hers in a long kiss.

Heat rose from her belly to her breasts in a satisfying wave. Her knees nearly buckled with joy.

"I thought you controlled the cord," she said when they came up for air, still locked in each others arms.

"Perhaps neither of us controls it. Perhaps it is a symbol of something deeper that we refused to recognize." He kissed her again, molding her body to fit neatly against his.

"Stay with me, Nimbulan. Please, help me make this clearing our home."

"If we are to stay, we must lay in some stores. There is a sack of seeds and roots underneath the bed in the hut," Nimbulan said. "Magic has kept them in stasis, so they won't spoil. If we're going to be here any length of time, we'd best start planting the garden. Can you dig if I plant? I don't think I have the strength yet to do the heaviest work." He walked slowly back to the one-room home with the very wide bed. Last night they'd slept there, side by side, Amaranth between them or on top of one of them—as they'd slept on the trail. Nimbulan hadn't touched her. Amaranth was too good a chaperone for that.

Tonight the flywacket would sleep elsewhere, Myri decided.

"I don't know if I like it that you are a Battlemage, Nimbulan. But you intrigue me and make me feel safer than anyone has before. You must be a very special man."

* * *

Myri's joyful planting song dwindled to a questioning note as a cloud dimmed the Spring sun and then passed on.

She looked to the Northeast and sniffed the damp breeze. She almost tasted the warm growth and new life abundant in the forest around her. Her song returned to her lips, soaring high. A sense of rightness with the world swelled her heart and added speed to her digging.

Nimbulan looked up from where he dropped triangles of yampion root into the freshly turned earth two rows to her left. He laughed with her and joined her song. They'd made love last night, and the three nights before. Joyous, wondrous, abandoned love, growing in intensity with each joining. She needed to sing about that, too.

"When you stand like that with your face uplifted to the wind, you remind me of someone," Nimbulan said. "But for the life of me, I can't remember who." He shook his head and resumed his planting.

"Someone you know? My family, perhaps?" If he knew her family, she could meet them, talk to them, fill in missing pieces of her memory.

"I must not have known her well, or I'd remember. Don't worry about it. If it's important, the name and the face will come to me."

"I'd like to find my family someday." Someday, when exploring their love wasn't quite so new and fragile.

She'd dreamed of flying again last night. The sensation of wind beneath her outstretched arms felt as natural and as harmonious as singing with this man beside her. She tried to imagine the two of them soaring effortlessly across the bay on a warm current of air; the crisp bite of thin air cleansing her mind and body of old fears and urgencies.

She hunched her shoulders and folded her elbows in memory of tilting wings to catch the next updraft. . . .

" 'Twas only a dream," she sighed. "But it felt like a memory." She pushed the shovel into the ground.

The scent of brine alerted her to the next change in the weather. Tall trees blocked her view of the Great Bay. She blinked three times, a trick Nimbulan had taught her, and found her FarSight ready to scan North, through the forest, and over the horizon.

Dark clouds boiled on the horizon, where the bay met

the open sea. Tonight the rains would soak their small garden and nourish the seeds and roots they planted.

The hair on her arms and the back of her neck bristled. Her sense of safety and privacy vanished. She whipped her head back and forth, sniffing the air for the "difference."

"We aren't alone," Nimbulan whispered.

"We must be. The barrier remains intact," she answered.

"Is someone coming near?" He rose slowly to his knees, still protecting the vulnerable area around his wound. He raised his left hand, palm outward, fingers slightly curled and rotated it.

"I sense weariness and fear. One stumbles and . . . and I share pain with her. Almost too tired to feel the pain. Another helps. But he is tired, too." Awareness of the two lives invaded her empathy.

"They need you. Nimbulan struggled to his feet. Once upright he walked over to the nearest barrier and touched it with the flat of his palm.

The barrier swirled into a dozen visible colors, extending outward from his hand. The trees outside the clearing seemed to lurch and right themselves slightly to the left of where they had been.

Myri closed her eyes. The world returned to the same place as before. She opened them again and the trees continued to shift until an arch opened in the barrier, outlined by a narrow band of the swirling colors. On the other side of the barrier stood two children, a boy and a girl with identical mud-brown hair tinged with red and sprays of freckles across their noses. They both stared at Nimbulan with wide gray eyes.

CHAPTER 27

Moncriith dragged at the leash of a baying dog. The stupid creature couldn't track its own shit, let alone an elusive witchwoman and two grubby children determined to elude their fate.

He was close to Myrilandel. He knew it, could smell the demon magic in the air. The villagers had said she was nearby.

Where else would those two cursed children run but to the witchwoman. She was the only one in these parts who would give shelter to the brats.

Except possibly the Rover chieftain. He sought Myrilandel, too. Moncriith had to find the witch before the Rover whisked her into Hanassa or some other impossible place.

"Sieur, we've passed that split tree with the boulder growing out of the center three times." The sergeant assigned to Moncriith wiped his brow with his sleeve as he stared at the tree in question.

The other soldiers huddled together behind their sergeant, shoulders tensed as if trying to make themselves invisible by reducing their size.

"Fools! Of course we're going in circles. The witchwoman has laid a dozen false trails. We have to branch out and look for signs of passage beyond this circle." Moncriith pushed his own growing anxiety aside with his forceful tones. He knew the eerie feeling permeating these woods was a cloaking spell. No one would venture closer to the witch's dwelling because of the growing sense of unease generated by her evil.

Magretha had generated the same miasma of impeding doom in the woods surrounding her house. A house where she had seduced young men with promises of great magic and never-ending sex.

Moncriith had been naive enough to believe himself the first and only young lad to share her bed.

Magretha had been as false as her foster daughter.

Flushed with lust and newly awakened power, Moncriith had believed Magretha and pledged her his love. His parents had encouraged the match, even though Magretha at thirty—a very beautiful thirty—was fifteen years older and fifteen years more experienced than Moncriith. A magician in the family, particularly one powerful enough to become a Battlemage, offered a chance for a steady income and a way out of the constant grind of hunger and hard work. The entire village hoped Moncriith would be powerful enough to protect them from the marauding armies that had plagued Coronnan for two or more generations.

But Magretha had betrayed Moncriith. She had seduced his father and two of the village elders, as she seduced every man who crossed her path. Moncriith had discovered her lying in his father's arms, both naked, in the throes of passion. While he stood in the woods, aghast and ashamed, the two village elders joined him, awaiting their turn with Magretha. Their lewd jokes had roused Moncriith's youthful anger and righteous outrage. Moncriith unleashed his newfound and uncontrolled magic. He sent a firebomb into the thatch of Magretha's sturdy home. Rain hadn't fallen in nigh on three moons. The dry straw and aged timbers erupted in flames and smoke so fast, the inhabitants hadn't a hope of escape.

Magretha and Moncriith's father should have died, locked in each other's arms at the height of their unbridled lust. But Myrilandel, no more than six at the time, had dragged Magretha from the flames, leaving Moncriith's father to die.

The stench of burning flesh had sickened Moncriith and brought home to his grieving mind the enormity of his crime. He'd run away to the nearest monastery, pledging the rest of his miserable life to repentance and service to the Stargods. At the gateway of the temple he'd pledged never to use again the magic that Magretha had awakened and shown him how to use.

All priests of the Stargods must first be magicians. So Moncriith had turned to blood magic rather than draw power from the ley lines embedded in the Kardia. Most often, he used his own blood, relishing the pain and the power that pain brought him. He should have been the most powerful Battlemage of all time, continuously drawing strength from the blood and death of a battle.

The elders of the temple had banished him on the night of his ordination as a priest. They would not sully their hallowed halls with blood.

But they harbored demons. Only demons could make the elders turn against Moncriith and his vision of the infestation of evil into all traditional magic.

The vision drove him to scour Coronnan free of the pestilence of the demons who used human bodies to house their spirits. Myrilandel led the demons now that Magretha had died—finally purged of her possession by holy fire.

How else had a child so small rescued Magretha? Why else had she rescued the treacherous witch and not Moncriith's father?

* * *

"Master Nimbulan!" Powwell flung himself forward, hugging the magician's knees. He wanted to wrap his arms around the older man's waist and hug him tight, but the woman was in the way. "We've found you at last. Kalen said you were alive. I didn't believe her. But she convinced me. We ran away from Master Ackerly and her father. We ran away to bring you back. They searched for us but we hid. Then Sieur Moncriith found us and fed us and kept us warm. He wanted to find you, too, but we ran away again. He wants to hurt you."

"Powwell? Slow down. One thing at a time." Nimbulan eased them into the clearing, toward the little hut at the center. "How did you find me? I've been gone for moons."

"It was Kalen all the time. She knew where to look. She knew we'd find you in the East. You have to come back to the school with us. You have to make it all better."

Only when the heat from the central hearth in the hut

engulfed Powwell did he realize how cold and wet he was. How tired he was of sleeping rough and eating rougher. How dangerous Moncriith and his preachings were. But if he was cold and tired and ready for the comfort of a real bed and hot food, Kalen must need it more.

Dark circles beneath her eyes made her look like her face was always dirty. She didn't smile or laugh any more, and she certainly didn't play magic tricks on him the way she had back at the school.

Powwell released Nimbulan and assumed a straighter, more mature posture. He wrapped an arm around Kalen's shivering shoulders. He had to take care of her. No one else would.

"Come, tell me your adventures, Powwell. And you, too, Kalen. Then we'll decide what to do with you. Your parents and Ackerly must be frantic about you."

"How did you know to come East?" the woman asked from the doorway. Kalen hovered there twisting her hands in her skirt as if frightened of everything.

Kalen looked up at the woman. Determination firmed her chin and cleared her eyes of all traces of her tiredness. "*They* told me."

"They?" Nimbulan asked, exchanging a worried glance with the woman.

"The voices in my head. They told me to come East and find you."

(Your family is complete. Come to us. Follow the path only Myrilandel can see.)

A large black cat stalked into the hut, fluffing his wings for all to see.

Powwell's jaw dropped. A flywacket! A real, live, *flywacket!* Nimbulan had found a creature that lived only in legends.

(I am Amaranth, Myrilandel's familiar,) the flywacket announced directly into Powwell's mind.

"I . . . I'm Powwell. This is Kalen," he stammered an introduction since it seemed warranted.

(We must trust the little ones. All of us are needed. The path opens to you at dawn,) Amaranth told them all.

* * *

Nimbulan watched Myri walk up the trail. Her lovely shape was outlined by her skirt with each long, confident stride. He longed to reach out and hold her close, kiss her, love her. The slender silver umbilical that connected them grew stronger every day until he was sure he could reach out and pull her closer to him by tugging on the magical cord.

But they had a long trek into the mountains to find the mysterious guiding voices, and the children watched every move he made with avid curiosity—when they weren't trying to catch Amaranth and make him show off his wings.

Nimbulan decided to question them once more rather than contemplate Myri and how she found the path that appeared behind them but never before them.

"How did you two meet?" The similarity in hair and eye color, the position of their freckles, and the shape of their tip-tilted noses was too much coincidence for them not to have a common parent or grandparent.

Nimbulan had met Powwell's mother when he recruited the boy for the school. A shy woman who'd been seduced by a man displaced by the wars. She might have been beautiful if loved and allowed to bloom with joy, but years of hard work and being outcast for bearing a bastard child had etched premature worry lines into her face. Hunger had worn her to a thin shadow of the beauty of her youth. She had never taken another lover.

Powwell's mother had been shunned for loving a man not her husband. Rover women regarded children as wealth, regardless of the father or their marital status. The old pagan practice of random matings at Festival and measuring wealth in the number of children hadn't died out with the teaching of the Stargods.

The depredation of war took more lives than the sacrifice to Simurgh had in the old days, before the Stargods. Lives that could only be replaced by numerous children. Powwell and his mother should have been honored rather than cast out by family and village because she slept with a man outside of Festival or marriage.

"Kalen's parents brought her to the school," Powwell said, helping the girl over a fallen log. "Her da was a merchant in Baria and lost everything when the town was sacked. They'd been on the road for months, hungry and down to their last few coins. Kalen has talent, lots of it. So they brought her to the school to have one less mouth to feed. They ended up staying to help run the school."

"A merchant, eh?" Was that the connection? Or had a different man seduced both women? The family resemblance was strong enough that Kalen's father might very well have sired Powwell, too. He'd made promises and never kept them because he was already married. Or about to marry. Probably Kalen's mother had a hefty dowry, more attractive than Powwell's mother's small inheritance. Did Kalen's father have gray eyes and freckles?

"Stuuvart traded for better food, and Ackerly offered the services of students for healing and soil replenishing. Sometimes he took money, a lot of the times he could only get cloth and parchments and stuff. And Kalen's mother is a great cook." Powwell looked longingly at the pack Nimbulan carried. Undoubtedly his growing body cried out for food. The lessons Nimbulan had set both children earlier to test their skills had depleted their energy reserves as well.

Kalen hadn't spoken more than a few words since yesterday. Nimbulan wondered what lay behind her act of wide-eyed innocence.

"So why did you find it necessary to come searching for me, if you believed me dead." Nimbulan turned and faced the children squarely. This was the heart of their desperate flight from the school.

"Kalen discovered that your niche in the crypt was empty."

Nimbulan knelt down so that he was level with the girl. He tried to look her directly in the eye. She suddenly found a tall everblue tree fascinating and wouldn't look at him.

"Why were you exploring the crypt, Kalen? Surely there were better places to play," Nimbulan asked gently.

The girl looked at her feet and bit her lip. Powwell had the same bad habit.

"You can trust him, Kalen," Powwell urged.

"I wanted a place to hide," she whispered.

"Hide from what?" Nimbulan asked.

She darted a worried glance at Powwell then back to

the ground. "Ackerly wanted me to do terrible things with my magic."

Myri joined them and held the child close against her side. "If she doesn't want to talk about it, don't push it. When she's comfortable enough with us to talk, she will. Don't upset her." She glared at Nimbulan.

Nimbulan returned Myri's stare with love. He recognized the blooming of her maternal instincts and wished they could have children of their own. Children with her pale blonde hair and beautifully expressive eyes. They showed hints of purple now, blue when she was sated with sex, fiery green when she healed. He longed for children he could teach to carry on the legacy of honorable magic, neutral in the realm of politics. The lack of his own children became a deep and empty ache.

He mentally shook himself free of the delusion. Denied children of their own because of their magic, they could only accept and love the ones the Stargods brought to them. Powwell and Kalen.

"It's important that he knows what Ackerly is doing, Kalen." Powwell encouraged the girl. "If you don't tell him, I will."

Kalen's eyes flashed in anger at the boy. Powwell backed off and dropped his gaze to the ground. The boy might speak for them both, but clearly the girl was in control. Interesting relationship.

"Ackerly was teaching me to work a summons through a glass and a flame. He wanted me to try sending witchfire with the summons. He wanted me to burn whole armies. He wanted me to murder innocent people with magic and then collect gold for it. He's evil, and Moncriith is right when he says demons control magicians. I don't want to be evil. I don't want to hurt people!" Kalen buried her face in Myri's skirt. Huge sobs sent shudders down her small body.

"If Moncriith is right, then why were you so eager to get away from him?" Nimbulan asked. He touched the child's back with a comforting hand. Her sobs eased a little.

"Don't press her, Nimbulan," Myri said, stroking her hair.

"Moncriith is as evil as Ackerly. He wants to burn all magicians, not just the evil ones. He does it to fulfill a vision from the Stargods—or so he says. Ackerly does it for gold. Moncriith wanted to burn me, too, after we found you. That's why we ran away from him. I don't want to be a magician, I wish I'd never been born."

"Don't ever say that, Kalen. Don't even think it!" Myri knelt down and faced her, nose to nose. "Moncriith made me feel the same way. I spent my whole life running away. Now I have found a home and a man who loves me." She reached a hand to Nimbulan and blushed. "Moncriith is wrong, Kalen. Magic isn't evil. It's how we use it for good or ill that matters. As long as you use your magic for good, you are good."

"That's why I started the school, Kalen. I wanted to teach magicians how to act for good, for peace, so that we could end the wars and make magic a tool of Life and Healing, not of destruction. Magic is a wonderful gift. We must use it to help those who don't have the gift rather than for our own power and glory. Moncriith has a magic gift. He think's he's using it for the good of all, but he's not." Nimbulan explained to himself as well as Myri and the children.

"Moncriith thinks all magicians are worthless, except for himself." Powwell spat on the ground. "He wants to be a priest-king of Coronnan. I think he wants to be a god-king instead."

Nimbulan could see the boy's quick mind working, putting pieces together.

"All people have value, Powwell. Those who have magic, and those who don't. All of us were created by the Stargods for a reason. Sometimes it's hard to find the reason and make the most of it. But we have to try." *I have to take the Rover ritual back to the school. I have to continue my work. I can't do it alone. Will Myri go with me, or will she cling to her new home?*

CHAPTER 28

Myri took Kalen's hand and started forward on the path. Her little fingers felt cold against Myri's palm. Questions clouded Kalen's eyes. She needed time to absorb all the things they'd said about magic and self-worth. Myri hoped the little girl could believe it in time.

Saber ferns, rotting limbs, and rocks blurred and drifted out of Myri's vision to reveal a path of sorts. Kalen kept looking forward and back, off to the side, through wide-open eyes then half-closed lids, straight on and out of the corners.

Myri almost laughed at her puzzlement. She had no idea why none of her companions could see the path.

A broad alpine meadow opened before them. Off to the right, the landscape opened up to reveal peak after snowy peak jutting into the stunningly blue sky. The urge to fly swamped Myri's senses, demanding she let go and soar upward.

Amaranth screeched as he glided past her and pounced on something in the lush grasses. He emerged from the greenery, wings half-furled, shaking his empty paws clean of damp soil. With all of his cat dignity and arrogance, he perched on a rock for a much needed bath. Bright sunlight gave his black fur and feathers a dark purple sheen—a darker shade of the same color of wildflowers that hovered like a mist above the greenery.

He paused in his ablutions, head cocked as if listening. His head reared up, ears flat. He chittered in excitement.

"What is it, my friend?" Myri gathered him into her arms, scratching his ears affectionately.

He nuzzled her chin once and squirmed to face forward, paws resting on her arms in preparation for launch.

"Something awaits us," Myri said.

"Did Amaranth tell you that?" Nimbulan turned a full circle, scanning the meadow with eyes and magic senses. He suddenly stilled. "Something is waiting and watching. In that tumble of boulders and fallen trees." He pointed to the wall of cliffs that enclosed three sides of the meadow. A stream cascaded down over a tumble of boulders at the base of the cliff into a brook that meandered through the grasses. At the edge of the meadow, the stream plunged over the precipice in a wide waterfall.

Amaranth burst upward in a thunderous flap of wings. "Merawk!" he cried over and over. He dove and looped, flipped and soared in a wondrous display of acrobatics. As he swooped down for the third time, claws extended, he grabbed Myri by the hair, tugging upward in an invitation to flight.

"Let go, you silly flywacket. I can't fly," she protested as she laughingly disconnected his talons from her fair hair.

(Can, too!) Amaranth squealed and flew off again.

Dreams of flight. More than dreams, memories lashed through all her senses. She lifted her arms as if they were wings. The wind caught her sleeves. She closed her eyes and relived the sensation of soaring. Had Amaranth's dreams invaded her mind?

Suddenly, the puffy white clouds shifted. A ray of sunlight struck the jumble of rocks. Light arced out and up, filling the meadow with rainbows.

The children squealed in delight and danced about, trying to catch the pretty colors.

"Our oldest legends, before the days of the Stargods, tell us that rainbows are symbols of peace and goodwill," Nimbulan said in wonder. He turned a slow circle, eyes wide with amazement. "This isn't possible. Light doesn't refract through air this way. It needs a prism source. That waterfall isn't big enough to provide enough water for a rainbow. There must be crystal all about his meadow. Only a massive amount of crystal would make this happen."

"Look!" Powwell gasped and pointed above the little waterfall and the jumble of rocks.

Myri looked and saw only water and boulders and a few common plants.

"Dragons!" Kalen whispered. "A full nimbus of crystal dragons."

"I can't see anything but the rainbows," Nimbulan said.

"Who told you there are dragons here?" Myri stared at the little girl rather than the wonder of the rainbows. Memories pushed at her, demanding attention. Memories of . . . The familiarity vanished. "And how did you know to call it a nimbus and not a herd?" She knew a mating group of dragons was called a Nimbus. The dragons invented the word.

How did she know that?

"They told me," Kalen said, eyes open with genuine awe this time.

"Who told you?" Something akin to panic swelled within Myri's chest. She wasn't sure if she let it burst, it would free her of her forgetfulness or push it down again and find solace in not knowing.

"They told me." Kalen pointed to the sky above the waterfall. "The dragons told me, just like they told you."

"How long have the dragons spoken to you?" Myri didn't dare breathe. If she gave in to the longing to join the dragons, she'd have to remember everything, and challenge everything she knew about herself, including her new-found love for Nimbulan and the children.

"They spoke to me right after I discovered Nimbulan wasn't in the crypt. They led me to you and the clearing and your house. The clearing is going to be my home, too. We're all going to live there like a nimbus of humans and be happy."

Finally Myri swallowed the panic in her breast and looked where Kalen pointed. Letting her magic talent flow freely, without plan or push, her eyes followed Amaranth's antics in the sky. He traced the outline of a huge dragon. Glimmers of crystal wings and body outlined in a faint swirl of rainbow colors jumped into her vision.

Amaranth leaped to another point, and she saw a second dragon, silvery in body and outlined in green. Several more creatures appeared before her, each bearing a different hue on wing veins and spinal horns. Only the massive central dragon held all the colors around the edges.

Myri's heart beat double time. Her lungs labored to draw air. "I see them now," she admitted. Joy replaced her anxiety. Lightness filled her until she thought she could lift free of the Kardia and soar with the magnificent crystal beasts.

(Welcome home, my child. You all have much to learn. Come, eat your provisions, drink from the stream. We will begin to teach you a new form of magic when you are rested.)

Warmth and love folded around Myri as if the dragon had wrapped her in soft wings, like she would one of her own dragonets.

* * *

"The dogs have found something," the sergeant blurted out, rushing through the underbrush toward Moncriith. "The trail leads straight through the woods, no apparent path at all, but the scent is strong and the dogs are eager to make up for lost time."

"Then we must be off. The witchwoman and those children must be brought to justice before the Spring campaign season begins."

"Yes, Sieur. Children, Sieur?" The seargeant tugged at his maroon-and-green tunic as if it suddenly fit too tight. His face paled and a tightness thinned his lips. "We have never hunted children before, Sieur."

"I will make an example of both of them. They deserted my just cause to warn the chief demon of my pusuit. They forsake the people of Coronnan so that they may enjoy the power of demon magic. They won't enjoy it long. Their deaths will prove to the lords once and for all that they can't go to war with demons in their midst. And without demon magicians to protect their troops, they will think long and hard before entering battles."

"Coronnan will know unity at last." The sergeant parroted Moncriith's doctrine. His eyes remained fixed upon some distant point beyond Moncriith's shoulder. "Freedom from war and freedom from enslavement to demon magicians. Moncriith is the prophet of the Stargods. Only he knows the truth." He saluted the Bloodmage automatically and turned woodenly back to the task of finding Myrilandel and the children.

Moncriith smiled to himself. The guards Kammeryl

d'Astrismos had assigned to him were deep under his control. They'd never have a thought of their own again. He'd see to it even if he had to draw their blood to reinforce his spells. All Coronnan would bow to him, unquestioningly, before the end of the campaign season. His followers already regarded him as more god than priest.

* * *

(The words you speak matter not. Only that you say them in unison and the words contain the essence of your requirement. Speak together as you shape the magic you have gathered into the form of your spell.) Shayla, the all color/no color female dragon, directed Nimbulan and Powwell. The silvery young dragons with primary colors on their wing tips rested on nearby boulders and clifftops—too old to cavort like children, too young for their fur to be transparent crystal. All four of the dragonets were male.

Each of them sported a different color, no two alike. Shayla, the lone female, maintained the all color/no color crystal sparkles along her spinal horns and wing veins as well as her entire body, each hair as clear as crystal. The spiral horn sprouting from her forehead caught the light, swirled it away from the fine fur of her body, and flung it around the meadow in a dozen rainbows. The prismatic arcs terminated at a spot just behind her. The casual eye swept with the rainbows around the dragon, never seeing her magnificent beauty. Nimbulan found it impossible to look at her long. Yet he couldn't look anywhere else.

He drew a deep breath. Powwell did, too. They released the air at the same time and recited the simple spell formula.

"Wisp of flame, burning bright
Travel far beyond my sight
Bring to view the other true
Pass the word of magic might"

Nimbulan concentrated on the tiny candle flame on the other side of Powwell's apprentice glass, held proudly by its owner. Magic energy pulsed around them in unison with their heartbeat. A visible aura of power blended around both their forms, binding them together. They watched through the glass the vision of the flame skipping across the meadow behind them. Without turning to watch with physical eyes, they monitored the progress of the flame until it burst into the still pool at the edge of the stream.

Through the glass they watched Myri and Kalen from the perspective of the bottom of the pool. Their features took on focus with the slight distortion of looking upward through water. Kalen reared back her head, startled. Myri peered closer, puzzled and curious.

Nimbulan mouthed "I love you." She smiled and returned the silent greeting.

The vision faltered, then cleared. All he could see was a burned-out candle wick standing behind the small scrap of precious glass he held in his hand.

"We shouldn't have been able to do that, Powwell. Myri wasn't using any of her magic senses to channel the flame. And she looked into water, not glass. The spell couldn't have worked with one magician alone using the old magic."

"Let's try it again. I'll work with Myri. You combine with Kalen." The boy dashed across the full length of the meadow to join the women.

A brief conversation ensued that Nimbulan couldn't hear. But Kalen's exhausted posture told him volumes. The new procedure drained her of energy. He didn't understand why. Magic was merely fuel for an inborn talent. Weren't Kalen and Myri gathering the dragon magic at all? He'd already checked that there were no ley lines near this meadow to interfere with the new procedures.

They'd quit soon and have some dinner. He needed to try the spell one more time, to make certain he had the formula memorized. Maybe after Kalen and Myri ate, they'd be more receptive to gathering dragon magic.

The dragon nodded agreement. Nimbulan clutched Kalen's hand as he lit the candle once more with a snap of his fingers. The new magic flared easily from his fingers.

His belly growled with hunger. Dragon magic also demanded more bodily fuel to hone an inborn talent than the old forms. One more time with the summons spell, then he'd eat.

"You've memorized the words, Kalen?" Nimbulan asked.

She nodded, breathing deeply as she'd been taught. They spoke the words together.

The magic remained inert. The flame stayed firmly rooted to the candle.

"Let's switch again, Powwell. Kalen's too tired. Send Myri over here." Nimbulan called across the meadow toward the streambed where they crouched.

A few moments later, with Myri's hand clutch lovingly in his own, they recited the words again. Nothing happened.

"What's the matter, Shayla? What are we doing wrong?"

The dragon shrugged her massive shoulders in a curiously human gesture. The dragon's long, spiked tail swished impatiently, back and forth in the grass. She had already swept a clear circle around her with the wicked spines. No part of the dragon came close to touching, or harming any of the humans.

"I'm the problem. I can't do it." Myri turned her back on Nimbulan and Shayla.

Nimbulan wrapped his arm around Myri's waist and pulled her head onto his shoulder. "We'll rest a while and try again." He dismissed Kalen and Powwell from their perches at the edge of the brook.

Kalen visibly drooped with fatigue and disappointment as she curled up in the forearms of the now-reclining dragon. Shayla's wings fluttered and stretched into a protective posture—as if Kalen was one of her own offspring. Kalen drifted off to sleep almost immediately, curling into the dragon's warmth. But Powwell looked as bright and alert as ever. He dove into the pack of provisions, pulling out a fistful of jerked meat. He made a face at the dry journey food but bit deeply into the tough fare.

(Fresh meat will replenish your body better than that. *The little ones will hunt for you.)* Shayla dipped her head as her telepathic speech fell to a whisper so as not to awaken Kalen.

"You are all so beautiful," Myri said as she watched the

smaller dragons launch into the air. "Why didn't I know before that you were the voices who guided me through life?"

"How long have they been urging you to come to them?" Nimbulan asked, spreading a blanket on the grass near their packs, just outside the circle of Shayla's tail sweep.

"Nearly a year now. I kept delaying while I stopped to help people who needed healing."

"Like you stopped at the battlefield. I'm glad I had the chance to see you work before we were thrust together again by fate."

"By fate or by dragon lure?" She laughed and caressed his cheek with her palm.

"Maybe both. I do remember a voice in the wind telling me to go East. I'd find what I sought in the East. This dragon magic is better than Rover ritual."

(We waited for you both to grow and mature into the vision of united magicians and united mundanes. You had to recognize the need before you could use the tool,) Shayla said, nodding her head at their clasped hands. The pastel colors of her eyes suggested a smile—if a dragon could smile.

Nimbulan kissed Myri's forehead as he eased her down onto the blanket.

A smile lit his mind. Myri's white-blonde hair and pale eyes reminded him of Quinnault! The curious elongated shadows he'd seen on Quinnault's face had looked curiously like the muzzle of a dragon.

"You sneaky creatures. You've been priming all of us for this moment. Maybe using us is a better word. How many of Quinnault's words of peace came from you?" He laughed in admiration of their foresight—or precognition. How much of past and future did dragons see?

Shayla nodded her head slightly. A light chuckle of approval and agreement whispered across his mind.

"What if I can't gather their magic?" Myri interrupted his speculation.

"You will. It just takes a bit of searching to find it. The air is filled with it. Breathe it in, like a heady aroma then concentrate and push the air deep into your being, behind your heart."

"I've tried again and again. I can't even smell the Tambootie in the air that you and Powwell can. Kalen can't find it either. What if this new magic belongs only to men?"

(She may be right.) Shayla speared them with her big crystalline eyes. Looking directly at the refracting light drew Nimbulan out of his body, deep into the sparkling colors, so like the colored umbilicals he'd seen in the void.

"We will try again," Nimbulan insisted. "Myri must be a part of gathering and combining magic. You dragons singled her out of all humans to be your link to us. And I need her to be a part of everything I do. In this life and the next." He kissed her again, long and full.

The world drifted away. Only he and Myri remained, their bodies, minds and souls entwining like a spiral of sparkling light illuminating the void.

"Can't you two do anything but kiss?" Powwell loomed over them, hands on hips, a disgusted, but fascinated scowl on his face. "Dinner's here. The dragons brought a deer. They even gutted and cooked it for us. But we'll have to skin it. I'd love to ride a dragon while they hunt. Their fire must reach a hundred leagues!"

(Far less than one league, child. Barely two dragon lengths,) Shayla chuckled.

"Have you something to dig roots with? The dragonets will roast them for us, too. I'm hungry. Can you really throw flames that far, Shayla? I bet you'd end a battle real quick with just one blast." Powwell said.

The dragon stilled and almost faded from view.

(Do not suggest that dragon fire be used as a weapon. We have vowed to teach you to control your magic and your battles rather than blast you away with our anger.)

Shayla came back into view, her rainbow horns and wings glowed brighter than before. She bent her head as if listening intently to the young man. *(Now that you gather dragon magic, you will need dragon food. Enjoy the meat we provide you.)* A curious expression came over the dragon's muzzle, a mirror image of Powwell's hungry gaze at the deer carcass.

Myri laughed, breaking away from Nimbulan. Nimbulan chuckled, too. Adolescence must be catching up with Powwell for him to be so concerned with food. Nimbulan faced his fiftieth birthday next Winter. He shouldn't be so hungry his stomach felt like it was wrapping around his spine.

"There are fresh greens growing on the bank of the brook, Powwell. Pick those and eat them raw. 'Tis the wrong season for roots." Myri stood, brushing off her skirt.

"Raw vegetables! Ugh." Powwell stuck out his lower lip and tongue, scrunching up his nose in distaste. A young dragon did, too.

"You ate my ma's greens all the time, Powwell," Kalen informed him. She stretched and yawned from her nest in the dragon paws. "And you liked greens back at the school well enough to ask for more."

"But your ma boiled them in soup stock and dressed them in vinegar and spices. Myri wants us to eat this stuff raw! A man needs his food cooked."

"A man needs nutrition any way he can get it. We'll eat the greens raw." Nimbulan tried to look sternly at Powwell. Memories of his own childhood view of good food and "women's food" tickled deep inside him. He wanted to bellow with laughter and good will.

His good humor continued through the improvised meal. He and Powwell ate ravenously. Myri and Kalen only picked at their food. "Why don't you and Kalen watch for a while, Myri?" Nimbulan suggested. "Perhaps you can learn something to make the task easier."

"I feel like I should remember how to do it." Myri turned haunted eyes up to him. "I want to remember how to do it, just like I want to remember how to fly. When I don't want my past to touch me, events and people parade before my mind's eye with annoying regularity. When I need to remember, I can't find any part of myself in the past."

"Don't push it, Myri. Memory is like quicksilver. It looks tangible until you touch it. Then it spurts away, breaking into hundreds of sparkling, unrelated entities," he soothed.

(You must remember, my child,) Shayla said. *(Without you, all our efforts are for nothing.)*

Suddenly, the dragon reared her steedlike muzzle in alarm. Steam seeped out of her nostrils. Her eyes shifted rapidly from nearly colorless to a wild array of primary colors, never lingering on one for more than two heart-beats. With a loud blast of sound, almost above human hearing, she burst upward into flight.

CHAPTER 29

At last the trail dog put his nose to the Kardia and yelped with excitement. Moncriith breathed a sigh of relief. Myrilandel and the children had tried to fool him by walking down the center of a stream, but the dogs had found where they left the water. The dog dragged him through a brambleberry thicket. Thorns snagged and tore his new red robe—bright red, closer to the color worn by priests than of old blood.

"*Simurgh* take you to all the living hells!" he yelled at the dog as his cuff clung to yet another bush. This one was sticky and tried to wrap itself around his arm.

He stumbled and ran, desperately clinging to the animal's leash. A long branch of the clinging shrub detached itself from the main trunk with a sickening slurpy sound.

The dog yelped again and dashed forward.

They were close. Moncriith sensed Myrilandel's presence just ahead. The witchwoman wasn't alone. The evil magic he smelled grew to enormous proportions. She must be hiding in the demon lair! Not far now. After all these years of tracking demons, he would finally rid Coronnan of all of them at once.

A doubt wiggled into his mind. How would he handle several large demons at once? Did he truly know the strength of a demon? He buried his misgivings where he'd hidden his memories of Magretha and his father. The Stargods had chosen him to rid Coronnan of the demons. The Stargods would not, could not fail him now. Not when he was so close.

The dog stopped running so abruptly Moncriith nearly tripped over him. Frantically the animal dug at a hole in the ground. Dirt flew behind him, pelting Moncriith with large clods and small rocks.

"*S'murghin'* useless beast. First you can't find a scent at all, and now you track a path even a striped lapin couldn't follow into a mole hole!"

More frantic yelps from the other four dogs sounded in the near distance. They, too, had caught an elusive scent and converged on the same mole hole.

Moncriith dropped the leash from his sweating palm in disgust. Five dogs digging in one tiny hole in the center of a tangle of brambleberry vines would lead his quest nowhere.

He thrashed his way clear of the thorny vines that reached out and grabbed him as he passed. "What is wrong with your dogs?" he asked the nearest guard.

The young man blushed and stammered, unable to meet Moncriith's gaze.

"I'll tell you what's wrong with them!" Moncriith shouted. Heat flooded his face and sent twitches through his hands. "Your dogs . . ."

The forest stilled. No bird song lightened the heavy air. The tiny rustlings in the underbrush ceased. A pricking sensation sent the fine hairs on the back of Moncriith's neck standing on end.

"What?" Moncriith searched the forest for the source of danger one and all sensed. Even the dogs had ceased their digging and yelping. They stood with their neck ruffs erect and teeth bared in silent growls.

A huge shadow blocked the sun.

"Yikkiiiii. . . ." The lead dog tucked his tail between his legs and ran downhill. The others burst from the thicket, pelting in different directions as if *Simurgh* himself pursued them.

"A—a dragon, Sieur!" A guard pointed upward. All color drained from his face. His mouth flapped open and shut several times before he could speak again. "It's hunting, Sieur. Hunting us."

"Nonsense." Moncriith tried to present an aura of calm. Lumbird bumps erupted on his skin and his mouth went dry. He followed the guard's pointing finger and nearly fouled his trews.

He saw the outline of a dragon above the trees.

"Stargods, preserve me." He crossed himself again and again. The shadow did not go away.

A sense of peace flooded his mind, replacing his anxiety. The frustration of the past days of searching vanished. He smiled in triumph. He had already killed all the demons and Myrilandel and Nimbulan. He must return to Castle Krej with the good news. Immediately.

* * *

Nimbulan searched the skies for signs of Shayla in flight. A few moments after her departure, the female dragon flew back into the meadow with a wild screech that sounded oddly triumphant. She clutched the carcass of a tracking dog in her front paws.

Nimbulan looked questioningly at the bloody animal.

(This creature picked up your trail with its sensitive nose. It led men too close to this meadow. We cannot afford an interruption until you have learned what we have to teach you.)

"How close?" he asked. Televarn? Only a Rover as tenacious—obsessed, Myri had said—as Televarn had the audacity to follow them into the wilderness.

(The one who pretends to priesthood cannot find you. The other dogs have scattered in fear. The men wearing the clothes all alike ran with them at sight of me. Only the one in new red persists, and I have given him a dream that will take him back where he started from.)

"Moncriith!" Myri paled. "He will remember. He has no other reason for living than to watch me burn." She stared at the dragon with less effort than Nimbulan could.

(If he remembers outside the dragon dream, then you can, too. You must remember how to gather dragon magic.)

"Why me? I can't do it, but Nimbulan and Powwell can. Why me?"

(You are the one we trust. We have guarded you for many years, waiting for you to forge a covenant between dragonkind and humans.)

"If you want her to remember, then she must have done this before," Nimbulan mused. "If she did it before, she would have a memory, but all her memories come and go, as if she were breaking through a spell. A very strong spell that is renewed each time she tries to break free. Did you impose the spell?" Nimbulan forced himself to look Shayla directly in her eye. With effort he maintained his sense of self and kept the dragon within view.

(Dragons have limited magic. Our defenses have always been in our size, our flight, and our fire. Against human magicians these are not always enough.)

An old grief assailed Nimbulan. Reflected in Shayla's eyes he saw men battling across a wheatfield near the River Coronnan. At first he thought he saw the battle last Autumn when he had been forced to kill Keegan. Then, he noticed the style of uniforms dated back twenty years—to the time when an out-of-control spell had burned the field and all who stood within it. Druulin, Boojlin, and Caasser had died in the hellish fires that day.

Nimbulan and Ackerly had escaped death only because Nimbulan had finally broken Druulin's binding spell on Ackerly the night before. The cunning old man had known that Nimbulan could break any spell placed upon him. But the spell placed upon another—especially one that held death in the breaking would defy him for a long time. Druulin also knew that Nimbulan wouldn't leave without Ackerly. So the spell had been placed upon the lesser magician. Nimbulan took ten years learning to break the spell. They had run away to take service with Kammeryl d'Astrismos the night before the fateful battle.

His perspective shifted to an aerial view. The Kardia no longer supported his feet. He looked around and discovered himself flying alongside Shayla—arms outstretched like wings, the wind buffeting his face and keeping him aloft. His stomach lurched with the unaccustomed sensation of flight.

A vague tingling ran up and down his leg. He shared Shayla's pain as magic gone awry pierced them both. His belly cramped as Shayla began her premature labor.

Anger at the irresponsible magicians below boiled within them both. They opened their jaws wide, sending forth a blast of dragon fire. He watched as flames engulfed the people below, spread to the dry wheat, and up the few trees. He heard Druulin and his assistants scream in agony as fire took them.

He took no satisfaction in the revenge. The ghost of dead baby dragons haunted both of them.

Suddenly he was free of the hypnotic contact and knew who he was and why he stood in this mountain meadow learning a new form of magic.

(We can give you dreams of what has happened or what you want to happen. Rarely, we can give you a glimpse of what will happen. Nothing else that we can tell you is within our power. Yet we are a source of magic for those who choose to accept our covenant,) Shayla said.

Knowing her grief, Nimbulan wanted desperately to be among those who formed the covenant between dragonkind and humans, to use Shayla's magic for peace and control of those who wielded magic indiscriminately and harmed innocent bystanders. Caasser had thrown the spell that wounded Shayla—a spell Nimbulan had devised and taught his fellow magician.

Nimbulan looked at Shayla and her children with new sympathy. "I take responsibility for those who hurt you. I was not at the battle, but I could have been. I could have woven the spell that cost you the lives of your babies.

(Will you work to end the irresponsible use of magic?)

"I so swear by the Stargods and all I hold dear."

The dragons didn't respond immediately. Nimbulan searched Shayla's eyes for some indication that he had been accepted by them.

He fell into the glittering whirlpool of Shayla's eyes. Dizziness overwhelmed him. Then he awoke, sitting in a thronelike chair padded and covered in blue and silver, the signature colors of his magic. Around him, other magicians sat in similar chairs, each covered in different colors. He recognized none of the men, all much younger than he. Except . . . was that Lyman to his right, his face shadowed by the torches stuck into wall brackets directly above him? In the center of the circular stone room rested a table unlike any he had seen before. One solid piece of black glass. No forge in all of Kardia Hodos could generate enough heat to burn away the impurities of black sand to create true glass of a quality to stand up to daily use. Only one source of clean sand existed that could make the small glass lenses used by magicians.

No man could afford a table of solid black glass.

(No one man could afford the table, but a commune of

magicians in covenant with the dragons could request dragon fire to forge such a rare symbol of their combined power.)

Abruptly, Nimbulan was back in the meadow, standing next to Myri, facing Shayla, a live dragon who promised them a way to create peace. His hand still tingled with the cold, smooth feel of black glass. . . .

"Can you give Myri a dragon dream of her past so that she will know how to gather your magic?" He pressed his temple to push away the lingering memory of the magicians working in concert around that magnificent table. The magnitude of the spell they shaped awed him.

Beside him, Myri gasped and shook her head in denial of those memories.

(Myrilandel is not ready. When the time is right, she will know what is important. Her lineage and her childhood will become clear.)

"What about the near past? The days that come and go without my awareness, though I march through them?" She clung to Nimbulan's hand, her sweating palm nearly slipping away.

(The near past is under your control. When you can accept what you have done and what has been done to you, you will remember.)

"But I need to know!"

"Think of the quicksilver, Myri. The images will come when you need them." But Nimbulan wasn't sure. He'd seen several people so traumatized by the wars and the ghastly deeds perpetuated in the name of right that they chose never to remember. Not even their birth name. Some invented exotic pasts that had nothing to do with reality but recreated the person into someone they would rather be than themselves.

Who was Myrilandel? Could Moncriith's delusion of demons spring from his interpretation of the dragons that protected her and guided her? Only the dragons knew for sure. They trusted Myri, believed in her, depended upon her for a most important mission. He committed himself to do the same.

* * *

"I still don't know if the dragons warned me that the villagers would betray me. They may have sent Moncriith to follow us," Myri said as she and Nimbulan headed back to the clearing. The clearing, with a small hut they had called home for a time. A home where they could live safely, privately, raising Kalen and Powwell.

"If you don't trust the villagers, we'll have to wait until we reach the School for Magicians to be married," Nimbulan said. "Powwell said that two retired priests had signed on to the faculty."

She didn't want to go with him. The dragons had promised her a home. She'd found that home. But Nimbulan was not destined to be part of her family in the clearing. He had greater things to accomplish at his school.

But if she didn't go with him, she would be alone again.

I am tired of being alone.

Amaranth landed on a branch above her head. The rising wind made him clutch at his perch with fully extended talons. *(You aren't alone. You have me. You have the dragons. We are your family,)* he said.

She looked at Nimbulan, felt the heat of his hand holding hers as they walked. Ahead of them, Kalen and Powwell skipped and capered down the path toward home. Love and joy filled her heart at the nearness of them. The physical pleasure of touching another human being for no other reason than to touch overwhelmed her. She raised her hand, still linked with Nimbulan's and kissed their entwined fingers.

He smiled down at her and returned the gesture. "We will be married at the first opportunity, Myri. I promise."

I need him, Amaranth. Just as I am incomplete without you and the dragons. I must go with him. We *must take this new magic back to the other magicians. This is what the dragons planned for us all those years ago. I have to leave my home.*

(You will come back.)

Yes, Amaranth. I will come back. We will all come back when we have completed our task. She held out her arm as a new perch for her familiar. The flywacket spread his wings just enough to glide down to her. He retracted his talons at the last moment and landed softly upon her forearm, then siddled up to her shoulder. He wrapped his fluffy tail around her neck for balance and nuzzled her cheek. His purr sent warm comfort through her entire being.

"We're here!" Powwell called just ahead.

"I can see the roof," Kalen added.

"I'm hungry," said Powwell.

"You're always hungry." Kalen punched him in the arm.

Myri looked up at the overcast sky. "There will be rain soon. I can smell it on the wind. We'd best hurry."

(You are needed,) dragon voices invaded her head.

She wrapped her hand around Amaranth's muscular body, strengthening her contact to him. Beside her, Nimbulan stilled, waiting for the rest of the dragon's message.

(Fishermen in trouble.)

"Will the villagers accept my help or betray me?" she asked the sky. She couldn't see any dragon outline against the rapidly gathering clouds. Spring often brought sudden storms—short in duration but violent while they lasted.

A sense of urgency pushed aside her doubts and fears. Men were in trouble. Her feet needed to fly down the steep path to the village right now. Without delay.

What stores of herbs and poultices did she have in the hut? Her mind raced to the few remedies she had left. She lingered over the list, overruling her anxious feet. Was she strong enough to help? Her healing spells for Nimbulan had drained her badly.

"I'll take care of you afterward, Myri. I heard the command as clearly as you did. Go. I'll gather some herbs and the leftover bandages. Don't worry. I'll come as fast as I can," he said, urging her forward. "Remember what I taught you about the ley lines. Stand close to the Equinox Pylon where the lines cross and use the strength of the lines to fuel your healing."

"Follow me, Amaranth." She urged him off her shoulder so that he could fly and not hinder her own run to the village.

(Go. Now. You cannot be late.)

Amaranth launched himself upward, pushing his wings

downward with powerful strokes. *(We come,)* he announced.

The wind whispered of small boats swamped by waves and hungry rocks reaching to slash and impale new victims.

CHAPTER 30

Myri's bare feet found the path into the village without really knowing where she ran. Her mind was with the gale that whipped the waves to a crashing froth. The uncaring air was too busy shifting from here to there to pay attention to the men who were in trouble. Myri found no trace of their life energies. She lifted her arms, letting the wind catch her sleeves. The sensation of almost flight gave her greater speed.

A week ago, when she and Nimbulan were drained of all strength, this same journey in reverse had taken days. Now with her health restored, and the urgency of the dragons pushing her forward, she ran the distance in less than an hour.

Her magic tether to Nimbulan's heart stretched but did not break. For the first time in nearly a week, she was separated from him by more than a few arm's lengths. Loneliness assailed her already.

Her talent pulled her forward. She had to run with it.

The dozen cottages huddled together on the edge of the bluff above a narrow gravel beach looked smaller, shabbier, abandoned since she'd left here a week ago.

She looked out over the bay for physical signs of the men in trouble. Rain squalls and low clouds obscured her view of the waters beyond the cove. Waves rose too high, too fast to reveal what might hide in the troughs. Only small boats with crews of three or four could maneuver through the Dragon's Teeth, the jagged outcropping from the bay floor that changed currents at will and disguised depths.

Myri headed for the dark and smoky pub. All of the villagers would gather there to organize a rescue or mourn the dead.

Tension hung with the gloomy smoke and the silence in the crowded pub. Doors closed against the storm intensified the stale and murky air. A few men sipped at mugs of ale. Anxious women stared into their cups lest they catch the eye and the worry of another. No stories of daring deeds and monster fish trapped in the nets passed around the cave. No lewd jokes or grumbling of what might have been.

Yoshi, the simple boy, poked sticks into the central fire, silently watching the glowing embers. He was big and strong, in his early twenties, but his mind had never grown after a bout of brain fever when he was ten. The same fever that nearly claimed him last winter. He took orders well, but had few thoughts of his own. He didn't look up at Myri's entrance. A sure sign of his preoccupation.

"Who is missing?" Myri asked as she stood on the threshold. The anxiety of the men and women invaded her heart. She scanned the group, counting heads, lumping family groups together.

"Rory's boat of four," Karry replied. "Kelly has three in his." Years of pitching her voice to be heard over a noisy throng made her near whisper seem a shout.

Amaranth crept between Myri's feet to curl up by the fire. His purpley-black fur absorbed the meager light of the central hearth, draining it from the rest of the cave. A grizzled old man shifted his stool away from proximity with the flywacket. He crossed himself in the manner of the Stargods, then surreptitiously placed his left wrist over his right and flapped his hands.

Yoshi didn't know enough to be afraid of the witchwoman's familiar and reached out a hand to caress the cat. Amaranth nuzzled his outstretched palm, but didn't purr. "Rory be smart," Yoshi told Amaranth. "He'll not try for home in this weather. Knows the Dragon's Teeth won't let him land till the wind slacks and the tide changes."

Karry poured another round of ale from pitchers. Her smile trembled, then reasserted itself, too wide, too fixed.

"Something's wrong." Myri leaned out the door, hesitant to throw herself into the business of rescuing the men, needing to help and obey the compulsion within her to heal. The rising storm and tricky currents threatened her life more than the drain of a normal healing.

"They're coming through now!" Nimbulan shouted as he ran down the cliff path.

"Get ropes and blankets," Karry ordered the men. "Yoshi, build up the fire and find bandages!" Turning to Myri, she whispered, "Who's he?"

"My friend." Myri smiled her love for Nimbulan, then turned and raced for the steps cut into the bluff leading to the beach and the jagged rocks that had claimed more than one life. Karry would organize the villagers here in the pub, but they wouldn't hasten to venture forth into the crashing waves. Could any of them swim? Probably not.

She met cold, wet gravel at the base of the bluff with her bare feet. Spring was barely here. The storm could still contain a last blast of Winter. Myri acknowledged the season with a regretful wish for her clogs and woolen socks. But foot coverings would hinger her movements. She needed freedom to rescue the men in the bobbing boat just visible in the trough between two waves. One boat, riding low, not two.

Would they find safety or death in their mad attempt to return home?

She peered through the thickening cloud layer that blended with the sea. Sheets of rain brought the horizon closer. The fury of the sea seemed to push the speck of black that was the boat, farther away from the shore.

An opening between waves revealed the much closer outline of the boat, overcrowded with seven men. Too close to the Dragon's Teeth. The stern sank lower yet and the bow tilted in the wind.

Nimbulan appeared at her side. His arm clasped her waist and brought her close to him. The warmth of his body brought a moment's relief from the chill rain. "You can't be thinking of going after them."

"I must. They'll die. I'll follow them into the void if they die before I help them." She closed her eyes against the vision of death that awaited in the waves among the Dragon's Teeth.

"Then let me help the only way I can. I can't swim." He looked regretfully toward the boat. "I'll send a rope to them by magic. They can lash the rope to the bow and we can all pull them in." He indicated the men standing hesitantly on the edge of the cliff. Powwell and Kalen stood in front of the villagers, ready to jump to Nimbulan's and Myri's orders.

Powwell raced down the path to join them.

"The rope will get tangled in the rocks," Myri protested, eyeing the narrow channel between them.

"Maybe I can levitate the boat enough to clear the worst of them."

"Do you have the strength to work?" she shouted above the wind. "Can you and Powwell combine to keep the spell going?"

Nimbulan shrugged. "Like you, we have to try."

She watched them take the regulation three breaths. Nimbulan's eyes went blank and rolled slightly upward. Then he raised his hand high over his head. The rope held by the men on the cliff uncoiled and spun outward, toward the foundering boat.

Myri followed the progress of the rope end with her own talent, willing the fishermen to lash it tight to the prow of the overcrowded vessel. When she sensed the rope in place, she waved her arms to the men who had drifted down the path to the gravel beach. As if with one mind, they pulled, leaning all of their weight into bringing the boat ashore.

She shifted her mind back to the men in the boat. A tall wave washed over them. They clung to the sides precariously. A huge spire of rock loomed directly ahead of them.

"Quickly, Lan, lift them high and to the right!"

He closed his eyes in fierce concentration. Half of Myri's concentration remained with him. The other half monitored the panicky fishermen.

Were the dragons flying nearby, giving the magic power Nimbulan and Powell needed to sustain the spell?

She watched the fishing boat edge past the pinnacle of rock. Their tremendous relief came to her in a rush.

Nimbulan was tiring. Strain whitened the little wrinkles around his eyes. He couldn't sustain the levitation much longer and Powwell was far too inexperienced to take over the spell.

The next massive wave dashed against the boat, carrying it away from Nimbulan's waning spell directly into the rock. He sank to his knees in exhaustion, clutching his arms across the wound in his belly.

Seven men went under. Their cries of despair stabbed at her heart. Her mind shared the shock of cold, the gulping of too much salt water, the lack of air, the weight against tired limbs and the first hungry bites of the Dragon's Teeth.

Myri shed her bodice and skirt as she dove into an oncoming wave, reaching out in long strokes to carry her toward the drowning men.

Another giant wave rose between Myri and sight of the men. Achingly cold water enfolded her, numbing her limbs and her mind.

The men's fear pulled her forward.

* * *

Nimbulan's heart leaped to his throat as Myri dove into the roaring waves. Her slender body, clad only in her shift, took on the sleek form of some water-born creature. She seemed to expand, turn silvery, tinged with purple. The waves parted for her graceful undulating movements. For a moment he lost sight of her. How could anyone—anything—survive the swirling currents that smashed up against the jagged rocks?

He despaired of ever seeing her again, feeling her quiet presence at his side as he woke in the middle of the night, hearing her gentle laughter at his awful jokes, finding the *right* rhyme to accompany his spells. His world emptied of all emotion. He couldn't give way to grief now. He had to be ready to help her at the first sign of trouble.

If he ever saw her again.

There, nearly invisible against the rising blackness of water, he caught sight of a darting form in the water. A white blob of a face appeared at the wave's crest, gasping and choking. Myri's long white arm that looked amazingly like a silvery wing, reached out to curl around the man's neck. The man fought her grasp briefly, then collapsed into the water's embrace.

Moments later, Myri dragged the man up the gravelly shore. Her body once more the same as he had watched dive into the waves; a slender woman wearing a drenched shift that might as well have been as transparent as a dragon wing. Tiny rocks cut into her bare feet. The greedy sea absorbed the thin rivulets of red, sucking them away.

He ran to her, catching her in his arms as her knees crumpled. He clutched her close against his chest, pushing his remaining warmth and strength into her. Others pulled the choking man to safety.

"The others," Myri said as she turned within his embrace. "I must save the others."

"Take some deep breaths. Clear your lungs," he ordered.

"I'll be all right as long as I know you are safe here, on shore. In the water, it's . . . I'm . . . I can't explain. It's like I become the water. The dragons are with me, telling me what to do, how to avoid the rocks and changing currents. I wonder if I am part dragon the way I understand them."

"Merlep mew!" Amaranth screeched as he plunged into the next wave, his wings tight against his body, claws extended.

The sight of his diving body triggered a memory in Nimbulan. He saw again the black creature flying into the column of flame that guarded the abandoned monastery.

Stargods! Amaranth had joined with the guardian spirit to test Nimbulan and Quinnault. Amaranth? Why hadn't he been with Myri?

The spirit had disappeared. Briefly, he wondered if Amaranth was the guardian or had absorbed it.

"I have to go. Amaranth can't keep him above water for long." Myri twisted from Nimbulan's arms and dove into the next huge wave.

In the trough, between crests, the white blob of another face showed briefly. The dark speck that might be Amaranth, swam beside the man, front talons and mouth clamped into the collar of his shirt.

Before Nimbulan's eyes, the flywacket grew and faded into transparency. His wings stretched out and out and out, to become life-saving floats.

A dozen terrifying heartbeats later, Myri reached the unconscious fisherman and began the exhausting process of dragging him back to shore.

Lightning flashed across the sky, blinding Nimbulan for an eye blink. When he looked back to find Myri, he couldn't distinguish her from Amaranth. They both seemed half dragon in the weird light. Then Amaranth retracted the spectacular transparent wings and dove into the next wave, once more a black flywacket.

Myri remained silvery and unnaturally buoyant until she reached shallow water. When she stood up, dragging the half-drowned fisherman, she was fully human once more.

Nimbulan shook his head free of the hallucinations and dashed to help her bring the fisherman ashore.

Three more times Myri and Amaranth pulled men from the jaws of the Dragon's Teeth. Three more times, Nimbulan watched helplessly as they performed impossible feats of strength and agility within the crushing currents. Each time they dove, he was certain he'd lost them forever. The emptiness of his life without the witchwoman and her familiar nearly choked him.

The fifth time Myri dragged a fisherman onto the beach Amaranth crawled out with her, bedraggled, exhausted, miserable. They both collapsed against the sharp gravel, in danger of drowning in two inches of water that swirled about their faces. Nimbulan scooped up the flywacket, who now looked like an ordinary half-drowned cat, with one arm while he grabbed Myri around her waist. He tried lifting her clear of the water. Burning pain slashed across his partially healed wound.

Yoshi and Powwell dashed to grab Myri as Nimbulan lost his grasp of her.

"No more, Myri. Don't go into the water anymore." Yoshi said as he carried her to safety.

Powwell tucked a blanket around her. He looked back to Nimbulan. Awe and concern flashed across his eyes in rapid succession.

"Two more. There are two more men out there!" Myri cried.

"You can't save the last two," Nimbulan said as he cradled Amaranth against his chest. Kalen threw another blanket over them both.

Myri struggled briefly against Yoshi's tight hold of her, then collapsed, a limp, dead weight.

"They're dead. It's too late," she said, looking regretfully back to the angry waves.

"You did what you could. You saved five men who would have died without you." Nimbulan brushed wet hair out of her eyes with his fingers. Briefly he regretted Yoshi easily managing her weight. Then common sense asserted itself. He was in no shape to carry her. He'd be lucky to make it up the cliff path without help.

"Five. Only five." Myri moaned her grief.

Villagers rushed forward with blankets and chattering concern. Nimbulan allowed a stout woman to take Amaranth. She wrapped the cat in the folds of rough wool, rubbing his fur dry, pushing her face close to the animal's while she cooed praise and comfort.

Yoshi set Myri back on her feet as Kalen and Powwell draped a second blanket around her shoulders. All three of them rubbed the coarse weave against her arms, back, and legs to stimulate her body's natural heat.

Another woman gave Nimbulan a dry blanket and ushered all of them toward the warmth and shelter of the pub. The smell of hot soup and cider drew him to the pool of light spilling out from the doorway.

"Thank you." Myri kissed his cheek, then rested her head limply against his shoulder. "Knowing you were waiting for me, helping me, almost protecting me, made the job less frightening. I've never had anyone wait for me like that." She looked up as if scanning the ceiling of the pub for evidence of the dragons. They had helped her, too, she had said.

"I will always be here to help you, Myri." He paused at the doorway to the pub. Both of their stomachs raised loud grumbles at the onslaught of the enticing smells and promise of protection from the storm inside the pub.

Gently they laughed, pressing their foreheads together in wonderfully private intimacy.

"Does that mean you will go with her to the cleansing fires?" Moncriith asked from right behind them.

CHAPTER 31

Powwell trembled at Moncriith's words. How had the Bloodmage found them? The dragons had given him a dream that would take him back to Castle Krej.

Beside him, he felt Kalen go stiff with anger. Her eyes opened wide in her innocent act—something she hadn't done since they'd found Nimbulan and Myri.

"The children led me to you, Nimbulan, so that I can fulfill the vision provided me by the Stargods. When I awoke from whatever enchantment you and the the witch put on me and found my men and dogs scattered, nearly witless, I realized I had not killed any demons after all. So I decided to seek the children instead of the witch. Once I remembered that I had kept threads of their old clothing smeared with blood from their small cuts and scratches, all I had to do was link blood to blood and I found them." The Bloodmage chuckled at his own cleverness.

Guilt washed over Powwell. He should have known Moncriith could find them through the clothes they had disgarded at Castle Krej.

"The witch and her consort must be burned to cleanse this land of demons." Moncriith raised his arms to the cave ceiling in a dramatic gesture that Powwell had seen all too often. It had no more meaning to him than if the man scratched his backside. But the people crowding the pub looked up wide-eyed and silent.

Only when he saw the cave ceiling did Powwell realize he was underground again. The smoke and smell of too many bodies crowded together, robbed him of air. He felt the weight of all of Kardia Hodos pressing on his head and chest. All trace of magic deserted his body with his growing panic.

He was defenseless, helpless to join his magic with Nimbulan to oust the Bloodmage.

Kalen took his hand in hers. An image of a flower-strewn field open to sun and wind flashed from her mind to his. He relaxed a little and listened.

"Don't be ridiculous," Nimbulan scoffed. He turned his back on the priest and stalked into the depths of the cave, keeping a half-drowned Myrilandel within the circle of his arms. Powwell noticed how his shoulders had tensed and his grip on her had tightened. Whispers erupted throughout the pub.

"Nimbulan will know what to do. We should stay close to him," Powwell whispered to Kalen as he breathed a little deeper. The ceiling of the cave still seemed awfully close to his head.

Kalen darted a look at Moncriith that Powwell didn't understand. "You need to stay by the door so you can breathe, Powwell," she answered. Resolutely, she eased him through the shadows toward the doorway.

He wanted to rush to Nimbulan. He also wanted to get out of this cave. But Moncriith stood in his way, blocking the entrance.

"You can't ignore me anymore, Nimbulan. I have the authority of Lord Kammeryl d'Astrismos," Moncriith shouted as he stepped past the doorway into the pub interior.

A hush grew outward from his words. No one moved. The only sound in the cavern was the crackling of the fire and the swish of Amaranth's tail against the rough wool of its nest in front of the flames.

"What do you want from us, Moncriith?" A stout woman stepped forward from the center of the crowd. She stood with her ample arms planted on her hips in a defiant stance.

"Out of my way, whore. I have cornered the demon that corrupts all of Coronnan. My vision will be fulfilled. She must burn."

"Not *s'murghin'* likely." One of the fishermen staggered to his feet. "Myri saved five men from certain death. She saved us when no one else could. Every last person in the village will defend her to the death." He coughed heavily then stood straighter. His wet hair still dripped into his eyes, and his hands shook with cold where he clutched a blanket around him. His face looked very pale from shock. Powwell had seen men in his condition after a battle.

Murmurs of assent rippled around the room. One old man even raised his fist in defiance and shook it at Moncriith.

"He's going to lose this time," Kalen whispered in Powwell's ear.

"I have soldiers waiting to follow my orders. Soldiers who will burn this entire town and all of you with it. Will you sacrifice your lives to die with the witch? Will you sacrifice your souls to her? She has already stolen the souls of five men who should have died and joined the Stargods. You think she saved your lives, but she stole them. You will be her slaves in evil for all eternity, never dying, never knowing free will!"

"Steed shit!" the heavy woman shouted above Moncriith's ranting. "Lord d'Astrismos fought hard to win this village back from Lord Baathalzan and the Kaaliph of Hanassa before that. We provide Lord Kammeryl's table with bay crawlers and his troops with bemouths. No other village dares hunt those killer fish, though one will feed half an army." The woman returned Moncriith's stare measure for measure.

Kalen yanked on the woman's skirt for attention. "He's lying. The six soldiers ran away. They won't return from Castle Krej unless compelled by the lord or magic." She pitched her voice to make sure the others heard her as well, then scuttled back to the doorway to hold Powwell's hand again.

"Fetch your soldiers, Moncriith," Nimbulan said, his voice deceptively calm. "Myrilandel and I will be long gone by the time you return." He removed his arm from Myri's shoulders, flexing his fingers. His left hand came up, palm outward, fingers slightly curved, ready to weave a spell—if he needed to.

Powwell walked boldly across the crowded room to stand beside his teacher. The safety of fresh air near the door didn't compare with his need to stay with Nimbulan. He placed his hand on his teacher's shoulder and joined his magic to the older man's. Power welled up within him, ready to burst forth in whatever spell Nimbulan chose.

Myrilandel stood straight and defiant. She seemed to glow from within, like the dragons. Amaranth roused from his nest by the fire and joined her, pacing a protective circle around all of them. His black fur seemed to absorb light where Myri reflected it back.

Moncriith raised a fist in defiance of Nimbulan. He held three strands of Myri's hair, a few bloody threads, and a long splinter of wood, also bloodied. "I have something from each of you four demons. I bind you with magic. You cannot resist my commands!"

A wave of red energy undulated from Moncriith's clenched hand. Powwell suddenly felt heavy and sleepy. He needed to drop his hand from Nimbulan's shoulder to hold up his head. But the decision to move any muscle was too much effort.

Suddenly, a web of light shot from Nimbulan's hand. A giant fishnet of eldritch power wove around and around Moncriith, containing his magic within the web. The pulses of red energy ceased. The heaviness left Powwell.

He stood straighter with no effort.

"You can't do that! Kardia magic cannot defeat blood magic," Moncriith protested.

"We have found a new magic that allows us to combine our powers to overcome any one magician, no matter what source of power he uses to fuel an inborn talent," Nimbulan explained.

"You'll never get magicians to cooperate. This battle isn't over yet, Nimbulan."

"Leave now, Moncriith. Go back to Lord Kammerly d'Astrismos and tell him that if he goes to war this Summer or any Summer, he will face the combined might of many magicians and many lords." Nimbulan flipped his wrist and wiggled his fingers in a walking motion. The web of magic pulled Moncriith back toward the door. Wind and rain pelted the Bloodmage as he grasped the doorjamb to keep from being dragged outside.

"You haven't seen the last of me yet. Any of you. I'll be back with an army and the Lord d'Astrismos. You'll all die for your sin of sheltering this witchwoman. She's a demon, I tell you. She plays with evil. Repent now, and follow the path of the Stargods," Moncriith bellowed so loudly Powwell wanted to put his hands over his ears. The Bloodmage's knuckles turned white where he clung to the edge of the doorway. His feet kept pulling him outside.

"If the path of the Stargods means following your sick hatred, I'll take Simurgh any day." A grizzled old man crossed his wrists and flapped his hands. The waving of his hands imitated the ancient winged god who demanded human sacrifice. His crossed wrists warded against the return of that particular demon.

"Get out of our village and don't come back." The stout woman raised her fist as if she intended to plant it in the Bloodmage's jaw. "Myrilandel is our witchwoman, one of us. She belongs to us, and we'll take care of her. Go meddle in someone else's business, Moncriith."

"You'll regret this. All of you." Moncriith turned and exited slowly, as if his dignity and honor hadn't been questioned.

Chewed up and spat out, Powwell thought. *We'll have to deal with him again. I hope there are more of us then and we know what we're doing with this dragon magic.*

* * *

"Thank you. Thank you all," Myrilandel said shakily. Tears streamed down her face. "I was sure you would join Moncriith in throwing me to the flames. The last village where I lived turned against me and my guardian. They burned Magretha while Moncriith laughed. I ran away, but Magretha was too old and ill to get very far. I watched her burn from a distance and couldn't do anything to save her. I truly tried, but I wasn't strong enough to fight Moncriith and the village turned against me. Forgive me for doubting you." She stumbled into Karry's open arms, weeping uncontrollably. All of the fear and strain of the past poured of her in a flood.

" 'Tis we who must thank you, Myri. You saved five good men. Men who will live to fish again, live to provide for their families and the village. Now enough of that blubbering. Time to get some hot soup into you." Karry escorted her to the padded chair by the fire.

Myri looked back to Nimbulan, needing to draw him

into the loving warmth of the village. She saw hot brightness in Powwell's eyes. Kalen clung to the boy's hand again. Her chin trembled a little uncertainly.

Nimbulan stood slightly apart from the crowd. He nodded to her then turned to Powwell and Kalen. Myri felt a slight tug on the silvery cord that bound her to Nimbulan with love now, as well as healing. She needed to fold herself within his arms again but knew that would come later. For now she needed to form a new connection with the villagers who had sheltered her all Winter and now welcomed her as one of their own.

When the voices had whispered of betrayal, they must have meant Televarn stabbing Nimbulan. These people would never turn on her.

"Where is Televarn?" she asked Karry in a whisper. "I know he was here."

"Left in a hurry after we told him he wasn't welcome and we wouldn't tell him where you were. I think he went to Hanassa. Good place for thieves like him." Karry spat toward the fire.

"Thank you, Karry. You have saved me from him as well as Moncriith. I am glad to call this place home."

(You have work elsewhere, child. Dangerous work that only you can accomplish. We will help you in the coming battle. A terrible battle that may cost you the one you love. Only you can save him, but your talent will be useless.)

* * *

Myri fingered the wide skirt of the new gown that molded tightly to her breasts and waist, then drifted loosely around her hips and legs. She'd chosen the fabric from Karry's store because it was the same color as Nimbulan's eyes; the soft green of new oak leaves. She'd memorized every nuance of his eyes, fearful of losing him. The dragons had warned her.

"Since you are heading back to Lord Quinnault's stronghold, you could wait and have a real priest bless your marriage there." Karry smiled hugely as she fussed with the hem of Myri's new dress. "Not that I want to miss this celebration."

Amaranth played hiding games with the hem where Karry lifted it slightly to finish the last few stitches.

"I want Myri and the children to have the protection of my name and rank before we set out on a long journey," Nimbulan insisted. He leaned against the bar of the temporarily empty pub, arms crossed, admiration and love pouring from his glorious green eyes. A brief shadow passed across his face. He blinked and resumed his admiration of Myri in her wedding gown.

"I traveled across half of Coronnan on my own, Lan. The children did, too. I don't have to take your name for protection. If you want to wait for a real priest, we can." She met his gaze and nearly lost herself in the intensity of his stare. She still couldn't believe he had asked her to marry him. Living with him, following him anywhere across the continent, would have satisfied her. For as long as she had him, she wouldn't leave him.

Amaranth pounced from his hiding place beneath Myri's skirt onto Nimbulan's boot. He batted one cat paw at an imaginary shadow. Then he curled up on Nimbulan's feet for a brief nap, clear proof that he had adopted the magician as Myri's equal in his affections. Myri saw only the flywacket's unwillingness to be separated from him.

Her heart ached with the knowledge that she might lose him to the next battle. How would she live without him?

She banished the terrible thought, unwilling to let her fears mar the beauty of the day. Her wedding day.

"The marriage will only last a year if you don't find a priest to bless it before the next Vernal Equinox," Karry reminded them as she knotted the last stitch in the hem of the dress.

Myri prayed they'd have that year together, at least.

"I've not seen any prettier brides, Myri. The color suits you, though it's the most common of all dyes and most brides want something different and special for their wedding gown." Karry stood back, assessing the gown and the bride with a huge smile on her face.

"I want this wedding, Myri. I want the laws of man and the Stargods to acknowledge what we already hold dear." Nimbulan stepped to her side and raised her palm to his lips. They stood together a moment in silence. He kept his eyes lowered to her palm.

Amaranth circled them both, purring loudly. His looping path wove an unneccesary binding spell—or was it protection? Myri touched the silver cord that bound her heart to Nimbulan's. That simple piece of magic pulsed with vitality. Amaranth merely echoed the bonds already in place.

Myri caressed Nimbulan's face with her free hand, relishing the warm tingles that traveled from his kiss all the way through her body. Her knees weakened. 'Twas always the same. She had no control when he touched her. If they didn't get on with the simple village ceremony soon, she'd tear his new tunic and trews from his body and make love with him on the bar. She vowed to herself not to let a day go by without making love to him and telling him of her joy in him. She wouldn't let him go to his grave doubting her feelings.

"Such scandalous thoughts, my love?" he whispered to her. He raised one eyebrow, as if he also contemplated the quickest way out of their new clothes—gifts from the villagers in thanks for saving Rory and Kelly and the other fishermen.

"You read my mind?" she whispered back. He didn't do it often. He had said that he hated violating another person's privacy, yet every once in a while the rapport between them was so perfect he couldn't help overhearing her thoughts. The magnificence of that rapport and the magnitude of his talent still awed her. She suppressed her fears lest he read those as well.

She didn't deserve to keep him to herself. All of Coronnan needed him and the new magic the dragons gave him. He must fight the coming battle. She hoped desperately that she had the strength to save him afterward.

"I could read your mind," Karry snorted, repressing a laugh. "You'd think you two were youngsters just discovering the delights of Festival." She handed Myri a nosegay of wildflowers. Nimbulan settled a crown of similar posies on her head. He dropped a quick kiss on her lips, a brief promise of more to come.

"In a way, Karry, we are experiencing our first Festival. Our first Festival together." Nimbulan offered Myri his arm.

She clung to him.

"Save the sentiments for the priest who marries you for all time. He's the one you have to convince that you want to stay together beyond the first few tumbles in bed." Karry moved to the doorway, opening it to the morning sunshine. "Remember, this common law ceremony lasts only a year."

"Its good enough for most people in Coronnan who only see a priest once a year," Nimbulan replied. "I never considered before what villagers do for religious sacraments or for healing. We must take magic away from the battlefield and bring it back to the people."

"You'll have a lot of hard work ahead of you, then," Karry snorted. "Not much trust of trained magicians. We like our witchwomen better. They belong to us, not to some lord. Granny Katia told of a time when we had a priest. This village was important because of the triple Equinox Pylon. But the wars came, and the lords took our priest to serve their armies 'cause he was a magician of sorts."

"That must change. Magicians must belong to all people of Coronnan, not just the lords. But we have to start the changes with the lords and end this endless civil war. We'll leave with the children for Lord Quinnault's keep right after the ceremony. He has a priest in residence." He led Myri toward the Equinox Pylon where the entire village, including Powwell and Kalen, waited. Amaranth scampered to join them.

A huge black cloud covered the sun, plunging them all into shadow. Cold darkness descended on the bright morning. Myri shivered at the terrible omen.

CHAPTER 32

"My Lord Quinnault, I demand justice for the loss of my daughter. These islands fall under your authority. Only you can give me justice." Stuuvart stalked the length of the Great Hall, speaking in tones that demanded attention.

Ackerly hurried in his steward's wake, anxious that his side of the story be heard. He surveyed the hall carefully as he stretched his short legs to keep up with Stuuvart. The lord, his steward, three servants, and five dogs populated the larges room in the keep. The numerous retainers and tenants must be out plowing and planting in the early Spring sunshine. He could tell what he knew and hope it wouldn't pass to the general populace.

Ackerly made a mental note to remind the lord how much the presence of the School for Magicians added to his prestige and held together his mutual defense pact. The two lords who had recently signed Quinnault's treaty did so only because Ackerly had agreed to add his magicians to any defensive action needed. He was still looking for a way to make the lords pay him for those services, but Quinnault had reminded him that the school was housed on one of his islands rent free.

Quinnault de Tanos looked up from the parchments he studied with his own steward. The lines around his pale eyes creased with concern. His long, thin face seemed longer yet as he massaged his chin with his left hand. No trace of his pale, blond beard shadowed his face.

"One of my students ran away from my steward, Lord Quinnault, more than two weeks ago," Ackerly explained to his landlord. He wouldn't call her Stuuvart's daughter. "She was willful and unruly and hated her lessons. Only now does Stuuvart seriously look for her, now when he wants more money from me. Money I do not have to give him. What is of greater concern to us all is Lord Kammeryl d'Astrismos. He has declared himself king and marches his army North to confront any who challenge him. Rumor places Moncriith, the Bloodmage, within his ranks." Ackerly bowed his head in a gesture of humility. Anything to keep Quinnault de Tanos from worrying about that blasted child.

If he'd been able to train Kalen properly, she'd be worth at least a gold piece for each battle. Combined with Rollett and Maalin, he could up the price to about six pieces of gold per battle. Without the girl's ingenuity and creativity with fire, the two journeymen were only the equal of a mediocre Battlemage.

"I know of Lord Kammeryl's pretensions," Quinnault said.

Of course he knew. Ackerly had told him after one of his brief communications with Moncriith.

"D'Astrismos claims the right of kingship from his genealogy," Quinnault continued. "I have always suspected the insertion of the Stargods at the top of his family tree to be false, but that is not important now. The presence of a Bloodmage has yet to be verified. No one has reported lost livestock, prisoners, or pets that could be sacrificed for such an evil magician. How could a man draw power from the pain of another?" Quinnault shuddered a moment. Silence reigned in the room as he looked to each man present for an explanation.

After a moment he returned his gaze to the plans on his desk. "Have you looked for the child before this? Did she have reason to run away?" Quinnault studied Stuuvart in that direct way of his. Practiced scoundrels were known to babble everything they knew under that gaze. If they could remember who they were or what the question was after the lord's rapid leap from subject to subject. Ackerly avoided that gaze whenever possible.

"The child was well behaved, a loving and devoted daughter until we enrolled her in this man's supposed School for Magicians." Stuuvart pointed accusingly at Ackerly. "Almost immediately, she rebelled and fought the use of her talent. She hated Ackerly, but she remained devoted to her mother and younger siblings. She would not have run away unless provoked. I wonder that perhaps Ackerly found a way to hold her for ransom. He has not mounted a serious search for her."

Ackerly glared at the steward. He hadn't cared about Kalen until the question of money came up. Now he was using her absence to demand coin in redress, coin he should have offered for her return.

"My lord," Ackerly said with his hands open before him in a gesture he meant to show his honesty. "Kalen was a very intelligent child with a great deal of talent. I tried to teach her the necessity of control of that talent. She was frightened badly by the impostor Moncriith before she came to my school. She had been mistreated by Stuuvart, who claims to be her father but isn't. She had no true reason to run away after she came into my care. Granted she was quiet and didn't make friends easily, but she was more afraid of her talent and Stuuvart than truly rebellious. If Moncriith does indeed march with d'Astrismos, it's possible he kidnapped Kalen. We both know his attitude toward traditional magicians—especially females."

The only difference between a female magician and a witchwoman was the formal training all magicians underwent to gain control of their talents. Moncriith wouldn't see that control as a difference. He wanted to burn them all.

"You have a point, Ackerly. I shall send a message of inquiry to Lord Kammeryl. One of your journeymen can do the honors. Do you know if Moncriith uses a traditional method of summons—a flame through a glass?"

"*I* heard that Lord Kammeryl d'Astrismos has denounced magicians and intends to win the crown without a Battlemage," Stuuvart said. "You'll have to send your message by fleet steed and rider. It will take weeks to get a reply. I'll go myself. With your permission, sir."

"Don't be ridiculous. No one can win a battle without a Mage to protect the troops from other magicians," Ackerly protested.

"If only Nimbulan hadn't died. He always seemed to be able to keep track of what was happening in all corners of Coronnan." Lord Quinnault shook his head sadly. "He'd know who marched with d'Astrismos. He'd also know why the little girl disappeared."

"But Nimbulan is dead," Ackerly replied. "He'd never have been able to build up the school as you and I did—to make it big enough to provide defense for your united lords. He'd not have attracted the large numbers of tenants who have settled and will defend your islands. He'd be so lost in a Tambootie trance, he'd forget to eat or teach his classes, or look in his glass for the information we seek. The addiction to the drug of magic ruled him, my lord. Perhaps it's best the weed took him." Ackerly paused a moment in a pose of grief before continuing. "I'll send the message myself. I don't need to know a specific magician's address." He already knew when and where to contact Moncriith, and that Moncriith had found and lost Kalen and Powwell. But he wouldn't let that bit of information slip to Stuuvart.

"That won't be necessary, Ackerly." A strange voice interrupted. A voice from the past that shouldn't have ever spoken again.

"With my head and my heart and the strength of my shoulders, I renounce the presence of this ghost!" Ackerly crossed himself hastily as he mumbled the prayer. Then he looked to the source of the voice and crossed himself again. "Nimbulan!"

The dead had come back to haunt him. Shabbily dressed in peasant clothes, a day's growth of beard, and slightly grubby, Nimbulan alive would never have allowed himself to fall into such dishevelment, unless deep in the throes of his addiction. He must be dead. He had to be dead! The overdose of Tambootie mixed with Timboor had killed him.

Maybe this was an impostor, cloaked in magical delusion?

"Nimbulan!" Quinnault stood so fast his chair crashed backward and skidded across the floor.

"You can't be here, you're dead! I buried you myself." Ackerly found himself backing toward a doorway that led to the interior of the keep. The door to the courtyard was filled with magicians and apprentices trailing in Nimbulan's wake. And right beside him, close enough to be a family unit, walked Myrilandel and the two missing children.

"Apparently, Ackerly, you buried me too hastily and

not deep enough," Nimbulan replied. A wry smile creased his otherwise grim face.

"Where have you been, my friend? Why were you gone so long? What brings you back? How? But . . . ?" Quinnault rushed forward and clasped the Master Magician's hand with both of his own.

He'd never greeted Ackerly with such enthusiasm. Never called him friend. Never acknowledged Ackerly's help and guidance.

"One question at a time, Lord Quinnault." Nimbulan returned the lord's affectionate greeting. "My adventures were long and numerous. Suffice it to say, I have perfected a way for two or more magicians to join their magic, compounding the effect of a spell. Without the Tambootie. I have no more need of drugs to enhance my magic. I have a better way. Henceforth, no solitary magician will be able to stand against those who join me. We will remove magicians from battles and politics. We have a chance for peace." Nimbulan raised his left hand, palm outward, fingers slightly curled, little finger bent almost to the palm, as if ready to capture the threads of the Kardia and weave them into a spell. The habitual gesture confirmed that this was indeed Nimbulan and no impostor. The perfectly proportioned hand with more than ordinary grace couldn't be imitated.

"Stuuvart, Kalen stands before you and you do not welcome her. A moment ago you demanded justice for her disappearance." Ackerly reminded his steward of why they had come to Lord Quinnault's hall. He needed to get back to an ordinary topic, one he could deal with while the rest of his mind worked furiously. Why wasn't Nimbulan dead? The Timboor mixed with the ink on the letter should have killed him if the additional drugs in his cup hadn't.

"My daughter clings to another woman as if she were her mother. She hides from *me,* her beloved father." Stuuvart glared at Ackerly, daring him to contradict his legal claim on Kalen. "What happens here? Who are these people?" He beat his clenched fist against his forehead, effectively hiding his facial expressions.

"Yes, Nimbulan, introduce us to your friends. Then tell us your adventures over food and drink. You must refresh yourselves." Quinnault raised his hand to signal a servant. Then he clapped the magician firmly on the shoulder, a smile spreading across his face.

"My lord, may I present to you my wife, Myrilandel. My apprentice, Powwell, I believe you have met—and Kalen, Ackerly's apprentice, who discovered I was missing from the crypt and ran away to find me." Nimbulan gathered the three into the circle of his arms as if they were his own children. "And this is Amaranth, my wife's familiar." At last the witchwoman raised her face from the cat she held quite tightly in her arms.

"My sister's name was Myrilandel," Quinnault said as he kissed the woman's hand. "Unfortunately, she died when only two. I thought the name unique to my family."

"I grieve for your loss, my lord. I was an orphan. I have no knowledge of my parents or why I was named Myrilandel, only that I came to my guardian with the name."

Her voice was the same melodic whisper Ackerly remembered from the hospital tent last Autumn. He wanted to lean closer to capture every last nuance of her words. He needed to reach out a hand and touch her to make certain she was real, to smell her flowery scent, to follow her anywhere. . . .

No wonder Moncriith thought her a demon. She could enchant the most hardened of hearts.

"Before we settle in for a proper discussion of our mutual goals, I think you should know that the islands are soon to have some rather awesome visitors." Nimbulan spoke with the commanding authority he used only on the battlefield. All within the room heard and turned their attention to him.

"If we are to have guests, I would like to take my daughter home to her mother and give her a good meal and a bath. There is much to prepare at the school before we can offer lodging and meals. How many should we prepare for?" Stuuvart reached to clasp Kalen by the shoulders. The girl shrank away from him, trying to hide behind Myrilandel's skirts.

"Our visitors won't require anything of you, Master Steward." Nimbulan placed a reassuring hand on Kalen's shoulder. The little girl relaxed a little, but didn't move closer to her mother's husband.

"Will they be staying with me?" Lord Quinnault looked as if he were calculating the stores in his cellars.

"No, my lord. Our visitors require nothing from us in the way of hospitality. I doubt they would fit inside either building." That wry smile threatened to break through again. Myrilandel smiled, too.

What was Nimbulan up to? In years gone by, Ackerly was privy to all of his master's schemes. But now he'd been shut out, ignored. He deserved better than this. After all, he'd made the school a profitable and popular business. Nimbulan would never have been able to recruit nearly fifty apprentices and fifteen faculty. Nor would he have found the funds to make the school self-supporting.

"Tomorrow morning, five dragons will grace us with their presence. For they are the secret to combined magic."

Everyone in the room grew unnaturally still.

"Dragons?" Ackerly asked the question for all those present.

"Dragons, Ackerly. I went in search of myths and found my future. The dragons are real and ready to form a covenant with us."

"If this isn't some Tambootie-induced delusion, then the dragons are more likely ready to dine on all of us. Lord Quinnault, I suggest you lock Nimbulan and his wife in your deepest dungeon for their own protection. I ask only that you give me back the children. I am their master and have more legal right to their raising than their mothers." Ackerly stalked out of the keep, heading for *his* school. He didn't truly expect *his* children to follow.

CHAPTER 33

Nimbulan emerged from the central door of the old monastery at dawn the next morning, still yawning. Myri clung to his arm, barely able to contain her excitement. He looked across the sky for evidence of the dragons. Not that he expected to see the nearly invisible creatures themselves. If he caught a glimpse of a rainbow arcing down from where the sun struck their wings, he'd be lucky.

"I guess we'll have to wait a bit," he said stifling another yawn.

"I don't think so." Myri giggled, pointing upward.

He followed her pointing finger to the top of the residential wing—right over the suite he had appropriated for himself and Myri. Shayla perched on the peak of the roof.

The dragon peered at him with one multifaceted crystal eye. She cocked her head in a listening posture very like the one Myri adopted.

Nimbulan broke the mesmerizing eye contact. He needed his wits about him today, not another dragon dream.

Four smaller dragons—the twenty-year-old adolescents—silvery as moonlight, swam in the river, guarded the causeway, and eyed the fields of fat cows near Quinnault's keep. Five full-sized males sat, reclined, and hovered over other portions of the island. Curious. None of the males had been present during the training session in the meadow.

"Your mates joined you, Shayla!" Myri called and waved.

(The need to control magic brought them out of their solitude. We will see if the covenant we reach is enough to keep them with me. 'Tis not natural for dragons to be

together. We will change our society only if you change yours.)

Quinnault ran across the causeway, splashing through the puddles left by the receding tide. He tucked his shirt into his trews as he rushed to join Nimbulan and the dragons. A servant ran behind him, proffering bread and cheese to his lord.

"I still don't understand why your dragons are suddenly concerned with the affairs of men when they have remained hidden and elusive for centuries." Lord Quinnault stopped abruptly behind Nimbulan. His eyes and mouth opened in awe as he stared at Shayla.

"They aren't my dragons. Myri is the one they listen to. They only tell me what they want me to know. With her they communicate freely." Together they watched Myri caress a young red-tipped dragon's cheek as if she petted a docile steed—a steed as large as a hut.

"He says his name is Tssonnin," Myri said over her shoulder to Nimbulan. "They always accord others the honor of using their names."

"Did I tell you that we rode dragonback from the Southern Mountains?" Nimbulan asked Quinnault, suppressing yet another yawn. "Shayla spoke to Myri the entire trip. They discussed all manner of issues, dragon and human, female and general. Myri rode directly in front of me, and I heard only her words. Nothing from the dragon. I think the young dragons spoke, too. Again, I was not privy to any of their comments."

Quinnault cringed as Tssonnin bent his head to scratch behind his steedlike ear with the barbed tip of his wing. The red-tipped spiral horn on his forehead came dangerously close to spearing Kalen who had crept up to be closer to them. "They will hurt her." He moved to pull her away.

"Doubtful." Nimbulan held Quinnalt back. "They adore children. And Myri has claimed Kalen and Powwell as her own. Myri is the one the dragons trust. She is the one they sought out and waited for."

"But why now? Why not when the wars first started?" The lord looked as if he barely restrained himself from dashing to rescue Myri and Kalen.

Amaranth joined the women and clambered up Tssonin's outstretched foreleg to perch on his shoulder. His long talonlike claws didn't penetrate the tough dragon hide. A few crystalline hairs fell free in the flywacket's wake. They glinted in the early sunlight. Three apprentices dashed forward to gather the hairs as souvenirs.

"Look, my lord, the children have no fear of the beasts. They seem to know instinctively how much the dragons treasure young ones. Now we must get to work. Do you wish to join us in the exercises to gather dragon magic? You might have a talent for it."

"I have so little magic my efforts will add nothing to your schemes."

"Perhaps. Perhaps not. This is an entirely different technique. I find it more exhausting than drawing energy from the ley lines. But you can't see ley lines, so maybe gathering dragon magic will be easy for you. Come. Try, at least. Sharing magic is an exhilarating experience. I just wish Myri were able to join us."

"Nimbulan?" Myri turned sharply. Her spine stiffened, and she looked as if she needed to flee. "Lan, Shayla says there is an army approaching from the South. A day's march away. They move only at night and remain hidden during the day so that Quinnault will have no time to prepare. Moncriith is with them."

* * *

"Wisp of flame, burning bright
Travel far beyond my sight
Bring to view the other true
Pass the word of magic might"

Nimbulan listened to the apprentices and masters chant the words of his simple communication spell.

Why did they take so long learning a simple rhyme? He'd never perfect the technique of joining their magic if they took hours on the easiest of spells. Kammeryl d' Astrismos and his army came closer with every tick of the water clock.

He hoped Rollett was able to infiltrate the enemy army soon enough to learn some important tactical information to aid Quinnault in the coming battle. The young journeyman magician would have to be careful and stay out of Moncriith's way.

Patience, he told himself. *You didn't learn magic in a day.* He remembered the years he'd struggled to create his spells. Old Druulin had made him keep his incantations and pieces of poetry to trigger those spells private, even from the master and Ackerly, his best friend. Druulin had stolen the rhyme for a simple invisibility spell and used it to sneak up on Nimbulan. The old man had knocked his young apprentice senseless with a mind probe. The lesson had been clear. Never allow another magician to learn your spells.

Secrecy among magicians was a major barrier he had to overcome. Mistrust among the older magicians who had come to the school might prevent this little communication spell from working. Only Ackerly seemed to grasp immediately the concepts of this new magic.

If only Nimbulan still trusted Ackerly. The man had evaded questions about the overdose of Tambootie and Timboor that had almost killed him, with sly hints and accusations against everyone except himself. He'd even blamed Nimbulan for endangering the apprentices with his experiments.

Ackerly was amazingly adept at gathering dragon magic. Nimbulan hadn't expected his assistant to be more powerful with the new system than he had with the old. Ackerly grasped the concept of gathering magic quickly and demonstrated the technique adeptly to the younger boys, something the older master magicians couldn't—or wouldn't—do.

They needed speed. Kammeryl d'Astrismos' army marched closer every minute.

Nimbulan would have gladly excused his assistant from the practice until he knew for sure who had poisoned him last Winter, but he needed his help.

Journeyman Gilby stumbled over the words of the spell. The entire circle of magicians and apprentices faltered and stopped in their recitation.

"Begin again," Nimbulan said impatiently.

When they were all competing against each other, keeping their spells private had been vital, lifesaving.

Now they all must use the same spell, in unison, and work in concert for the same goal.

The future he envisioned banished all barriers among magicians. They would share more than power during vital spells. They would share knowledge and pass it down to each successive generation.

At last the magicians worked their way through the spell three times without error. "Hold hands, men. The magic only works when you are in physical contact with every other magician working the spell," he directed.

Twenty bodies shifted and shuffled in embarrassed silence. Men didn't touch each other in their culture. Another custom Nimbulan must banish. Finally they were all joined, old and young, trained and raw. Ackerly, the last man in the line, placed his free hand on Lyman's shoulder, completing the circle. Lyman held his master's glass in front of the flames in the hearth.

"Together now, breathe in on three counts, hold three, release three." A tingle of energy ran up Nimbulan's arms. The room filled with power, begging him to join it. He watched the men's auras blend into one giant pulse. Arcs of many individual colors swirled and shifted until they were all one glowing dome of lavender/white energy. Lavender, Lyman's signature color. If Ackerly led the group, would his yellow dominate the aura?

They knew so little about why dragon magic allowed communal working and ley line magic didn't. Magic was strictly fuel, wasn't it? They didn't have time to puzzle out answers.

Nimbulan stepped back, physically and magically. He wasn't part of this spell. He needed to observe the effects from a distance. So he watched the auara as a reflection of available power. The single united aura grew until it filled the room and pushed outside the stone walls of the room.

"Again, breathe in, hold, release, hold." The united aura began to throb and reach outward.

"Once more. Breathe, hold, release, hold." The level of power in the room grew and multiplied like a living thing, replicating itself faster than they could think. All color vanished as the united aura whirled until it became the nearly transparent all color/no color of a dragon's hide.

"Chant the words of the spell, and send the flame to

Naabbon, Lord Hanic's new magician. Send the flame across the island, watch it skip over the river, guide it West by Southwest, across the grazing land, through the rich farmland up to the foothills." Nimbulan closed his eyes and imagined the progress of the flame. He'd sent a message along this very route the week before that fateful battle last Autumn. Then he had pleaded with Keegan to return and complete his training. His message had been ignored then. Would it be again?

His left hand reached out, palm forward, as if drawing the communal magic into himself. He forced himself to clench his fist and drop it back into his lap. He couldn't participate. He had to observe.

At last he heard Lyman reading the written text of the message Quinnault had worked out. A plea for Hanic to join the united lords in mutual defense against Kammerly d'Astrismos. United strength to combat those who sought war for the sake of war. If all stood together, they could defeat Kammeryl and negotiate a new government with a new monarchy.

They deliberately left the issue of a monarchy hanging. Hanic had to believe himself eligible for the crown, though Quinnault's alliance had already asked the lord of the islands to rule.

Lyman's words trailed off. Nimbulan opened his eyes to see, what, if any, reaction came back through the glass. Because he was not joined to magicians performing this spell, he saw nothing through the glass but magnified flames. He could only judge the response on Naabbon's end from Lyman's face. A map of time-earned wrinkles around the old man's eyes crinkled. A smile curved upward, revealing amazingly sound teeth.

"Agreed, Naabbon. Your lord will march tonight to reinforce Lord Quinnault as he defends his lands against Kammeryl d'Astrismos and the Bloodmage."

Ackerly removed his hand from Lyman's shoulder. The spell dissolved.

"We did it, Master Nimbulan." Lyman stood up from his crouched position before the fire. "We blasted young Naabbon with so much magic we dragged him out of his bath. He spluttered and gasped, but he couldn't break the summons. He had to stay with his glass, walked it down the corridor—him dripping bath water the whole way and naked as a lumbird—into Hanic's bedroom. Woke the lord up and got the agreement. He couldn't break the summons!"

* * *

Moncriith studied the army of Lord Kammeryl d'Astrismos. Far less than the one thousand men the lord advertised as his following. No need. Moncriith could handle any magician Quinnault de Tanos found.

A niggle of doubt crept into his mind. Nimbulan and the boy had overpowered him. He'd had thread from Powwell's cloak, strands of Myrilandel's hair, and a splinter from Nimbulan's old staff—purchased from Televarn before the Rover chieftain disappeared into Hanassa. All of the souveneirs had tasted the owner's blood. His spell should have been more powerful than anything they threw at him.

Except he had nothing from the girl child—Kalen. She'd thrown her old and ragged clothes into the hearth fire rather than let Moncriith have them. Perhaps that was the problem. She had been excluded from his spell and able to help Nimbulan in some way. Either that or the bit of Nimbulan's staff had been false. Rovers were known to lie about everything. Except, Moncriith suspected, the Rover had a grudge against Nimbulan and wanted him dead.

When next Moncriith met Nimbulan and Myrilandel, he would have an entire battlefield of blood and pain to fuel him. They would not survive his next attack. Would not survive long enough to have their marriage sanctified in a temple of the Stargods. Demons couldn't be allowed to profane the sacraments.

When Nimbulan and Myrilandel fell, so would the rest of the magicians and the demons that controlled them. Moncriith would be the only magician left in Coronnan. He would rule through his puppet, Kammeryl d'Astrismos for a time. The self-crowned king would die, too, when Moncriith no longer need him.

His vision had become so real, he reached out a hand as if to grasp the image of himself as anointed priest-king of all Coronnan. No one would dare defy him once he ruled.

He smiled at the army that awaited his command. One

of them was Nimbulan's spy. The young man from the school harbored a demon spirit disguised as a magic talent. Moncriith smelled the evil creature on the wind.

Moncriith needed sacrificial human blood to begin his battle spells.

An example must be made now, to all magicians, that their powers and interference would not be tolerated. His army would destroy the one who hid among them. That death would give him tremendous power to neutralize Nimbulan before he managed to summon demons.

"Bring me the demonsniffers," he ordered the young sergeant who stood beside him on the knoll. The two women and one old man who could smell magic in a person, but had no other magic talent themselves, had formerly been called "witchsniffers." Moncriith gave them a more important role in this army—to root out spies and enemy magicians. They would have the privilege of marching at the fore of the army as they massed for battle tomorrow morning, but only after they brought him the impostor. Only after his maddened crowd had torn the magician limb from limb.

CHAPTER 34

"Master, come quick. We need you!" Journeyman Gilby ran into Nimbulan's study without knocking. He skidded on the smooth slate floor, catching himself on the doorjamb.

"I can't step away from the workroom for five minutes without all of you flying into a panic." Nimbulan looked up from the pile of old journals he'd come to fetch. Over the years he'd kept faithful records of his life, including the numerous incantations and cantrips he used to trigger spells.

"What is wrong, Gilby? Take a deep breath and calm down. Then tell me in simple words." He motioned to his journeyman to sit in the chair beside him. The chair where Myri should be. He missed her company every minute of the day. She was on the mainland with the few girl apprentices, none of whom could gather dragon magic.

Gilby shook his head and gulped air. "A summons, sir. A desperate summons from Rollett. He used a flicker of witchlight and a cup of water. It's all he has while spying on Moncriith. He says there are witchsniffers after him and a mob screaming for blood. His blood."

"Quickly, back to the workroom. This will take a very delicate touch. I pray we have learned enough to help the boy from this distance." Nimbulan snapped his journal closed and reached for an older one from his own journeyman days.

Where was the entry he'd made about delusions? He'd read the rhyming phrases only yesterday. He scattered books across his desk in his haste to find the book. Where? Three volumes hit the floor with thuds and skids that must have broken the spines of the bindings. He ignored them.

No book was as valuable as Rollett's life.

Why had he sent the boy to spy on Moncriith? He should have sent a mundane, someone who wouldn't rouse the Bloodmage's suspicions, or gone himself.

He couldn't lose another apprentice so soon after Keegan's death. He wouldn't let war take another person he loved.

"Here!" He grabbed the book he sought, rifling through the pages as he hurried down the hall. "We haven't time to memorize the spell. I'll read it aloud, phrase by phrase, the group will repeat each phrase with me. I hope it works. I pray we are in time." He looked out a window as they nearly ran down the corridor. No sign of any of the dragons. They were close—he sensed their presence in the constantly renewing source of magic power. But he couldn't see them. Would the spell be stronger, more easily controlled, if the magicians linked hands around a dragon?

No time to find out.

They found the assembled magicians, journeymen, and apprentices milling about the workroom in confusion.

"In a circle, grab hands. Apprentices stand outside and observe. Break the circle if something goes wrong. A fire and a glass. Where's my glass?" Nimbulan marshaled his magicians.

"An infusion of strengthening herbs, Lan, before you begin. It will help settle your nerves and focus your magic." Ackerly stood at Nimbulan's elbow with a mug of steaming brew. Nimbulan took it from him gratefully. Leave it to Ackerly to think of such a minor thing that could save the entire spell.

The stream drifted past his nose as he raised the mug to his lips. The musky sweet aroma made his muscles freeze. "You put Tambootie in the infusion."

"Yes, Lan. Like always. You need the drug to fuel your magic and channel your energies." Ackerly blinked at him in puzzlement. His wide gray eyes revealed none of his emotions. He'd also found the armor to protect his thoughts from Nimbulan's probe.

"No, I don't need this demon brew. I've broken free of

the cursed drug. All I need is dragons. That's all any of us need to fuel our magic." Impatiently, Nimbulan handed the mug back to Ackerly. He scanned the group to ensure they were ready for this important rescue attempt. Their glazed eyes and vague expressions sent his heart sinking into his gut.

"How many of them drank of your evil infusions, Ackerly?" He grabbed his assistant's tunic at the throat, shaking him in frustrated anger. "They're useless like this! We're going to lose Rollett to Moncriith's mob because you dosed them all with the Tambootie."

"We've always used the Tambootie," Ackerly protested. He surveyed the stain on his tunic where he'd spilled the infusion. A dark brown stain with green and pink tinges, just like the fresh leaves of the tree of magic, spread outward across his chest.

"Those flecks and burrs in the infusion. That's Timboor. Timboor is poison!" Nimbulan jerked away from Ackerly as if touching the liquid were as dangerous as drinking it. "You set out to poison us all, just like you . . . You poisoned me last Winter and left me for dead in the crypt. You tried to murder me!" The certainty of Ackerly's guilt hit him hard. He couldn't believe it, didn't want to believe it. The evidence lay before him, spilled on Ackerly's tunic.

"Nonsense, Master, your wife gave me the herbs for the infusion," Ackerly scoffed, backing toward the door, the incriminating cup still in his hands.

"My wife hasn't been on this island since before sunup. I'll deal with you later, Ackerly. Gilby, you and Powwell, Haakkon, Zane . . ." No, not Zane, he couldn't gather dragon magic. "Jaanus and Bessel, you haven't drunk any of the poison yet. Join me. Push the others aside. We'll help them after we rescue Rollett. Maalin, you stand aside as control and guide."

Three deep breaths brought their talents into concert, just as they'd practiced.

"Shadows and mist gather near
Cloak and shade in pictures clear
Those who seek through smoke and fire
Will not see, through magic's spire."

Not great poetry. But the intent was there. Nimbulan recited the formula line by line. His five companions echoed his phrases in unison. The magic built to a whirling frenzy, demanding release. He felt a tiny surge of power from the apprentices, quickly controlled by Gilby's deft blending of energy.

"Steady, men. Hold it steady. With me, through the glass, to Rollett." Together, their minds flew into the image of flame on the other side of Nimbulan's large Master's glass. Like an arrow carefully aligned to a target, they sped with the flame across the leagues to the grassy rolling hills to the South. They bypassed Lord Kammeryl's organized and disciplined troops for the rambling campfires and scattered tents near the perimeter of the army.

The noise of hundreds of angry voices burst through their focus. One magician faltered in the quest. Another pulled him back into the group consciousness. Thoughts, dreams, aspirations—all were available to any in the group who wished to probe deeper, just as in the Rover ritual. But there wasn't the time or malice to invade a man's privacy here.

Rollett? they whispered physically and mentally. *Where are you boy? Rollett!*

An image flickered at the edge of their vision. As the tool of a solitary will, the magic arrow turned a sharp corner and sped to the feeble call of one in need. The mob turned and followed their spell, the three in front sniffing with all their senses.

Hurry, Rollett. Gather the magic in the air. Roll it into a formless mass inside you. Let us penetrate it and make a new you.

Shouts of rage and near recognition drew closer. The witchsniffers moved faster, honing in on the "scent" of powerful magic.

At last the communal magic found a target. Their arrowlike spell penetrated and exploded on impact. The essence of Rollett, his personality, his soul, his magic, burst free of the confines of his body, scattering to the four winds.

* * *

Ackerly stuffed his clothes haphazardly into a travel pack. He would be halfway to the mainland before Nimbulan thought to look for him. Anxiously, he flung the pack onto his bed and knelt on the floor by the high narrow window of his solitary cell. He pried at a loose flooring stone with his belt knife. The thin surface of slate lifted free of the square pattern of similar pieces. Beneath it, Ackerly had removed the slab of granite foundation to make a safe hiding place. He thrust his arm elbow deep into the recess until his fingers closed around the neck of a burlap bag.

Using both hands, he heaved the heavy sack onto the floor beside him. Hastily, he untied the knots with a tiny spell. So much easier to do with this new dragon magic. Gathering the ethereal energy from the air made him as powerful a magician as any other single man in the school.

Never again would he have to follow in the wake of a more powerful man, hiding in the background, performing all the menial chores delegated to servants. He had amassed the gold bit by bit for the last thirty years. Between the gold and the dragon magic, he controlled as much or more power than any man in Coronnan.

More. Because he knew how to negate the dragon magic, making Nimbulan and his precious Commune useless.

Kammeryl d'Astrismos would pay much for that knowledge. So would Moncriith. He'd summon the Bloodmage with the nature of the spell seeking to rescue Rollett as soon as he was safely on the mainland.

Ackerly cast aside the clothes he'd already assembled, filling the empty pack with the sack of gold instead.

Should he take Kalen with him? She was now outcast from the school because she couldn't gather dragon magic. She had always been outcast from Stuuvart. A brief longing for companionship with the only child he suspected he had sired almost sent him in search of the girl.

No. She couldn't gather dragon magic, so she couldn't augment his own powers. Moncriith would probably persecute her, too. They were both better off alone.

Looking up and down the corridor outside his room

with all of his senses, he slipped outside the ancient monastery and headed to the sheltered cove where he kept a boat. By this time tomorrow he would be the most powerful and respected magician in all of Coronnan.

* * *

Myri looked up from her search for a sprig of fennel. A single sprig was all she needed to protect Nimbulan in the coming battle. A shiver of danger prickled the hair on the back of her neck.

"Look at all those people running around in circles!" Kalen whispered to Myri. They and the two other girl apprentices lay flat at the edge of a hilltop overlooking the army camp. Their baskets overflowing with healing flowers and leaves—none of them the precious fennel. Myri had taught them songs of thanksgiving to the Kardia for the gift of each plant. As they plucked leaf and flower, a second song sealed the healing properties into it, to be released only when added to an infusion, ointment, or poultice.

Myri picked out Moncriith's distinctive figure with ease, below them on a knoll at the edge of camp. His back was to them as he faced his camp. He always stood on the highest point around and surrounded himself with people who stared *up* at him as if he were all three Stargods incarnate.

"What do you suppose they're doing?" Kalen asked.

Myri looked for a pattern in the way the people below them massed behind three figures who held their hands before them, seemingly sniffing the air.

"Witchsniffers!" Myri nearly choked on her own fear. Dizziness swept over her, giving her view of the scene a second layer. She'd watched this scene before. A piece of a memory fell into place in Myri's mind. She and Magretha, the old scarred witchwoman, had watched a similar scene from the shelter of a treetop. The milling throng below them always looked forward, never up. After an uncomfortable night catching a little sleep wedged into the fork between a stout branch and the tree trunk, she and her guardian had descended in silence and fled to a distant village—one that needed a witchwoman, and hadn't yet learned to blame an ugly old woman with burn scars on one side of her face and back for every ill that plagued them.

"We'd better run. They'll find us soon enough." Kalen edged backward on her belly.

"Not yet. They seek someone closer. See how their hands stay straight out in front of their noses. If they sought someone beyond their camp, their hands would sweep in wide circles until they found a scent on the wind." Myri held the girl in place.

Amaranth let out a piercing squawk of distress above her. His outline looked like nothing more than a large black raven or hawk in shadow. His cry sounded more birdlike than cat, but deeper and more resonant than any bird.

Above his circling silhouette she caught the glimmer of a transparent dragon wing. The larger animal radiated concern into her mind.

Myri, she greeted the dragon, giving her name. Dragon manners seemed to require free exchange of names.

(Shayla,) the dragon replied with her own name. *(The one they seek belongs to Nimbulan. We cannot allow the arrogant one to succeed this time.)*

The female dragon wouldn't dignify the Bloodmage with a true name. The arrogant one. A good description of Moncriith.

"Whoever they are hunting needs our help. We have to come up with a plan," Myri said to her charges. She turned her attention back to Moncriith and the witchsniffers.

"They keep going back to the same tent, around and around it. The circles get narrower every time." Kalen pointed to a small canvas shelter barely large enough to hold one man.

It wasn't the last tent within the perimeter of the camp, but very near the edge, as if the owner were a latecomer or wished a rapid exit.

"And look at Moncriith." The little girl stood up, hands on hips, an expression of outrage on her face. "He's cheating. Look at his aura. He's amplifying the emotions of the crowd following the sniffers. He's the one crying for blood and making them think it's *their* wish."

"Rollett is down there." Myri remembered clearly that Nimbulan had sent the young man, Lan's most trusted journeyman, to spy on Moncriith yesterday afternoon. Rollett had been eager to test his skills as an observer, as well as his ability to disguise himself. A simple delusion, altering only hair and eye color, required enough magic to alert a witchsniffer. "How, Shayla? How can we help him?"

A prickling on the back of her neck warned her of danger. She ducked, drawing Kalen and another girl back down to the grass. An arrow of magic whizzed past them, speeding directly for the tent that must belong to Rollett.

The shimmering spell spun as it flew, sending out tiny rainbows. It paused briefly, turned abruptly, then plunged faster and faster toward the tent. The silent impact sent shards of colors radiating into the air like a sunburst. When the tiny points of light drifted to the ground like colored snowflakes, the tent was gone. Vanished in an eyeblink.

Above them, Shayla heaved a sigh of relief.

Myri looked closer with all of her senses. A dome of transparent magic now covered the space where the tent had been. Its presence was discernible only by the distortion of light around it—like looking at a dragon.

The witchsniffers paused in their seeking. Their arms began a new dance of sweeping wide circles. They'd lost their prey and now sought a new direction, following a similar dome of transparent magic that drifted to the East of camp.

"We have to provide a diversion, or they'll find him for sure." Kalen jumped up again. She closed her eyes and frowned in concentration as she drew energy from the Kardia.

Myri felt the pull of a ley line to the North of them. She, too, drew on it to fuel a spell. *Land in the next valley, Shayla, and mount Rollett on your back. No one in the camp will see you. They'll all be looking at us,* she said to the dragon.

(Agreed. Amaranth will guard you until I return for you.)

Beside Myri, Kalen wove a delusion around herself. With each heartbeat she grew taller, broader. Her simple leather tunic and trews shifted toward red tones, stretched into a blood-red robe. Her features took on masculine coarseness. In a moment, an exact replica of Moncriith stood on top of the hill. Then Kalen, beneath the disguise, raised her hands, palms outward in a traditional gesture of benediction. Only the slightly downward curving little and third fingers indicated that she captured threads of the Kardia and wove them together to create her appearance.

The witchsniffers looked up, their seeking arms stopped circling. Fingers and noses pointed accusingly at the new Moncriith on the hill, in a direct line with the original figure. From the vantage point of the mob, the sniffers were pointing at their leader as the source of magic they should seek out and murder.

"Oh, you wicked child!" Myri laughed.

"I can't hold it very long. I don't know how to . . ." The delusion collapsed. Only a very tired little girl in scratched journey leathers remained, hands to knees, head bowed, panting raggedly.

The witchsniffers faltered again in their quest.

"If you can't sustain the delusion, I'll have to try." Myri gathered the threads of energy in her fingers and spun them around her. From memory she painted a portrait of her enemy on her own face, recreating his signature robes and untrimmed hair and beard.

The seekers found the scent again and marched forward, a confused and angry mob in their wake. They surrounded the knoll where the real Moncriith stood, hands held out in mute appeal. He screamed something at his followers. Fear laced his tones.

Myri fought to sustain the spell. Fatigue threatened to drag the delusion back into the Kardia where it originated. She only needed to hold the spell a little longer. A little longer. Just until Rollett escaped.

Her contact with the ley line drained away. The threads of magic she held within her fingers threatened to tangle.

She gritted her teeth and found the strength to hold the spell. Sweat broke out on her brow. Moisture trickled down her back.

She looked carefully at the scene below her. Moncriith and his three witchsniffers charged up the hill toward her. Shouts of rage filled their voices. Murder glinted in their eyes.

CHAPTER 35

"Did we do it?" Nimbulan asked the magicians who slumped near him. Their hands still linked them together, but the fire in the brazier had gone out and the magic drained away.

"I don't know," Gilby whispered through gritted teeth.

The others shook their heads in confirmation of losing track of the spell. Their stomachs growled in unison. They had used tremendous amounts of energy to throw the magic.

"We have to try again," Nimbulan ordered. "We have to make sure Rollett is safe." Fire burned across his still-healing knife wound. He ignored the nagging pain and rekindled the fire with a snap of his fingers. He held the glass up before the flames. All he saw was fire, slightly magnified. Frantically, he cast about him for more dragon magic. He sensed none in the air around him. Had they used up the entire supply?

Rollett was still in danger. Nimbulan had to do everything to save him. Ley lines still permeated the area. He reached for the nearest one and ran into a solid wall of resistance.

"No, Nimbulan." Old Lyman placed a surprisingly strong hand upon his wrist. "We must forget ley lines altogether. That is why the shadowed guardian of this place sealed the well of Kardia magic. If communal magic is to succeed, we must never again resort to solitary sources, no matter how desperate the need."

Nimbulan blinked rapidly, trying to bring the old man into focus. "Rollett is still in danger. I can't let him die like Keegan."

Lyman blurred and stabilized, blurred again, mist or smoke cloaked his outline. Finally, his form came back into focus. Nimbulan blinked once more. Slowly. Hard. When he opened his eyes, Lyman had resumed his place on the other side of the circle from him. Had the old man momentarily taken on the form of the shadowed guardian, or had fatigue and pain played tricks with Nimbulan's vision?

"Rollett's life is now in the hands of the Stargods. We did what we could," Lyman said.

"You might add the dragons to your list of thanks. More specially, Shayla." Rollett himself wandered into the room, looking slightly dazed, limping and cradling his left arm in his right hand. His dark curly hair stood out around his head as if he stood in a strong wind.

"Rollett!" Nimbulan flung himself at the young man. Jaanus followed suit, embracing his classmate and his master. "You're safe, boy. You're safe," they repeated over and over.

"Yes, yes, I am," Rollett murmured, amazed at his good fortune.

"How? Tell us all. We need to know the details in case we have to repeat the procedure." Lyman took control of the emotional outbursts.

"I felt your summons. My cup of water throbbed so violently, I thought it would shatter with the force of your demand that I join your spell. I held it up to my flicker of witchlight and suddenly the world seemed to explode with colors. Like lightening growing outward from the water. But it didn't spread very far. When I could focus my eyes, I looked around, and everything within my tent shimmered with that odd iridescent light that you see when you look directly at a dragon and find yourself looking beyond it." He looked around the room for confirmation that they understood.

A twitter of tension-breaking laughter flickered around the room.

"Well, I took a chance and peeked outside the tent," Rollett continued. "The witchsniffers and their mob stopped and veered off in a new direction. I slipped out of the tent, and walked as fast as I could in the opposite direction. I wanted to be as far from them as possible. But when I looked back, the tent was invisible. I just stood there in amazement when one of Moncriith's pet sergeants ran past me. He couldn't have been more than an arm's length away, but he didn't see me!"

Nimbulan's heart lightened with relief. He lost a little sensation around the edges as he took in the import of his journeyman's tale. They had used dragon magic to make the boy as invisible as a dragon!

"Then what happened?" Nimbulan prompted, eager to know why Rollett had included the dragons in his list of thanks, other than their wonderful gift of communal magic.

"I ran. I ran as fast as I could over the top of the next hill. I tripped and fell, but I got up and kept running." He winced slightly and shifted his weight off his right foot.

Jaanus rushed to get him a high stool. Rollett sank onto it gratefully, still cradling his left arm. He stretched out his long legs. His torso slumped a little as if he suddenly realized how tired and hurt he really was.

"Halfway down that hill I tripped again and rolled. That must have been how I wrenched my shoulder. I could hear the shouts of the mob. Their blood lust was up and nothing was going to stop them. They were coming my way again, I don't know if they sensed me or not. I thought I was done for, but I suddenly stopped rolling. Something very big stopped me. Shayla."

Everyone in the room nodded. They all knew precisely how big Shayla was. As wide as two sledge steeds and as tall as two more. Several tons of dragon presented a formidable wall to run up against.

"She didn't speak to me, but I knew a compulsion to climb up onto her back. It was a struggle with the ankle and the arm, but I managed to hold onto her spines, and half a heartbeat later we were airborne."

Nimbulan lived again the bunching of dragon muscles between his legs, the tremendous wind generated by the first downstroke of powerful wings. The sensation of his throat sinking to his belly as the Kardia fell away and they broke free of the pull of gravity. Shayla had insisted she and her consorts bring him and Myri and the children back to the island. He hoped to experience those thrilling moments of true flight again some day.

"We stopped on the other side of Moncriith's camp and plucked Myrilandel and the girls from a hilltop. The mob seemed to be pointing at them and getting ready to run after them. But one sight of that dragon and they all turned tail and ran. All except Moncriith. I saw him whip out his knife and slash his forearm to begin a spell." Rollett swayed briefly with relief and pain. "Shayla flew high and fast, and we stayed ahead of whatever he threw at us."

"Let me send for Myri. You need to have her look at your injuries." Nimbulan pressed the young man's uninjured shoulder in reassurance.

"Sorry, she's not here," Rollett replied. "On the way back we flew past Lord Hanic's army. They're on their way here, but I don't know if they can get here before Kammeryl does. Shayla took Myri back that way. Maybe they can hurry them along. I'll have to hunt up Ackerly to look at this shoulder. Maybe Guillia can fix me a poultice for the ankle."

"Ackerly." All thought and movement ceased in Nimbulan. In the rush of the spell and the excitement of Rollett's return, he'd forgotten Ackerly. For a moment, disbelief riddled him with guilt for his harsh words. Ackerly couldn't have betrayed him, tried to murder him with an overdose of timboor. They'd been friends and colleagues for too long. They depended upon each other for too much. They had saved each other many times. Shared too much of their lives.

"Shall we bring the man to the refectory for judgment or take him to Lord Quinnault?" Jaannus asked reluctantly.

"I suppose we should take him to the lord's hall. These islands still belong to him. He has the right of governance among us. But I hate to turn over a magician to a mundane," Nimbulan said.

"He's Quinnault the Peacemaker, not Kammeryl the destroyer," Lyman reminded him. "He'll understand that Ackerly is still human, with a man's motives and failings and not a demon. We have to obey the laws if we are to set an example for the rest of the kingdom and bring about peaceful living under the law."

"We can't let personal feelings get in the way of the law." Nimbulan hung his head in a moment of grief. "The evidence suggests the man tried to murder me. He must face the law as represented by Lord Quinnault de Tanos."

* * *

"I wish I could fly," Myri said. Idly, she twirled a long stem of grass in her hands while she leaned against Shayla's flank. The grass was very like fennel, but not the precious herb of protection she sought. Maybe if they sought farther North, in a warmer, drier clime, they would find what she needed.

Below the hillside where they perched, Lord Hanic's army hurried along the trader road. If they marched all day and night, they might arrive in time to bolster Quinnault's small defensive force. But then they'd be too tired to fight.

Myri wondered what she could do to prevent the battle, as she stroked Amaranth's sleek black fur. He snoozed in the nest of Shayla's curled forelegs. The flywacket seemed more at home there than he did in Myri's lap lately.

"I have dreams of flying." Myri returned to her original thought. If they had one hundred dragons, they might be able to fly the army to the islands. With such a great show of force Kammeryl d'Astrismos would have to retreat and rethink his battle plans.

(You must forget your dreams of flight, my child. Your destiny no longer lies with the dragons,) Shayla replied. *(You are happy with your consort. You must remain with him, not fly with your nimbus of dragons.)*

"I love Lan very much. I don't know what I'll do if he dies in this battle."

(You will survive. We promised you a home and family. You must weave no more magic, to save even the ones you love,) Shayla said.

"The spell I wove to distract the crowd from Rollett was only a delusion. A simple spell," she defended herself.

('Tis not the strength of the spell that will harm your baby. Any spell will change its destiny before it has a chance to make its own. You were victim of one spell too many. Don't do that to your own child.)

"Baby?" Myri sat up straight, her spine rigid, not touching the dragon in any way. Shayla's presumption that she carried a child was much more important than the fleeting glimpse of her past. "Witchwomen cannot conceive, and magicians cannot sire."

(Granted, this blessing is rarely given to those of your kind. Magicians have poisoned their bodies with Tambootie for many generations. This prevents them from fathering children. But you are not like most witchwomen and Nimbulan has rid his body of the Tambootie. Together you have made a new life. Do not deny what your heart and your body tell you are true.)

"You and your consorts eat of the Tambootie tree, heavily, and produce many babies."

(The Tambootie is a part of dragonkind—both native to Kardia Hodos. Humans came from elsewhere a long time ago. We cannot live without the Tambootie. But what mutates within us to produce the magical energy men may gather, is a slow poison when consumed by men and women.)

"I have never taken the Tambootie, and yet I have not conceived before this. Why now?" Gently she touched her belly with sensitive fingertips. Too soon to detect any swelling. She didn't dare probe the life with her magic, not when Shayla had specifically warned her not to weave any spells at all.

(Witchwomen have too much control over their own bodies and do not voluntarily conceive. They have strong instincts that tell them who will be a good father and who will not. Magic and solitude to study and perfect their talent is more important to them than husbands and family. You have that control, my child, and sensed that the time is right. The man is right. Your heart overrode your mind and let you conceive. A new era begins for humans in this realm. Your child will be among those who spread the benefits of dragon magic and prevent the carnage that has plagued both humans and dragons for too many years.)

"Men will always go to war."

(But they will not fight with magic. One last battle will settle the place of magic in your realm. After the last battle, magicians and dragons will control all magic. Mundanes will control the battles and only look to magicians for wisdom.)

"One last battle," Myri mused. She started to stand then

sat back down again, leaning hard against the recumbent dragon. "I don't know if I can deal with the aftermath of a battle. I can't throw any healing spells for fear of damaging the baby. How can I not heal suffering men?"

Amaranth awakened with a squeak and moved to her lap. He butted her hand with his head, demanding a caress, offering comfort in the same gesture.

"I have to find the fennel before then. It is the only thing I know that will protect Lan if I can't use my magic to save him."

(Trust Lyman. He is one of us. Amaranth will show you what to do when the time comes.)

"I wish there were a way to avoid this."

(We are too late to intervene. See that man to the Southeast of where we sit?)

Myri shielded her eyes from the lowering sun. The silhouette of a man burdened by a heavy pack became visible on the ridge. "I see him."

(That is the gold man.) Shayla gave him no name. That could only mean the dragons feared or distrusted him. *(The man who loves gold more than he loves life.)*

Myri recognized Ackerly's distinctive gait and posture.

(He flees Nimbulan's wrath to the camp of the enemy of dragons. He will make certain there is a battle. Now you must survey this ground and plan ahead. Come, I will take you to the battlefield.)

A short dragon flight took them to a different hillside overlooking a vast plain spreading more than a league toward the river.

"Here?" Myri looked more closely at the flat ground surrounded on three sides by low hills. The rises on the East and West ends of the meadow rose more gently than where she stood. She turned a slow circle, pausing as she looked South where a chain of hills undulated upward in a familiar pattern.

"Here." She resigned herself to the inevitable. "They fought the last battle here. Last Autumn, when I first met my husband."

(They fought the same battle here twenty years ago. The battle that loosed uncontrolled magic into the skies and nearly killed me. But this will be the last battle fought on this land.)

"Strange that here I find a single stalk of fennel." Myri plucked the elusive plant and cradled it in her hands like a living baby.

* * *

Nimbulan warily eyed a burly lieutenant wearing the colors of Kammeryl d'Astrismos' personal guard as the man marched up to the dais where Quinnault presided over a celebratory meal. The day was nearly finished and they had accomplished so little other than Rollett's rescue. Now the various forces seeking power and control over Coronnan were poised for an inevitable convergence. A very destructive clash.

Tonight the magicians and mudanes gathered in celebration of the successful rescue and one last attempt to make merry before they faced death in battle on the morrow.

"In the name of His Majesty, Kammeryl the First, descendant of the Stargods, King of Coronnan, Master of Hanassa, and Lord of The Great Bay, I demand the surrender of this keep, its surrounding islands, all tenants and leaseholders, boats and vessels, and all buildings," the soldier bellowed for all within Quinnault de Tanos' Great Hall to hear. He held a parchment at arm's length as if he read the document. He allowed it to roll shut with a snap before finishing his statement. Proof to Nimbulan that this man, like all mundanes had never been taught to read.

"But I do not recognize *Lord* Kammeryl's authority as king. Nor do the seven lords who have signed my mutual defense treaty," Quinnault said. He turned mild eyes up to the soldier for a brief moment, then returned to his meal as if that were much more important than the prattling of the soldier. Only the twitching of his fingers against his table knife betrayed his emotions.

Nimbulan silently applauded the lord for his cool exterior. The soldier had to know that all of the united lords were too far away to send aid in time. Quinnault's only hope for victory in battle lay with Lord Hanic, if he arrived in time. If he decided to help Quinnault and not Kammeryl.

The soldier's face colored briefly. He sucked in his

cheeks and squared his shoulders. "Refusal of His Majesty's demands will bring quick and terrible reprisal."

"Tell Lord Kammeryl the united lords will discuss this matter with him directly and not through an underling." Quinnault waved his hand in dismissal. His long fingers made the movement graceful and compelling.

Myri used the same gesture when she finished feeding her flusterhens in the clearing. Nimbulan clutched the little bag of fennel seeds Myri had given him on a thong to wear around his neck. Then he reached the same hand to squeeze her shoulder. Her love protected him more than any plant.

The soldier stood his ground. "No discussion or delay is permitted. Either you accept the orders of your rightful king or you do not."

"Before we can acknowledge Kammeryl d'Astrismos as rightful anything," Nimbulan said, "His Lordship must return the criminal Ackerly to Lord Quinnault for lawful judgment." He stood from his chair on Quinnault's right, pressing his fists against the table until his knuckles turned white. Anger at his assistant's betrayal and his own lack of foresight closed his throat.

Myri covered his hand with her own. Calm spread through him.

The soldier paused, ducking his head and touching his right ear lobe with his right middle finger.

"He's being coached," Nimbulan whispered to Quinnault. "Every word we say is heard by a magician in Kammeryl's camp. They are instructing him now. Every time he touches his ear, he activates the communication spell."

"We must get rid of this messenger." A moment of fear crossed Quinnault's eyes.

"How? If we capture and detain him, we have issued a challenge to Kammeryl's authority, bringing immediate reprisal. If we break his contact with Kammeryl, we challenge him. If we stall and send him away we outright deny his right to rule. Your choice, Lord Quinnault de Tanos," Nimbulan said quietly. "Every choice is designed to bring about a battle that will decide our future."

Quinnault deliberately turned his back on the soldier. "I have never fought a battle before. I maintain no army, I have no weapons. But I'll be damned if I acknowledge a warrior who sees war as the solution to all problems as my king."

"Then we must fight a battle. But on our own terms. Kammeryl has made a mistake in not attacking us covertly."

"The islands are easily defended. He wouldn't get very far."

"Then he must draw you into open battle. *We* must choose the time and place. Dismiss the messenger," Nimbulan replied sadly. Myri's hand on his tightened convulsively. Her healing talent would be needed many times over if the Commune of Magicians failed. He worried already that she would kill herself trying to save Quinnault's followers.

Quinnault turned back to face the now-grinning messenger. The soldier's middle finger caressed his earlobe again.

"I believe you already know our answer. Return to Lord Kammeryl at once." Quinnault raised his hand, palm outward in a gesture of goodwill.

Startled by the lord's gracious attitude, the soldier backed out of the Great Hall, half-bowing in respect. Kammeryl d'Astrismos would have executed the messenger bearing distasteful news.

"Now, how do we fight this battle, Nimbulan?" Quinnault stared at his half-eaten meal. "I have no army. Hanic is not here and not a certain ally if he arrives in time. My other allies are spread across all of Coronnan and can't arrive in time. How will I face Kammeryl d'Astrismos and the Bloodmage?"

CHAPTER 36

The sun had not yet broken the horizon when Myri felt the rush of dragon wings as the great beasts rose into the sky. They circled the battlefield where two armies prepared to face each other with weapons and magicians. Myri and the three apprentice girls waited on a hilltop behind the chosen field of battle.

Where was the third army? Lord Hanic could have been here, if he chose.

She turned her face into the wind, cherishing the power of the moving air. Her shoulders rotated as her arms lifted to grasp the freedom of flight. If she flew with the dragons, she could observe every movement on the field and warn Nimbulan through the silver cord that still connected her heart to his.

(We watch for you. Do not fly. Remember your unborn child,) Shayla warned her.

She picked up Amaranth, needing his purring warmth to replace her need to fly. "Why, Amaranth? Why is the desire for flight so strong in me?" she whispered to the flywacket.

Nimbulan had ordered her to remain well back of the coming fray. At the first sign of trouble for the Commune and the forces of Quinnault, she was to flee with the girls, as far and as fast as she might. She would rather be at his side for every one of his last moments.

"I have to protect the baby from the battle as well as my own magic. The baby may be all I have left of him after today." She hadn't told Nimbulan about her pregnancy. It was still too early for her body to provide proof that she carried a new life within her. Who would believe that a witchwoman and magician had managed the impossible?

She held Amaranth tightly, burying her face in his fur.

He squawked at her fierce hug and struggled in her arms, eager to join the dragons in flight. Uncharacteristically, he pushed at her with his back paws, talons unsheathed. Unable to restrain him, Myri released him to the soaring freedom they both craved.

Up and up the black flywacket spiraled in wider circles. He stretched his neck and wings, growing longer, wider, sleeker with each movement.

Myri blinked against the increasing daylight. Amaranth paled. She lost sight of him against the emerging sun. He screeched his joy. She followed the sound of his voice. A shaft of sunlight caught the last of the purple/black fur as it transformed into silvery crystals tipped with lavender.

Memories flooded her. Memories of flight, of diving into the Great Bay to hunt bemouths, the huge fish that terrorized sailors who washed overboard, but could feed an entire village for a week if captured. She remembered watching as her mother, Shayla, brought her and Amaranth, her twin, to the edge of a burial ground in the dark of night—at the site of a human tomb.

Shayla was her mother! A lifetime of seeking her heritage fell into place. Tears streamed down her cheeks. Mixed joy and fear at finally knowing sent her to her knees as she relived the last time she saw her mother in dragon form.

(One of you must choose to inhabit the body of this human child. There can only be one purple dragon alive at any one time. One of you can no longer live with the nimbus,) Shayla had instructed on that long ago night.

Myrilandel—then Amethyst—and Amaranth had quibbled and argued over the great honor to become human, to grow and learn, to guide other humans to live in harmony with dragonkind.

In the end, Amethyst had managed the shapechange faster than her brother. Amaranth was so lonely and bereft without his twin, his otherself, he had taken the form of the flywacket and become the human child's familiar. Shayla had deposited them both near the home of Magretha, a witchwoman with a longing for a child and the magic potential to teach Amethyst all she needed to know.

But remnants of Myrilandel's spirit had lingered in her not-quite-dead body. Dragon memories disappeared in the face of very strong human memories of name and personality. The two spirits in the same body compromised on forgetfulness.

"I remember how to fly now. Amaranth, wait for me." She lifted her arms again, willing the change to overtake her.

(No, my child. Amaranth is the only purple-tip dragon now. You must stay human. You must remain Nimbulan's consort and helpmate.) Shayla said.

"Why? Why must there only be one purple-tip when we were born twins?" Myri almost cried with regret that she could not fly. A small piece of satisfaction also dwelled within her. She couldn't leave Nimbulan. She had to remain human for him, for their child.

('Tis the way of dragons. For as long as dragons have claimed this planet, purple-tips have been born as twins. Their destinies are special and separate. One may remain with the nimbus, the other must seek to fill a vacancy in the world—a vacancy that if left empty will endanger all dragons.)

The need to fly temporarily overrode her emotional bonds with Nimbulan. She'd come back to this human body later. But she *had* to fly now! As a dragon, she'd be able to protect Nimbulan. She spread her arms once more, willing them to form wings. No, the wings must sprout from her back. The pronounced bone structure along her back must elongate into the showy march of purple-tipped spines.

(Do not forget your child, Myrilandel. Purple dragons are very rare and very special, but they are neither male nor female. If you revert now, your child will be lost forever. There will never be another. Will you kill Nimbulan's child so that you may fly?) Shayla asked.

Myri lowered her arms and hung her head. Her hands curved protectively around her still-flat belly. "I can't become a dragon again and aid my husband by giving him dragon magic. I can't use my talent to heal those who will be wounded. What am I to do? I can't just wait and watch and do nothing while men die!"

Kalen reached up and held her hand in mute sympathy.

(You will be needed. Amaranth will show you. Anyone, even a mundane, can gather magic from a purple

dragon. But you must be touching him when the time comes. And you must be very careful. Lyman will help you.) Shayla's voice faded as the dragon turned her concentration to the spells Nimbulan and his enemies prepared.

* * *

Nimbulan stood on the knoll at the East end of the battlefield. He rested his foot on the magic-blasted stump, one elbow on his raised knee. The view before him was much the same as it had been last Autumn—as it would have been to Druulin twenty years past.

Two armies faced each other, each grouped around the slight rise where their Battlemage prepared to direct the course of the battle. Behind the mages, assistants, apprentices and messengers waited to assist.

He didn't need to be an empath to feel the tension roiling through the air. Men on both sides paced restlessly, checked and rechecked weapons, fussed with steed harness. They spoke in whispers, then snapped at each other in loud shouts over trivia.

Nimbulan had seen it all before—with and without the magical enhancement to his sight that allowed him to view details across the entire plain. With luck and the help of the dragons, he would never have to see it again.

This time Nimbulan opposed his oldest friend and former assistant, Ackerly, instead of a beloved apprentice. This time he had a nimbus of dragons hovering in the sky above. This time he had Myri to go back to at the end of a long day.

He straightened from his contemplative pose. Instantly his assistants, Master Magicians, journeymen, and apprentices, jumped to the ready. Anticipation fluttered in his belly while apprehension sharpened his already-heightened eyesight and sense of smell. The scent of fear wafted up from the ranks of farmers and laborers hiding behind a delusion of armor and weaponry. A few had fought in battle before. A very few compared to the numbers gathered in the attacking army.

A trick of the light quadrupled the men's shadows in Quinnault's army. Kammeryl d'Astrismos would have a hard time accurately estimating the number and strength of the troops. But would the trick fool Ackerly and the Bloodmage?

"This is the last time," he declared to himself. "This must be the last battle."

Across the way, Nimbulan spied a bustle of activity around Ackerly's robed form. He wore bright yellow today, the signature color of his own magic rather than Nimbulan's blue.

A second magician in formal robes of scarlet stepped to the front. He held up the carcass of a butchered goat for all to see. His ritual knife dripped red. The Bloodmage. Moncriith. Fear, pain, and the spilling of more blood on the field of battle would fuel his magic above and beyond the endurance of most solitary magicians.

Would the combined might of the communal magic be enough to defeat him?

"Never again, Bloodmage. Your kind will never practice magic in Coronnan again," he vowed.

Nimbulan raised his hand, palm outward, fingers slightly curved, little finger crooked in a half circle. The temptation to spin the threads of the Kardia nearly overpowered him. "Force of habit." He shook his hand free of the tingling ley lines radiating over the entire surface of the planet.

"Gather dragons,
gather guardians,
magic bright and dear.
Gather power,
gather union,
Join the vision clear."

He commanded the men and boys assembled behind him. He felt the shuffling and aligning as they all joined hands. Rollett and Lyman each placed a hand on his shoulder to bring him into the chain of mounting power. His hands were free to throw the spells he devised in the course of the battle.

Across the way, Ackerly wove his hands in an ancient pattern to call forth firebombs. The Bloodmage drew an arcane pattern in the grass at his feet with the bloodied ritual knife.

A moment of inadequacy flashed before Nimbulan. He'd done this before as chief Battlemage for a powerful warlord. But never before had he performed this chore with so much at stake.

"Peace," he reminded himself. "We earn peace with this one last confrontation."

A dragon rose up into the sky from behind him. The rising sun caught the crystal outlines, showering the field with rainbows. He scanned the wingspan. Red. Rouussin. Nimbulan had learned all of their names, all of their histories last night. As they had learned his. The magicians and dragons worked today in true communion.

The big male dragon craned his neck, peering directly at Ackerly and the Bloodmage.

The Bloodmage recoiled, throwing his right arm, still holding the knife, over his eyes to shield him from the beneficent light.

Ackerly laughed at the man's fear. The traitorous assistant swelled his chest as he gathered the tremendous amount of dragon magic in the air.

Between the two knolls, the army of Kammeryl d'Astrismos edged backward, bunching up in disorderly knots. They cowered away from the dragon, looking to the officers mounted on their flanks and to their rear for direction.

Good. The space between the two armies widened appreciably, giving Nimbulan room to work his spell.

"You want to play with fire, Ackerly? I'll give you more fire than you bargained for." He wished he'd had time to devise a specific tactic rather than randomly counter whatever the enemy threw at him.

Lyman began the first line of the spell. Then all of the gathered Commune repeated the words in unison. Power built within them. Nimbulan spoke the words by rote, paying little heed to their meaning, concentrating all of the massing energy into powerful arrows that would explode the firebombs into tiny fragments that lacked enough heat to ignite anything.

Ackerly launched his balls of flame. They whizzed over the heads of Kammeryl's army, arcing upward, then descending toward the farmers and craftsmen who made up Quinnault's forces.

Nimbulan threw his probes into the bombs. Tiny arrows of light sped toward the dozen flaming missiles.

Moncriith shouted a chant of discordant sounds.

Nimbulan's probes ran into a solid wall of magic, finger-lengths from their targets. The balls of flame continued forward. Quinnault's men ducked and held their few shields over their heads.

Nimbulan launched a new round of arrows on a shorter flight path. Spell met spell in a blinding flash directly in front of his eyes. He blinked and shook his head, trying to clear it of the dazzle blindness.

Below him, Quinnault's army sagged in relief, but they didn't break formation. Nimbulan let go a tiny sigh of satisfaction. The men were loyal. They wouldn't break easily.

Moncriith smiled briefly in acknowledgment of Nimbulan's quick thinking. He launched a spell of his own. A dense cloud formed above the center of the field. Lightning flashed within the roiling darkness. The mist sent out seeking tentacles toward the ranks of Quinnault's men. Each thrusting coil of blackness was tipped with searing green fire.

Kammeryl's army surged forward in the wake of the cloud. Quinnault's men threw up their hands and shields to protect their heads from the fires and jerked backward in a wave.

Nimbulan countered the cloud with a gush of water gathered from the nearby river. It dissolved and scattered harmlessly. He still had to deal with the seasoned troops rushing forward, weapons raised, battlecries ululating from their throats.

Quickly he levitated a cache of metal throwing stars at the attackers. The razor-sharp weapons faltered in their trajectory and dropped harmlessly to the ground. Neither Ackerly nor Moncriith had countered the spell.

Who? Who else interfered with this battle?

* * *

Kammeryl's forces swept closer.

Nimbulan tried to resurrect the throwing stars with a

rapid series of hand motions. He had to levitate them before they buried themselves deep in the Kardia, never to be used again.

The throwing stars remained inert.

"Quickly, Nimbulan, shatter their weapons. Do it before they kill anyone." Myri tugged anxiously at his arm.

He didn't stop to question her presence. He didn't dare think about the danger she might be in.

The first rank crashed into Quinnault's amateur defenders.

"Metal grow brittle
fragile become
shatter like spittle
dive into the loam."

He threw the hastily invented poem at the clashing armies.

Swords and pikes, lances and shields all crumbled into thousands of pieces. As directed, the shards of metal sank deeply into the top layer of dirt, just as the throwing stars had.

Men from both armies looked in dismay at their weaponless hands, at missing armor, and finally at their Battlemages for explanation. They shuffled back and forth in indecision.

"Shayla says you can only use the magic for defense. You can't attack," Myri cried, still hanging onto Nimbulan's arm. "The throwing stars couldn't obey your spell."

"Defend?" He looked at her, a little dazed at the concept. He'd always worked for strong warlords who considered the best defense to be an overwhelming offense.

"Look above you, men," Moncriith shouted across the field. Magic augmented his voice so that all could hear. "Look at the demons that force this battle. Do you wish to be slaves of the demons? Do you wish to lose your souls as well as your lives to them? My magic is stronger than theirs. I have neutralized Nimbulan, the greatest Battlemage of our time. I have ended his powers and shattered your weapons! Now I will liberate the souls of all those who have died on this field in times past. They shall no longer be the tools of the demons."

"He's using magic to make all believe his lies," Lyman whispered in Nimbulan's ear. "If we can show the people how he lies . . . *Stargods,* he's doing it!"

Nimbulan looked where the old man pointed. Mist boiled up from the river banks. The dense fog rolled inland too rapidly to be natural. Within heartbeats, the stifling moisture enveloped Nimbulan and his Commune.

Shifting clouds within clouds distorted images within a few inches of Nimbulan's nose. Trees and outcroppings took on engorged dimensions. They seemed to move and shift from place to place as distance and time lost all meaning.

The gray water vapor brightened to green smoke, backlit as if by natural fire. Coiling tendrils writhed and formed faces in the fearsome mist.

"Armies of the dead. They march toward us through the fog," one of the young apprentices screamed. He broke the link with the magicians on either side of him. The power of Communal magic dissipated into the mist.

Ghostly faces solidified, clothed in the armor of twenty years ago. Horrible wounds of lance and fire showed through rents in rotting tunics in the colors of lords long-dead.

Druulin, face and hands horribly burned, stared directly at Nimbulan. Accusing. Demanding retribution for betrayl and desertion.

Nimbulan's body and will froze in the face of his master. He hadn't died with Druulin twenty years ago because he and Ackerly had deserted their master. They had been cowardly and disloyal. They deserved to die now. Die as horribly as Druulin had. . . .

"Stargods, he's conjured the dead from previous battles fought in this field." Lyman's hand jerked against Nimbulan's shoulder as if to ward himself with the cross of the Stargods.

The ward broke the mesmerizing stare from Druulin's ghost. Nimbulan closed his eyes and mind to the horrible accusations of his mentor.

"Stay linked!" Nimbulan ordered. "We cannot fight the Bloodmage individually. We have to stay together."

Above him, dragon wings beat against the stagnating air. The fog faded but the dead continued to march forward, intent on killing any who stood in their way.

"Misty wraiths, lost in time,
Seek your fate in love benign.
Go your way, your life fulfilled,
The void restores your spirits killed."

He chanted an invitation for the displaced ghosts to find their way back to the void and their next existence. The magicians behind him repeated the incantation.

They recited the spell a third time, together with growing confidence.

The fog thinned. Ghostly faces dissolved. The screams of terror faded in the ranks of soldiers caught between the two Battlemages.

"See the lost souls demons have betrayed and prevented from finding their next existence. I send them away in peace," Moncriith proclaimed.

"A little late, Moncriith," Nimbulan said as he gathered his wits to face the next attack from the Bloodmage.

The slight river breeze that dissipated the mist took on a musky, sweet scent. Real smoke replaced the mist. The smoke of burning green Tambootie mixed with timboor.

Nimbulan raised his hands to place a barrier between himself and the deadly smoke. No power tingled in his palms. He had no magic left to protect his troops or his magicians. He gasped for breath and took in a lungful of the poisonous smoke. In a moment, he'd begin hallucinating.

He thrust Myri behind him to protect her as much as he could.

CHAPTER 37

Ackerly fanned the flames higher on his bonfire of fresh and aged Tambootie limbs. The green flames licked hungrily at the fuel. Smoke poured upward in a spiraling column. The wind was already from the West, born in the cold mountain range, seeking the warmer flatter plains of Coronnan. He needed no magic to send the smoke directly into Nimbulan's face.

Years of suppressed resentment for his childhood friend and companion built with each puff of smoke and burning log. "Your respect for me was measured against the size of my talent, Nimbulan." He stabbed at the fire with a fresh stick, building the flames higher, high enough to burn the green wood with the deadly sap still in it.

"You measured everyone against your own magical talent and none of us matched you, so you were superior to all. You used everyone you came in contact with—made them clean up the mess you left behind. You had to be the best, so only your desires, your talents, and your wisdom mattered. But where would you be if I hadn't arranged your business affairs, taught the apprentices, kept you fed, and made sure you had a tent to sleep in? Well let me tell you, Nimbulan, I can gather magic now, as easily as any of your Commune. I can work any spell I want with very little effort. I'm as good as you. Better. Because I also have the gold. Gold to buy people and luxuries and respect. That's something you'll never have. No one will respect you unless you possess gold and are willing to make more gold. Only gold matters to mundanes."

He threw another stick into the greedy flames. The fire burned too hot. The smoke climbed too high before spreading out and engulfing the opposing magicians. He called up more wind. Harder to do that now. Why?

The dragons, dimly visible above the battlefield withdrew. The magic disappeared with them. Ackerly delved into the store of magic within his body. The Commune hadn't figured out how to do that yet. He'd stumbled on it by accident. Only he knew that unlike the old magic, this new power could be stored for later use. The dragons didn't have to be present for him to work magic.

"I'll see you in chains before this day is done, Nimbulan. And I will rejoice because you will be my servant and your dragons will help me. Dragons like gold. They hoard and treasure it. My gold makes me one with them. Only me!" he chortled as he danced around the fire. He made a full circle, skipping and hopping, clapping his hands.

Moncriith looked at him strangely.

"You have your rituals, I have mine," Ackerly yelled back at the man with knife scars all over his face, hands and body, from where he'd drawn blood to fuel his magic.

Moncriith didn't understand true power either. His scars marked him as a powerful Bloodmage. He created fear wherever he went. But he had no gold. Only gold bought power.

As Ackerly laughed again, the wind shifted. He gulped a great draught of the smoke. Dizziness shifted and fractured his vision. He covered his mouth with his sleeve and breathed deeply through the fabric.

Some of the poisonous smoke leaked through. Tears streamed down his cheeks as he coughed heavily, trying to rid his body of the smoke and yet still breathe. He felt as if he'd stumbled into one of Lord Kammeryl's torture devices. Iron bands constricted his chest, pressing tighter. Tighter yet. Squeezing the life from him. Tighter.

Ackerly tried desperately to erect a barrier between himself and the deadly smoke. His store was empty. There was no more magic in the air to gather.

His lungs froze in the poisonous smoke.

(We refuse you the magic. You do not work for unity and peace,) a disapproving voice came into his mind.

"Help me!"

(You must help yourself.)

Darkness took Ackerly's mind. Pain kept him awake.

The smoke grew thicker. Dirt pressed into his mouth and nose. Air. I have to have air. . . .

At least my gold is safe. No one will find it in three hundred years.

* * *

Moncriith took a whiff of the noisome air. Memories of his own trial by the Tambootie smoke swirled around him like coils of suffocating mist. His visions of demons had been prophetic. They took the form of women, naked from the waist up—voluptuous women with pale skin and fair hair. Magretha, his first love with her lush and welcoming bosom. Other lovers, all whores. All the demons he saw in the smoke had hideous lower halves with numerous snakelike limbs that coiled around throat and heart, crushing him to near death while titillating his male parts to excruciating fullness. At the time, he'd been frightened for his very soul. Now with the wisdom of experience and time, he knew the monsters for what they were. Demons that plagued Coronnan and made magicians their slaves.

Myrilandel was their leader. 'Twas her face he'd seen surrounded by a cloud of pale, almost colorless hair in those smoke demons. She had taken human form, but he knew her and his lust for her could be countered only by cleansing fire.

Moncriith saw her standing next to Nimbulan, slim and beautiful, with hair as pale as moonlight. Her beauty and feigned innocence had been designed to capture men's hearts. 'Twas Myrilandel's demonic influence that caused Magretha to betray Moncriith with other men—his own father. 'Twas Myrilandel's demonic spirit that had driven his anger and hurt at the betrayal into a killing rage. But for her, he would have run away from Magretha and his father. Myrilandel had driven him to use magic to murder them.

But the demon had pulled Magretha from the flaming hut, leaving Moncriith's father to die a terrible death. Myrilandel must suffer the same death by fire. Magretha had. He'd finally tracked her down and consigned her to holy fire. Now it was Myrilandel's turn. She was to blame. She had to be the cause of all his grief. Myrilandel had tempted him. Forced him. Betrayed him. . . . He couldn't have done those terrible things to his own father. He wouldn't. . . .

But he had.

"No more false memories!" He held his head in both hands, driving away the guilt and self-doubt the sight of Myrilandel always brought to him.

He held his breath. If demons took command of his body and mind, he'd lose control of his grand plan for today and tomorrow and a hundred tomorrows. The Stargods had given him a vision. The temple elders were in error.

His eyes crossed and his vision blurred. He blinked rapidly, clearing them of the poisonous smoke. The dragons in the sky multiplied before his eyes, splitting into dozens of small demons that dove straight for his face, talons extended. The colored spines and wing veins blackened. The smaller demons opened their mouths, fangs dripping poison into his eyes.

Weird coils of numbness spread from his lungs to his fingers to his knees and back to his heart. Instinctively, he gulped air. More of the poisonous smoke poured into his lungs. The demons of his hallucination tore at his eyes and lungs, rending his flesh into bloody strips. Everywhere they touched him turned to ice.

He choked and spat. Not enough air! He clawed at his throat and chest to rid him of the things that wrapped cold fingers around his heart and lungs, squeezing. Squeezing the life and the magic from him.

He drew his pain deeper into his body, letting it sharpen his senses and fuel his inborn magic talent. With a mighty effort he drew a spiral with his finger, starting at his mouth and expanding outward. Glowing lines of red magic followed the path of his finger. He willed the magic to draw the killing smoke from his lungs. Two tiny puffs of gray mist exited his body with his next breath.

He needed to inhale. Air, more air! The smoke took the air out of his lungs as well.

Darkness surrounded him. A tunnel of bright light robbed color and definition from his failing sight. He closed his eyes to separate himself from the demons. The world righted. The dragons resumed normal proportions and numbers. Then he knew that Ackerly's Tambootie smoke had created the demons, not the dragons themselves.

Air and smoke exploded into a sunburst, blotting out everything else.

* * *

Nimbulan kept his arm around Myri as he watched Shayla and Rouussin thrust their great wings up and down. They stirred the air. The Tambootie smoke blew back toward Ackerly, dissipated, faded, mixed with clean air from the river and mountains.

Myri rubbed her eyes, clearing tears away with her sleeve. Nimbulan did the same. Together they scanned the battlefield.

Chaos reigned below them. Hundreds of inert bodies lay in the trampled grass, sprawled where the smoke had caught them. Only Kammeryl's army retained their positions, sagging against their pikes and lances, bleary eyed and coughing, but upright. Quinnault's tenants, pretending to be an army, gradually roused from the choking smoke first. They used pitchfork and shovel handles—now devoid of metal—as braces to hold themselves upright while they coughed their lungs clear. None of the troops, from either army, seemed fit for battle.

On the hilltop to the South, a ragged line of men was outlined. None moved to help or hinder either side.

Lord Hanic had arrived, but he held back, waiting for the tide of battle to turn. Waiting to commit his troops only to the winner.

Nimbulan saw nothing of the Kammeryl d'Astrismos who claimed the crown, or his mounted officers.

The dying fire on the knoll opposite him demanded his attention. Ackerly lay beside the glowing embers, his hands holding his throat. His aura hovered above him, separated by several arm's lengths.

The departing aura proved the man dead. Grief blinded Nimbulan momentarily. Grief for the years of companionship, shared youths, and friendship. He couldn't let his emotions cloud the debacle forming before him. Ackerly had betrayed him and suffered from his own foolishness. The winds were too capricious to use smoke as a weapon. Too many uncontrollable factors influenced the direction and intensity of smoke.

The Bloodmage was missing from the knoll. Hastily, Nimbulan searched the field for signs of Moncriith. He supressed the extra heartbeats that bounced in his chest. Moncriith on the loose, possible crazed by the smoke was too dangerous. Nimbulan had to account for the Bloodmage.

Tambootie smoke was debilitating to everyone, magician and mundane. His enemy was out of commission at least temporarily. But where had he gone?

"Thank you for clearing the air with your wingbeats," he called to the dragons. Then he turned to the three apprentices designated as runners between his position and the army command post. "Quickly, send a message to Lord Quinnault. He must ride out in front of his troops. If they see him acting calm, they'll take confidence in him. Tell the lord he must remind the troops not to attack. We are here to defend only."

"A barrier. If you could create a wall to keep the armies separate they couldn't kill each other," Myri said, her eyes lighting up with the idea.

"Of course. But Kammeryl would still seek a way to prove himself the greater warrior. That is the only kind of leadership and rule he understands." Nimbulan closed his eyes and formed the image of an invisible wall running North and South across the entire width of the field. To his surprise, his body responded with a coil of magic ready for forming. He had stored the magic from an earlier gathering rather than dissipating after the last spell. A smile crept across his face as the barrier fell into place.

A few of the seasoned troops on the front lines pressed against the wall and withdrew, puzzled looks on their faces. A mounted officer raced to the front from a clump of trees off to the left. The steed's hooves dug up great clumps of turf as it galloped forward. The beast stopped short, skidding the last few lengths before the wall. The rider nearly plunged over his mount's head in reaction.

When he righted himself, he reached out with tentative fingers and pushed against the almost-visible barrier. He jerked it back as if burned.

Lord Kammeryl d'Astrismos emerged next from the clump of trees. He rode a magnificent, white war steed, heavier boned and stronger than standard cavalry beasts. A golden circlet on his armored helm announced to one and all his claim to be King of Coronnan.

"Ah, so that's where he's been hiding," Nimbulan murmured.

"I believe it's called strategic vantage point for directing the battle," Lyman said, hiding a smile behind his hand. His extra long fingers stretched nearly to his ear. "It also makes retreat easier should it become necessary."

Kammeryl d'Astrismos also pushed against the wall. He let his hand linger, daring the pain to throw him away.

"Fight me!" Kammeryl yelled at the top of his lungs. "Make this a fair battle. Fight me with weapons and tactics I can counter."

"We do not attack. We only defend," Nimbulan replied in a voice pitched for all to hear.

"Then defend yourselves from *ME!* I challenge Lord Quinnault de Tanos, the traitor, or his champion, to single combat."

"I am the Peacemaker." Quinnault took up the lord's challenge. "I cannot ask my people to fight for the sake of fighting. Your quarrel is with me, Kammeryl d'Astrismos. Let your battle be with me and let the innocent of Coronnan stand aside, free and unharmed by us." He strode out to face his enemy without helm or armor, only an ancient sword in his left hand. His fair hair glinted in the sunlight, as pale and fine as Myrilandel's.

Suddenly Nimbulan saw the resemblance to Myrilandel in Quinnault's posture, profile and coloring. Could Myri truly be the lord's long-lost sister? When? How? He didn't want to think about the incredibly dark forces needed to reanimate a dead body.

No time for questions, only time to help and guide Quinnault before he lost the entire war in single combat with Kammeryl d'Astrismos.

Nimbulan withdrew the barrier.

* * *

Myri watched Quinnault stride to the front of his troops, sword in hand, sunlight glinting on his fine, fair hair. A quick glimpse of his profile, with his long face and proud nose echoed her own image in the metal mirror Nimbulan had given her.

"He is my brother. We stole his sister's body to give me life because there can only be one purple dragon alive at a time," she whispered to herself and to her mother flying the skies above her. She didn't know if Nimbulan heard her words and didn't care. He was her husband and had a right to know.

(Yes. Myrilandel was on the brink of death. Bleeding in her brain from a defect at birth,) Shayla replied. *(Her coma was so deep her family thought her dead and placed her in their stone tomb. Had they buried her, we would not have been able to free her in time. Your dragon vitality awakened the human child's natural talent. Together, you healed the weakness in her brain and stopped the bleeding.)*

"But because she wasn't quite dead, her spirit lives on inside me. That is why I couldn't remember. The two spirits vied for dominance and finally compromised on forgetfulness."

(Yes.)

"I can't let my brother die, Shayla. I have to stop him." Suddenly she knew that her certainty that Nimbulan would die this day was misplaced. Quinnault de Tanos, her only living blood relative, was the one destined to die.

(He makes his own destiny.)

"I must stop him. He is my family. The only human family I have."

(You have your husband and your child. Kalen and Powwell look to you rather than their own mothers. Save yourself, Amethyst.)

"I am Myrilandel. Amethyst must die and be forgotten. I cannot be a dragon anymore. Amaranth is the only purple in all the nimbi of Coronnan. I claim Quinnault as family now." Myri ran down the hill. She knew only that she had to stand beside her brother in this most important deed in his life. And when the time came, she would use every resource available to save him, including her magic talent.

Nimbulan caught up with her. Together they ran to help the lord who controlled the fate of Coronnan with his ancient, slightly rusty sword.

CHAPTER 38

"Don't be a fool, Quinnault." Nimbulan grabbed the lord's arm to hold him back from carrying through with his challenge. "You know nothing of weapons and combat. He'll make mincemeat of you in a matter of moments. Choose a champion. Perhaps one of Hanic's men." He pointed to the line of men silhouetted on the hill.

A wry smile touched one corner of Quinnault's mouth. "I'm the son of a lord. I wasn't always intended for the priesthood. I have trained with weapons. But I admit it's been a long time since I held a sword. And never as fine a one as my father's." He surveyed the length of the weapon that had been spared Nimbulan's metal shattering spell. The magic had destroyed only the metal carried by the men on the field, not those who waited and directed from behind.

Intricate runes decorated Quinnault's slender blade. A moonstone glowed in the pommel. Decorative as it was, it was also a working weapon, meant to be used. A telltale line of rust around the pommel indicated how long the weapon had remained idle and how recent was the polishing that made the runes glow in the growing sunlight.

"He outweighs you by fifty pounds, his reach is longer, and he's a practiced warrior," Myri added her own argument.

"Once he was a warrior. Now he's a general. He hasn't engaged in combat in years. And he's used to easy living with his fine wines and fancy food. I've been building bridges all winter, eating the same rough but hearty food as my tenants." Again that half smile lightened Quinnault's set visage. This time the smile almost reached his eyes.

"My lord, I am your sister." Myri clasped Quinnault's

hand over the sword hilt, staying his headlong rush into combat. "I wasn't quite dead when the family buried me."

"I guessed something like that happened, Myrilandel. We will talk later. If I survive." He patted her hand lovingly. Again that wry smile lit his face but not his eyes.

"You know something, Quinnault. Tell us why you won't choose a champion to fight this battle for you. Don't lie to us." The man's calm shook Nimbulan, more than Myri's revelation. He kept his hand on the back of Myri's waist to brace himself against the coming shock. He thanked the Stargods she had come with him, yet he was frightened out of his wits that she stood so close to the line that could become a battle front at any moment.

"I know that I have proclaimed my cause as peace, not conquest. If I win, all of the families who have lost men and land and crops and the will to live during a war, will flock to my side. The people are ready for peace. They will grasp it any way they can. Kammeryl has only recently declared himself king. He offers the people nothing but more war. If he wins, they will depose him, and I will still win."

"But you'll be dead." Myri clung to Quinnault rather than wipe her tears away. "I have so much to tell you, brother."

"I know some of it, Myrilandel. I pray that we will have the time to rediscover our mutual past." Quinnault caressed her hair, lovingly, as he would a small child. The child sister he remembered? "But if Kammeryl kills me, I will become a martyr to the cause of peace. We all know that a dead martyr is worth a hundred live rabble-rousers. Make sure the people remember me and not Moncriith and his demons."

He turned abruptly and walked to a place near the center of the field, his troops behind him, Kammeryl's army before him, and the crowds of camp followers and neighbors lining the hillsides around the field. The people of Coronnan cleared a circle for the two combatants, roughly one hundred arm's lengths across.

Kammeryl rode his magnificent steed to one side of the cleared space. He pulled the crowned visor down on his helm and loosed his sword. No king would attend a battle carrying a lance, pike, or ax. Only a sword symbolized the honor of a man who ruled.

A common soldier from Kammeryl's ranks rushed up to Quinnault, offering his own boiled leather helmet. Not much protection, but better than nothing—the offer more valuable considering the source.

"Take it, Quinnault. Please take it. And the breastplate the next man offers," Myri whispered, clutching Nimbulan's arm so tightly she nearly cut off the circulation to his hand.

"Interesting that the offers of assistance come from my enemy's army," Quinnault said, that half smile tugging at the corner of his mouth. He donned the borrowed protection. Three men rushed to help him with the buckles of the chest and back leathers.

Myri stepped forward to help. Nimbulan held her back.

"The Stargods control the outcome of this duel, Myri. We can only watch," he replied, patting her hand, but not loosing her fingers. Somehow he needed that slight discomfort to remind him what these men fought for.

"You can armor him with magic, Nimbulan. A thin bubble that no one else can see," Myri pleaded. Her eyes never left her brother.

"If I could, I would. This must be a battle between the lords. One of them must prove his right to govern by the outcome of this battle. If I help now, then Quinnault's victory or defeat will be mine, not his. If he uses his own magic to protect himself, then the victory or defeat will be for magicians and not Quinnault. No one must interfere." Sadly, Nimbulan pulled Myri close against his chest. "You don't have to watch."

She drew her face away from the protective folds of his formal robe. "I must watch. I must know the moment of his death or his living." She turned within the circle of his arms, resolutely facing the field of combat, filled with anger and fear.

"You will do anything to win, Kammeryl d'Astrismos. Even entering single combat asteed while your opponent has no mount or armor," Quinnault taunted. "Your honor will be in question for as long as you live. As well as your prowess at arms. Every lord with a strong companion will know that you are afraid to face me, an untrained warrior, a former priest, on equal ground."

Kammeryl snarled an incomprehensible animal sound of fury as he kicked his steed into a full charge. The visor restricted his vision. Quinnault neatly sidestepped out of the path of the white steed. At the last moment he dipped his sword and severed the saddle girth. The tip of hammered steel nicked the steed's side. The animal reared and screamed. Kammeryl lost his balance as his saddle slipped and gravity dragged him toward the Kardia. He was too skilled a rider to fall, dismounting lithely at the last moment, sword at the ready, visor pushed back for better line of sight.

Quinnault widened his stance, grasping his sword with both hands. The blade did not waver. But Nimbulan saw the tension in his neck and in between his eyes.

The first blow from Kammeryl came quickly, without warning. A powerful downward stroke meant to split open his opponent's thin leather helmet and his skull beneath. Quinnault blocked the blow, and the next, never having time to recover and strike one of his own.

Slash and thrust, duck and parry. Quinnault led Kammeryl in an exhausting and dangerous dance around the circle. Slash, thrust. Sidestep, jump, and roll. Blow after blow, they wove their way around the circle once, twice. A third time.

The older, stouter warlord breathed heavily, but still he pressed the younger, more agile lord to his limits.

Quinnault parried another blow and retreated closer to the silent watchers. His aura remained closed. Nimbulan couldn't read the man's emotions or physical state. But then, he never could. Kammeryl stepped forward, raising his sword for another strike. His aura seethed with red-and-orange fury. Black spots surged and faded within the envelope of light.

The wry half smile lighted Quinnault's face once more. He must have seen the aura, too, known that Kammeryl's temper would get the better of him; known that the man's inner balance was always precarious.

Quinnault wasn't strong enough to deflect the rapidly twisting blade aimed for his gut. Bright blood stained his tunic across his middle. He staggered, clutching at the wound with his free hand. His sword dangled uselessly from a rapidly weakening left hand.

Kammeryl moved in closer for a killing blow. Confidence slowed him. He wanted to savor the moment of his adversary's death.

Nimbulan wanted to close his eyes, knowing the battle was over. Firmly he made himself watch. For at the moment of Quinnault's death, he would have to begin the campaign to proclaim him a martyred saint in the name of peace.

Quinnault ducked and rolled. Kammeryl's blow barely touched his shoulder. As Kammeryl brought back his sword again, his raised arms lifted his body armor, revealing a vulnerable crack in his middle. Quinnault thrust his sword tip toward the bared midriff, but he was rapidly losing his strength. The blade went no farther. Kammeryl laughed, raising his sword higher.

"You're dead, Peacemaker. You're dead already. I see the light fading from your eyes. I could stand here and watch you bleed to death. But I'll be merciful and make it quick." As he brought the weapon down, he bent forward to guide the blade to the fallen man. Quinnault thrust upward with the last of his strength.

Both men collapsed. Their blood mingled and stained the beaten grass beneath them.

* * *

Myri wrenched herself away from Nimbulan's convulsive grasp. The sight of her brother's blood brought her talent into full, insistent preparedness.

(Don't, Myrilandel. Don't risk your child,) Shayla reminded her.

"I must save him. I can't watch him die," Myri protested.

(Then let Amaranth help you. Gather his magic for your healing spells.)

"Women can't gather dragon magic." She ripped Quinnault's tunic open, exposing the wound. Then she pressed a strip from her skirt against the gaping edges of skin, praying the pressure would slow the bleeding.

"Anyone can gather magic from a purple-tipped dragon. Even women and mundanes, provided the dragon in question is willing." Old Lyman, the mysterious magician who seemed to know more about dragons than Myri did, chuckled as he reached pale hands to help add pressure to the wound. "In another existence, I was called Iianthe—the last purple-tipped dragon before Amaranth and Amethyst made a premature entrance into this world. After that I drifted for many years as the guardian spirit of the beginning place until Nimbulan called me forth in the name of peace. Amaranth is willing to give magic to this spell. I must guide you both."

A swoop of wings fanned the air before Myri could question the old man whose fingernails appeared slightly lavender where the blood pulsed beneath them. The crowd pressing close to Myri and her patient gasped and fled backward. A gentle thud behind Myri announced the landing of her familiar, now in full dragon form.

"I am not a healer, but I will direct the flow of magic through you so that it does no harm to your baby," Lyman whispered.

(Give me your hand, Myrilandel.) Amaranth's mental voice came to her, deeper and more mature than she had ever heard him. It sounded very like Lyman's voice did to her ears.

She had no time to reflect on the oddity. Beneath her hands, Quinnault's life hung in the balance.

"Amaranth, you're too big to cuddle in my lap like you used to when I worked a healing." She stretched her free hand to grasp his extended forepaw. "I think I need both hands for this." She studied the red-soaked skirt she still pressed into Quinnault's wound. She sensed his life slipping away. They didn't have much time.

Amaranth waddled closer, not nearly as graceful on the ground as in the air. Gently, he extended one wing to cover her like an iridescent veil while his muzzle rested lightly on her shoulders. The other wing extended to Lyman.

Energy tingled along Myri's spine and into her arms. Stronger than the ley lines, this magic begged to be used for good. Her talent wrapped around it.

Both hands free to hold the wound in place, she let the magic flow freely into her brother. A healing *Song* honed and directed the magic. Her vision followed the healing into the gaping folds of skin, down into the muscles, repairing tears here, rejoining severed blood vessels there. Her mind lost track of what she *Sang,* only aware that a lilting tune hovered near her ears.

She sensed other people joining, adding more and more magic to the power she felt. The gathered soldiers and commoners must be touching Amaranth, compounding the magic. The spell remained at the same level, not amplifying like Nimbulan's dragon magic. Her husband used rhymes to bring his magicians into a spell. She had no poems ready that described the intent of the spell.

What? What could she use to join these people to the spell?

An old ballad fairly leaped to her lips. She molded it into a *Song* of healing.

A dozen other voices grabbed the melody and joined with her. A deep well of harmony amplified the energy running from the dragon through her into her brother. Other hands grasped her shoulders, hair and back, linking her to the common people of Coronnan as well as the purple-tipped dragon.

Suddenly she was a part of each person who touched the dragon. Their hearts beat as one. Their minds mingled, sharing hopes and plans for the future, all of them centered on the man who lay bleeding to death beneath her hands.

She repeated the melody, uncaring of the words, only knowing that the notes needed to blend and flow in a way that all could sing it with love and hope and unity. As the melody rose and swelled on the breeze, all of them became a part of Quinnault de Tanos and his rapidly healing body, giving him their love as well as the little bit of magic allowed them.

Myri's love for all of them grew with the *Song* and the healing magic.

Soaring on a high note, she directed them all to the core of the wound. Together they patched his internal organs, rebuilt the nicked rib, joined the major artery, then slowly backed out, blending muscle tissue together on their way.

The music turned joyous.

Lord Quinnault opened his eyes.

"Our king lives. Long live King Quinnault!" The shout

rippled through the crowd who had given this man back his life.

"I was afraid they'd make me king if I lived. Maybe you should let me die," Quinnault quipped.

"Never, brother. You must live for these people. You belong to all of them now," Myri replied. Tears of joy streamed down her cheeks.

Hands broke their connection with Myri and Amaranth. The magic dwindled, drained out of her. Movement flickered around the edges of her vision. The people danced and celebrated. One and all they acknowledged Quinnault their king. The wars were over. Peace had won.

Somewhere in the background she heard/sensed Lord Hanic joining the celebration with his men.

"Sorry we were late. Delays crossing the ford. I lost some men who ran from a cloud shadow they swore was a dragon."

She crumpled into the blood-soaked ground, exhausted. Her stomach felt funny, half cramped, partially upset. She clutched her belly desperately, praying she hadn't lost the baby in saving her brother's life.

CHAPTER 39

Nimbulan gently laid Myri on their bed in the old monastery. He pulled a rough blanket over her. Gradually her shivers subsided as he stroked her hair and held her hand. He checked the silver cord of magic connecting his heart to hers. The gentle bonds pulsed with life and vigor stronger than before.

A breath of relief swept over him. For a few moments, he'd feared that her talent would sever the tie to him in favor of her new patient, Quinnault.

At this very moment, the Lord of the Islands, no, he was now King of Coronnan, was being tended by retainers and healers of all levels of society. Hasty messages of the day's events, especially the proclamation of kingship by the common people, had been sent to all the lords. He sincerely hoped that news of Ackerly's death and the Bloodmage's failure to penetrate the defenses of the Commune would do more for the cause than the death of Kammeryl d'Astrismos. Within a day or two, the leaders of Coronnan—noble and magician—would all descend upon the small keep in the heart of the delta islands to verify that the wars had ended. The lords would probably confirm Quinnault's kingship since he now commanded the loyalty of Kammeryl's army as well as his own islanders. Most of Hanic's men had also sworn their loyalty to Quinnault as king.

Hanic was still wavering, waiting for a consensus from the lords.

While a great fuss was being made over Quinnault the Peacemaker, only Nimbulan remembered Myrilandel, the witchwoman who had saved the new king from certain death. Granted, a great many people had participated in that final spell. But Myrilandel, and only Myrilandel, had known what to do.

"Make sure that Quinnault drinks plenty of water and small beer. We healed the wounds, but magic cannot replace lost blood. He needs fluid to rebuild it," Myri whispered.

"Hush, now. He's in the hands of the best healers in the country. They will see to him. You must take care of yourself, Myri. Kalen will bring you some broth in a few moments. You must promise to drink it all. You must get strong again, soon, for I don't know how I will live without you, love. We will be married by a priest as soon as I can arrange it. A forever marriage, blessed by the Stargods." He traced her cheek with a gentle fingertip, memorizing each plane and angle.

She kissed his palm and closed her eyes with a satisfied sigh.

"Tell me what happened to the others, Ackerly and . . . and Moncriith." She grasped his hand with greater strength than he thought she had left.

"Ackerly is dead, suffocated by the Tambootie smoke and his own strangling hands," he said sadly.

"Commit his body to the pyre with honor and respect. Please, Nimbulan." She held him tightly when he would have turned away.

"Ackerly betrayed me and his students. He tried to kill me, twice. He sabotaged the spell to rescue Rollett from Moncriith's witchsniffers. He . . ." He couldn't go on. Memories of all their years together kept intruding on his sense of outrage.

"For the man you want to remember him as, please, give his death the respect you yourself would want." Her big eyes, almost colorless with fatigue, pleaded with him.

"I promise. He shall go to the funeral pyre wearing his formal robes and carrying his staff—the symbol of his status as a magician." Nimbulan bowed his head, allowing himself to grieve honestly for his old friend.

"And Moncriith?" Myri tucked both her hands beneath the blanket, giving way to a great shudder.

"We don't know. No one has seen him or his body."

"I fear that he lives and will return to plague us all."

"If he does, the entire might of the Commune of Magicians will protect you and all innocents that men such as he seek to persecute."

She looked at him then with mingled trust and skepticism. "Men like Moncriith will always find a way around institutions of authority."

"Sleep, now, Myri and don't worry about the future. Or the past. Sleep and regain your strength. There is much to celebrate. I want to share the joy with you, as my legal wife." He kissed her brow and watched as her eyes closed and her breathing slowed to the easy rhythm of sleep.

Silently, he prayed she wasn't right this time. Coronnan had enough troubles without worrying about Moncriith. He'd have to make sure the new government had strong and just laws for all the people so malcontents like Moncriith had no injustice to use as a springboard to power.

* * *

"If you demand I start a new dynasty with a new name, then I won't make Castle Krej—named for one of Kammeryl's supposed ancestors—my capital," Quinnault said. The mildness of his tone belied the tension in his knuckles where he grasped the arms of his chair.

Nimbulan scanned the new king of Coronnan with just a touch of *Sight*. His normally pale skin carried a tinge of blue rather than healthy pink and his fine hair hung limply where it had pulled free of its queue restraint. No other signs of illness or weakness showed.

"Castle Krej is an easily defended fortress, Your Majesty," Lord Hanic replied."It is yours by right of conquest. For your own safety, you must retreat there with an army combined of all our forces. As general of the united army, I will guarantee that you are protected."

No one had declared Hanic leader of anything.

"No." Quinnault speared the tardy lord with a glance. "I will no longer be dependent upon an army, any army to protect me. Peace and justice will be my protection. We will build a city here amongst the islands at the head of the Bay."

"But it isn't safe. The islands can't be defended," Lord Sauria said.

"I intend to reign over a country at peace. Defense is no

longer my primary concern. We need a new city. Here will be a center of commerce when we reopen the shipping lanes in the Great Bay. My home will be a palace, open to lords and merchants and petitioners. I have had enough of fortresses and wars."

"Perhaps we should call the new city, Dragonville in honor of the dragons that give us the means to enforce peace without armies," Nimbulan suggested.

"I'd rather call it Coronnan City. The monarch and the capital city must belong to all, rather than the king owning all." Quinnault stood and began to pace, hands behind his back, shoulders slightly hunched like wings tucked up, head thrust forward, sure signs of his returning vitality. No trace of the draconic shadows masked his face. These thoughts were his own. "Don't any of you understand? We are trying to build a united country with laws and justice. No one of the lords will be more powerful than the others. No king will be a despot, but rather a first among the equal lords. And all people, noble, common and magician, shall be subject to law. Therefore, the king can't own more than any other lord, preferably less, to maintain a balance." He paused to look each of the assembled lords in the eye. There were only twelve of them left. A century ago there had been more than twenty.

"I agree to take the surname of Draconis and pass it to future generations of kings. But I insist that the capital be Coronnan City. It is a city of people, the very people who shared in my healing. They are what makes Coronnan great, not me."

Silence hung heavily in the Great Hall of Quinnault's keep. No noble had ever heard of such an outrageous idea. Nobility had always meant privilege and ownership. Nimbulan silently applauded this bold move.

"Responsibility must be the primary tenet of kingship and nobility." Quinnault pulled a small book from the pile of texts, maps and parchments on the table. "That idea was first put forth by the Stargods, in this sermon, recorded by one Kimmer. He calls himself simply a scribe from the South." The new king looked over the stunned faces of his assembled lords.

"I won't bore you with the entire text. Suffice it to say, I intend to govern alongside you lords with the idea that we are, one and all, responsible for every living creature within our boundaries."

"Does that include the dragons?" Nimbulan asked, ready to move on to the issues Myri had told him concerned the creatures who made this all possible.

"Yes," Quinnault replied."If we are going to rely on communal magic to enforce our laws and control solitary magicians, then we must ensure the safety of the dragons and their continued presence within our boundaries. Demon hunters like Moncriith can't be allowed to harm them in any way."

"There are only six full-grown dragons in the current nimbus and five youngsters. That figure includes Amaranth the purple-tip." Nimbulan recited the statistics Myri had relayed to him. "Dragons throughout the rest of Kardia Hodos are solitary creatures and may not agree to become a part of the nimbus. Our nimbus needs to increase their numbers to provide us with enough magic to be readily available at all times, no matter where the dragons currently fly. Shayla has requested a provision of livestock to feed them and plantations of the Tambootie tree, the source of their magic." Nimbulan waited, holding his breath to see if the lords would willingly give up parts of their wealth to help the dragons thrive. Previously they considered the beasts to be dangerous predators or demons—if dragons existed at all.

"Will a tithe from each lord be enough?" Quinnault cut through any objections before they could be voiced.

"I think that will do. As long as the herds and plantations are spread out. The dragons must range widely to stretch their wings." Nimbulan hid his embarrassment at the next request behind a cough. "And, ah, the dragons have another requirement to seal the covenant."

Quinnault looked up a little startled, as if he knew the next demand would be outrageous.

Nimbulan signaled the servant at the door to admit the three magicians who waited there. They marched in at a stately pace. Lyman carried a precious artifact, resting upon a wide pillow covered in fire green silk. A cloth of gold velvet shielded the heavy object. They paused beside Nimbulan's chair until he stood and joined them.

"As newly elected Senior Magician of the Commune of

Magicians, the nimbus of dragons, currently resident in Coronnan have directed me to offer to the people of Coronnan this crown." Nimbulan whipped off the velvet covering to reveal a crown of precious clear glass, forged by dragon fire in the form of a dragon's head, set with gems—ruby, emerald, sapphire, topaz, and amethyst—the colors of the dragon wingtips.

"It is beautiful!" Quinnault gasped.

"More than beautiful, it is unique and special. No other monarch in all of Kardia Hodos has a crown so valuable, nor so heavy with responsibility. The dragons will be present at your coronation, and the crowning of each of your successors. You and your line rule by the grace of dragons and you will be addressed as 'Your Grace' for that reason. If any man breaks the covenant with the dragons, they will withdraw their grace and the crown—The Coraurlia."

"That is a name I do not know." Quinnault couldn't take his eyes off the glittering crown. Sunlight from the high windows struck the glass, sending rainbows arcing throughout the room.

"The Coraurlia has been imbued with special magic," Old Lyman said as he fiddled with the golden cover cloth, opening it to form a sack with a drawstring and carry-strap. He held the sack open while his two supporting magicians carefully deposited the crown inside.

"You, King Quinnault de Draconis, must keep the Coraurlia on your person for the next three days until your official coronation. During that time, the crown will be imprinted by your aura. Until the day you die, or are deposed by the dragons and the Commune combined, no magic will touch you for good or ill. Mundane weapons can penetrate the spell, but with difficulty. This is the best protection we can give you."

"What about the rest of Coronnan? What will be our protection from magical attack? Your Commune can't be everywhere. In the past decades we have supported numerous Battlemages and their assistants very well. Now that we don't need them, will they retaliate against us, before the Commune has a chance to enforce the new laws?" Lord Hanic stood to make his point, fear written all over his face.

"All magicians will be invited to join the Commune," Nimbulan replied.

"But what about those magicians who can't or won't gather dragon magic?" Lord Baathalzan stood, adding his insistence to the request.

Nimbulan had no answer. He'd assumed all magicians would gladly join him and conform.

"Any magician who practices outside the Commune has no place in the Coronnan we are building," Quinnault said.

"Your Grace." The Lord of Sambol bowed in deference to the new king. "We twelve lords of your Council recommend a law exiling all magicians who will not or cannot join the Commune of Magicians. We recognize dragon magic as the only lawful magic. This law must include all former Battlemages as well as witches and other magicians of minor talent and informal training. *And* they must remove themselves from Coronnan by the time of your coronation."

A general cheer of acceptance resounded around the room. The sound built as it bounced against the stone walls, hammering into Nimbulan's ears.

He sat heavily in his chair, stunned. Myrilandel, his beloved wife, could not gather dragon magic.

"What about the purple dragon?" Nimbulan grasped at the only possibility that presented itself. "Anyone can gather magic from a purple-tip."

"But there is only one purple-tip in all of Kardia Hodos," Hanic said. "I understand one must be in physical contact with it to work magic. It cannot be everywhere and I understand it prefers the form of a flywacket, which doesn't give off magic to be gathered. No. Our definition of dragon magic doesn't include the purple dragon. Exile or death for *all* solitary magicians." Baathalzan resumed his seat with dignified satisfaction that his primary concern had been addressed.

They were right. For the good of all Coronnan, solitary magicians had to be exiled.

Nimbulan stared into nothingness. *Myri, oh, Myri, what will I do without you?*

* * *

"I now pronounce you husband and wife, mated together for the duration of your lifetimes. The Stargods acknowledge your vows of faithfulness. Let the people respect them as well." A priest robed in bright red recited the formula of the marriage blessing in some haste. He looked at the long caravan forming outside the School for Magicians before sealing the ceremony with the cross of the Stargods.

All around them steeds stamped, people shouted, sledges groaned with the weight piled high upon them. In the midst of the frenzy, the priest presided over a hasty union. He turned and left the couple without waiting for them to seal their vows with the traditional kiss.

Emptiness washed over Myri. This should be the happiest day of her life, not the saddest.

"Come with us now, Nimbulan. Please," Myri pleaded with Nimbulan one last time, though she knew he must stay in the city. He must help rebuild Coronnan and the create the Commune. Her brother, King Quinnault, couldn't do it all.

She would survive without Nimbulan. She wasn't sure the new Commune, King, and Council of Provinces would.

"The clearing will protect you, Myri, until I can come to you. I moved some lines on the new map so that you will technically be outside the boundaries of Coronnan. I will come to you as soon as I can. I just wish I could find a safe haven for you closer to the city," he said while clutching her hands within his own. He searched her face as if etching the image into his memory.

"I know you will come, my love." She turned her head away to hide her tears. And her guilt. She hadn't told him about the baby. She needed to know for certain that she wouldn't miscarry, as so many witchwomen did. Shayla had told Lyman—he was almost as much a dragon as Myri—but no one had told Nimbulan. At first she waited for the right moment. A quiet time when they wouldn't be interrupted. Then the Council had issued their edict of exile.

To tell him now would divide his loyalties even further between herself and the new government. His dream of peace was too important to all of Coronnan. She couldn't do it now. She would wait until she knew for sure. Then, when he joined her in the clearing, she would tell him. This parting was hard enough on both of them.

Her chin quivered and the ache in her chest choked her breathing.

"Don't hide your tears, Myri." Nimbulan captured her chin between two gentle fingers. "I love you. I'll come soon. Kalen will keep you company." He kissed her tears as they fell.

Stuuvart had blithely abandoned all claim to Kalen as his child as soon as the edict of exile was made known. Guillia had hugged the girl fiercely in a tearful embrace all through the brief wedding. Now she reluctantly let her daughter lift her pack onto the sledge. Myri tried to summon anger at the absent Stuuvart to replace her lonely suffering at parting from Nimbulan.

"I'm going with them, too," Powwell announced, marching up to the last sledge in the long caravan headed South and East. He carried a simple pack bulging with books and clothes and food.

"Your place is here, Powwell," Myri said. "The Commune needs every magician who can gather dragon magic to help enforce the laws."

"Stupid laws. I won't be part of a country that forces you and Kalen into exile. I'm coming with you." He set his chin in a stubborn attitude that wouldn't budge. "You'll need a man to help with the heavy work."

"Then I charge you, Powwell, to look after Myri and Kalen, and to protect them. You must perfect the summons spell quickly so that you can keep in contact with me," Nimbulan ordered the boy. "You are nearly fourteen now. A man, and I trust you."

"Yeah, sure." Powwell jumped on the back of the sledge next to Kalen. He crossed his arms and glared at his former master.

"I wish it could be otherwise, Myrilandel. I wish we could be together." Nimbulan held her close until their hearts beat in rhythm.

"As do I, my love. I wish we could be together always, in our own home, with our family." She turned her face and kissed him long and full, putting all of her regret and sorrow into her embrace. She tasted salty tears. His or hers, it didn't matter. If only she could cling to him a little longer, hold his warmth a little closer, make love with him one more time. . . .

Shouts and whistles to sledge steeds, and a general shift of people forward, signaled the beginning of the long journey. Traders and exiles alike settled into the line of march.

Myri flung her arms around Nimbulan's neck, holding him as long as possible. Gentle hands pulled them apart. She slid her hand down his arm, caressing his fingers, cherishing his touch for as long as possible.

"I love you, Myrilandel. I'll come to you soon," Nimbulan whispered.

"I love you, Nimbulan." The silver umbilical that bound them together stretched thin but did not break.

EPILOGUE

(The Covenant is broken!) Shayla's last communication reverberated through Nimbulan's ears three days after she and her nimbus had departed abruptly from Coronnan City.

At the same moment as she spoke, Nimbulan's contact with Myrilandel through the silver umbilical snapped.

Now he trudged up the path from the village to the clearing. Footsore and saddlesore, he rested briefly against the split boulder with an everblue tree growing out of the center of it. He'd ridden from Coronnan City at a breakneck pace. Five steeds had floundered under his prodding to move ever faster. The last of the beasts had gone lame two leagues outside the village.

The magical barrier that protected the clearing should be within sight—if the barrier were visible. Winter mud slowed his passage along the trail. More than half a year had passed since he'd said farewell to his wife. Too long. He'd allowed the concerns of the King and Commune to chain him to the capital for too long.

Hastily he finger-combed his hair, trying to make his weary, mud-splattered appearance a little more presentable. Regretting even that delay, he stepped up to the barrier, closed his eyes, and pushed with his left hand. He met no resistance.

Puzzled, he stepped across what should be the threshold of the clearing. No tingle of magical energy. No resistance. Nothing.

He looked through the screening trees. Nothing had changed from the first time he'd seen the place. The thatch on the one room hut sagged in the middle, the door still hung slightly crooked, the kitchen garden was overgrown with weeds. Two flusterhens scratched at the center of the clearing in search of food.

"Myri?" he called. His voice echoed through the emptiness of the clearing. "Myrilandel," he shouted louder with both voice and magic.

No answer.

(The Covenant is broken!) The dragons were gone. He was no longer connected to his wife.

And yet the dragon magic persisted in the air. What was happening?

Why, oh why, hadn't he made sure Powwell or Kalen could work the summons spell properly before they left Coronnan City? Neither of them had perfected the spell in the last three seasons. Myri had never been able to learn it. Communication had been sporadic and incomplete at best.

"Myri!" he cried, desperate to see her again and know she was safe. "Myri, Kalen, Powwell. Somebody please answer me."

Nothing.

"Where are you? You can't be gone." He dashed into the hut, thrusting the door open so hard he nearly jerked it off its frame. "*Myrilandel!*"

Empty. The hut was as empty as the clearing, with no sign it had been inhabited at all in the last year.

"Where are you?" he whispered into the emptiness. "Were you ever here?"

Loneliness landed on his shoulders like a lead-weighted cloak. A headache pounded in his temples. He tried to remember her face, her tall, slim body and fine hair so pale it looked like colorless dragon fur. The purple shadows under her fingernails. The way she buried her face into the fur of her black flywacket.

All the images faded from his mind. He forced them back, holding on to them with the desperation of a deserted lover. The memories slipped through his grasp as if they'd never been.

His heart ached as tears choked him.

"Were you real, Myrilandel, or just a dragon dream?"